AN INDECENT PROPOSAL

"You really can't judge people by their looks."

"I can, and do," Julian asserted. He smiled devilishly, and refilled his goblet from the silver pitcher. "You, for instance—"

"Spare me, please."

"You'd never bore a man. You have just the sort of mouth a man would love to taste beneath his own, and enough light in your eyes to promise passion. And your hair is magnificent. I would love to see it down and curling around your waist. I would like to run my hands through it—"

"Please stop it, Julian."

"Stop it? No, I think not. As a matter of fact, I think we may have found the solution to our problems."

Ivy wished he would move back. He was too close, too beautiful, with his stormy, intense eyes and elegant hands and shining dark hair. She couldn't breathe, couldn't speak.

"I want to keep an eye on you. You wish, for reasons known only to your devious little heart, to stay at Wythecombe Keep. I offer you a bargain, Ivy."

"What?" she whispered, her voice quavering.

"You may stay...as long as you wish. But you stay as my mistress. You warm my bed. You attend to my needs. I let you stay, and your body is mine—whenever I wish, however I ask."

ENCHANTED TIME

Amy Elizabeth Saunders

LOVE SPELL NEW YORK CITY

LOVE SPELL®

September 1995

Published by

Dorchester Publishing Co., Inc.
276 Fifth Avenue
New York, NY 10001

Printed in the United States of America.

To my grandmother, Eva Tucker, with all my love.

Chapter One

Looking back on it, Ivy told herself that from the beginning, there was something magical about the day.

Perhaps it was the fog—though fog was nothing new in Seattle, especially in December. But it wasn't a dreary, oppressing fog.

It was a fog that whispered in, floating in wisps around the barren treetops, shading their stark branches. It softened the street lamps, creating halos of light around them. It dusted over the wreaths and evergreen boughs that decorated the shops and galleries of Pioneer Square, like a sparkling fairy mist.

True, the day had begun like any other. Ivy arrived at her antique store at exactly 9:30 A.M., had a quick coffee from the espresso shop across

9

the street, made a short, thorough check of the displays and merchandise, and opened the door at exactly ten, ready for a day of business.

As she did every day, she stepped outside to admire her storefront.

The store window glowed like a fairyland. Passing holiday shoppers inevitably slowed their hurried progress and lingered for a moment or two, captured by the scene.

A Victorian trunk, lined with faded floral paper, spilled open like a pirate's treasure chest, brimming with antique lace, delicate cameo pins, painted fans, and silver mirrors. Two teddy bears, their charm not diminished by their worn spots and missing hair, lay tumbled amid torn wrapping paper and ribbons, as if their new owners had just opened them and been called away. An Edwardian tea set, painted with sprays of wine red roses, sat on a gleaming tea table, a few faded Christmas cards scattered between the plates.

And behind it all, the Christmas tree, sparkling with hundreds of white lights, covered with the odd prisms of old chandeliers, antique dolls in faded dresses, gleaming pocket watches, and bejeweled hat pins.

Satisfied, Ivy steeped back from the display, burying her hands into the pockets of her wool coat.

Perfect. She could easily have paid someone else to arrange the windows, but she loved doing it herself. From the packages beneath the tree to the garlands of fragrant pine that hung above the store entrance, from keeping the books to haunting estate auctions, it was her own business.

Ivy gave a final appraising look at the display window and up at the worn brick of the building, where fresh evergreen garlands hung beneath the sign.

Enchanted Time, the sign said in simple letters.

She left the cold air of the outside and made her way back into the store, where the familiar, rich smell of polished wood and evergreen boughs and cinnamon tea warmed the air. And there was another fragrance too, the one that she loved best—an indefinable aroma of the past that seemed to cling to the silver vases and old furniture and hatboxes. It was the smell of times gone by, the scent of a more graceful era.

She shrugged off her brown wool coat and carried it to the tiny back office, stopping to flick a speck of dust from the faded back of an old rocking horse. She straightened her gray wool skirt, touched her hair with quick fingers to ensure its confinement, gathered her ledgers and receipt books, and made her way back to the showroom.

Her desk was a beloved horror of the Victorian Gothic Revival, dark and bulky, carved with pseudomedieval hunting scenes. She settled in comfortably and opened her books.

She raised her head briefly at the sound of the

door opening, greeted the customers with a quick smile, and returned to her books.

Lookers, probably, she thought. During the month of December, the serious buyers stayed away from the antique stores and galleries, preferring to shop during the February slump, when prices dropped. She might unload a few trinkets and toys, but the real treasures—Georgian wardrobes and Shaker tables and faded Victorian carpets—those sales slumped with the arrival of the holiday shoppers.

She began adding the neat rows of figures in her books, smiling with satisfaction at the profits.

The front door opened, ringing the sleigh bells that hung from the polished handle.

"Ivy!"

She smiled at the distinguished old gentleman who came barreling through the door: Winston Arthur, who ran the Arthur Gallery—by appointment only—across the brick-paved street.

He entered with great aplomb, cashmere scarf and camel-hair coat announcing his affluence to anyone who cared to notice, and made himself comfortable on the Queen Anne chair next to Ivy's desk.

"And how is my titian-haired tycoon faring?" he demanded.

"Steady and sure." Ivy indicated the books before her. "Very typically December. Lots of small sales. Mostly lookers."

Winston shuddered. "Perish the thought. You

should get rid of all the little things and concentrate on paintings, or furniture. Show by appointment. That way, you only deal with the serious shoppers."

"I love the little things," Ivy protested with a smile. "And lookers often buy, Winston."

Winston raised a dubious gray brow. "It would free up your time," he pointed out, as he inevitably did. "You work too hard. Get out, enjoy life, Ivy! You're far too young to spend your life buried away here."

"Nonsense," Ivy smiled at the old gentleman. "I like being buried here." She gazed out the front window, where the pale fog softened the facades of the old buildings.

Across the store, the two women shoppers were quietly discussing an old quilt, faded, but in good condition. They looked at the price tag, hesitated, and then left, the smell of the cold sea air drifting in as the door swung closed behind them.

"Lookers," Winston remarked in contemptuous tones.

Ivy thought about pointing out that not everyone was born with the proverbial silver spoon in their mouth, but decided against it.

"Tea, Winston?"

"A quick cup, thank you."

Ivy made her way to the back office and poured the tea into fragile cups of Chinese porcelain, switched the cassette tape to its other side, and carried the steaming cups back to her desk. The sound of Christmas carols wafted through the shop, Julie Andrews singing "Silent Night."

"Not that dreadful cinnamon stuff, is it?" Winston demanded, his patrician nose quivering over the cup.

"Mine is. Yours is Earl Grey."

"Good." Winston took an appreciative sip. "Are you going home for the holidays, dear?"

Ivy almost choked on her tea. Home. That was a joke. She wondered what it would look like to Winston—the cluttered trailer house outside of Las Vegas, her loud, drunk mother leaving overflowing ashtrays on the fake wood tables, her newest stepfather sitting in his undershirt watching wrestling on the dusty TV. What his name was, Ivy couldn't remember. The only distinguishing characteristic he seemed to have was his inordinate pride in the blue tattoo of a hula dancer that graced his forearm. After a few beers, he would flex his muscles and make the tattoo dance.

"No, I think I'll stay here, Winston. Take care of the shop."

Winston looked appalled.

Ivy was sure that Winston's family home was as dignified and elegant as he was. The kind of place where people spoke in hushed, gentle voices, where old ladies with pearl chokers smiled at little girls in velvet dresses with lace collars. The kind of home she had always dreamed of.

14

"You're more than welcome to join us, dear. We're celebrating at my sister's home this year."

"No, thanks. I've already made plans." It was a lie, and Ivy wondered if Winston knew it. She hated going to other people's homes for holidays. It was something she had done in her college days, going home with one roommate or another. It didn't help. She always felt awkward, an outsider.

"Suit yourself, but the invitation stands. Heavens, is it three already?" Winston set his teacup carefully back on its saucer and rose to his feet. "I have a couple from Mercer Island coming to see my walnut chest of drawers. Buyers, not lookers," he added. "New money, I think, but they seem nice enough."

Ivy repressed a smile at Winston's unconscious snobbery. Old money, new money... who cared? It was better than no money.

Winston held open the door to admit a customer as he left, a woman with an improbable red wig brighter than Ivy's own conspicuous copper hair. He lifted a brow at the woman's earrings, plastic Christmas bulbs that actually glowed. "Looker," his expression said clearly. He gave Ivy a quick wave and was gone.

Ivy gave the woman a perfunctory smile and opened her books.

"Oh, my, isn't this lovely?"

Ivy glanced up at the wigged woman, who was beaming at a table of shimmering German glassware nestled in fresh pine branches.

"Thank you." Ivy began adding a figure of tidy columns.

For a few minutes, the woman wandered through the store, humming loudly along with the Christmas carols.

Ivy looked up again as the humming approached her desk and stopped.

"May I help you?"

The woman beamed at her, the wrinkles around her eyes deepening. "I thought I might be able to help you," she announced. She reached into the large bag she carried and began searching. "I have something you might be interested in." .

Ivy wondered if the woman might not be a little crazy. It wasn't unheard of in the heart of the city. Pioneer Square was an eclectic mix of antique stores, art galleries, nightclubs, and tourist traps, where importers of Persian rugs and proprietors of elegant restaurants mingled with vagrants and tourists, gallery owners and aspiring rock bands.

"A little something that's been in our family," the woman added, resting her canvas bag in the middle of Ivy's desk.

Ivy wondered about the sort of people who sold their family heirlooms. She knew that if she had any, she would treasure them. The closest thing her mother had to an heirloom was a burnt wood plaque that hung above the screen door. It said: *If this trailer's rockin', don't bother*

16

knockin'. Ivy cringed whenever she saw it. Fortunately, it had been a long time. She had left home the day she graduated from high school, and taken the Grayhound to Seattle, with nothing but a battered suitcase, 150 dollars, and a paid scholarship to the University of Washington.

"I really only buy in lots, or by appointment," Ivy informed the old woman, whose synthetic, flame-colored curls were almost buried in the open bag.

"Don't bet on it," was the muffled reply.

Ivy suppressed an impatient sigh and fixed a polite smile on her face. "If you'd like to call and make an appointment—"

"Here." The woman seized a large, square package from her bag, and her wrinkled fingers caressed the brown paper for a moment before she dumped it on Ivy's desk.

Ivy ignored it, wanting to stand her ground. Customers tended to treat her like some kind of junior salesgirl. Probably her size, she often thought, which gave her an almost waiflike look. And the red hair didn't help. She dealt with the flaw of her height by dressing her slender body in severely tailored clothing, and her riot of red curls were scraped into what she hoped was a dignified roll.

The wigged woman obviously wasn't intimidated.

"I think you'll be surprised," she chirped, tapping a spotted finger on the package.

It was probably quicker, Ivy decided, to look at whatever the woman had and dismiss her.

She unwrapped the brown paper and stopped.

It was a book.

Not just any book, but probably the oldest book she had ever seen. A tingle raced down her spine, the familiar sense of excitement she felt whenever she'd found something special.

There was no title, just a dark leather cover, ancient, peeling and cracking in places. The binding was hand-sewn with meticulous stitches, fraying and falling out in places, but still in remarkable condition, considering . . .

Considering it was the oldest thing she had ever held in her hands.

She could feel the age of it, the antiquity. She glanced up to speak to the red-wigged woman, but she had wandered across the room and was peering through a box of antique postcards, laughing softly to herself.

Gingerly, testing the strength of the binding, Ivy opened the book, trying to keep her thin fingers steady.

The pages were parchment, handwritten. A book made before the printing press was common.

She stared at the front page. The ink was faint and faded, the letters curiously shaped, but after a few moments, she was able to read the curious, ancient hand.

Susanna of Denbeigh, it read, *Wythecombe Keep, 1530.*

Ivy's arms prickled with an odd chill.

It should be in a museum, Ivy thought, her heart racing, or locked in a library someplace.

Beneath the first line, another, in different writing.

Given from Alyce Ramsden to Juliana Ramsden, anno domini 1564.

Her pulse quickened.

Real, not a clever forgery. She had no idea of the value of the thing. She thought briefly of calling David, who dealt in antique books in a store off Jackson Street, but decided against it. He could outbid her too easily.

And yet another line of archaic script, a little brighter than the first.

To Margaret Ramsden, from Juliana, 1589. Wythecombe Keep.

That was all.

Ivy stared at the names, mesmerized. *Susanna. Alyce. Juliana. Margaret.* Who were they? She scanned the dates again, trying to absorb it. These women had taken pen in hand and written on these pages when Henry VIII disavowed the Holy Church, when Shakespeare wrote *The Tempest*, when Elizabeth the virgin queen held reign, and when the Tudor line died with her, passing to the Stuarts.

She was holding history.

Slowly, carefully, she turned the first brittle page, and then another, and another. It seemed to be a book of herbal recipes—cures for fever and hysteria, posies to ward off the plague or encourage fertility, recipes to sweeten the air and banish illness.

"Do you want it?"

Startled, Ivy looked up. Her hand went to the severe collar of her blouse.

"Yes. Yes, it's very . . . unique." Ivy looked down at the book, her heart tripping quickly. "Are you sure you want to sell it?"

She had a policy of being honest with her customers, especially those who looked as if they couldn't afford her not to be. This woman, with her tattered coat and worn polyester pants, was definitely not wealthy.

"Sell it? Why ever not? I can always write another, if I choose."

Ivy could hardly believe the ludicrous statement. "Are you sure? It's very, very valuable," she explained gently.

"One hundred dollars. Cash."

Ivy was genuinely horrified. Obviously, this woman with her blinking earrings and lurid wig had no idea what she held. The temptation was overwhelming. Yet how unscrupulous it would be to take advantage of someone's ignorance. Almost like stealing.

The old woman snapped her fingers. "Make a decision. One hundred dollars. If you say no, I'll take it to the bookstore I saw down the street. You have one chance. Say yes or no, and it's done."

"Yes." The word escaped before Ivy could think.

"Good. I think you'll enjoy it."

Speechless, Ivy stared at the book. Hers. This ancient, precious piece of the past. Her hand, looking very small and pale, rested on the dark leather cover.

"Miss?"

Ivy had already forgotten the woman with the wig.

"My money?"

Like a sleepwalker, Ivy opened the drawer of her desk, unlocked her cash box, and counted out five 20-dollar bills.

"Enjoy it," the woman said.

Ivy opened the book and stared at a set of directions regarding the proper distilling of rosewater.

She looked up when the sleigh bells on the door jangled, and saw the woman disappearing down the foggy street, where the streetlights glowed in misty halos through the sea-scented mist.

For a few minutes, she simply sat, unable to believe her fortune.

Susanna of Denbeigh. 1530. Juliana Ramsden, 1564. Wythecombe Keep.

Who were they, the women who had collected the recipes and cures and passed them down? She would find out; she would research it in libraries. She would find where Wythecombe Keep had stood—perhaps still did, for all she knew.

She stared out the front window of the store

and saw the lights on at the gallery across the street. She picked up the telephone and dialed, her fingers feeling shaky.

The voice that answered the phone was deep and well modulated, a voice from a 1930s movie. "Arthur Gallery, how may I help you?"

"Winston? It's Ivy, over at Enchanted Time. Listen, you've got to see what I've just bought. It's incredible, really. A museum piece. Can you come?"

"Give me five minutes, dear, and I'll be there."

Satisfied, Ivy hung up the phone and ran her hands over the book, marveling at its presence.

"Incredible. Simply unbelievable. I take back everything I ever thought about lookers." Winston turned the vellum pages slowly, reverently, lifting his gray brows as he peered through his glasses.

"Do you think it's genuine?"

"Of course it is, you silly girl. I taught you better than that, didn't I?"

Ivy thought of the nights when she was working her way through college, inventorying the priceless furniture and carpets in Winston's gallery, attending estate auctions with him. What he regarded as too trivial for his attention, Ivy invested in, waiting for the day when she would open her own store. Yes, Winston Arthur had trained her well.

"You can feel it, can't you?" Winston continued. "What it may be worth, I have no idea. It's not my forte. Of course, as I always say, it all depends on how badly someone wants it. Anything can be sold for a fortune to the right buyer."

"I'd never sell it," Ivy exclaimed.

Winston raised his head briefly, a little surprised at the passion in her voice. "Well, that happens, occasionally. Something comes along that one can't consider parting with. Consider yourself lucky that it only took a hundred dollars. May I have more tea?"

"Of course." Ivy hurried to the back office, refilling Winston's cup while he perused the pages of the book, a thoughtful look on his face.

She was stirring in his customary teaspoon of sugar when he began laughing.

"What?"

"Come and see," he called.

Ivy hurried back into the cluttered storefront, almost spilling the tea in her haste. "What on earth, Winston?"

He looked up with a chuckle and lifted his reading glasses.

"Just look at this, Ivy. How marvelous. It seems that one of your ladies from Wythecombe Keep fancied herself a witch!"

Bemused, Ivy took the book carefully and frowned at the open page.

"To change the weather," she read slowly, frowning over the unfamiliar, crabbed letters and faded ink, "stand facing west, and speak these words."

23

"Go on," Winston urged. "It's really very poetic."

She read very slowly.

> "A day of damasked rosy heat
> Or ye barren boughs of cold
> A fairy spring of rainfall sweet
> Or trembling leaves of gold;
> Presume no more to go your way:
> I bid thee hasten at my say."

"If not a necromancer, a poet," Winston remarked.

Ivy touched the page with gentle fingers, wondering which woman had written the words, and when. Had she genuinely believed that the rhyme would alter nature's course? Was she a fey, frustrated poet?

"I congratulate you," Winston announced. "You've found a genuine treasure."

"I have, haven't I?" Ivy sat slowly, feeling a warm flush of pleasure. For a few minutes, she and Winston sat in comfortable silence, sipping their tea and smelling the fir tree and cinnamon smells of the cozy store, while Bing Crosby sang over the stereo, dreaming of a white Christmas.

Ivy caressed the precious book. Lucky. She was so incredibly fortunate. This precious heirloom made her feel somehow connected to the unknown women who had written it, as if she were descended from them, part of their family. And her store, small but perfect, an answer to her childhood dreams of gentility. And her friend Winston, a true Old World–style gentleman, who had helped her to shape her dreams.

"I have everything I could possibly want," she said aloud. "I'm the luckiest woman in the world."

Winston raised his brows. "I'll admit it's a marvelous find, dear, but there is more out there."

Ivy laughed. "Like what?"

"Oh, just little things. Swiss bank accounts. Trips to Europe. Real estate. A husband and children."

They laughed together.

"Maybe someday. For now, things are going too well to bother changing them."

"Just don't wait too long," Winston advised, his smile only half joking, "or you'll end up an old confirmed bachelor, like me." He replaced his teacup on Ivy's desk and stood, gathering his overcoat and gloves. "I'd better be going, or I'll be late for the symphony. And you know how—"

He stopped abruptly, and Ivy followed his startled gaze to the front window.

It was snowing. A sudden, heavy snowfall, without warning. It came fluttering down from the sky in lush white clouds, and descended on the old lampposts and brick streets; it blanketed the parked cars and barren trees. Across the street, it settled like a powdered wig on the stone lion that guarded Winston's door.

Over the sound system, Bing Crosby's melodious voice wished them a white Christmas.

Winston raised a brow at the sudden change. "I wish that you'd not put that tape on before you read that incantation. Perhaps we should have heard 'April in Paris,' or something warmer."

Ivy glanced sharply at the book on her desk, and then back at Winston.

He was joking, of course.

"Honestly, Ivy, don't get superstitious. You're in the wrong business to be that fanciful. It's a coincidence. Quite a startling one, I'll admit, and more than a little annoying, but a coincidence all the same."

Ivy's smile felt weak. "Of course it is. You know me better than that. It's just been such an odd day."

"Profitable, not odd," Winston corrected. "Well, if I'm going to drive tonight, I'd better set off now. And just as a precaution, dear, don't read that spell again. I shudder to imagine what could result."

"Oh, stop it." Ivy stood briskly, slid open the drawer of her desk, and laid the book carefully next to her cash box. Enough of that; it was time to get back to business. "Have a good night, Winston. I'll see you tomorrow."

"Not unless this snow lets up," Winston informed her, and made his way out into the white-frosted street, glaring up at the heavens as if to chastise them for this inconvenience.

Enchanted Time

Ivy watched him cross the street, his silver hair gathering a dusting of white, his coat flapping in the sudden breeze.

She turned back to business. She rearranged a child's bed of full of antique bears, hung some feathered hats on an oak hall tree, and straightened the silver writing stand on her desk.

A young couple came in, laughing and dusting snow off of each other's shoulders, and spent 300 dollars on a lampshade that wasn't a Tiffany, but a lovely imitation.

Ivy allowed herself a fleeting moment of envy as they left and made their way down the snowy street, as delighted with each other as they were with their new lamp. They would go home, she thought, and give the lamp a place of honor in their house, and for years afterward, they would smile and say to each other, "Do you remember when we bought that? It was just before Christmas, and it snowed."

"One day," she promised herself. "When I have time."

She opened her drawer and reached for her cash box, pleased with the 300-dollar check.

The book sat there, mysterious and enticing.

Ivy glanced at the empty store and told herself to get back to work.

She gave another longing glance at the book.

"Fifteen minutes," she told herself. "It can't hurt to take fifteen minutes off." She made herself a cup of tea, turned the hot plate off, and settled in at her desk.

27

She turned the pages of the book slowly, drawing her leaded crystal lamp a little closer as she squinted at the faded ink.

She learned that sweet woodruff would purify the air, and that angelica warded against evil. She learned that wrapping a person in red flannel and laying them near a fire was good for chest ailments.

Strawberry leaves, in tea, were good for an easy "travail through childbirth." The bark from a walnut tree, with rosemary, would add "a fyne gloss to dark hair."

She looked again at the poem she had read aloud. "To change weather, stand facing west and speak these words."

She glanced up, and got a quick chill as she realized that she had indeed been facing west, toward Elliot Bay.

"Bull hockey," she said aloud, and turned the page, briefly glancing through a set of instructions for planting an herb garden, using the phases of the moon to ensure success.

Two pages later, another poem.

"For fortune which was lost," Ivy read quietly. Only two lines, this time.

"What fortune hath been given, but to slip
away
I call thee back, in twofold, before the
end of day."

Ivy looked up, half expecting coins and earrings, lost car keys and hairpins to rain from the

28

heavens. She sat for a moment, tense, expectant.
Nothing happened.

She laughed aloud at her own silliness and put
the book back into the desk drawer. "Get a grip,"
she told herself, and went back to work.

It was less than an hour before it happened.
The woman who had been in with her friend earlier returned to buy the quilt.

"It's the oddest thing," the woman told Ivy as
she laid the heavy fabric on the desk. "I told myself it was just too extravagant, and was on my
way home. So there I am, driving through the
snow, and I suddenly had the urge to come back.
I just knew I couldn't sleep tonight unless I had
this. It's really weird."

"Not really," Ivy reassured her. "Old things are
like that, aren't they? Sometimes they just grab
you, and you have to have them."

Like my book, she added silently, and froze as
she remembered reading the charm for lost fortune. Oh, stop it! she told herself. And 700 dollars isn't exactly a fortune. But it's a lot more
than I expected.

She wrapped the quilt carefully in tissue and
placed it in a large white shopping bag with Enchanted Time printed across it. She handed the
woman back her Visa card.

"Thank you, I hope you enjoy it. And happy
holidays."

"Thanks, I will. And Merry Christmas to you."

There, Ivy told herself, that's it. Just a normal

sale. No big deal. Anyway, that silly poem said something about twofold. If I sell two quilts today, then I'll worry.

"You know . . ."

Ivy turned back to the front door, where her customer stood, one hand on the handle, the other clutching her shopping bag.

"This is the weirdest thing. That other quilt over there, the pink and green one?"

"Double wedding ring pattern, about nineteen twenty," Ivy answered automatically.

"I want that one, too. I just have to have it. Isn't that the strangest thing?"

Ivy looked from the book on her desk to the snow-covered street and back to the woman, who was already digging in her purse for her credit card.

"It is." Ivy's words were slow and careful. "It really is the strangest thing."

The next few pages of the book seemed normal enough. A few remedies read as a little odd, such as pigeon's blood as a cure for arthritis, but given the era, probably not that peculiar after all.

Ivy had locked the store, taken the more valuable items out of the display window, totaled the day's receipts, and emptied the cash box into the safe.

She called for a cab to her apartment, and was told that the snow was holding things up, but they'd be there.

She dimmed the lights, set the alarm, and sat down to read while she waited.

Perhaps it was the snow, perhaps the coming holiday, but the passing people in the street seemed jollier than usual. Lawyers carrying briefcases, a group of young people on their way to a show, a man and woman, already in evening clothes, maybe going out to dinner, or a party at an art gallery, or even to happily ever after in their careful finery.

Ivy looked after them, noting the way the woman looked up at him, the tender, graceful way he touched her cheek with his gloved hand.

"Don't pout," she told herself. "There are worse things than being alone."

She turned back to her book and read a recipe for dandelion wine.

She turned the brittle page and drew her breath in at the sight of another verse, written in a clearer and more graceful hand than the other two had been.

She started to close the book and stopped herself.

Don't be stupid, she told herself, and read on:

I have sought thee over time and land,
And found naught but more seeking.
I have sought thee through dawn and dusk.
I have sworn that I would seek no more
By my sorrow is undimmed.
Most certain is my heart
That I long for more than longing's sake.

31

Amy Elizabeth Saunders

And so I call thee;
I speak to the other half my soul,
Whose body grants heat to my winter
Whose breath cools summer's fire,
You, who are lost
Somewhere between dawn and dusk
In enchanted time.

Enchanted Time.

Ivy's heart raced like the feet of a frightened rabbit.

"They're only words," she whispered. A coincidence. A fluke.

And yet she shivered as if touched by ice; the hair on the back of her neck prickled.

She turned the page and read, "To reverse the spell . . ." To her surprise, her hands began to tremble, and the book dropped to her desk before she could finish reading.

A sparkling, tinkling sound caught her attention, and she whirled around.

The Christmas tree was shivering like a living creature, the white lights sparkling with a frantic shimmer, the crystal prisms that covered the branches swaying as if in a breeze.

She grabbed her keys, but her hand was shaking, and they fell to the page of the book that lay open on her desk.

The room seemed to sway, and she leaned forward to steady herself.

The air seemed alive. It hummed in her ears with a soft, golden sound. Shelves of glassware shimmered and trembled, but didn't fall. The antique bears in their brass bed seemed to quiver, and the cameo brooches on their velvet cushion sparkled as the jewelry case began shaking.

Ivy cried out and reached for her keys again, but they seemed far away, even though she knew they were on the desk in front of her. The room was bright, unnaturally bright.

She felt light-headed, as if she might faint. She reached for the phone, and her hands felt useless, almost like air.

"What in the hell is happening?" she cried out, but there was nobody to answer her, and suddenly, there was nothing but empty darkness.

Outside the antique store, an old vagrant stopped his grocery cart long enough to peek in the window, mesmerized by the swaying, shimmering lights. He opened a bottle of wine, took a healthy swallow, and wiped his chin.

"O, Chrishmash Tree, O Chrishmash Tree," he sang at the window.

From somewhere in the store, a blinding flash of gold light exploded with a Fourth-of-July glitter, and the old wino jumped back.

"Whew!" He pressed his cold red nose against the window, squinting to see in.

The store sat dim and quiet, a lamp casting a soft circle of light over a dark, empty desk.

"An' Happy New Year to you too," the old vagrant announced to nobody. He checked his bottle to make sure the lid was on tightly, tucked it beneath his tattered coat, and continued down the cold city street, pushing his shopping cart through the snow.

Outside the store called Enchanted Time, a few more snowflakes fell from the dark sky, shimmered in the light like shards of silver, and fell to the earth, unheeded.

fang Obsession Continues

Chapter Two

She'd never slept so soundly. It was a solid black, heavy, almost drunken sleep—except, of course, that Ivy never drank.

Slowly, her brain began to form coherent sentences.

Must've stayed up too late. What time is it? Should get up and turn up the heat. . . .

It was the cold that registered first—the slow realization that her fingers were stiff and icy, that she was shivering. And then the wind, biting her face and shoulders, stinging her with the strong scent of salt air.

Did I sleep with the window open?

And then, simultaneously, the thoughts came that A: something was very wrong, and B: she was outdoors. The ground felt hard and rocky beneath her aching back, and the wind that rushed over her body was too fierce, too stiff, to be coming through a window. A loud, pounding roar in her ears, the ruthless wind, the cold . . .

An icy splash of water rushed over her legs, the coldest water she had ever felt. Her mind couldn't quite grasp it, but the shock of the cold was enough to spur her body to action.

She scrambled away like a terrified animal, sightless and mute, too frightened for coherent thought, guided only by the instinctive drive to escape the cold water.

She stopped abruptly as her vision cleared, and her mind began to absorb the scene before her.

Beach.

Breathing hard with painful gasps, she swung her head in one direction and then the other, her tangled, wet hair lashing against her cheek.

A sheltered cove, with hulking rock formations rising from the pebbled beach.

She felt the small rocks beneath the surfaces of her palms, and biting into her knees.

A towering cliff before her, its jagged face rising high into the gray sky. A few patches of defiant green clinging to the surface, some scrubby trees toward the top of the precipice, their twisted, gnarled branches bent by the stiff wind.

The roar in her ears grew louder, and another icy wave rushed at her feet. She scrambled forward on her hands and knees, with a frightened noise that she didn't recognize as her own voice.

36

She twisted and stared back at an endless sea, darker than the heavy sky above it. It roared its way in cold waves toward the rocky shore, foaming around a few dark, jagged stones.

She closed her eyes, catching her breath with a painful, sharp gasp, and looked again.

Nothing had changed.

Shaking, she dragged herself to her knees.

Nothing made sense, except that something was horribly, sickeningly wrong.

So wrong as to be impossible.

Shock. She must be in shock. She was cold, and her body shook with it; she could feel the wind and the wet and the rocks, she could see the rocky cliffs and the dark, pebbled ground, but none of it made sense.

Had there been an accident? An earthquake? Why was she here?

The only answer was the eternal sound of the wind and ocean, the measured hiss of waves breaking over the beach.

Think, Ivy, think! Ah, that's a good sign, you know your name. You live at the Lindquist, on Ninth Avenue, you were born in Reno, Nevada. You're 25 years old. . . .

Her hands were like ice, knotted into fists against her mouth. Her eyes shot from ocean to cliff to rocks to sky, searching for an answer.

Think! The last thing I remember is . . . what? Working. The store, talking to Winston, drinking tea. Snow. The Christmas tree . . . the book.

She'd been reading the book. A poem. And

then the room had started shaking, and her body had shimmered with glistening, golden light, and then . . .

This.

The wind buffeted her hair, and she clawed the damp strands away from her cheek.

She stopped in the middle of the motion, staring at her own sleeve.

She didn't know it. Deep green, thick fabric, almost like a brocade. A full sleeve, three-quarter length. A turned-back cuff of white lace circled her slender forearm, stained with water and sand. She knew at a glance the lace was handmade, in a pattern she'd never seen before.

She raised her arms with a slow movement and stared down at herself. She stayed there, unmoving, for an endless moment, her arms stretched out like a supplicant.

She was wearing a dress she had never seen before, a dress of green, so dark it was almost black. A deep, rounded neckline, with more of the handmade lace falling from it. A slightly flared peplum at the waist, and very long, full skirts, tangled around her knees, the fabric darkened by the seawater that had splashed her.

"Why?" She hadn't meant to speak out loud, but the cry burst from her throat. Despite the plaintive, terrified sound of it, she felt better at hearing her own voice, knowing that it was hers. She looked at her hands again, to satisfy herself that they were her own, and they were. Thin and small, with a few freckles sprinkled across them.

She tried to think how she had arrived on this desolate stretch of beach, and found no answer.

Perhaps she'd been kidnapped, hit on the head by some crazed criminal, dressed up, and left.

It seemed unlikely.

She stared wildly around her, trying to identify the area, but it didn't look like anywhere she'd been before.

Don't panic. Think . . . what should you do next?

Walk. Get out of here. If she had indeed been brought here by some costume-loving serial killer, it wasn't a good idea to hang around.

She rose unsteadily to her feet, the heavy, wet fabric of her skirt clinging unpleasantly to her bare legs. The cold hurt her feet, and her hands were a mottled red and white from it.

There had to be a phone nearby. A town, an oceanfront hotel . . . something. She could call Winston.

She took a few stiff steps and hesitated, shivering.

She had no idea which way to go.

She stopped and leaned against a hulking rock, barely feeling the wet, hard surface against her back. Her eyes were hot: her throat felt tight. She struggled against the fear that rushed through her body, fear as sharp and bitter as the wind that stung her cheeks.

Just walk! she ordered herself sharply, and started forward again. The pebbles cut into her tender feet, and she winced, but kept walking.

She tried not to think about the strange dress she wore, the terrifying sense of isolation. The wind made a mournful sound as it whipped through the cove, and a sea gull's mocking cry sounded, muffled by the sound of the surf.

And then, over the rhythmic hiss and slap of the waves, she heard another sound. A steady, faint beat, slowly growing louder.

She stopped and listened.

The sound of something striking the ground, coming closer around the curve of beach before her, hitting the rocky turf with a steady, growing thud, getting closer and closer . . .

She gave a choked cry of fright as the horse and rider appeared around a rock formation. The back of her hand was pressed tightly against her mouth. Her heart gave a sickening lurch, dipped, and raced again.

The man on the horse appeared almost as startled by her appearance as she was by his, and for a few long moments they stood still, each staring at the other, while the wind whistled between them.

He was a ghost, or an escapee from a Reformation drama, or a hallucination. Maybe he was from one of those anachronistic organizations she had read about, where people costumed themselves like characters from the past and playacted at living in a time gone by.

He sat perfectly still, his gloved hands tight around the horse's reins. His hair was very dark, almost black, and fell in waves over his

40

shoulders. He wore a jacket—or should it be called a doublet—of faded black, slightly frayed at the cuffs, buttoned in double rows of buttons to the waist. His sleeves were carefully pleated at the shoulder, and slashed to the wide cuffs, revealing full white sleeves beneath. His breeches were of the same dark, worn fabric, tucked into scuffed, loose boots, cavalier style. His collar was slightly open at the neck, a wide, falling collar trimmed with lace.

A seventeenth-century gentleman, a dark and vivid painting by Rembrandt, come to life.

Stunned, Ivy stared at his face. There was nothing of a Rembrandt painting about that—none of the broad, comfortable lines of the Dutch. Dark eyes with an almost foreign tilt at the corners, a lazy shape that was in sharp contrast to the intense glitter of his gaze. A haughty nose, with an aristocratic arch in it. A dream of a mouth, firm and full, and a sharp, strong jawline. It was a face that was part prince and part pirate, alluring and dangerous.

Was it this man who had brought her here? Her costume-drama, serial-killer madman?

After a moment, it began to sink in that he was staring back at her with an expression as confused as her own.

She took an involuntary step backward, her hand still pressed against her mouth. She stumbled slightly, impeded by her heavy, wet skirts.

"Good woman, are you hurt?" His voice startled her, the first human sound she had heard since she had awakened.

Unable to answer, she simply stared.

He threw a long leg over the back of his horse and slid down easily, the horse's reins and trappings jingling softly with the motion.

"Are you lost?" he asked. It was a pleasant voice, low and calm, with a ring of authority to it.

After a moment, Ivy nodded.

He quickly crossed the rocky beach between them, his boots crunching. Even as he approached, he was unfastening the heavy cape that was flung over his shoulders.

"You look fair frozen."

Ivy shrank from his grasp as he reached out, but he simply draped the long cape around her shoulders. There was nothing menacing about his face, she realized. The frown simply appeared to be one of concern and confusion.

The cape was of gray wool, lined with soft silk, warm from the heat of his body. Ivy stared up at him, shivering.

"How came you to be here?" he went on. "Were you separated from your party? Where were you going?"

With a conscious effort, Ivy took her hand from her mouth. Slowly, feeling dazed, she shook her head.

"I don't know," she whispered after a long pause. "I can't remember."

Her voice was hoarse, and shook when she spoke.

"What? Nothing at all?" His dark brows narrowed; he spoke as if he had a right to know.

Ivy shook her head.

Frowning, he turned and stared up the beach, first one way, then the other.

"You have no baggage? No horse? You've seen no one else?"

He turned back to her, and she noticed that his eyes were gray, like the rock and the ocean and sky, as if he had been made from the colors of the earth around them. She found herself noticing the stitching down the front of his doublet, the filigree buttons of silver that ran down the careful pleats. His gloves had wide cuffs, the supple leather folded over.

He studied her just as carefully, but seemed to find no answers to his questions.

"Your name?"

"Ivy."

He lifted a dark brow. "This is passing odd. Is it Lady Ivy? Mrs. Ivy? Or just Ivy?"

It was like a riddle, one that she had no answer to. She elected not to answer.

He took her by the elbow, and she shrank away from his height.

"God's grace, mistress, you needn't fear me," he exclaimed, and he sounded offended. "I mean you no harm. Look you, you are wet, you are cold, you may be ill, and most assuredly you're lost. Let me take you back to the keep, and my lady grandmother can see to your needs. I can make inquiries around the village, and see if we

43

can sort out your muddle."

She wondered if she had stumbled into some bizarre play or an elaborate joke. She thought about running, but had no idea which way to go. The hand on her elbow was firm, pulling her across the beach.

Ivy allowed herself to be led over to the horse, a tall, black animal with a white mark on its forehead. She thought briefly of objecting, but her tongue felt useless, and her mind was having trouble forming coherent thoughts.

None of it was real—the beach, the horse, the tall, beautiful man with the dark hair streaming from his patrician brow.

Bits and pieces of his speech echoed in Ivy's head. . . . *This is passing odd. . . . God's grace, mistress . . . my lady grandmother . . .*

And yet it was real. The way the horse's breath showed in the air, and the distant cry of the gulls, and the soft creak of leather as he swung into his saddle. He reached down, and his hands were strong and firm as he lifted her up and pulled her onto the saddle behind him.

Awkwardly, Ivy clutched at the saddle, noticing the baroque designs tooled into the dark leather, the decorative silver swirls on the harness. She felt very unsteady, very high from the ground.

She noticed, for the first time, the dull light of the sun showing through the cloudy skies, struggling to break through. Everything was too vivid to be simply a dream.

"I pray you, don't fall. You don't feel very sure of yourself. Put your arms around my waist." *I pray you* . . . Again, the odd speech.

Ivy didn't answer. She simply sat, still and shocked, as the man guided his horse across the rocky beach and up a twisting path that climbed the hillside.

He seemed sure of his way. His waist was solid beneath her arms, and the horse seemed to know the path well. They climbed the rocky, wooded hillside, and the beach disappeared from view.

"Do you remember coming down this way?" he asked suddenly, looking over his shoulder at Ivy.

"No," she answered quickly, certainly. None of it was familiar—the rocky path, the twisted, dark evergreens or barren branches of the winter wood. As the horse climbed higher, the sound of the surf grew fainter, the smell of salt air less pungent.

"Well, you must needs have. This is the only path down. Unless of course, you came from the sea. And this is a damned unlikely place to make a crossing."

Ivy glanced back over her shoulder as the horse turned a switchback, and caught sight of the sea between the trees.

"Why?" she asked. "Crossing to where?"

Behind her, she felt the man tense. Did her voice, her speech sound as strange to him as his

45

did to her? Or was it the question that surprised him?

"Nowhere," he replied after a moment. "Unless of course you were headed north to Ireland. But God knows that no man in his right mind would try to go to Ireland now. It would be like escaping Hades for Hell."

Ivy felt much the same as she had when the first cold wave had splashed over her. England. She was somewhere in England. Along the west coast, if she remembered her geography correctly.

The sky grew brighter as they reached the summit of the hill, and the horse led them to an expanse of grassy flatland, bordered with misty trees. The path joined to a wider road, dirt with tufts of rough grass growing in it.

The book. It was the book. I was reading that poem . . . that spell . . . and then here I am. It can't be real, and yet it seems real. What did it say, that poem?

The road turned into a wooded grove and then, abruptly, seemed to end in a circle of pale sky.

"Look you," said the dark-haired gentleman, stopping the horse abruptly and gesturing at the view that suddenly spread before them. "Do you know this place? Have you been here before?"

Ivy drew in another breath—this time stunned by the beauty of the view. They were at the top of a steep bluff, staring down into a valley below.

To her left, the sea spread out in an expanse

46

of dark, smoky blue until it disappeared beneath a soft blanket of fog. The sun had appeared at last, and only faint traces of mist softened the silhouettes of the dark trees that climbed the hill below them.

In the valley before her lay an enchanted village, houses and buildings of gray stone winding around cobbled streets. Their chimneys and gabled roofs and church spires rose from the treetops, reaching up toward the brightening sky. It was a beautiful, happy-looking village, nestled in its snug little valley, protected from the fierce winds by the two promontories of land that cradled it.

Breathless with a strange excitement, Ivy stared at the picture-book village, the sweeping, fog-shrouded sea.

And on the hillside opposite them, as in all good fairy tales, stood a castle. The village houses climbed up the hillside and then thinned, and then there was only one road leading up to the great castle walls.

It was built of the same gray stone as the cliff that it stood upon, so that it appeared to simply rise out of the earth it was built upon, out of the stone and the sea and the soft greens and browns of the trees.

The single road that led to the great gateway seemed to beckon, to tell the traveler that this was journey's end. And the ancient castle itself seemed to shimmer as the last of the fog drifted around the four rounded watchtowers that rose from the crumbling walls.

"Oh." Ivy exhaled with a long, unsteady breath, forgetting her fear, forgetting even the dark-haired man that held her on his horse. "Oh, it's beautiful! It's stunning! That castle . . ."

"Do you like it?" the man asked, and there was a note of surprise in his voice. "The old monster. It's my home."

"Oh, how wonderful!" Ivy felt her fear lifting like the fog. "How lucky you are! Is it really?" He looked over his shoulder at her, and his dark eyes shone with a kind of bitter amusement as he gazed at the castle. His smile was a little mocking, giving him an almost wicked look.

"Yes, of course." The wind tossed his hair, and he shook it back with an impatient gesture. "Who would claim such a burdensome place if it were not theirs? I've lived there most of my years."

He turned the horse down the treacherous-looking trail.

"Wythecombe Keep," he added as an afterthought.

Ivy clutched his waist with both hands to keep from falling.

"I'm Julian Ramsden," he went on, as if he hadn't noticed.

Ramsden. The same name as in the book.

He appeared not to notice her surprise, and they were silent as the horse guided them down into the valley, where the sea and village and castle lay before them like a medieval tapestry of gray and green and brown.

Chapter Three

"See you anything familiar?"

The horse was carrying them through the village, over narrow streets of cobblestone. The winter sunlight was cold, and the breeze whipped in from the nearby sea, carrying a cold salt scent.

Ivy stared at the stone buildings, the roofs of heavy thatch or dark tile, the thick glass windows, and the smoking chimneys that scented the sea air with wood smoke.

Two small girls were playing in front of a cottage, in dark dresses with wide white collars. Their bulky skirts dragged on the wet ground as they dropped pebbles into a puddle. They looked up as Ivy and Julian passed by. Their eyes widened with curiosity, and something almost like fear.

Ivy wondered how it appeared to them—the lord of the manor riding by, tall and dark and dangerous-looking, with a bedraggled young woman behind him, barefooted and clinging to his back, wrapped in the heavy folds of his cape. She could feel the wet, tangled snarls of her hair against her face and throat. Perhaps the children had a good reason to stare.

I must look like a fright. I can only imagine the expression on my face.

Ivy attempted to smile at them, but they simply stared back, owl-eyed. She noticed their white linen caps, small and shaped to their heads, tied neatly under their chubby chins.

Incredible. A movie set, a living museum. She must be dreaming.

A young woman drawing water from a stone well glanced sharply at them over her caped shoulder and looked hastily away.

"Have you no memory of passing through here?" Julian repeated, and Ivy looked up to see him watching her over his broad shoulder.

"No. No memory at all."

The horse carried them between the cottages that climbed the hillside, onto a road of hard-packed earth.

"Your voice is strange," Julian observed suddenly. "I've lived in London, I've met men from all manner of places. But never have I heard speech like yours. Where are you from?"

"I don't remember." Ivy wondered what he would do if she told him the truth. Laugh. Have her locked up as a lunatic. Maybe have her burned as a witch. She decided that lying was the best option.

"Perhaps you were set upon by thieves. You don't seem to be injured, though. Were you traveling alone?"

Deciding to keep her strange accent to herself, Ivy shrugged. Her heart was thudding with a strange, hollow beat. Not exactly fear, though she'd be a fool not to be afraid. A feeling of fate at work, a feeling of anticipation.

The horse climbed higher along the hillside road, bordered with barren trees and rough clumps of grass, yellow and tired-looking in the winter light. The wind was faster up here. It tangled her hair into her eyes, and snapped the folds of Julian's heavy cape around her cold legs and bare feet.

She wondered if he was cold without it. She raised her face to look at him again.

She saw his stark profile as he turned his face and stared up the hill at the castle.

Like a sudden blow, disbelief struck Ivy anew.

She stared up at the huge gray walls rising out of the hill above them, at the battlements, the narrow windows cut into the stone. Three dark walls, built against the hillside. Four round towers at each corner.

The road ended at the castle entrance, an arch of stone between two smaller towers, huge wooden doors standing wide as if to admit them. The wind seemed to race down the road ahead of her to the gatehouse, through the massive doors, and into the courtyard, where who-knew-what awaited her.

Ivy drew a sharp, uneven breath. Her face felt tight; she felt like a frightened cat, ready to spring and bolt.

But there was nowhere to go—just the rocky, grassy field surrounding the dark walls, and the wooded hill, and the cold sea below.

She looked again at Julian and wondered if she should fear him.

His shoulders were stiff and straight beneath the black doublet; the wind whipped the folds of white sleeve that showed through the slashes. It blew his dark hair back from his face as he turned to look at her.

His expression was close, guarded. There was a bitter look in his gray eyes and in the tight lines around his perfect mouth.

"And here you are," he said, and his voice was very quiet, and slightly mocking, "at Wythecombe Keep, quite by accident."

A quiver chased through Ivy, and her throat felt tight.

"You must be freezing," Julian said suddenly, and the disturbing look was gone from his face. He simply looked worried, and devilishly good-looking. His hair was very dark against the gray sky, his noble profile distinct and well cut. "Let's get you out of the wind. Grandmother and Susanna will be in the gallery, I shan't doubt. They'll find you something dry to wear, and something to eat."

Who was Susanna? Ivy wondered to herself, but said nothing. Her hands tightened around Julian's waist as they rode into up the hill, through the arched entrance, and into the paved courtyard.

The courtyard was empty, surrounded by a horseshoe of silent buildings. Ivy saw a covered well, a chapel. No servant came to take the horse; nobody appeared to call a greeting. The place looked curiously deserted.

"Don't fall," Julian advised her as he climbed from the saddle. He reached up and pulled Ivy down after him. She felt very small and unsteady next to the tall horse.

"This way," Julian said, and she followed him to a wide staircase and up four broad steps to a double door.

He pushed it open, and Ivy stepped into the great hall of Wythecombe Keep.

It was a long room with a vaulted stone ceiling that made her think of a church. It was almost barren of furnishings—a long table, a few chairs, a bench against a wall. Light streamed in beams from a few high windows, bright trails in the dusty quiet. There was no sign of life, only a fire crackling in the huge fireplace.

Arched doorways led to unknown places in the castle. A circular staircase of stone wound around one corner alcove and disappeared.

It was beautiful and frightening.

Julian was casually removing his gloves and raking his hand through his tangled locks. He tossed his gloves to the table and looked over at Ivy.

"You looked shocked," he observed. "Well you might. It didn't always look like this, you know."

"It didn't?" Ivy couldn't imagine what else to say.

"No. Before the siege, it was as fine and comfortable as any place in London, or anywhere, for that matter. Rich carpets, chairs upholstered in good brocades, paintings and stools and books and plates. All gone, of course." His voice echoed in the vast, empty space.

"But why?" Ivy sounded very small and quiet.

"That's the price royalists pay for closing their gates to our noble Lord Protector Cromwell, didn't you know? Penalties paid to the Crown. My lands, my title, my money, and anything of value we owned. Gone." He turned away. "Sad, isn't it?" he asked, but his tone was flippant, as if it meant nothing, and the smile he tossed her was mischievous.

"Come along, Ivy-who-thee-may-be, and let's tend to your muddle. We shall see what my grandmother makes of this."

Ivy didn't know what to make of it herself, but she followed Julian across the room and up the twisting staircase, her heavy skirts dragging.

The stairs were narrow, the stone worn in the center from generations of footsteps. There was a silent, deserted air about the place, and Julian's pirate-looking boots seemed very loud.

She followed him down a long, cold hallway. They passed an open door, and Ivy saw that this room too was curiously empty.

At the end of the long hall, Julian stopped before a closed door. "The gallery," he announced. "It's my lady grandmother's favorite room. It's one of the rooms that was refurbished during Elizabeth's time, when the family was in favor and fortune smiling."

Elizabeth who? Ivy wondered, and realized with a start that he probably meant Elizabeth Tudor, the virgin queen.

He opened the heavy door and beckoned to Ivy. "Pray come, it's the most pleasant room in the keep."

Shivering in her wet dress and heavy cape, the stone floor cold against her bare feet, Ivy followed.

"My lady, I've brought a guest," Julian announced.

Ivy looked around, astonished. This room was warm and bright, as rich and comfortable as the rest of the rooms had been cold and stark. It was paneled and floored in rich wood, carved in elegant Renaissance patterns, and the sloping ceilings were plastered in smooth white.

Sunlight came through many-paned windows in gleaming wood frames, some with small designs of stained glass in their centers, and the light played over the cushioned window seats

55

and tasseled stools and chairs upholstered in jewel-bright colors.

Through the windows Ivy could see the wooded hills beyond the castle walls, and the endless sea.

If Wythecombe Keep had been plundered by Cromwell's troops, it would appear that they had missed this room.

Wondering, she turned her attention to the two women sitting by the fireplace. Julian was speaking to them in low, urgent tones.

One woman—his grandmother, she assumed—looked to be in her sixties or thereabouts. She sat in a tall-backed chair, queenlike in her posture. Her lined face was pleasantly curved, her dark eyes bright and interested as she looked from Julian to Ivy and back to Julian again.

She wore a gown of midnight blue velvet with a white collar, high-necked and falling over her shoulders, trimmed in thick lace. Her white hair was drawn smoothly back from her plump face, and disappeared beneath a cap of white lace settled neatly on the back of her head.

At a stool by her feet sat a young girl in her late teens—presumably Susanna—so like Julian in appearance that Ivy knew she must be a younger sister. She had the same gray eyes, the same full mouth and slanted cheekbones. Her thick dark hair was drawn into a smooth roll at the base of her neck and fell in soft ringlets around her face. She watched Ivy with lively curiosity, her eyes sparkling. Her wine red gown was made in the same fashion as the one Ivy wore—slightly high-waisted, almost off the shoulder, and trimmed with falling lace, with full sleeves slashed to show white silk, and trimmed with pearl buttons.

As Julian finished speaking, Susanna rose quickly to her feet and crossed the long room to seize Ivy's hands.

"I'm Susanna, Julian's sister. What a merriment to have a guest! Did you really have nothing with you? You may wear my things till we find your place. What a very odd thing, to be left on the shore! How came you to be there, do you reckon?"

Ivy drew breath to speak, but Susanna rushed on, her words almost tripping over each other. "We shall have to make up a bedchamber for you. Pity all the good beds are gone. Did you really ride through the village looking like that? How everyone must be talking—"

"All of them together could not speak as much as you, Susanna," her grandmother interjected, and Susanna gave a good-natured laugh and fell silent as Lady Margaret approached.

She held the book in her arms.

The leather cover was smooth and shining, not a stitch on the binding loose or worn, but Ivy recognized it as surely as if she had seen it a thousand times before.

The old woman held the book firmly against

her ample breast, one hand protectively against the cover.

Ivy remembered the words written on the first page. *To Margaret Ramsden from Juliana, 1589.*

Could this be the same Margaret Ramsden?

Lady Margaret's dark eyes were watching Ivy's face. "And here you are, young Ivy. I can't think but that fate brought you to us." She took Ivy's hand in her own plump, wrinkled one and turned it over, glancing briefly at the palm. "I think you'll stay a while," she announced, closing Ivy's cold hand in her own warm one. "What think you, Julian?"

"I think we'd better find out where she came from, and how she came to be here," Julian retorted. His tone was sharp, and Ivy looked up, forcing her gaze away from the precious book— the book that held the key to her return.

Was it her imagination, or was Julian staring at the book as well? He looked fierce, and Ivy wondered what had changed his pleasant mood. "I'll thank you to leave the matter in my hands, my lady. I need none of your meddling."

Lady Margaret made a mocking face at Susanna and Ivy.

"And as for you, Susanna," Julian went on, "where, pray, is poor Mrs. Sisson? Are you hiding from her again?"

He went to a side table, picked up a glass decanter, and took a sparkling wineglass from beside it. "You should be attending your lessons, sister, instead of hiding at your grandmother's knee, wasting your time with idle nonsense."

"Fiddle and twaddle, all in a muddle," muttered Lady Margaret.

The decanter of wine slipped from Julian's hands and shattered on the gleaming oak floor. The firelight shone on the shards of crystal and the spilled dark wine.

Susanna gave a delighted laugh, and Julian rounded on them with a face of thunder.

"God's nightgown!" he roared, and then stopped abruptly at the sight of Ivy's shocked face.

"Pardon me," he finished coolly, "I seem to be clumsy today." He drew a deep breath and glared at the three women. "Susanna, find Mrs. Sisson and attend to your learning. My lady, will you find our guest—"

"Ivy," corrected Lady Margaret.

"As you will. Find Ivy some dry clothing. Better yet, find a servant and let her tend to it."

"I don't mind," Lady Margaret replied.

"I don't either," Susanna put in. "Mrs. Sisson has been gone for near a week, Julian. She came down with the most unfortunate case of spots, and headaches all the time."

"And has left? For good?" Julian asked. "How many is that, Susanna?"

"A good many, I guess," the girl replied, looking not the least concerned.

"And no one thought to inform me?"

"You do get upset, Julian, whenever a governess leaves," his grandmother pointed out.

Julian glared at one woman and then the other.

Neither seemed intimidated.

"God grant me patience," he muttered, and stalked toward the doorway. He paused before his grandmother, and then, to Ivy's shock, he reached out and calmly confiscated the precious book from his grandmother's hands.

"Your pardon, my lady," he said, as graciously as if the deliberate act had been an unavoidable accident.

All three women stared at his back as he left the room, the heavy door slamming behind him.

"What a tyrant!" Susanna cried, her gray eyes dark with anger. "Pay him no mind, Ivy."

Lady Margaret looked down at her empty hands with a sorrowful look, and then gave a soft sigh and a shrug.

"Julian," said Lady Margaret thoughtfully, "has always had a bad temper. It will affect his health, I think. Come, Ivy, let us not neglect you. I think a warm bath and a fresh dress. Then food and a bit of sleep."

"Thank you," Ivy said softly.

"Not a bit. We're delighted to have thee, child."

Ivy looked up to see Lady Margaret and Susanna exchange quick glances. Margaret looked positively devious; Susanna's eyes danced as if she had just heard a wicked joke.

"Now we shall have a merry time," Susanna announced, tossing her dark ringlets. "I shall go find Doll and tell her to ready your chamber."

She laughed her sparkling laugh as she went.

Ivy wondered if they were all a little mad—laughing Susanna and her birdlike, sly-eyed grandmother, and Julian, with his sudden, unexplained rage.

And me, she added silently. Am I really here, or am I just dreaming this? And what is my place among these people?

"It doesn't help to worry," Lady Margaret said suddenly, and Ivy jumped. "We'll find your family, young Ivy. Now come, and I'll show you to your chamber."

Ivy glanced at a shelf of books as she left the room, wondering where Julian had taken the one she needed so desperately.

She followed Lady Margaret down narrow hallways of dark stone, shivering in the chill air. She wondered if she would be here long enough to find her way about, or if the enchantment would wear off, and she would find herself back at home.

"This should suit you," Lady Margaret announced.

Ivy jumped, wondering if the woman had read her thoughts, but Lady Margaret had stopped before a heavy door and was gesturing toward the room beyond.

Following her in, Ivy made a swift inventory of the chamber. It was small and sparsely furnished. A bed with a tall headboard of carved dark wood, canopied and curtained in dusty russet fabric. A table and chair sat before an empty fireplace, and that was all. Heavy, diamond-paned windows looked out onto the empty courtyard of the castle and the hill and sea beyond.

Ivy was grateful for the light, after the musty darkness of the corridors.

As she looked out, she saw Julian riding out through the arched gateway, his brownish black hair shining in the winter light, his full, long breeches tucked into the wide cuffs of his boots.

"Good," Lady Margaret said behind her. "This will give Julian something to do, apart from sulking about. Ever since the war he's had altogether too little to occupy his mind. He used to be quite a jolly young blade when he went up to court. City life suited him. And the politics. He loved the politics! I think he was actually looking forward to the siege. We held the castle against Cromwell's troops for almost forty days."

Ivy tried to imagine it. "Just the three of you?"

Lady Margaret's eyes almost disappeared when she laughed, and she looked quite girlish for a moment, despite the silvery hair and soft wrinkles. "Well, there were more of us then. We had our people for the stables and the priest and the steward, and all the house servants. It was very crowded, in fact. Not like this. We were the last castle in the county to fall. The Roundheads were in fits, I can assure you," she added proudly, and Ivy began to suspect that the old woman had actually enjoyed the siege.

"Now Julian is in fits," Susanna announced,

appearing at the door with her arms loaded with what appeared to be a bundle of clothing. She tilted her dark head and sent Ivy a mischievous smile. Ivy noted again the resemblance to Julian, the large, deep-set eyes, the prominent cheekbones. "He hates to lose, you know."

Ivy thought about that, the proud, almost arrogant way he carried himself, the authority with which he spoke. He didn't strike her as a man accustomed to losing.

"Did you find Doll?" Lady Margaret asked her granddaughter. "Poor Ivy will need clean linens, and blankets, and a fire. And warm water."

"She was sitting by the fire with her feet up," Susanna answered, and the way she rolled her eyes implied that this was nothing new. "I've brought Ivy some of my things," she added.

"When I was young, servants knew how to behave," Lady Margaret observed.

"That was a passing age ago," Susanna answered, sounding very cheerful despite her disrespectful observation.

"Young women knew how to behave as well," Lady Margaret added mournfully.

" 'Tis likely they did," Susanna retorted, sounding surly. "And they had dances and masked balls and trips to London and suitors to court them and new gowns as they wished." She dumped her bundle of clothing on the russet-covered bed. "I hope you don't perish of boredom here, Ivy. I think I may, before overlong."

"I don't think I'll find it boring at all," Ivy answered honestly. Terrifying, maybe. More than a little eerie. But boring?

"Where is that strumpet Doll?" Lady Margaret demanded impatiently, and as if in answer, the maligned Doll appeared in the doorway.

She was young, though not as young as Susanna, and her pretty, if somewhat petulant face examined Ivy suspiciously over a pile of linens. She had very green eyes, and her brown hair curled from beneath her white cap.

"I didn't know we were having guests," she announced in defensive tones.

"Now you do," Lady Margaret informed her in a sharp voice.

Doll gave an insulted sniff and began her business of changing the bed.

"Doll will help you change," Lady Margaret told Ivy, "as soon as the chamber is warmed. And then you should rest a piece before the evening meal. You look quite agitated."

"You should give her something for it," Susanna suggested, "before she takes ill. We don't want her dying, or any such trouble."

"What a rude child you are. Poor Ivy will think you've been raised by wolves."

"Julian has the temper of a wolf." Susanna's smile flashed again. "Mayhap in a way I have been."

"A soothing posset would be just the thing," Lady Margaret announced, ignoring her granddaughter. "Come with me, Susanna, and I'll teach you the proper way to brew one."

Susanna looked agreeable to the idea. "Fair enough. Ivy, when you get dressed, wear the plum-colored gown. I think it will suit your hair."

Lady Margaret swept from the room, her blue gown trailing behind her. After a moment Susanna followed.

Ivy was left alone with the silent maid, who offered her only a sullen glance as she went about the business of putting blankets on the bed.

Doll spoke not a word as she left the room, then returned with a pile of wood and an iron pot filled with smoking embers. She gave Ivy a resentful look as she built the fire.

Awkward and cold, Ivy stood in the middle of the room until the fire blazed up. She moved closer to the flames, holding her hands out to the crackling heat.

"By the by," Doll said suddenly, and Ivy looked over her shoulder to see her standing by the chamber door, her plump arms crossed over her laced bodice. "I'd be careful, if I was you. Anything the old woman gives you to drink, you better ask what's in it. The good Lord only knows what it might be. Not that I ever said such a thing, if anyone was to ask," she added, and left the room with a dark look.

Ivy swallowed as the heavy door banged closed. What could it mean? She sank to the wooden chair next to the fire and buried her face in her hands, grateful to be alone.

Amy Elizabeth Saunders

It was silent except for the hissing and crackling of the fire and, outside the thick stone walls of the chamber, the mournful sound of the wind as it rushed in off the empty sea.

Chapter Four

"I don't much care where she came from," Susanna announced. "Why fret, Julian? It's nice to have company. I get tired of seeing your sour old face."

"Old be damned, you monkey," Julian retorted, glaring across the long table. Even as a child, Susanna had been outspoken, and now she was simply brazen. It came of having her run of the castle, he supposed, and not having anything to do with herself.

"I listened in outside the door," Susanna went on, "whilst Doll was helping her dress. What a terrible accent she has! Do you think she's Dutch, Julian?"

"You ignorant child." Julian tapped the side of his goblet with a distracted gesture. "She doesn't sound the least bit Dutch. Or Irish, or Italian, for that matter."

"Perhaps she's a mermaid, washed up from the sea," his grandmother said with a light laugh. "What think you, Julian?"

"What utter rot." He took a long drink of wine and glowered down the table. "I'll thank you to speak sensibly, madam, and not trouble me with your ludicrous fancies."

His grandmother beamed at him as if he hadn't spoken.

"Like Venus, born of the sea foam," she went on.

"Venus is always fat, in paintings," Susanna put in, "and runs about quite naked."

"What did Mrs. Sisson teach you?" Julian demanded. "Certainly not manners, Susanna. That's hardly the kind of remark one expects from a well-bred young lady."

"Well, when next I go to court to visit the queen, I shall keep that in mind." Susanna's tone was petulant.

Julian resisted the urge to snap back. After all, it wasn't so hard to understand. At Susanna's age, she should be making her appearance at court. She would have been a prize, sought after and wooed. Chevaliers would have been writing poems to her beauty, and suitors sending her hothouse bunches of nosegays with fluttering ribbons.

And instead she sat there, trapped in a crumbling castle with only her grandmother for company, her brother and guardian stripped of his lands and title. She had no dowry, and no suitor so stirred by her beauty that he would risk the displeasure of Lord Cromwell.

"Wherever she came from, I think our little Ivy should stay," his grandmother said suddenly, interrupting his musings.

"I do not." Julian took another drink of wine. "Did you ever think, my lady, that she might be a danger to us?"

"She hardly looks it," cried Susanna. "Really, Julian!"

"Think," he urged them. "She simply appeared, exactly where I ride every day. No trace of anyone or anything near. She's not a peasant, you can tell by her hands. And she seemed uncommon clean. Where did she come from? And no more of your poetical fluff about Venus rising from the sea, please."

"What are you trying to say?" Lady Margaret demanded, setting her own glass down.

"She could be a spy," Julian suggested, lowering his voice.

Susanna gave a delighted whoop of laughter.

"It's not at all a jest, I assure you. The only reason I'm not in prison now is that I bought my way out. And Cromwell wouldn't mind an excuse to change his decision. Perhaps she was planted here to watch us, to see if we're involved in any kind of planned rebellion."

"I hope that we are not, Julian." Lady Margaret spoke quietly.

Amy Elizabeth Saunders

"Truth to tell, I wish we were. But no, my lady, it's all over. All the loyalists have been subdued. There is nobody left to fight."

For a few minutes, they all sat silently, the three of them in the dining hall where once there had been at least 30 every night.

"Do you know anything about her?" Julian asked, suddenly regarding his grandmother with a suspicious eye.

"She seems very nice," was the noncommittal reply.

"But do you know—"

The hall suddenly resounded with the crash of breaking glass and the clang of metal, and Julian leapt swiftly to his feet, reaching for his dagger.

Doll stood behind him, and at her feet lay the remnants of the dinner she had been carrying. Broken crockery lay in shards; the soup tureen lay in jagged pieces in a steaming puddle.

"I didn't do it," Doll said in a defensive tone.

Julian looked at the tilted tray in her hands.

"I didn't," Doll protested. "I was as careful as could be, sir. It felt like someone grabbed the tray and give it a pull, that's what. Frightened me half to death. 'Tisn't normal, that."

Susanna began to laugh and Julian turned to her, ready to enlighten her as to what was amusing and what was not, when Ivy entered the room.

Perhaps he had been away from court too long. Perhaps he hadn't spent enough time, of late, in the company of women. Perhaps comb-

70

ing the wench's hair and washing her face had made more of a difference than he could've imagined.

Whatever the reason, Julian thought, the waif-like creature he had found by the sea had suddenly been transformed into a bewitching young woman.

He noticed for the first time the sweet shape of her face, a heart shape, a kittenish broadness across the brow, tapering to a narrow, sweet curve of a chin. A small mouth, but perfectly curved and bowed. Very dark brown eyes, large and soulful-looking, thickly lashed, and they seemed even darker because of her complexion, pale and glowing, tinted with the same blush as a ripe peach.

And her hair glowed. Brilliant copper, sparkling highlights of gold, shining in a million little ringlets, like an Italian painting of an angel he had seen once. It was pulled away from her face, twisted and intertwined with satin ribbons, but everywhere small curls had escaped, and they moved softly around her slender neck and over her bare shoulders and down over the back of her plum-colored gown.

And he had not noticed her figure earlier in the day. He had thought her as scrawny as a child. But the tightly laced satin of her gown showed that despite her small stature, she had all the curves of a woman full grown—a perfectly delightful waist, and perfect shoulders, and the tops of her very white breasts showed round and soft over the top of her low-cut gown. . . .

"Sit down, Julian," Lady Margaret said, "it's only our little orphan."

"Born of the sea, like Venus," Susanna added, laughter bubbling in her voice.

"Mind your clattering tongue, you rude child." Julian sounded a little harsher than he had intended.

"Sit down, dear," Lady Margaret called, gesturing to an empty seat, and Ivy followed his grandmother's bidding without a word. Her smile was hesitant but charming, he thought.

He wondered again who she was. She didn't have the bearing of a peasant, and her hands looked like silk. Not a common jade, certainly. A woman of the streets had a certain walk, a bold and sure way of moving, as if she were already naked and displaying her wares for the world to see. Ivy carried herself too humbly, too modestly for that. Too fair to be a Gypsy. Not Irish, or Scot, to judge by her voice.

Doll came back into the room carrying a new tray, and Julian watched carefully as Ivy was served. She had manners, he could see; she accepted her plate graciously and waited for the others at the table to be served.

It made no sense.

Not a damn bit.

With each passing moment, Julian was getting the distinct feeling that something was afoot, something he wasn't privy to.

And he didn't like it.

Ivy felt as if she had been trapped in a weird dream. Perhaps it was the wine she drank, dark and rich and soothing to her frayed nerves. She rarely drank, except for an occasional glass of champagne at a wedding or an eggnog at Christmas. But she didn't want to call attention to herself by making any unusual requests, so she drank her wine.

The food was good—roast beef and good bread and preserved fruits stewed together with raisins—but she ate without really tasting it.

Instead, her attention was fixed on the three people at the table—the dark and brooding Julian, who watched her with a hawklike stare, and pretty young Susanna, who laughed about anything, even when it didn't strike Ivy as funny, and Lady Margaret, serene and gentle, who beamed over the table like a grandmother in a Norman Rockwell painting, as if this were the most mundane and ordinary of gatherings.

And she was fascinated, of course, by the dining hall—the high walls of smooth stone, the dark beams that crossed the high ceiling, the row of diamond-paned windows showing only the dark night beyond and reflecting the glimmer of the candles that glowed around the large, almost empty room.

There was a tapestry on one wall, as large as a garage door, of a medieval hunting party. Ivy couldn't wait to see it in the daylight, to examine the minute stitches that formed the slender women and beplumed suitors, the gangly hounds and hawks.

On the opposite wall there was a portrait, a dark-haired young woman with a solemn expression, in a pearl-trimmed Tudor headdress. She seemed to watch the four diners with her large, solemn dark eyes.

"My great-grandmother," Lady Margaret said suddenly, seeing Ivy's interest. "Susanna of Denbeigh. It's a very charming story. I shall have to tell you sometime."

I'll look forward to it," Ivy answered. *Susanna of Denbeigh—wasn't that the first name in the book?*

"They say she was a witch," young Susanna said, leaning forward over her plate and staring at Ivy with dancing eyes. "Now what do you reckon my mother was thinking, to have named her own daughter after a witch, Ivy? Do you believe in witches?"

"Of course she does not!" Julian stabbed at his roast as if it might still be alive. "And I'll thank you to stop that stupid, ill-thought noise, Susanna."

"Witches is everywhere," Doll said, suddenly appearing at Ivy's elbow, filling her wineglass from a silver jug. "Everyone knows that."

"Superstitious want-wits believe that," Julian snapped, his fingers tightening on his fork. "And

74

you, Doll, had better hold your tongue when you serve at my table."

Doll's pretty green eyes narrowed, and she gave her employer a sullen glance.

"I have it!" Susanna cried out, clasping her hands together. "That's it, Julian! No wonder Ivy appeared so suddenly—she's a witch, Julian!"

"She has red hair," Doll pointed out, as if that meant something.

"Do hold your tongue, Doll," Lady Margaret suggested.

Ivy felt sick. Everyone at the table, save Lady Margaret, was staring at her, hard. Susanna looked breathless with excitement, Doll suspicious, and Julian . . . well, Julian looked plain furious.

His dark eyes narrowed, and his mouth tightened; a muscle twitched in his jaw. He drew himself up to his full height and drew a deep breath.

"Oh, mercy," murmured his grandmother.

"Damn!" His voice roared out into the quiet hall and echoed beneath the high ceiling.

He glared at Susanna, and Doll, and, most unreasonably, at Ivy.

"What in the name of God need I do to be obeyed? Did I or did I not say I would have no talk of witchcraft within these walls?"

Doll looked terrified. Susanna's cheeks flushed red and her brows drew together. Lady Margaret continued eating, unperturbed.

"Did I or did I not?"

Amy Elizabeth Saunders

Susanna, glowering at her plate, muttered something.

"Am I or am I not the master of my house?"

"You're the master of something, but I don't like to say what," Susanna snapped, hurling her napkin to the table.

"Oh, no," muttered Lady Margaret.

"You impudent brat." Julian wasn't shouting anymore, to Ivy's relief, but there was a cold anger in his voice that made her heart race. "Have you no more brains in that head than a mewling infant? I have endured enough, Susanna. You and your stupid mouth may well be the undoing of all of us. Now hear me, and hear me well. You, and you, and you as well—" and he pointed at each person in the room, including—most unfairly, she thought—Ivy. "I will not tolerate one more word on this ridiculous subject. And anyone who thinks to defy me will leave this place."

"Oh, Julian," began his grandmother.

"Oh, Julian be damned to you," he retorted. " 'Tis no joking matter. What starts as a young girl's foolish talk leads to all manner of disaster. Tell me, clever girl, how many supposed witches have died this year alone because of harebrained gossips and silly old women's tales?"

"How should I know?" Susanna retorted, rolling her eyes and looking more like a twentieth-century teenager than Ivy would have dreamed possible.

"You will know, because I shall tell you, you ignorant creature. In Essex County alone, thirty

76

women hanged and burned. In all of England, twice that. In Scotland, they say a full hundred a year. In Germany, too many to count—and there are no laws against torture there."

"God rest their souls," Lady Margaret said softly, and for a long moment the room was silent.

"And you wonder, Susanna," Julian went on more quietly, "why I caution your indiscreet and prattling ways? These are dangerous times. I have warned you time and time again, and I say to all of you: no more. Not a breath of it. Susanna, you shall stay in your room for a fortnight and rethink your ways."

"A fortnight! Julian, you cannot!"

"I can and do, by God! You may stay there without company."

"Not even Grandmother?"

"Especially not Grandmother. She encourages this . . . stupid rubbish."

Susanna looked horrified and angry. Her red cheeks grew redder, and tears stood in her dark eyes. "I will not heed, Julian."

"You will, or you will take leave of my house."

Susanna stood, her eyes filling, and then she ran from the room, her wine red skirts flapping around her ankles.

Ivy sat silently, her head lowered. Having grown up in a house full of conflict and unreasonable tempers, she had learned quickly how to make herself unobtrusive.

"Julian, that was cruel," Lady Margaret said quietly.

"Cruel, my lady?" Julian retorted. "Is it crueler than hanging, my lady? And I'll thank you to remember that I am the master of this household, and that includes yourself. If you dare to gainsay me, you will not care for the consequences."

At last Lady Margaret looked angry. "Shame upon thee, Julian Ramsden!" she cried, her dark eyes snapping. "To speak so to your own grandmother! I never thought I should see the day. If you will excuse me, I find I have little liking for your company," she added in icy tones. "Forgive me, Ivy."

Ivy nodded, but Lady Margaret appeared not to notice as she stood and swept from the table.

"By the way, Julian," she added over her shoulder, "I used to change your dirty drawers."

Julian looked bitterly offended. "What utter rot," he said, and sat for a moment, trying to regain his dignity.

He did very well for almost an entire minute, until suddenly, and without warning, the leg of his chair snapped and broke, sending him crashing to the floor.

"God's nightgown!" he roared from somewhere beneath the table, and Ivy buried her face in her hands as sudden, unexpected laughter welled up inside her, and then broke.

Julian's handsome face appeared over the edge of the table, looking so thoroughly displeased that Ivy laughed even harder.

"I hope we find your family soon," was his comment. "The last thing I need is one more addlepated female around here."

Ivy's face grew warm, and she wished with all her heart that she was back in her shop, or in her cozy apartment, where she and only she gave orders.

She wondered what Julian had done with the precious book. If it was in the castle, she would find it. Until then, she would hold her tongue and make herself as agreeable as she could.

If she hadn't been so worried, she would have found it fascinating.

Sleep evaded her, and she sat by the fire in her chamber, looking at the gowns Susanna had left her. The plum satin she had worn to dinner, the heavy, warm sheen of the fabric, the lining of gold cotton sewn in with careful, tiny stitches. A skirt of heavy wool, a gold color like autumn leaves, and a matching jacket with wide satin cuffs. A deep blue gown of textured velvet with three-quarter–length sleeves that ended in wide lace cuffs. The sleeves were slashed from shoulder to cuff, and gathered at intervals with knots of gold cord and pearls.

She examined a corset, quilted of heavy cotton, that tied at the shoulders with ribbons, and swore not to wear it.

She stared into the flames, and wondered if Lady Margaret suspected that she had arrived here by supernatural means. She wondered if

Susanna really thought she was a witch, or was just chattering in her youthful manner.

She wondered if Julian believed his sister. He didn't believe her story of memory loss, that was obvious. He had watched her through dinner with suspicion written on every line of his face.

She found herself reliving the silent dinner, watching Julian as furtively as he watched her, noting the fierce set of his dark brows, the stone gray of his eyes, the way his dark hair flowed in long, loose waves over the broad shoulders of his black doublet.

She wondered why he wasn't married. In Ivy's experience, good-looking men were always married.

She wondered what he was doing at this moment—was he sleeping in the silent castle, or was he lying awake, wondering what to do about their unwelcome guest?

She paced the room for a while, dressed in Susanna's long white nightgown and a heavy robe of blue velvet, trimmed in dark fur.

She considered climbing into bed, but knew sleep was impossible.

At last she took the candle from the table by the fire and went to the door. Opening it, she saw that the hall was completely dark. It seemed that she could faintly hear the sound of the sea.

It was time to look for the book.

It seemed impossible that she would be able to find anything in the vast darkness. It seemed

more likely that she would lose her way altogether.

She found her way down the curving staircase
and into the great hall. The fire in the cavernous
hearth had burnt down, and glowed red and
gold in the darkness. Ivy hesitated.

There were the great doors leading to the
courtyard, there the corridor to the dining hall,
and that left her three other arched doorways,
all looking equally forbidding, that she had not
yet been through.

One seemed just as likely as another.

Go on, girl, she ordered herself. If you don't
find anything down the first, you come back and
start over.

Her bare feet sounded very loud on the stone
floors.

The hall was cold and dark. She passed by a
large room, empty except for a cushioned window seat. Her candle reflected its light from a
diamond-paned window as she held it aloft.

A stringed instrument—a lute?—lay on the
floor next to the window, a sheet of what looked
like music next to it. She wondered if Julian
played, couldn't imagine it, and decided the silent instrument must be Susanna's.

She moved on down the corridor and stopped
suddenly as she saw light showing from beneath
a closed door.

She listened but heard no movement.

Don't be a coward. Knock, and if anyone an-

swers, say that you lost your way. That's easy enough to believe.

She approached on silent feet and leaned her ear against the door for a moment, listening. Hearing nothing, she knocked.

There was no answer.

She took a deep breath, glanced over her shoulder, and pushed the heavy door open, cringing at the squeaking hinges.

It must be Julian's room, though he was nowhere in sight.

She saw a small room, like a sitting room, and beyond it a large bedchamber. A small fire crackled in the outer room, illuminating the patterned carpet, an upholstered chair, and a long, low table that seemed to be serving as a desk. It was littered with papers and pens, a few open books. Julian's black doublet was flung over the back of the chair.

Moving quietly, Ivy crossed the room and stared into the bedchamber beyond. The bed was large and empty, covered and curtained in dark blue, with a fur throw across the bottom. The headboard rose almost to the ceiling, carved with twisting vines, and each corner bore carved rams' heads, their eyes closed as if in sleep. Unable to resist, Ivy crept closer to the bed to read the letters that were carved into the design.

Nicholas and Susanna Ramsden, 1529.

An open cupboard across the room showed some doublets and the long, loose breeches that Julian seemed to favor. A large hat, beplumed like something from *The Three Musketeers*, lay on the floor, half crushed beneath a pile of clothing and discarded boots. A collection of empty glasses and goblets sat on a table, gathering dust.

Julian, it seemed, was not a housekeeper.

Ivy made her way back to the antechamber, gave another quick look and listen, and assured herself she was alone before going to the desk.

She glanced at the books that lay in plain view, but they were all the wrong size or shape. She went to move a pile of papers, and stopped, unable to resist reading the top sheet. The writing was bold and clear.

. . . dangerous and ill-thought action. I beg you, Julian, to consider—I have been your friend and your trusted companion since our schoolboy days, when we were young and brash and had nothing to lose but a few pieces of silver in a card game, or our dignity in a brawl. But this is no barroom fight, and if you stand your ground and bellow that you will fight to the end, you may indeed find your end. Your lands and money you have already lost. Your refusal to renounce your former king may cost you more.

Because our great friendship is known, I must tell you that Cromwell himself has ordered me to intercede—a task you must know I find no liking for.

He asks that you marry Felicity Astley, whose father holds the lands that once were yours. He sayeth that such a match would please him, were it to happen by spring, at the latest.

Before you shout and refuse, hear me. He has mentioned your lady grandmother, and implied that he has certain information that sits ill with him, that he is loath to explore further—unless his hand is forced.

Consider, then, my fierce friend—

Ivy stopped and was about to turn the page when a log snapped behind her, startling her.

Remembering her quest, she laid the fascinating letter aside and lifted the stack of jumbled papers, careful not to disturb their order.

Nothing.

She moved a book and glanced briefly at the rich embossing on the cover, then lifted another sheet of paper that was covered with tidy figures.

There was the book.

Buried beneath a stack of papers and books, away from prying eyes.

It had been so easy she could barely believe it, but there it was—the dark, smooth cover, the carefully made binding, already so well known to her.

Ivy exhaled, the sound loud in the silent room. She clutched her book to her chest—*her* book, she already thought of it that way—and murmured a silent thanks to God, or fate, or whatever had led her to it so easily.

Her hand shook as she opened it and began to flip through the pages.

To purify the air . . .
Chewing the seeds of Queen Anne's lace will
reduce fertility. . . .
If internal bleeding is suspected . . .
Rosemary water, if properly distilled . . .

The pages were crisper and cleaner than the last time she had handled them, the writing darker and easier to read, even by the dim firelight.

Feverfew should never be gathered when the
moon is waning. . . .
A most useful sleeping potion, but to be used
with caution . . .

And then there it was—the very spell that had brought her here.

Ivy's heart was racing as she saw the poem. She glanced wildly around the empty room.

She prayed quickly, hoping that the spell would work, that it would send her back to her shop as quickly and effectively as it had transported her here.

To her surprise, she felt a stab of remorse—she might never find out what had become of them all—silver-haired Margaret, and merry Susanna, and Julian, with his fierce, dark eyes and beautiful face. She hoped that he would regain his fortune and escape the wrath of the new government.

"Good-bye," she whispered, and her voice quavered a little in the quiet room. "Good luck to all of you."

She took a deep breath and began to read, softly.

"I have sought thee over time and land"—a whisper of a breeze seemed to stir around her— "and found naught but more seeking."

A tremor ran through her body. She swallowed and read on. "I have sought thee through dawn and dusk"—she felt a shimmer, a golden thrill. It was working, working!

"I have sworn that I would seek no more—"

"Or at best, if you do seek again, it had best not be in my bedchamber."

Ivy's heart stopped, and she gave a soft cry as the book was snatched from her hands.

Julian stood before her, the coveted book in his hands. He closed it with a sharp clap.

He was shirtless, his full breeches slung low on his slender hips. His long, full hair hung over the sculpted curves and hollows of his shoulders. His eyes were dark and narrowed as he stared down at her.

"I'm waiting," he announced.

Ivy opened her mouth to speak, but the right words didn't come. She closed her mouth, opened it again, and closed it once more.

"Very good," Julian told her. "Very clever, indeed. I've never seen anyone look quite so much like a fish. If you care to do a cat or a seagull, you may save it for another time, thank you."

"Oh, crap." Ivy threw her hands up and sank to the empty chair behind her. She tried to think of a time when she had felt so utterly helpless, but couldn't.

"Are you going to answer, or do your cod imitation again?"

Ivy's nerves were about as close to shot as she could imagine. No, they were shot. She was doomed. She was tired. She was lost in time, and utterly without recourse. Her feet were cold.

For what might have been one of the first times in her life, Ivy snapped back.

"Are you always so awful?"

Julian looked shocked. He probably was, that this intruder, this apparent thief, would take the offensive.

"Look," Ivy went on, not even caring what he might think, "I'm having a bad day. I'm lost, I'm tired, I'm miserable. And you—you and your damned sarcasm are really not what I need right now."

"What you need," Julian suggested in cool tones, "is a good beating."

"What you need," Ivy retorted, "is a good kick in the ass. You're rude to your grandmother, you're rude to your sister, you bellow like a spoiled child when things don't go your way.

87

You're the most arrogant, insufferable tyrant I've ever met."

Julian glared at her down the hawklike bridge of his arrogant nose.

"By God, you have a mighty nerve! You sneak into my house, you lie to me of your origins, you try to ingratiate yourself into my house, and you sneak like a spy into my bedchamber!" He leaned across the desk, and his face looked almost demonic in the firelight, all sharp angles and glittering eyes.

"Get out of my home."

The fight, the fire that had seized Ivy passed just as quickly as it had come. Her heart seemed to seize up; her hands froze.

"What?"

"Get out. Go. Now. If there's anything I despise, it's a spy. More than a spy, I mislike a thief. You, my sweet, are obviously one or the other. Now get out."

He meant what he said. It was obvious in his low, hard voice, in the tension of his face, in his tight posture.

He seized her arm, pulling her up from his chair. "Come, Ivy, or whoever you may be. Get your clothes and I will put you out the door myself, before you have a chance to do mischief in my household. And if you come back, by God, if you come within a mile of these castle walls, you will regret the day. Do you hear?"

He dragged her toward the door with one hand, and with the other tossed the precious book back to his table. It hit with a loud, hollow thump.

Ivy, still and cold with horror, looked back at the book, her only hope. Her head swam, she began to tremble violently, and, though she tried not to, she let loose a cry of despair that echoed through the empty castle.

Chapter Five

Julian dragged Ivy roughly from his chambers, shut the door behind him with a fierce kick, and pulled her down the dark corridor.

"Please . . ." Ivy's voice was strangled; even when she'd awakened on the beach, she had not known such panic. Perhaps her shock had protected her. But the shock was gone, and now she knew desperation.

To be put out into the cold winter night, in a world where she knew no one, had no skills, and no place to go . . .

She tried to imagine where she might go, what she might do. But there were no answers. She knew nobody; she was barely certain of where she was. Where would she sleep? How would she eat?

And, she was certain, her only way home lay written on the pages of the book, behind the closed door of Julian's bedchamber.

"And what did you think you were looking for?" he demanded abruptly as he pulled her into the great hall.

His voice echoed off the great vaulted ceiling, an eerie sound in the shadowed darkness.

"I lost my way," Ivy managed. The excuse sounded feeble, even to her own ears. "I saw the light in your room, and I stopped to ask—"

"And while you were there, you thought you might read my correspondence, and trifle with things that have nothing to do with you."

How long had he been watching her? Ivy searched for a plausible excuse. In the dim light from the great fireplace he looked very menacing, his eyes and cheekbones in shadow, his hair hanging over his strong shoulders. His grip on her forearm was unrelenting.

"I saw the books and thought that I'd like to read a little. I didn't think you'd mind if I borrowed a book."

"But I do mind. And, moreover, I don't believe you. If you think to fool me with your lies of being lost and unable to remember, think again. I'm done with your falsehoods."

"Why should I lie?" Ivy cried out, genuinely frightened.

"Any number of reasons. You are a thief, or a spy, or a—" he stopped abruptly.

A witch. Even though he had not said it, Ivy

felt sure that what was what he had been thinking.

"Please, please listen. I'm not, I swear it. I'm none of those things."

He stopped pulling her then and stared down at her, a hard light in his eyes. "Why should I believe you?"

"Because it's the truth. Please believe me. Oh, God, don't put me out to starve. Listen to me . . . I'm not certain where I am; I have nowhere to go. I don't even have a penny. I'll starve. Please, Julian, for pity's sake . . ." She hated to beg, but there seemed no alternative.

"Let me stay, at least until I can find my way home. I'll work, if you like. I'll help in the kitchens; I can't be any worse of a servant than Doll. . . . " She was about to cry, and she knew it. She blinked hard, her eyes stinging.

"Tell me how you came to be here." His voice was hard, his eyes suspicious.

"I can't." Ivy's cry was piteous.

He let loose her arm and leaned against the cold stone wall, watching her. His face was completely impassive, but his eyes seemed to bore into her.

Ivy swallowed and simply stood, her hands twisted in the fabric of her robe.

She was afraid to breathe. The wrong look, the wrong word, might decide him against her.

"I'll grant you two days."

Two days! Ivy wondered if she could secure

the book by then. Of course she could, now that she knew where it was.

Julian's next words turned her blood to ice.

"During that time, I'll try to find proof of where you came from, and how you came to be lost, and pray you that I find something. During those two days, you are not to leave your room. I'll lock you in myself."

Locked in! This was disastrous.

Speechless, Ivy stared at him. He looked pleased with himself.

"That's cruel," she whispered.

"Not a bit. I'm giving you a fair chance, after all. If there's even the slightest hope that you're telling me the truth, I'll find out. Cruel, indeed. You are fortunate that I'm not putting you out tonight."

Ivy was at loss.

Julian gave a mocking bow and gestured up the winding staircase.

"Please lead the way, my lady, and I'll escort you back to your chamber."

Silently, her heart in a tight, tense knot, Ivy turned and walked up the dark staircase. She looked back at Julian and, to her shock, caught a glimpse of Susanna standing at the bottom of the staircase behind him.

The young girl smiled, a warning finger to her lips, and silently moved around the corner and out of sight.

Bewildered and frightened, Ivy returned, defeated, to her small chamber. Julian was silent,

93

and the look he gave her was cold as he closed the door behind her and turned the key in the lock.

She had stayed awake long into the night, watching the fire and dozing fitfully. It was nearly dawn when she finally let sleep overtake her, and when she heard the sound of the door opening it took a great effort to open her eyes.

It was Doll, bearing a tray of bread and cheese. The maid looked as displeased as she usually did. She regarded Ivy with a sullen expression, utterly without sympathy.

"Now you're in it, aren't you?"

Ivy wondered what Doll had been told.

"Please, what do you mean, Doll?" Ivy made an effort to sound friendly. If she was a prisoner, she needed all the allies she could gather.

Doll pursed her full mouth and looked disapproving. She might be a pretty girl, Ivy thought, if not for her sullen ways.

"Why, sneaking about like a thief in the night, trying to steal from the master. He should take you straight to the sheriff, is what I say. If you were going to steal, you should have chosen another man to thieve from, is what I think."

Ivy sat up and hung her legs over the edge of the bed. Despite the fire, the room was cold. The winter sunlight came in through the diamond-paned window, cold and bright.

She reached for the heavy blue robe that lay across the end of the bed.

"I'm not a thief, Doll."

"That's not what I hear." Doll poked at the fire. "And you aren't a very clever one, at that. Why, you can't put anything over on Julian Ramsden. Or any of this lot here. They have the sight, you know."

"The sight?"

Doll stopped at the door, one hand on the handle, the other on her generous hip. "Aye, they know what you be thinking, like. They all have it. Now why do you suppose that I'm the only girl in the village will work here?"

Ivy reached for the silver cup that Doll had left on the table and took a swallow. She shuddered. Wine for breakfast. "Why, Doll?"

Doll tossed her brown curls and assumed a superior expression. "Everyone else in the village is afraid, is why. Now, there used to be enough pay up here to make people forget, but no more. There's just me left, and old Edith for the cooking, and Ben in the stables. And he's only a half-wit, you know. Doesn't have the sense to be afeared."

"Afraid of what?" Ivy asked.

Doll opened the door a crack and peeked down the hall before answering in a whisper.

"They be witches. All of 'em. The old woman, and Susanna, and Master Julian. They say . . ." Doll gave another furtive look around the room and leaned closer, her sly eyes gleaming. "They say that old Denby wasn't even his father. You can reckon what that means," she added significantly.

Speechless, Ivy shook her head.

" 'Twas Satan himself," Doll informed her, managing to look afraid as well as proud of delivering this crucial information.

"Oh, Doll! That's ludicrous!"

"Aye, it's a terrible thing," Doll agreed, the word "ludicrous" apparently lost on her.

The sound of hooves clattering out in the courtyard diverted her attention, and she moved to the window.

"Look." The buxom maid beckoned Ivy with a crooked finger, and Ivy crossed the cold floor on bare feet and stood beside her. "Just look at him. You can almost see it in him, can't you?"

Julian was riding his dark horse across the stone courtyard, his gray cape flapping in the winter breeze, the sunlight shining on his long, dark hair. He looked like a hero from an old movie, making his exit beneath the arch of the gateway.

"All I see is a very handsome man," Ivy said. "He has a face like an angel, actually."

"You see," Doll said, as if Julian's dark good looks were proof positive of his supernatural parentage.

"No, I don't see," Ivy said.

"They say Lucifer was one of the most beautiful angels, before he fell," Doll said, her green eyes following Julian.

For some odd reason, Ivy felt the urge to defend Julian from the sly-eyed maid and her superstitious gossip. "He's hard, and foul-tempered, I see that. And he's not reasonable, when he's made up his mind. But that hardly makes him the Prince of Darkness, Jr."

Doll looked very offended and a little suspicious. "I'm just saying what everyone in the village knows, and always has," she retorted. "You'll see, if you're around here very long." She tossed her curls again and headed for the door. "What you need," she added, "is a prayer book. I think he's got you under a spell, to take up for him like that. It's those looks of his. He smiles at a girl and she's done for. Ain't one can resist him."

"That, I'm sure, is simply a matter of testosterone, and not demonic powers." Ivy was more than a little tired of Doll's knowing attitude.

Doll looked thoroughly baffled.

"Testy yourself," she retorted at last, and put her nose in the air as she left the room.

Ivy heard the sound of a key turning in the lock, and she remembered that she was a prisoner and had just alienated a possible ally.

She stared out the window at the wooded hill beyond the gray walls, and the cold, endless sea, and the spires and rooftops of the village in the distance. She was trapped in this twisted fairy tale and had no idea how she would escape.

"Maybe Doll's right," she muttered, tearing off a piece of bread from her tray. "Maybe I need a prayer book."

*   *   *

"Ivy . . ."

She startled at the sound of the whisper that came through the keyhole.

The sun was setting; she had been alone all day with her imagination. She had imagined all sorts of things. She imagined Julian taking her to jail and having her hanged as a thief. She had imagined Lady Margaret bringing her the magic book and sending her back to the real world. She had imagined being trapped in the cold chamber until she was a withered crone, with hair as long as Rapunzel's.

She had slept, and wakened, and made an inventory of the furniture in the room, and was mentally cataloging the price it might bring on the antique market, when the whisper came through the door.

"Ivy!" The whisper came again, more insistent, and she left the cross-legged, cushioned stool she had been examining and hastened to the door.

"Who is it?" she whispered back.

A soft laugh. "Susanna," came the answer. "How fare thee, Ivy?"

"I'm fine. Frightened, though. Susanna, I wasn't stealing, and I'm not—"

"Hush and listen."

Ivy fell silent.

"I must hasten, before Julian comes and finds I'm out. Listen, Ivy, I can help, but you must do what I say."

"I'm listening," Ivy whispered through the key-hole.

"Good." Again the soft laugh. "Doll lost her key and cannot find it, to our fortune. I took your supper tray from her, and it's here outside the door. Julian is riding in just now, and I'm sure he'll be up soon and bring it in. Pay heed, Ivy."

"I am," Ivy assured her, wondering where this was leading.

"Make sure Julian drinks the wine from the pitcher. Do you hear?"

"Make sure he drinks the wine from the pitcher," Ivy repeated. A nervous thrill chased through her. "Why, Susanna?"

"Oh, don't fret, he won't die. Though, I confess, that was my first suggestion. The old tyrant. I've been stuck in my room all day, reading the most dreary book . . . you can't imagine. But Grandmother said no, you can't just poison people when you're in a temper. Pity, isn't it?"

"Susanna," Ivy interrupted, trying to curb her impatience, "what then? After he drinks the wine?"

"Oh." A bubbling laugh. "Then when he falls asleep, which shouldn't take long, come to the gallery and talk to my lady grandmother. That's all. Fare thee well, Ivy."

"Susanna," Ivy began, but she could hear the light sound of the girl's feet as she raced down the hall.

Ivy stepped back from the door and went to the mirror that hung beside it. She straightened her hair as best she could, cursing the wayward curls that escaped from the dark blue ribbons, and sat down to wait for Julian, her heart racing in a queer mixture of anticipation and dread.

She heard him before he reached the door, muttering curses beneath his breath about incompetent servants and troublesome women.

Ivy supposed that the latter included herself. Funny, she had never thought much about women's rights; she had always taken them for granted. But when she heard Julian proclaiming himself lord and master, and issuing orders to his sister and grandmother, she wanted to shout back at him and give him a lesson or two about equality.

That was funny too, because she'd never been a fighter. More of a coward, really. She'd run from her home, in college she'd run from any boys who expressed an interest in her, and she'd used her business to hide from real life. Now there was nowhere to run.

The key turned in the lock, and he entered the room, tall and dark and intense. He carried the tray of dinner awkwardly, like someone who had never carried a tray before.

"Did you find anything out about me?" Ivy asked. Of course he had not, but she knew it would sound funny if she didn't ask.

"Naught," was the answer. He set the tray on the table and settled himself in the chair next to it.

Ivy stared out the window at the sea, the landscape burnished in the autumn colors of the sunset.

"I have been to every inn, every tavern, every church, every house high and low within forty miles. And I've found nothing. Nobody has seen you or heard of you."

He looked tired, and his high cheekbones were flushed from the wind and cold. His dark hair lay tangled on the pleated shoulders of his doublet.

"Nobody even saw you ride through," he added. "I expected at least that much."

Ivy stared at the tray he had set down. The firelight flickered reflections off a silver pitcher. Two goblets stood next to it, both full. One had a single ivy leaf beneath its base. How clever. That one was meant for her.

Give Julian the wine in the pitcher.

Quickly, she picked her own goblet up and drank from it. The wine was heated and spiced.

"That's good," she murmured appreciatively, a little surprised.

Julian was watching her with his rain cloud–colored eyes. He looked tired and frustrated.

"It's very good," Ivy repeated. She set her goblet down and lifted the other goblet, her hand trembling a little. "Would you like some?" She tried to keep her voice casual.

"Aye, I thank thee."

It had been easy, too easy. He made no move to take it, and after a moment she realized that he was waiting for her to hand it to him. Like a prince, she thought, offering him the glass.

He took a long drink, and Ivy followed suit.

"As far north as St. Edmund's, as far south as Foley, and ten miles inland, over the moors," he said after he drank. "And not a word."

Ivy stood for a moment, awkwardly, and then sat on the cushioned stool before the fire.

"There's the possibility of shipwreck, of course," he added, "but I heard of no ships being lost." He took another drink of wine. "This is good," he commented.

Go for it, Ivy thought. She watched him carefully for any sign that the sleeping potion might be taking effect, but he didn't look tired at all, just thoughtful.

"Did anyone visit you today?" he asked. "My grandmother, perhaps, or Susanna?"

"Not a soul," Ivy answered immediately, remembering well that Susanna had been confined to her room. "Just Doll."

"That impossible creature," he muttered. "I suppose she gave you an earful of gossip."

Ivy was startled. Did he really have second sight? No, more than likely he was just familiar with the maid.

"She did," Ivy admitted, deciding that telling the truth was the wisest option, whenever possible.

"And what did you make of it?" he demanded, his dark brows narrowing.

Ivy shrugged. "Honestly? I think it's a lot of

nonsense. True, you're foul-tempered and dom-
ineering, and not very pleasant, but it doesn't
mean you're the son of Satan."

Julian looked very surprised at her forthright
opinion, and then to Ivy's great surprise, he
laughed.

He looked very different, smiling. His gray
eyes were bright and dimples appeared under
his cheekbones.

"What a thing to say, Ivy! I'm a little hurt. Do
you really think me so foul?"

He didn't look hurt in the least.

"Well, you're not my favorite person right
now. How would you like to be locked up in a
cold room all day, just for being lost and confused?"

He drank the rest of his wine in a single motion and refilled it. "There we are, back to the
beginning. I simply do not believe you're telling
the truth."

Ivy wished the sleeping potion would work.
Julian stretched his long legs and settled back in
the high-backed chair, looking down at her.
Maybe the wine was working. His cheeks looked
a little flushed, and his dark eyes had a warm
glow. He seemed relaxed, a little warmer and
easier than usual. She noticed again how handsome he was, like a painting of an Italian Renaissance prince.

Ivy noted that she felt a little flushed herself.

"The most logical conclusion would be that
you're a spy," he informed her. "That would be

just like Cromwell, to send a pretty young woman to distract me."

Pretty? Startled, Ivy raised her eyes to see if he was joking. She wasn't pretty. She'd never had any illusions about her looks. She was thin; she was pale. She'd never been considered pretty. She knew what pretty was, and she'd envied the girls in school who could lay claim to that label. They were noisy, confident creatures, with shining curtains of gold hair and healthy tans and expensive clothes, girls who lived in tidy suburban homes and had dates on Saturday nights, girls who roamed the malls in packs, searching for prom dresses.

Pretty was not a skinny little pale thing with a shock of red corkscrew curls, who stayed home with her nose buried in a book.

Julian looked perfectly serious. "You're blushing," he informed her.

Ivy took a hasty drink of wine and immediately regretted it. It was warm and rich and intoxicating, and she didn't want to let her guard down.

"Did you find anything interesting last night," Julian asked suddenly, "whilst reading my letters?"

Ivy thought about denying it, but he had her. "A little," she admitted. "I read that they want you to marry someone—"

"Felicity Astley," he supplied.

"Whatever. And that if you do, you get your lands back."

"You likely knew that before you read the letter," Julian remarked.

"I don't know a damned thing about it, and I can't say that I really care," Ivy retorted.

"I care," Julian informed her. "I care very much. I have no desire to be sold to the daughter of a stiff-necked Puritan, in return for what was stolen from me. By God, the insult!"

"Why, is she ugly?" Ivy was surprisingly relaxed, and interested. After being alone all day, it was good to have company. The room seemed warmer, and pleasant. The crackling fire warmed her back; the rich wine was soothing.

And Julian was fascinating to watch—the way he raised the glass to his perfect mouth, and the elegant motion of his hands, the way his hair fell on the rolled shoulders of his doublet.

It crossed her mind that if Julian were to marry, he and his wife would probably sit like this, drinking wine in warm, firelit rooms, laughing and talking together.

"No, Felicity isn't ugly. Just . . . tedious," Julian admitted with a rueful smile. "She does excellent needlework, and reads her prayer books, and manages her father's household very well. But I had hoped for something more."

"You'd get your land back," Ivy reminded him.

"Aye, that I would. And Susanna would have a dowry, and Grandmother would be safe from wagging tongues. And I, I would be under Master Cromwell's heavy thumb and careful eye. Marriage to Felicity . . ." He sighed. "Ah, if only

I had married when I was younger. Then I wouldn't be in this position now."

"Was there somebody special?" Ivy asked.

He smiled at her. "No, not truly. There were women, of course. When you're young, and rich, and handsome—"

"And humble," Ivy put in.

"Devil take thee," Julian remarked with a laugh, "whoever said I was humble? 'Tis not in my nature."

"No, I didn't think so," Ivy agreed.

"When I was at court, there were many women who would have agreed to marry me. But after a time I'd grow bored with them."

"And move on to greener pastures," Ivy added. It was easy to imagine, with Julian's good looks.

"Something like that," he agreed, looking not a bit ashamed. "It always seemed there was something missing. They were too shallow, or too serious, or too greedy. And some were just terrible lovers, though not many."

Ivy choked a little on her wine. "Shame on you, Julian. What an awful thing to say." She couldn't help laughing a little.

" 'Tis true. Though it doesn't happen often. A man can usually tell just by looking. Some women have no fire, no promise. And others, why, one look and you know they'd be a merry armful. And if you can't tell by looking, one kiss will usually tell."

Ivy drained the last few drops in her glass, a little taken aback by the turn the conversation had taken. She knew which sort she'd be. Boring, mousy, not even worth the telltale kiss.

"I think you're mean," she said, suddenly resentful of this good-looking, arrogant man who could make his way through women as if they were a box of assorted chocolates. "After all, you really can't judge people by their looks."

"I can and do," he asserted. He smiled devilishly and refilled his goblet from the silver pitcher. "You, for instance—"

"Spare me, please."

"You'd never bore a man. You have just the sort of mouth a man would love to taste beneath his own, and enough light in your eyes to promise passion. And your hair is magnificent. I would love to see it down and curling around your waist. I would like to run my hands through it—"

Ivy sat, still with shock. Her heart gave an odd quiver, a quiver that chased through her veins, followed by a rush of heat.

"You shouldn't tease me, Julian," she said after a moment, and her voice shook a little. "It's unkind."

The images he suggested wouldn't leave her mind; she could picture them together in the darkened chamber, his dark hands running through her hair and sliding over her naked body, tumbling her to the great bed and . . .

She'd had too much to drink.

Julian was smiling at her, and he leaned forward and took a curling red tendril of hair between his fingers, his knuckles brushing her cheek. "Teasing, indeed. I think it sounds perfectly delightful."

Ivy shivered. Her cheeks felt very warm; her body felt a sweet, shivering thrill. "Please stop it, Julian."

"Stop it? No, I think not. As a matter of fact, I think we may have found the solution to our problems."

Ivy wished he would move back. He was too close, too beautiful, with his stormy, intense eyes and elegant hands and shining dark hair. She couldn't breathe, couldn't speak.

"I want to keep an eye on you. You wish, for reasons known only to your devious little heart, to stay at Wythecombe Keep. I offer you a bargain, Ivy."

"What?" she whispered, her voice quavering.

"You may stay . . . as long as you wish. But you stay as my mistress. You warm my bed. You attend to my needs. I let you stay, and your body is mine—whenever I wish, however I ask."

Ivy felt her mouth drop.

"Think about it," Julian urged, and for a moment, Ivy felt as if she were, indeed, dealing with the devil's own offspring. " 'Tis not a bad bargain. I warrant you might be pleased with it."

She took a deep breath and felt outrage. The pleasant, friendly mood between them was gone. Now there was only anger and shame— and beneath that, a dark, rich desire that she couldn't deny.

"You go to hell, Julian Ramsden. I'd rather starve in the streets than sell myself like a cheap whore!"

He looked a little surprised. He also, to Ivy's fury, looked as if he doubted her words. After a moment, he shrugged and stood up.

"What so pleases you, Ivy. You have a day to decide. But I think you'd enjoy my bargain a little more than starving in the street."

"Think again."

"I will, and gladly. But I might say the same to you. I shall be back on the morrow, and hear your answer." He stood and bowed, and it seemed to Ivy that he was making a deliberate show of his fine figure, his long legs and slim hips and the thick hair that tumbled over his shoulders.

"Sleep well," he added, as if he knew that she would not. He left the room, and the sound of the key turning in the lock threw Ivy into a rage.

Lady Margaret raised her brows at her granddaughter.

"He said *what*? Are you absolutely sure, Susanna?"

"Of course I'm sure. I stood at the keyhole until I heard him making ready to leave, and then I hastened here."

They stood in a quiet, dark room off the kitchen, surrounded by shelves and cupboards filled with drying herbs and corked jars and mysterious bulging bags of rough fabric.

109

Lady Margaret stood over a steaming pot suspended over a low fire, stirring the contents. A large white apron covered her gown, and her silver hair was hidden under a modest cap. She and her granddaughter spoke in whispers.

"But it makes no sense! He should have been sleeping! Pray, Susanna, what answer did our Ivy give him?"

Susanna gave a soft giggle. "She did not strike him, but she gave him a fierce word or two. Poor Julian! I'm afraid he's not used to being refused."

"It cannot be," Lady Margaret repeated, her apple cheeks drooping in dismay. "It simply cannot be. He should have been asleep."

"Perhaps you got the ingredients wrong," Susanna suggested, taking an apple from a barrel and settling herself on a tall stool. "Or the words. You *are* getting a mite forgetful, Grandmother."

Lady Margaret bristled with indignation. "Off with thee, monkey! I'm as sharp as I was twenty years ago."

"You were old twenty years ago," Susanna observed around a mouthful of apple. She swallowed and looked thoughtful. "Tell me what you did."

"Why, not much. Chamomile, and skullcap, and tincture of St. John's wort, and a little tincture of damania. Dried violets, and some rose petals and cinnamon."

Susanna looked leery, and then her dark eyes began to dance. "It seems I remember learning that one, my lady. Tell me the words you spake over it before you put it in the wine."

"Chit! Do you think I have no memory at all? I said: 'Herbs of summer's lengthy days, gathered 'neath the full moon's gaze, in the wine so dark and sweet, then your pale blood shall heat. Where next your hungered eyes shall fall—' " Lady Margaret stopped abruptly, and her faded eyes grew very round. She swallowed and stared down at the steaming, cinnamon-scented brew on the fire as if it had betrayed her. "Oh, Sweet Mother of Sorrows," she murmured. "Oh, merciful heaven. What have I done?"

Susanna gave a noisy peal of laughter, and her apple fell from her hand and rolled across the flagstone floor into the darkness. "What have you done! Marry, Grandmother! What *have* you done? Poor Ivy! Poor Julian! They'll be so hot for each other that they won't sleep for days!"

"Mind your mouth, young woman."

But Susanna was laughing too hard to hear. "Put him to sleep, indeed! Oh, this is better than old Sisson's spots. This is better than when Julian's horse was walking backward!"

"That's enough out of you," Lady Margaret retorted in injured tones.

"This is better than when Felicity sneezed every time she spoke. Or the time that—"

"By my teeth, Susanna! Will you cease? This is terrible. What will we do?"

Susanna shrugged. "Put it right, I suppose. What would the words be for that?"

Lady Margaret wrinkled her brow and tapped

111

a finger to her lips. "Let me think. . . . I'm sure I can remember. Do I give him blue cohosh root?"

Susanna began to giggle again. "Well, that may make his monthly cycles more regular, but I'm not sure it will cool his ardor."

"Oh, mercy on us. Where did that rude boy hide my book this time, do you suppose?"

"In that wallow he calls his bedchamber, I expect. But I'll find it, Gran. Don't fret."

Lady Margaret shook her head slowly. "Children these days! Betwixt the two of you, I'll go to an early grave."

"Too late for that," Susanna teased.

"That's enough, girl. Take yourself to bed before Julian finds you're out of your prison. I'll try to remember a way to undo this mischief. What a tangle!"

Susanna jumped down off the stool, gave her grandmother a quick, hard hug and kiss on the cheek, and turned to go.

"There's one thing to be grateful for," Lady Margaret remembered, brightening.

"What's that, my lady?"

"At least poor little Ivy didn't drink any of the wine. Isn't it a good thing you told her not to touch the glass with the leaf beneath it?"

Susanna's smile faltered for only a second. "Yes, it certainly is," she agreed hastily. She managed to restrain her laughter until she was well out of her grandmother's hearing.

Chapter Six

There was a touch of ice in the winter wind. It stung Julian's cheeks, and hurt when he took it into his lungs. There was no sun today. Only dense, dark clouds that threatened an icy rain.

He noticed these things with only half his attention. His mind was preoccupied with thoughts of Ivy.

He thought of her over and over again with an almost feverish intensity. He thought of her mysterious appearance, he thought of her dark, enigmatic eyes, he thought of her odd voice.

What had possessed him last night to have made such an outrageous offer? He told himself that he never expected her to accept, that it was a clever move designed to make her show her hand. There was something so innocent about her; he knew full well she would never agree to become his mistress.

Unless she was a spy, of course, and ready to go to any lengths to maintain her position in the household.

He didn't like to admit, even to himself, that there might be a little more to it than that. The fact was, he burned to possess her. From the moment she had come down to dinner in that plum satin gown, all copper curls and glowing skin and delicate curves, he had thought of how sweet she would be, warming his bed.

It had been a long time since a woman had so enchanted him.

And then last night, he had looked at her, sitting next to the fire, with her hair lit by the glowing flames, looking up at him and laughing with her dark eyes glowing. Their conversation had been so easy, so comfortable and soothing. . . .

For a few minutes, he had allowed himself the ridiculous fantasy that she was his wife, that they sat together every night drinking wine and talking, and after a while, he could carry her over to the great bed and lay his naked body against her silken skin, and make love to her again and again, every night. . . .

Stupid thoughts, boyish thoughts that had no place in reality. And he felt a flush of anger, mixed in with the heat of desire, for allowing himself such wooly-headed dreams.

Before he had even considered what he was

saying, he had opened his mouth, and the outrageous offer came out.

And he found himself hoping that she would accept.

Even as he rode out into the winter winds, from bleak village to roadside inn, making his inquiries, he found himself hoping that he would discover nothing. That she had appeared as magically as she claimed, delivered, as his grandmother suggested, like Venus born of the sea, expressly for his pleasure.

He was still thinking of her when he reached Westford and rode through the fishing village. The men of the village had not taken their boats out that morning because of the threatening storm, and the town was unusually silent. In the other villages he had asked at the docks, at the inn, at the church—had any travelers been through the town? Had there been any inquiries of a missing young woman?

Negative answers, again and again.

And he felt his mood darkening. Not only was his search fruitless, he hated the looks the country folk gave him when he stopped and questioned them.

Fear. Curiosity. Suspicion. Even as they touched their caps and made their curtsies and called him "m'lord," their thoughts were clear.

They were speaking to Julian Ramsden, the fallen dark lord of Wythecombe Keep, the man rumored to be the son of the devil. He should have been used to it by now. Indeed, there had

115

been a time when it didn't bother him at all.

As a young man, studying in London, he had told his friend Christopher about it, and Christopher had laughed.

Wythecombe and the west country had seemed very far away from the glittering court and the masked dances and plays of London. When the story was repeated at that distance, it *was* funny, even to Julian.

Sometimes the villagers he queried didn't recognize him, and there were no darting eyes, no guarded expressions. But inevitably, as he was leaving the square, or the inn, or the crude cottage, the whispers would follow.

". . . Julian Ramsden. They say he be the son of Satan, himself. No, Bessie, don't thee look at him . . . you'll be cursed, for truth."

Utter rubbish. Stupid, superstitious prattle. He rode into Westford thinking with longing about his jolly, misspent youth, and how good it would be to drink and brawl and wench thoughtlessly, as only the young can.

The scene in the village square brought him up short.

There was a hastily constructed gallows, and three dead women hung from it.

The villagers crowded around, their expressions ranging from somber contemplation to self-righteous outrage to a sickening suppressed glee, the kind of look a sneaky child gets when he sees one of his playmates punished, a kind of secret delight.

116

Julian paused his horse and stared, sickened by the scene.

The three women were hanging, swaying slightly in the cold wind. The wind moved their hair and cloaks in an eerie imitation of life, an illusion belied by the unnatural stillness of their faces, the grotesque angles of their broken necks.

Some pious and caring soul had bound their skirts tightly around their ankles, so as not to offend the good people of the village with any immodest show of legs. The fact that those same good people were reveling at the sight of premature death revolted Julian.

And over the hushed murmurs and solemn voices of the macabre spectators, over the rush of the chill wind, rose the cry of a child. It was a mournful, animal noise of grief that shook him to his soul.

He moved his horse forward, not even sure why, through the crowds, to the gallows, and he stopped before the three dead women.

He saw then the source of the cries. A little girl, surely no more than five, standing at the base of the gallows. Beneath her ragged skirts, her thin feet were blue with cold. She shook like a leaf that clings to a tree in a storm. One final gust, and the leaf tumbles away, lost.

Her small, white face was turned to one of the dead women. Her blue eyes were wide, blank pools of grief, and out of her mouth came the mindless cry of misery, over and over. It was the sound of grief beyond words.

Nobody came forward to touch her, to pick her up, to take her away from the ugliness. They just stood, the good and moral people, letting the child scream her pain, while they congratulated themselves on a morning's work well done.

It enraged Julian.

"What has happened here?" His voice whipped out into the crowd, and everything fell silent, except for the wind and the mourning child.

"What is this? Who are these women, and what has been done?"

The crowd stirred, and he saw the faces changing, becoming defensive, settling into suspicious lines. The inevitable murmurs: "Julian Ramsden, of Wythecombe Keep . . ." The fear, the superstition.

His anger grew. It felt like a darkening thundercloud in his chest.

"Where is your mayor?"

At last a man separated himself from the crowd and stepped forward, his multiple chins held high above his wide, white collar. The face beneath the tall hat was belligerent, ready to defend his authority.

Julian noted the gravy stains on the wide Puritan collar and wondered if the man had enjoyed a good breakfast before the sickening execution.

"I am the mayor of this town, sir," came the answer.

"And what is this?" Julian bit the words off, scornful and cold, as he gestured to the hanging women, the howling child.

The mayor drew himself up to the best of his height. "It is, sir, exactly what it appears. A lawful execution, following a righteous and careful trial, as prescribed by the laws of England." A pompous nod followed this statement.

The crowd murmured appreciatively.

Julian wondered what would happen if he were to put his boot firmly into the face of the Lord Mayor Bastard. If he had not been so decidedly outnumbered, it would have been his first course of action.

"And what was the crime?" he asked, though he well knew what the answer would be. Out of the corner of his eyes, he could catch a glimpse of one of the hanged women, her golden hair fluttering in the breeze. He avoided looking. He didn't want to know—were they young? Were they pretty? Somebody's sister or grandmother? A sharp-tongued scold, a wandering vagrant, a young woman whose only crime had been come-hither eyes and an inviting body?

"They were witches, sir. God have mercy on their souls."

"More mercy than their fellow man," Julian responded quietly, but his answer was lost beneath the awful howling of the frightened child. The sound was more than he could bear.

"Who has charge of this child?" he shouted, surveying the crowd with fury.

They looked back with eyes of fear and resentment and suspicion.

At last, a woman too old or blind to know him called back fearlessly, "God himself does, now. She's the bastard of a witch. She's none of ours."

The golden-haired child mourned at the suspended feet of the golden-haired witch. Julian would bet his last farthing that the father was somewhere in the crowd, hiding behind his self-righteousness.

"And will none of you good Christian people"—he couldn't cover the mockery in his voice—"find the mercy to take her from this place?"

"It is a problem, sir," the fat mayor answered, stiff with dignity. "The child is an idiot, a mute, useless spawn. She may even be possessed of demons. What good man would risk having such a creature in his house to endanger his family?"

The crowd murmured assent.

Julian turned to look at the child. She continued her wordless cry, staring with blank eyes up at the hanging women. He noticed for the first time her unnatural thinness, the awkward, tense angles of her spindly arms, the precarious balance of her splayed legs.

The spawn of the devil. Well, he had been called the same. An idiot, they said. That well might be, but then, it might not. Possessed by demons. Bloody unlikely. And in all this crowd of good, merciful Christian people—for he was sure that was how they thought of themselves—

120

not one man or woman was willing to step forward, to try to ease this gut-wrenching grief.

If he turned and rode away, how long would the child live in this nest of hypocrites?

Without a word he urged his horse forward, leaned down, and scooped the child up.

She was light; her bones were fragile and brittle beneath his hands. Her golden hair was dirty and tangled. Her spine arched at an awkward angle as he held her tightly, and her thin arms twitched almost convulsively.

But the shock of the sudden motion stilled her cries, and at last the square was silent, almost eerily silent after the constant howl ceased.

He turned to face the people, the fragile child clutched tightly against him, and they stared back, shocked, outraged, frightened.

He found that he enjoyed the fear.

Good, you soul-lacking, hypocritical bastards. Look, and be afraid. Wonder what forces of good or evil you may have offended with your sickening pleasure, and may you find no rest on your pillows.

The mayor was staring at him with a mixture of dread and outrage.

"God have mercy on you," he said to Julian in a voice that gave the lie to what should have been gentle and good words.

"Keep your words of comfort for your people, you cold-hearted bastard," Julian returned calmly. "I think they are sorely in need of them."

The crowd parted as he rode through, the dark

lord clutching the cold, ragged child against his black doublet, his dark hair and dark cape wild in the wind.

He knew that he must look frightening in his rage, but for the first time, he was glad of the rumors of his unnatural parentage. He met each gaze directly, stared into every hypocritical, self-satisfied face, until he saw their gazes cloud with fear, until they looked away. Some of the oldest ones made the sign of the cross, even though that and all other papist habits were forbidden.

Good. Be afraid, as those poor women must have feared.

He heard the whisper behind him, "Satan's own come to claim his own."

He didn't care, his anger was so great. Let them think the worst, since the merciful words of their own God meant nothing to them.

The child in his arms was stiff and unmoving, paralyzed by shock or fear as they rode south and west, toward Wythecombe Keep.

Little Daisy was too numb to care much when the Dark Man took her away. She was numb with cold, and numb with grief, and she was having a hard time understanding any of what had happened.

She had heard of the Dark Man, and had even been told that he knew her mother, and would come to take her away. Old Ethyl, who lived in the next cottage, had often said that when her mother wasn't listening. For a long time after that, Daisy had kept a close eye on the men who came to visit her mother, but none of them showed the faintest interest in her, except to kick her out of the way, or push her out the door.

After a while, she didn't think about the Dark Man anymore. She was more concerned about staying warm, and eating, and if her legs hurt her too badly too walk that day.

She understood this much—her mother was dead and gone, the way birds sometimes died, or the kitten she had found once. Dead was gone; you never woke up. They had killed her mother, the Mean People, and nobody bothered to tell her why. People didn't bother talking to her, because she didn't speak back.

She remembered trying to speak, a long time ago. Her mother didn't like the sound of it. She put her hands over her ears and told Daisy to stop, so she did. Speaking was bad. She was bad.

Her mother was bad too, people said. They didn't care if Daisy heard them or not. Daisy didn't think her mother was any worse than anyone else. She hit her sometimes, and hid her in the chest sometimes, when men came and it was too cold to put her out, but she fed her. Sometimes, when her mother was alone and crying, she let Daisy hold her hand.

When they took her away, Old Ethyl said that the reckoning had come, that her mother was going to be with the Dark Man. So Daisy had followed, crying silently outside the jail window for two nights. Then she followed the cart that they carried her mother in, when they finally brought her out.

But the Dark Man had come too late. They killed her mother, and now she was alone with the Mean People, and there would be nobody to feed her.

She was so frightened, so terrified of her aloneness, that she forgot to be silent, and cried loud and hard when her mother died. So hard that she didn't even notice the Dark Man until he took her on his horse. Nobody had ever mentioned his horse, or the soft fabric of his shirt, as soft as the fur of her kitten.

He spoke rudely to the Mean People, and was unafraid of them.

Daisy was too tired and cold to care what might happen to her. It could not be any worse than being left here. She was cold, she hadn't eaten in two days, her legs hurt so much they felt as if they were on fire. If the Dark Man killed her, she didn't care.

But he didn't kill her. He carried her away on his horse, over the moors and down twisting cliff paths and by rushing streams and through villages she had never seen, or even imagined.

He stopped only once, at a place of great fallen walls in the middle of a wood. He helped Daisy down from the horse and set her gently on a stone wall and put the reins of the black horse into her hand. Her fingers hurt when he pressed them, though he was gentle.

"Don't let Bacchus run away," he said, and smiled at her.

It made no sense. The Dark Man could see that her fingers weren't working well today; he must know that if the big horse decided to run, she could never stop it. And his smile made no sense either. It was as if he were playing a joke on her, but not being mean.

There was nothing to do but try to hold the reins, and watch the horse, and hope that when she failed and the mean laughter came that it would not hurt too much.

So she watched the horse, and he watched her back with large, gentle eyes. Daisy liked animals, but she had never been so close to a horse before. Nobody had said that when the Dark Man came she would get to ride on a horse.

Oh, if only they had told her about the horse to begin with, she would not have been so afraid! It didn't matter, on a horse, if you stumbled and fell when you walked. On a horse, you moved as smoothly and quickly as anyone else.

While she sat with the horse, the Dark Man did a very strange thing. He went to a broken well, with vines and moss growing over the stones, and he loosened a couple of the rocks. Then he took a bundle from beneath his soft jacket. He took off the heavy cloth, and it was a book. He glanced at it briefly, wrapped it more tightly than it had been before, put it in the hole he had made, and replaced the stones of the well.

"There," he said, "that damned book can stay there, where it will do no harm." Then he came back and lifted Daisy back onto the horse, climbed on with her, and rode away from the ruined buildings.

Everything was so strange that day, she wasn't surprised when they rode up a twisting road, to the top of a great hill, and through the big gates of a castle.

The Dark Man spoke then for the second time since they left the village. Right before he carried her through the big door, he looked over and saw a carriage, and—wonder of wonders!—four more horses.

"Damn it all," he said. "What a foul day for the damn Astleys to come here."

Daisy hoped the Damn Astleys were not Mean People.

Julian tried to imagine a worse day for Felicity Astley and her father to come calling. He wasn't in the mood for it, but there they were, sitting in the great hall with Susanna and Lady Margaret.

They all sat, still and silent, while he explained the presence of the child as quickly and briefly as possible.

The little girl stood on her twisted legs before the fire, appearing not to understand a single word of what was being said. She simply stared, mute and pale, at the dancing flames.

"You were rather hasty," Lord Astley announced, when Julian finished his tale. "Most ill-thought, Julian."

Julian looked at Lord Astley, with his square, florid face, and wondered if the man had ever been cold or hungry.

Lady Margaret rose to her feet immediately and went to kneel by the silent child at the hearth. Her old, nimble fingers touched the cold, white face, the curled-up arms, the cold, spindly legs.

She turned to face her grandson. "I'm proud of you, Julian." Her voice was soft and even. "You showed courage and compassion, and your anger was righteous."

Felicity Astley looked unconvinced. Her prim, placid face showed a rare expression of unsettled thought. "But did you not think, sir, that these people might be right? What if the child is the offspring of a witch? And she might be possessed by demons." The blond curls that protruded from beneath her prim cap quivered as she spoke, and her blue eyes showed genuine fear.

Lord Astley cleared his throat. "Quite so, child." He crossed one plump leg across the other and smoothed the full fabric of his voluminous knee breeches. "That is exactly what I thought. And you, young Ramsden, can ill afford to be the subject of rumor."

"I'm prepared to risk village gossip, sir."

"You'd best be," Susanna agreed, "if you continue bringing in orphans, Julian. First Ivy, now this one! What is her name, Julian?"

"I haven't the least notion," he admitted, distracted by the mention of Ivy. For a while, he had forgotten about her, locked in her bedchamber. She was probably furious.

"Do they have names, creatures like this?" Lord Astley demanded, looking askance at the scrawny, trembling bundle of rags.

Lady Margaret fixed him with a stern look. "All God's creatures have names, sir. Even the least of them."

"Wouldn't have her in *my* house," Astley muttered, stroking his tidy little pointed beard. "Probably flea-ridden."

Julian had to admit that was likely.

"Then she must needs be bathed," his grandmother replied in brisk tones.

Astley looked distinctly uncomfortable at the mention of bathing, and Felicity blushed down to her high collar.

"What have you," muttered Astley, and turned to Julian. "We must needs speak in private, young man. I bring you a message from Lord Cromwell."

Julian wondered if the day could get any worse.

Astley sat across from Julian, surveying the cluttered table with disdain. He was also surveying it with curiosity, seeing what he could learn from the scattered papers and books.

Julian was relieved that his grandmother's accursed book was safely out of the house, especially after what he had seen today. That was one thing Astley couldn't use against him.

"What news from Lord Cromwell?" Julian asked. He disliked Astley, mistrusted him, and saw no reason to while the time away with pleasantries.

"First a word with you, young Ramsden."

That irritated Julian too, "young Ramsden," in that pompous tone, where once it had been "my lord," with fawning bows. Well, one was as bad as the other, he supposed.

"Go on."

Astley drew together the fur-lined edges of his coat and gave an elaborate shiver. "Damn, my boy, but it's cold in here. Can you call in a servant to add to the fire?"

All my servants are working in your household, you old ox, Julian replied silently. "I hardly think we'll be here long enough to justify the trouble." Julian knew he sounded rude, and didn't care.

"Very well. I shall be blunt. My Lord Cromwell has been most generous with you, in allowing you to stay in your home—"

"The home my family has lived in since the time of the Conquerer," Julian deftly put in.

"Er, yes. However, he is most displeased at your lack of cooperation with the new government."

"Why," Julian asked, "should he be interested in the service of a conquered royalist, when he has so many upstarts willing to dance attendance on him, like so many fat little lapdogs?"

The lapdog remark struck home. Astley's red face grew redder.

Take that, you pretentious son of a sheepherder, Julian thought, knowing that the thought was unworthy of him, but enjoying it anyway.

"He suggests that since you have no wife or child to depend on your care, a post in the army might be suitable."

Trump card.

"A post in his lordship's army?" Julian echoed, and his voice was very soft.

"Aye. The Irish, you know. So troublesome."

"I have no interest in slaughtering women and children, and driving starving men from their lands, Astley. It doesn't strike me as an honorable occupation."

"You have some ungodly ideas, boy. The Irish are a barbarian horde, controlled by their Roman masters."

Julian took a deep breath and made an effort to keep his voice calm. "One hears such things. They all have horns, and they eat sweet little English children for their evening meals, and ask the Pope's blessing upon the flesh. Don't take me for an idiot, Astley. I want no part of it."

Julian wondered if his sarcasm was lost on Astley, for the man nodded solemnly when he spoke of the Irish dining on children.

"That, of course, leaves you in a tight position.

130

It would seem that your only other option would be marriage."

What a clumsy politician you are, Astley. You want my castle and the prestige of the family history, questionable or not.

"Felicity," Lord Astley announced, in case Julian had missed the obvious point, "will bring a dowry of twelve thousand pounds. Half paid upon marriage, the other half paid at the birth of your first child."

The amount stunned Julian. He wondered where Astley had gotten money like that. The man was too clumsy to be lying. Julian's ability to detect a lie was almost uncanny.

"Twelve thousand pounds," Julian repeated softly, despite himself. He tried not to look at the frayed cuffs of his doublet, the barren and dusty room. He tried not to think of Susanna, who could easily go to court and make a brilliant marriage for a drop of that money.

"Of course," Astley finished, "If Ireland more appeals to you, his lordship kindly offers his protection to your grandmother and sister until your return."

Bastard. Julian knew that the offer of protection, when offered to a loyalist, was simply the taking of hostages.

"I wouldn't tarry long if I were you, Ramsden. His lordship would like to see the country settled, everything in place. And I would like that too."

Julian wondered if his grandmother had the

ability to turn Astley into a pig. Or an ox. No, a pig, that he could deliver to some nice, starving Irish family.

He didn't like being cornered or threatened. Even less, he misliked violating his own principles.

"I shall consider the offer of your daughter, sir." The words were cold and joyless.

"We are beyond considering, Ramsden. As of this interview, you are either betrothed to Felicity or a soldier of his lordship's army."

"The devil take you," Julian said very, very softly. He leaned back in his battered chair and rubbed his eyes. He was tired. It had been an ill day.

"Very well, Astley. You may bear the happy tidings to Felicity." *Until I find a way out of this mess.*

Astley's broad face lit with joy. "A very clever move, Ramsden. Felicity will be overjoyed. And since you are to be my son-in-law, there is something I would ask of you, please."

"Good God, man, what more do you want? My blood?"

Astley frowned. "Keep a civil tongue, please. I understand that you have . . . a woman in the house."

Damn Doll and her wagging tongue. "An orphaned cousin, sir. A distant cousin, but my moral responsibility, I assure you."

Astley had obviously heard otherwise. "It seems you have a taste for orphans, Ramsden.

You cannot keep bringing them home like so many stray pups."

Julian fixed the man with a cold glare. "Heed me, Astley. You have me by the balls, to be crude; you and that brewer's son Cromwell. But I will be master in my own home. I will marry your daughter, but I am not your lackey. Are we clear?"

Astley's face flamed. "You must guard your tongue, boy. It may be the death of you." He made his way through the room with his oxlike, lumbering gait, and Julian was alone. He heard the carriage leaving, and after a few minutes, thunder rolled, and the room darkened as rain began to pour down the heavy windows.

And to Julian's surprise, he found that he wanted nothing more than to be with Ivy, to sit in front of the fire and share a cup of wine with her and listen to her soft, peculiar voice, and to forget about Astley, and Felicity, and his responsibilities to his sister and grandmother.

Chapter Seven

Ivy resented being a prisoner only a little less than she resented the way Julian intruded into her thoughts.

Even in sleep she wasn't safe. She had been dreaming about him when she first opened her eyes. Exactly what she'd dreamed she couldn't remember, but they had been evocative dreams full of music and color and heat. When she woke up she was breathless, and her body was bathed with a sheen of sweat that had nothing to do with the temperature.

"Damn you, Julian," she said to the empty room.

It was a cold morning, and the wind that fluttered through the chamber made the bed curtains sway and touched her damp skin with cool fingers.

It was the sound of the door closing that had stirred her, and she saw that someone—Doll, presumably—had left her a tray of food—a steaming pitcher of wine, pies filled with good but unknown meats, and cold roasted chicken and bread.

Thankfully, Doll had also taken away the chamber pot and left a clean one in the adjoining alcove of her room, and also a steaming bowl of water to wash in.

She splashed the rapidly cooling water on her heavy eyes, wishing for a shower and a bar of soap. She wondered how the people of the castle managed to keep their health—as far as she could tell, they ate few vegetables, drank no water, and daily baths were out of the question. The drafts that wafted through her chamber kept it cold despite the constant fire, and she sat close to the flames while she brushed out her hair.

The chill air, scented with the smoke from the fire, made her feel as though she were on a camping trip—hurrying to dress, shivering in the cold, not feeling entirely clean.

What little light came through the heavy windows was dull and gray. She wished she had been transported to a warmer climate. Of course, then she wouldn't have met Margaret, or Susanna . . . or Julian.

Julian. She glanced at the chair he had been sitting in the night before, with the flames dancing on his sharp cheekbones and his thick, dark hair. She thought of the quick brilliance of his rare smile.

Pretty—he had called her pretty. Ivy rose and crossed the room to stare in the mirror. The glass seemed a little smoky, casting her into soft focus.

Was it her imagination, or did she look different?

It must be the dresses, she decided. The dark fabrics and rich lace suited her more than twentieth-century clothing, and the tight bodices and low necklines made more of her figure than the severe styles she favored at home.

You may stay . . . as long as you wish. But you stay as my mistress. You warm my bed, you attend to my needs. I let you stay, and your body is mine. Whenever I wish, however I ask.

"Damn you, Julian," she repeated.

She searched her mind for a solution, but none presented itself. She wondered what he would ask if she consented. Would he be a considerate lover?

It was stupid to even think about. It was out of the question.

And yet the images kept running through her mind. She wondered what he would look like, divested of his dark doublet, and what his skin smelled like, and if he would take her to his cluttered room, or take her here in hers.

If she became his mistress, would he grant her freedom? Or would he keep her locked in her room, like a sultan's favorite locked in the harem, and unlock the door only when he came to visit?

She imagined it: being kept in her room for days and weeks, seeing only Julian, until utter boredom would consume her, and she would live for the times when she heard the key turning in the lock. He would come into the room, and pull her gown from her shoulders, and cover her body with kisses that blazed like fire, and pull her onto the bed—

Shaken, she stopped her fantasy in mid-thought. What was wrong with her? She should be furious, or frightened. She should be planning her escape, not indulging in erotic fantasies about the man who had taken her liberty.

She glanced again at the mirror and saw that her cheeks were flushed with color and her eyes shining.

"Enough!" she said aloud. "You're about eight thousand miles and three hundred years away from home. This is neither the time nor place to be thinking about sex."

She went to the window and stared out, but clouds and fog obscured her view of the sea. There was only the stone courtyard, dark and wet, and the silent buildings and empty windows.

Was Julian there, somewhere in the castle? Was he thinking of her? When would he come for her answer, and what would it be?

She didn't know.

She poured herself a glass of wine, hoping to soothe her nerves, but that only seemed to make it worse. Images of Julian kept sneaking into her mind until her body became heated.

It might have been different, she thought, if it wasn't blackmail. If she had been born into this world and met him in a more conventional way—at a ball, or at court, or however he usually met women. Would he have wanted her then? Would he have told her she was pretty, wooed her with gentle words?

Would she have resisted?

No, to be honest. She thought of his proud, almost arrogant stride, and his sculpted features and dangerous, piratelike good looks. Funny, she thought, how the men who looked like they'd be bad for her were the ones who seemed to appeal most.

Bored and restless, she took another sip of wine, the same hot, spiced wine she had shared with Julian, to judge by the flavor.

Within moments, Ivy was lost in another daydream, where she and Julian met in a summer landscape of gleaming green and gold, and he told her that he loved her with all of his heart.

She slept in the afternoon, overcome by the lethargy that solitude inspires, and woke to the sound of the key turning in the lock.

She sat up hastily, pushing her unbound hair from her face as Julian entered the room.

He closed the door quietly behind him and

leaned against it, looking at her with an inscrutable expression.

"Sleeping already? It's not yet sunset."

He spoke as if they were friends, as if this were the most normal of situations. As if, Ivy thought irritably, he kept women locked in rooms and blackmailed them every day. For all she knew, he did.

"What else is there to do? I've nobody to talk to; nothing to read. I may go out of my mind with boredom."

"Marry, you're peevish-sounding," he said, and sat in the chair before the fire. He stretched himself with an easy grace that rankled her. How calm he seemed, how casual. And after her thoughts had been rolling and boiling in her head all day.

"You'd be peevish too, if you were a prisoner," she informed him, swinging her legs over the side of the bed.

"I daresay," he agreed, seeming not at all ashamed. "Pour me a little wine, pray thee. I've had a long day."

He didn't look it. His skin glowed with a healthy color, and his tilted eyes sparkled.

"Pour it yourself," Ivy retorted.

He looked taken aback, as if he wasn't used to being spoken to like that, but then he laughed and poured himself a goblet full. "Shrew," he called her, but his low, pleasant voice made the word sound like a caress, and his smile was so charming, so damned movie-star perfect, that

Ivy couldn't take offense.

He sipped the wine, gave a happy sigh, and tossed his hair off his forehead. He put his feet up on the tasseled footstool, and cast her a smile full of mischief.

"You do look like you've had a bad day," Ivy said. "What have you been doing? Out ravishing maidens since sunrise?"

He laughed softly. "You must learn to curb your sharp tongue, or the villagers will tie you into the scold's chair and give you a dunking. No, Ivy, today I actually rescued a maiden. If you want to call her that."

"What do you mean, Julian?" she asked, intrigued by his serious expression as well as his words.

Briefly, he described what had happened in Westford that morning—the women condemned by the witch-pricker, the crying child, the hypocritical villagers.

Ivy felt herself growing cold as she listened.

"Oh, Julian! My God, how horrible! What would have become of her if you hadn't taken her?"

Julian shook his head and shrugged. "They likely would have left her to starve. Self-righteous bastards."

Ivy shook her head in disbelief. What a strange, barbaric world she had fallen into. A frightening place, where people would let a child die because of their fear, where a self-appointed

140

holy man could condemn women to hang. She shivered at the thought.

"It wasn't very wise of me," he added, his eyes darkening. "There are enough rumors of demons and witchcraft surrounding Wythecombe Keep. It was passing stupid of me to fuel the fire."

"What else could you do?" Ivy asked. "Leave a child to die?"

"No, I couldn't. But what's to be done with her now, I can't imagine. I hate to burden Grandmother with her, and Doll says a prayer whenever she looks toward the little ragtag creature. Rumors will be flying about the village, I assure you. I pray that the witch-pricker stays well away from here."

"Oh, but he wouldn't dare—"

"A creature like that," Julian interrupted, "will dare anything. These are dark times, Ivy. I curse the day the butcher Cromwell came to power. Whatever faults Charles may have had, he was a tolerant man, God rest his soul. Now men are carried away with this puritanical religion, and they look for demons and traitors under every stone."

Ivy didn't know what to say. Only a few minutes before, Julian had appeared not to have a care in the world. Now bitterness darkened his eyes.

"Cromwell won't live forever," she told him, "and the Stuarts will reign again. Then you'll get

141

your land back, and things will be the way they were before."

Startled, Julian looked at her and gave a quick, sharp laugh. "Heigh-ho, little Ivy! You say that like a soothsayer! Take care not to say such things in front of anyone else, or the witch-pricker shall be at the gates."

"I can hardly say anything to anyone," Ivy pointed out, changing the subject abruptly, "if I'm kept locked in this room. You're the only one I see, Julian Ramsden."

"True enough," he agreed. "I feel much safer that way."

"I don't."

"You're safe enough. Safer then you'd be out in the streets. Especially if you wander about prophesying the death of the lord protector."

Ivy thought about the scene he had described, the three women hanging in the village square, and shivered. Perhaps he was right.

"Speaking of which," he said, leaning forward, "have you an answer for me?"

Ivy sat silently, dropping her eyes. "Do I have a choice? Aside from being sent away to beg in the streets, I mean?"

He considered, with a thoughtful expression. "In truth, yes. I have a nose for the truth, Ivy. It's a gift, you could say, or perhaps I'm just more observant than most. So I give you this choice as well: tell me who you are, and how you came to be here, and I shall rethink my first offer. Hand me an outlandish tale, and it stands."

"Great," Ivy muttered, wondering if anything could be more outlandish than the truth.

He sat expectantly for a few moments, and when he realized that she was offering no explanation, his eyes began to sparkle as if it was a fine joke.

"What a pleasure," he exclaimed. "I believe I have a new mistress. By God, it's been some time. What say thee?"

If only he were repulsive, or ugly. How easy it would be to say, "I'd rather starve, thank you."

But he wasn't. He was exotic and dashing; he was the best-looking man she had ever seen. And she liked him, oddly enough. He wasn't all bad. He was able to laugh at himself, and under his arrogant exterior he had a heart, and a brave one. She thought of the way he'd taken the crippled child from under the noses of the angry villagers, and brought her to his home without a thought of what it might mean to his neighbors and family.

Not the action of a cold or brutal man. It was brave, the action of a man with honor.

If only she could hate him. But the fact was, she felt something in her heart that went beyond the heat her body felt for him, beyond the physical fever that seized her when she thought of him.

"I've thought of it all day," she admitted.

"And?" He looked happier now, his eyes bright with curiosity. Handsome devil, so sure of himself.

143

Ivy swallowed and sat a little straighter. The fact was, he had her. She really had no alternative, but damned if she'd let him have an easy victory. She still had her pride and her dignity, and she'd not give those up.

"What can I say, Julian? That I'm ready to go out into the streets and starve? You know damned well that I have no place to go. I wouldn't think a man like you would stoop to mistreating a helpless woman, but there you go. You have, and you've won. I hope it makes you proud."

He looked insulted. "Asking an attractive woman to be my mistress is hardly mistreatment, sweet."

"That's your opinion. If you have no more pride than to blackmail women into your bed, fine. I lose. But I warn you, I won't enjoy it."

He raised his dark brows. "Marry, Ivy! What a thing to say. I think you will."

"Like hell. I'll do it because I have to, not because I want to."

"What? Is the idea of lying with me so repulsive to you?"

Ivy stared at him, his sharp, aristocratic face and elegant figure. *No*, she wanted to say, *it's probably the best offer I'll ever have, and you're so damned attractive it almost hurts. I wish I hated you, I wish I didn't dream of you at night, and I wish that you'd made the offer because you cared for me, instead of using me as a whore to ease your boredom and lust.*

144

"It sounds easier than starving," she lied. *You arrogant jerk. I'll die before I let you know how badly I want you.*

"You hurt my pride," Julian told her, in a soft, mocking voice that said she hadn't bothered him a bit. "And I'll prove you wrong, you imp. You'll enjoy it. I'll make sure of it. You'll like it, and you'll ask for more."

Ivy wanted to slap him, and at the same time, his words started a slow, languid heat somewhere deep inside her.

"And I won't be locked in this damned room anymore, do you hear? If I'm to be your mistress, I want the benefits of the position."

He looked startled. "What? Don't bother asking for carriages or jewels or your own establishment, for I can't afford it. This isn't London, and I'm a poor man."

"I realize that. All I want is the freedom of the castle, and to go out sometimes." *So that I can find that damned book and be rid of your beautiful, arrogant face before I fall in love with you, you selfish pig.*

"What's to prevent you from running?" Julian demanded. Ivy supposed that would be intolerable to his enormous ego.

"If I had anywhere to run to, do you think I'd agree to this disgusting arrangement?" she cried.

He leaned back in the chair, looking at her with a cool, calculating expression. And then he showed her his best, wickedly appealing smile.

145

"No, perhaps you wouldn't. But Ivy—don't give me this 'disgusting' nonsense. Your eyes don't say disgusting. They say you want me, and badly, and I'll bet you my last shilling that you like it well."

"You'll lose," Ivy snapped, her cheeks flaming.

"I'm bored with losing," Julian said, standing and stretching. "I've lost my title, I've lost my money, I've lost my battle with Cromwell and Astley, and I don't intend to lose any more." He took the key to her room from his pocket and tossed it to her. "It's done. You have the freedom of the castle, and you're mine. We'll see you at dinner." He turned to go, looking very pleased with himself. "Oh, and put your hair up before you come down. The way it is now makes you look quite wanton."

"In keeping with my new job," Ivy remarked.

Julian appeared not the least ashamed, and tossed her a merry grin as he left the room.

Her heart beating an odd, quick rhythm, Ivy turned slowly and confronted herself in the looking glass.

"What are you doing?" she whispered. "What in the hell are you doing?"

Her reflection was a stranger. Where was the prim shopkeeper with her well-ordered life, safe in her tasteful gray cashmeres and tightly twisted hair?

The woman who stared back at her was an unfamiliar creature, with dark eyes that glittered from a pale, glowing face, her red curls corkscrewing around bare shoulders and pale décolletage.

The image disturbed her, and she turned away. Nothing was the way it had been before. The life she had built so carefully was gone, and now even her very self seemed changed.

"The prisoners have been freed from the tower!" Susanna sang out when she saw Ivy entering the dining room. "Marry, Ivy, what has happened to evil King Julian? He's being so merciful—perhaps he's ill."

Ivy couldn't restrain a laugh. Susanna was such an irrepressible creature, so charming with her shining eyes and dark good looks, that it was impossible not to laugh when she did.

Lady Margaret beamed as Ivy approached the table. "How good to see you, Ivy. 'Tis odd, how soon I came to like your company."

It was true, Ivy realized. She felt the same. Lady Margaret and Susanna were so genuinely happy and likable that they already felt like friends.

"So, Julian has decided that you're not a Roundhead spy," Susanna observed. "How very perceptive of him."

"It's a good thing you don't have the opportunity to go to court," Julian observed, walking into the room behind Ivy. "You have the most indiscreet tongue, Susanna. You'd be clapped into irons within a week." He took Ivy's arm in a familiar way and walked to the table with her.

"Here, Ivy, you shall sit at my right hand."

Ivy cast him a curious glance. Was this how she was going to be treated, then? As if she were a legitimate member of the household? She hadn't expected that.

"It's good to see you smiling, Julian," his grandmother said. "A welcome change. I thought that after this afternoon, you'd be in a sulk."

"I don't sulk, you old scold," Julian retorted. "How dare you imply such a thing?"

Doll came into the room, bearing a tray of roasted birds. She shot Ivy a resentful look and set down the tray with a sullen thump.

"Dinner," she announced, and strolled from the room, scratching her hip.

Lady Margaret threw her hands up with a despairing gesture, which made Susanna laugh.

"What is this world coming to? When I was young—"

"About the time of the Crusades," Susanna put in.

Lady Margaret gave her granddaughter a stern look. "Enough from you, monkey. Tell us, Ivy, how are you faring?"

"Very well, thank you."

"Did Julian tell you about our new orphan?" Susanna demanded, attacking her food with vigor. "Mmm, I love duckling stuffed with oysters, don't you?"

"It looks very good, thank you. And yes, Julian told me about her—where is she?"

"Sleeping," Lady Margaret answered. "She'll be lucky not to take ill. I'd like you to look at her, Ivy, and tell me what you think."

"I'd be happy to, though I don't know how much help it will be."

"Another opinion is almost always welcome," Lady Margaret announced.

"Even Felicity Astley's?" Susanna cried. "She seems to think we're harboring the daughter of old Scratch! She fair ran out of here today. The silly cow."

At the mention of Felicity, Julian tensed.

Ivy glanced at him. He was scowling at his plate, and he tore a bite of bread from a loaf with an almost savage gesture.

"Oh, Susanna," Lady Margaret said with a tired sigh, "you do have a habit of saying the wrong thing." She rubbed her eyes with a tired gesture, and the wrinkles in her plump face settled into sad lines as she looked at Ivy.

"Our Julian became betrothed today," she announced in mournful tones.

Ivy felt a sudden, sharp pain. She stared at Julian.

His eyes were as dark as the ocean; there was no pleasure in his face. "Against my will," he added.

Ivy didn't know what to say. She looked around the room, which had seemed so pleasant a few seconds ago—the table crowded with pewter and silver, the sparkling fire lighting the beautiful tapestry, and the portrait of the dark-haired Tudor woman who watched them all with a glint of mischief in her dark eyes.

Susanna glanced around the table. "I've said the wrong thing again, haven't I?"

"It's a definite skill you have," her brother agreed. "Pity, it was a jolly meal till then. But don't despair. I shall think of a way out of it. How, I can't think now, but I vow that I shall. Until then, I have brighter news."

Lady Margaret smiled across the table. "Well-aday, Julian, I am glad of it. What could that be?"

Julian looked from Ivy to his sister to his grandmother, his eyes glinting as if with a marvelous joke.

"Ivy," he announced, "has agreed to become my mistress. What think you?"

Ivy choked on her wine. How could he!

Lady Margaret's jaw dropped, and her hands froze over her plate.

Susanna's dark eyes widened, her napkin covered her mouth, and she gave a shocked, short whoop of laughter.

Ivy felt her face burning. Her ears flamed. She was speechless.

Julian beamed at them, looking like a little boy who had successfully planted a frog in his teacher's desk drawer. "Pass the salt, please," he said.

"Oh, Julian," his grandmother said, shaking her silver head slowly. "Oh, Julian."

Susanna burst into giggles. "Marry, Grandmother! How did this come to pass?"

Ivy felt like a scarlet woman. Why, why would Julian say such a thing? How could he announce it as if it were pleasant dinner conversation?

Susanna was laughing fully now, her pretty face brilliant pink. Lady Margaret stared at her grandson, and her old face began to quiver with indignation.

"You asked me if she could stay," Julian pointed out.

"Why . . . why . . . mayhap I did, Julian. But *this*! I never thought . . . stop that stupid laughter, Susanna, I vow I can't think. Oh, Ivy, you poor little thing!"

Ivy felt her face turning even redder at this unexpected sympathy.

"Don't be silly," Julian said, still completely unruffled. "I expect I shall make her very happy."

"She doesn't much look it," Susanna observed. "She looks as if she might fall on the floor and die of shame."

Ivy thought it very likely.

Lady Margaret fluttered her hands and turned her eyes toward heaven. "This," she announced to the ceiling, "this is what comes of sending your children to London, Denby. I told you and told you, but would you ever listen to your poor mother?"

Susanna looked up at the ceiling, as if expecting to see the ghost of her father lurking about, and shrugged.

"Now see what you've done, Julian."

"And I was right!" Lady Margaret cried. "Back he comes, with his hair not cut and hanging down like a spaniel's ears, and those boots that look like they're about to fall off his feet, and breeches big enough to fit three men into—"

"More likely three women, in Julian's case," Susanna interrupted.

Lady Margaret took no notice. ". . . and strutting like a popinjay, all full of brash city manners. And look what your son has done now! This is what you learn in London," she belabored the invisible Denby. "You learn to corrupt innocents and flaunt your shameless behavior under your poor old grandmother's nose!"

The old woman settled back in her chair with a fiery glare in her eye. "The young these days," she muttered.

"If you've finished tormenting my poor father's ghost," Julian said, "may I get a word in?"

Stiffly, Lady Margaret nodded.

"Very well." Julian looked around the table at the three women—his outraged grandmother, Susanna, who was watching avidly with barely suppressed glee, and Ivy, still and silent, her pale face stained with a wash of brilliant crimson.

"I'm no fool, my lady. Something is amiss in this house, and well I know it. As do you, and you, and you," he added, giving all three a sharp glance. "Something is afoot, and I have no idea what, but it would behoove all of you to tell me. I get the distinct feeling I'm playing the fool, and anybody that would like to enlighten me may do so now. Who knows? If the explanation is reasonable, I may change my mind, and respect your tender sensibilities."

"You're a dog, Julian," Susanna said in an affectionate tone. "Wait till Felicity hears this. She may well refuse to marry you."

Julian looked pleased. "That could hardly hurt, could it?" He glanced up the table at his grandmother, and sent her a brilliant smile. "My lady? Have you anything you'd like me to know?"

Lady Margaret glanced at Ivy and looked away, but not before Ivy saw a quick look of guilt.

"You're outrageous, Julian." She looked at her plate, and then back at her grandson with a defiant air. "I have absolutely nothing to tell you. Nothing at all, do you hear? Now I'll thank thee to stop this dreadful game."

Julian appeared to be enjoying himself tremendously.

"I shall stop this game when everyone in this room has their cards on the table. Until then, I hold the trump."

For a few minutes, silence filled the room, and then Julian pushed his chair back and extended his hand to Ivy. "Come, sweetheart. We have business, I believe."

Ivy gave him a beseeching look, which had no effect on him at all.

"Pray thee, come, Ivy."

She glanced back at Margaret and Susanna, but neither met her eye. Her face hot with fury and shame, she followed Julian from the room.

Chapter Eight

As soon as Julian and Ivy were out of sight, Lady Margaret rose from her chair, taking a candle.

"Lord have mercy. Hurry, Susanna, you must help me, before we're found out."

Susanna rushed after her grandmother, following her through the kitchens, where Doll was napping with her head on the worktable. Edith was bent over the huge fireplace, offering them a view of her ample backside, and didn't even notice as they scurried past, down the back corridor, and into the room that Lady Margaret referred to as her "apothecary."

"What, does Ivy know?" Susanna demanded.

"Nay, I think not." Lady Margaret closed the heavy door behind them and lit a few more candles.

154

Susanna breathed in the familiar, pleasant smells of drying herbs and flowers and spices, and settled herself on the wooden stool next to the fireplace while her grandmother stirred the ashes and added a few more sticks to the small blaze.

"Why the hurry, if Ivy doesn't know?"

"Because if she tells Julian the truth about how she came here, he'll know for certain. And then we shall have trouble."

Susanna frowned, brushing her dark ringlets back over her shoulders. "Do you really think he would separate us, my lady?"

Lady Margaret was rooting through an assortment of bottles and jars. "I know he would, dear. Not because he's cruel, but because he's frightened. Look what he witnessed today. It will only strengthen his resolve. You'll be off to that French convent so fast you won't know what happened."

Susanna gave an elaborate shudder. "What do you intend for them, then?"

Lady Margaret poured a bottle of wine into a pitcher, and then dumped the entire contents of the small bottle into it. "In for a penny, in for a pound, I say. We'll give them more of what we gave them by mistake, and then some."

Susanna's eyes widened, and she smiled. "Will that keep Ivy from telling him how she came here?"

Lady Margaret sighed, stirring the pitcher. "If we get this to them on time, they'll neither of them be able to think about how she came here. They'll have too much else on their minds."

"You'd best say a charm for luck," Susanna suggested. "For it sounds risky to me."

"Oh, mercy, I should, should I not? Let me think, how does that go . . . something . . . oh! Oh, this is it, I'm certain." Lady Margaret looked very pleased with herself as she held the pitcher aloft in what she hoped to be a mystical stance and chanted:

> *By all the stars in midnight's sky*
> *By all the hares are in the wood*
> *And roses bloom in sweet July . . .*

Her voice trailed off, and she looked uncertain.

"You've forgotten," Susanna proclaimed, twirling a curl around her finger. "I thought you would."

"I have not, you monkey. It's . . . the last line is . . ."

Susanna stifled a yawn.

"As many hares are in the wood . . ." Margaret said, furrowing her already furrowed brow. "Come by dawn, with fortune good! Is that it?"

Susanna shrugged. "For all I care, it could be 'I'd truly like a velvet hood,' or 'the oyster soup is very good.' Honestly, Grandmam, let's hurry."

"And I thought Susanna had a clattering tongue," Julian cried. "Pray, Ivy, give me a moment's peace."

156

Ivy had no intention of doing so. "Did you even think how embarrassed I'd be? Did you? For decency's sake, Julian, you didn't have to announce it to your family!"

She sat in Julian's bedchamber, perched indignantly on the edge of a faded chair, her arms folded across her chest. "And then to haul me off here as if I were some cheap tramp from a twenty-dollar massage parlor! Like a T-bone you picked up at the supermarket! Like a blue light special from K-mart! Like a damned—"

"Ivy?"

She stopped, breathing hard with fury.

"You sound as if you're speaking English, but I've no idea at all what you're saying. Calm thyself, please."

She was about to tell him that he'd be lucky if she stopped long enough to draw breath, when the knock sounded on the door.

"Come in," Julian called.

It was Doll, bearing a pewter pitcher of wine. She gave Ivy a resentful stare as she thumped it to the table, followed by two glasses.

"Doll, I didn't ask for that." Julian appeared put out by the intrusion.

Doll, in her usual sullen fashion, rolled her eyes instead of answering, and slammed the door behind her.

"We really must replace that girl," Julian murmured, raking his hair from his forehead with an exasperated motion.

Ivy looked daggers at him.

"Oh, cease, Ivy. Here, drink your wine and take a breath."

Still glowering, she did so, taking care not to touch his hand when she accepted the glass from him. It appeared to amuse him.

"Now, if you'll let me have a word. I beg your pardon. I never intended to humiliate you. To be truthful, I never intended to go that far. I just couldn't resist. They're up to something, those two. I wanted to see if they'd confess."

"At my expense," Ivy cried. She was surprised to find tears in her eyes. "Do you know how humiliating that was?"

"That wasn't my intention, Ivy. I really didn't think it would go that far. I thought one or another of you would confess, and save your virtue."

"Confess what? I'd never seen either your grandmother or your sister before I met you. You've embarrassed me and upset poor Lady Margaret for nothing, Julian."

"I don't think so."

Oh, the infuriating calm of him! Ivy swallowed her wine, barely even tasting it.

"After all," he continued, and his voice was as warm and caressing as a summer wind, "here you are in my chambers. And your anger has put the most delightful color in your cheeks. You're very appealing, really, when you hold your tongue for a moment."

Ivy raised her eyes, about to give him a sharp answer. She fell silent, looking at him, and the words died on her tongue.

He sat in a chair opposite her, leaning toward her, an elbow propped on his knee. His eyes, as soft and gray as fog, were regarding her with obvious pleasure. "Ivy, you needn't look at me like that. If you think I'd force you against your will, you're very wrong. I've never had to force a woman. It would be quite insulting to my honor."

"Not to mention your colossal ego."

"I made you an offer, and you accepted it."

"What else could I do?" Ivy demanded. "Where else could I go, Julian?"

"From whence you came, presumably," was the cool reply.

Ivy thought of her lovely store, the polished wood and shining glass cases of jewelry and glassware, her cozy apartment with its wicker furniture and flowering houseplants. It was always spring in her apartment.

"If I could, I would," she said softly.

When she looked up, Julian was watching her carefully over the brim of his glass.

"Ofttimes," he observed after a moment, "I get the notion that you are speaking in half truths. Something is being kept from me, and I won't rest until I know all of it. What do you want from me, Ivy? From any of us? What brought you to Wythecombe Keep?"

She dropped her eyes to her lap and stared at her hands, pale against the blue satin of her skirts. What would he say if she told him the truth?

He reached forward and took her hands between his own. Strong hands, with long fingers. They were warm, and oddly soothing. How long had it been since a man had touched her like that? The last time she'd had a boyfriend had been her last year of college. He'd been a music student, and his passion for Stravinsky had far outweighed his passion for Ivy. He had left for the East Coast almost immediately after graduation, and Ivy had waited in vain for a promise, a commitment that never came.

But Tyler and his cello were happily committed to the Boston Symphony, leaving her with the feeling that she wasn't good enough . . . not good enough for marriage, not good enough for his family, not good enough for the things that other women seemed to get so easily.

"Such a sorrowful countenance," Julian murmured. He turned her hands over and stroked her palms with his thumbs, his touch as soft as a bird's wing.

Ivy sat silently, a strange, lethargic calm enfolding her. She felt as if she were falling into a dream. None of it seemed real—the way the flames flickered off the stone walls, and made the blue satin of her skirt catch the light, and lit Julian's dark hair with a burnished halo.

The touch of his hands against hers was hypnotic. She stared at the way their hands looked together—hers small and pale, his darker and larger. The white cuff of his shirt showed beneath the velvet sleeve of his doublet.

He was near enough that she could smell him—an intoxicating spicy scent, a little like sandalwood, and fresh air, and the not unpleasant muskiness of his skin.

She studied his face carefully—the proud, high forehead, the thick brows that slanted above his dark, tilting eyes. That impossibly beautiful mouth, the top lip drawn as carefully and symmetrically as if with an artist's hand, the sharp creases in the corner that became dimples when he smiled, the bottom lip full and sensual, bespeaking a man who loved the good things of life.

A movie star's mouth. A lover's mouth.

She noticed for the first time that his nose bent slightly to one side, an imperfection that didn't detract at all from the noble and aquiline look of it.

"What are you thinking, sweet?"

Ivy's gaze moved to his eyes, and he was watching her with eyes like twilight, soft and beguiling.

"Your nose," she answered honestly, and her voice sounded unsteady. "It's crooked."

He smiled and showed his dimples. "Does it displease you?"

Ivy shook her head. Her mouth felt unsure of itself, not quite able to form the words in her mind. *No, it pleases me very much. You have a beautiful face, exactly what a man should look like, and the way your hair falls down your back, and the way your hands feel over mine—as if they belonged there. Nobody's hands could feel like this, and it makes me wonder if our bodies would feel as perfect together.*

She had never been so intoxicated by a touch. Her body felt soft and warm, perfectly relaxed, and each touch of his fingers sent a tremor of heat through her body, a slow, gradual warmth that seemed to melt her fears and uncertainties like the spring sunlight melts the frozen winter earth.

"How well you suit me," he said, his voice hushed and tender. " 'Tis an odd thing. Your simplest touch drugs me like summer wine."

An echo of her own thoughts.

They sat there for what might have been a moment, or a year, simply looking at each other's eyes as if awed by what they saw, intoxicated by the rising warmth between them.

Whether Julian leaned toward her or she to him, Ivy would never be able to say. It was the only thing to do.

Their lips met, softly at first, as if to taste the other. His mouth was warm, delicious, tenderly caressing hers. His hands moved to her face, her cheek, her temple, the soft tendrils that curled around her ears.

The soft warmth that had been building in her sparkled and moved like light upon the ocean, a million radiant lights that rushed through her veins.

A sound escaped from her throat, and he pulled her tighter into the kiss. Her mouth opened beneath his, and the heat of his tongue moved against her own, hot and velvet smooth.

The light in her veins became the deep, dark heat of a summer night, languid and beautiful. Her hands moved to his hair, and it fell through her fingers like silk.

Their mouths met again, and there was no awkwardness in the kiss, no question of where do I put my nose or should I tip my head this way or that or is my breath fresh enough. It was as easy as drawing breath, as perfect and natural as the wind moving through the treetops.

They drew back for a moment and stared at each other, their faces reflecting wonder.

Julian touched the side of her neck and brushed a strand of hair away from her face. "Such beauty," he whispered. His words hung in the air, filling her ears and heart.

She was beautiful. He found her beautiful. There was nothing dishonest in his voice, in his darkened eyes. Julian Ramsden, the most beautiful man she had ever seen, her enchanted cavalier, her dark lord. He found her beautiful, and she believed him.

For the first time in her life, Ivy was beautiful.

He pulled her gently to her feet, and she followed without resistance. He bent his head to the hollow of her throat, and she shivered at the sensation of his mouth, hot and soft, pressing kisses in the hollow where her pulse beat.

163

If he let go of her waist, she might have fallen. There was not an ounce of resistance or strength left in her, only the warm, languid fever that caused her to melt at his touch.

In the back of her mind, the voice of reality nagged at her—this man wasn't her lover or her friend. He was an egotistical, manipulative tyrant, using her body to obtain a confession from her.

"Don't, Julian," she whispered, but the words didn't sound very convincing.

He pulled her closer. "Don't what?" he whispered back. "Don't do this"—and he pressed his mouth into the warm hollow behind her ear, his breath like a hot wind—"or don't do this?" He moved his hand over her breast with a soft, teasing motion.

The admonishing voice in the back of her mind faded and was silent.

Her body seemed to melt against his; the sensations poured over her like warm rain—the silk of his hair against her neck, the hardness of his shoulder beneath the warm velvet of his doublet, the feeling of her breasts pressing against his chest. His hips were tight against her, the satin of her gown moving between them.

They kissed again and again, and each time their mouths seemed hungrier. She was hardly aware of his hand in the laces and hooks at the back of her gown until she felt it slide from her shoulders, whispering against her skin as it fell to the floor. Her shift followed effortlessly, and

Julian's ragged sigh fell on her ears like poetry.

His hands traveled over the bare skin of her back, the curve of her waist, and onto her breasts, and the sight of his dark hands on her pale body was an image of erotic beauty beyond anything she had ever imagined. Her breasts seemed to swell and ache at his touch.

"Beautiful Ivy," he whispered, and his breath furled against her ear, hot and intoxicating. He pulled the ribbons and pins from her hair, and it slid down her back like a cool cloud, glowing in the firelight like the very fire that seemed to glow in her veins.

He carried her to the great bed, lifting her easily and laying her down tenderly. His eyes never left hers as he tugged at the laces and fastenings of his doublet and breeches.

When Ivy had been with Tyler, his nakedness had almost embarrassed her. He seemed pale and vulnerable, as uncomfortable without his clothing as he was without his glasses.

With Julian, it was different. As well as his dark doublets and cavalier boots suited him, his bare skin seemed to become him even more. His chest and arms were graceful and perfectly muscled, the dark hair of his chest tapered down to his perfect stomach, his thighs and legs were beautifully trim and muscled from years of riding. His dark hair shone in the firelight; his eyes glowed as he lay beside her.

Ivy was lost at the touch of his body lying full against hers. His skin was like satin caressing her body, and she felt him hard and hot and pressing against her thigh.

Unbidden, her hand reached for him with a gesture so natural that it would have surprised her, if she could have thought.

His breath exhaled against her neck, a warm wind that carried her further into the spell of her desire.

They explored each other's bodies with wonder and hunger—hot hands sliding over smooth backs, mouths tasting necks and eyelids. A hundred kisses were given and taken, and returned again with blinding heat.

When his fingers finally moved to the soft heat between her legs, Ivy cried out with the sweetness of the sensation. They skimmed over her, light and smooth, then with increasing pressure, until her body swayed and moved at the motion of his fingers, guided by the heat and friction.

She opened to him like a flower unfurls to the sunlight, welcoming him to her body, silently beseeching him with touch and motion to relieve the fever that engulfed her.

When he at last entered her body, she gave a cry of unrestrained joy. He filled her with heat, with a silken hardness that felt like nothing on earth. Her arms clung to his shoulders as if she would otherwise fall away; she buried her face in his neck and her mind filled with the taste of his skin, the scent of him. Every inch of her body sang with sensation.

She felt as if his very spirit had fused with

hers, and they moved together in absolute shared communion, a ritual as blindingly beautiful as had ever existed, or ever would. It was a darkness as perfect as a midnight sky, a brilliance like sunlight, a place where nothing existed but the two of them.

It wasn't long before Ivy gave herself up to the heat and darkness, and she fell into the sensation until she was nothing but feeling. Her world was gone as she was shaken by wave after wave of beautiful light, and through her delirium she heard Julian utter a primitive, fierce sound of triumph and joy that echoed her own.

Shaking, dizzy, and stunned, they clung to each other as the madness receded, trembling hands clasping together, moving slowly to each other's faces as the world became real again.

It happened slowly. Gradually, Ivy became aware of the sound of the fire, of the cold breeze that wafted over her skin, cooling the glistening sweat that beaded there.

And Julian—he lay next to her, a hand between her breasts, staring at her as if dazed by what he had felt.

Ivy lay unmoving and silent, unwilling to move or speak or break the spell that had bound them. The curtained and canopied bed was her haven, a perfect world.

After what seemed an eternity, Julian spoke.

"You're cold," was all he said, but there was a husky tenderness in his voice that caused Ivy's heart to skip a quick beat.

Silently, she sat up while he pulled the heavy blankets and linens aside. She wondered if he would send her back to her room, or expect her to stay. She wondered if it had felt as magical to him as it had to her. She wondered if he could ever love her.

He climbed beneath the bed linens and beckoned her with an outstretched arm.

She slid next to his body without question, the covers warm from the heat of their bodies. He pulled her head to his chest, and she laid her cheek against the soft hair that covered it, breathing in the scent of his skin. She laid a hand against his neck and felt the pulse that beat there.

Softly, his hand stroked her hair with a soothing, quiet touch.

She thought how strange it was, that she felt as if she had always slept thus. How comfortable it was, how right.

Dazed, she drifted in and out of sleep, aware of his lips touching the crown of her head every now and then. She wondered what he was thinking, but kept her silence, unwilling to shatter her euphoria.

After a time, she fell into the sweetest, happiest sleep she had ever known.

Upstairs in the north wing, Daisy was sleeping so heavily that when she first heard the noisy laughter, she ignored it and snuggled deeper under the heavy blankets. Oh, it was warm. She had never been so warm.

The laughter rang out again, high and merry, beckoning her from the warm cocoon she slumbered in. For a moment, she wondered what had happened to make her mother laugh so hard in the dead of night.

Then she opened her eyes and remembered.

She wasn't in the cottage at all. The cottage was gone, somewhere over the moors and the cliffs and past the rushing streams and beyond the little villages, and she was in the castle of the Dark Man.

Her arms and legs didn't hurt so much anymore. Maybe because she was warm.

She sat up in the big bed and looked around, more curious than frightened. The White-Haired Woman had put her into this bed.

Daisy sat for a long time, remembering. The White-Haired Woman had put her into a big tub of warm water, which had frightened her at first. She thought that it might be like a dunking, something that the Mean People did to women who were scolds.

But it wasn't. The woman had just washed her with the sweet-smelling water, speaking in such a gentle, soft voice that Daisy could hardly believe it was meant for herself. After a while she quit struggling and let herself be bathed.

And the Laughing Girl came in to watch. She laughed, but it wasn't the kind of laughter that hurt. Daisy was used to people laughing at her. The village children laughed when they pelted her with mud or threw rocks at her. Once they had told her they wanted to play with her and then pushed her into a ditch and laughed when she couldn't get out. That was mean laughter, and made her cry.

But the Laughing Girl wasn't like that. She was beautiful, like a red bird or the sweet flowers that grew by the big cottages in the village. She had eyes like a foggy sky, and shining dark hair, and she wore a dress of the same deep red as the summer flowers. No thorns, just deep, soft red. Daisy wanted to touch the dress, to see if it felt soft like the flowers, but she didn't dare.

She was happy just to look, and listen to the laughter.

"All sticks and twigs!" the Laughing Girl had cried, running a soft hand over Daisy's arms. But not mean.

They had dressed Daisy in a long white gown of the softest fabric she had ever felt. The sleeves hung over her hands, and it trailed far past her feet.

"No more fleas," the White-Haired Woman said, and Daisy saw that it was true. She didn't itch a bit anymore.

She wondered where the fleas had gone—did they listen to the woman and simply hop away?

Then the Laughing Girl left the room and came back with food. Daisy stared at it, unable to believe it was for her, and finally the White-Haired Woman fed her with a spoon—golden soup with white meat and herbs in it, and bread—bread like Daisy had never seen before. Gold outside, and soft and white inside, like clouds.

It had been like a dream, the nicest dream she had ever had.

And then they put her in a bed that was big enough for a whole family, and covered her with blankets of soft, fine cloth. "Go to sleep, you little bundle of twigs," the Laughing Girl said, but she said it as if she was fond of little bundles of twigs.

For a long time, Daisy could not sleep. She stared at the room, over and over again. The floor was of wood, but cut into pieces that fit together in a dizzying pattern of dark and light, light and dark. There were glass windows, and she could see the darkening sky beyond them, until the Laughing Girl covered them with the lengths of autumn-colored fabric that hung there—fabric with patterns of golden vines and leaves. There was a fire too, red and gold, in a fireplace of pale stone that shone as smooth as ice, and wood around it, dark and beautiful. And white candles in tall candle stands that shone soft and golden in the enchanted room.

The Laughing Girl made music on a stringed instrument such as Daisy had seen in the village on May Day and at fairs. But that music had never been so sweet. The Laughing Girl sat, like a bright, sweet flower in her red dress, and she sang about summer days and a woman who would not say yes, and a song about a fairy queen who fetched a man away to her kingdom.

Perhaps, Daisy thought, that is what happened to me. And then the warm soup and the warm blankets and fire and music lulled her away to the sweetest sleep she had ever known.

Now she woke to the sound of laughter. After a moment Daisy knew it was the Laughing Girl, somewhere outside the great door.

She wasn't afraid.

The fire was low, and the candles were gone, but she could see well enough. She climbed out of bed slowly. She fell once, tripping over the long white gown, but there was nobody to see or laugh, so she just got up and kept going.

The latch on the door was hard to open, and the door was very heavy, but Daisy managed.

She stepped out into the hall, which was very long and dark and cold, but she was used to cold. From somewhere down the hallway she could hear the laughter ringing through the darkness, and she could see the dim glow of light. She made her way down the hall, slowly and carefully. She stumbled once, and stopped to rest.

Now she could hear them clearly, The White-Haired Woman and the Laughing Girl.

"Oh, Grandmam! What have you done now?"

"Stop laughing, Susanna, and help me! Oh, if Julian sees this . . ."

"I knew you'd get it wrong. I knew it. Oh, mind, there goes another one!" This was followed by a peal of laughter.

"Catch him, Susanna! Oh, mercy upon us. I don't see how this happened."

Susanna, Daisy thought. The Laughing Girl's name was Susanna. She picked herself up and began to make her way toward the light and laughter.

Susanna was laughing again. "Heigh-ho, there's another! Do you suppose they're in the hall as well?"

"By my foot, Susanna, catch them, and help me put them out before you wake the house. How did this happen?"

As Daisy made her slow way toward the voices, she saw something move in the darkness. She stopped, hoping it was not a rat. Daisy liked animals, but she didn't like rats.

But it wasn't. It was a rabbit. It came loping toward her, down the wide hall. A big, pale rabbit with ears alert. It stopped when it saw her and sat, as silent as herself, regarding her with black eyes and twitching nose.

It didn't seem afraid. Animals were often like that with Daisy. She often thought that it was their shared muteness that made them not fear her.

After a moment the animal bounded past, its furry tail bouncing off into the darkness.

Daisy continued toward Susanna's voice.

"By all the stars in midnight's sky, by all the hares are in the wood," Susanna was chanting. "I think you said it wrongly, Grandmam. You were supposed to bid luck come, not the hares."

173

"Welladay, Susanna. What a clever girl. I should have kept Julian home and sent you to university."

Predictably, Susanna laughed.

Daisy rounded the corner at the end of the vast corridor. There was a short flight of stairs there, and she stopped abruptly, staring.

Susanna was there, in a long white gown like Daisy's own, with her hair unbound and shining black. The White-Haired Woman was there too, in a long robe of rich brown trimmed with fur. Her hair too was unbound. It looked like white clouds, illuminated by the candle she held aloft.

And rabbits.

There were rabbits everywhere.

Susanna held two beneath her arm. They were squirming, and kicking with their funny long feet, and she was trying to catch another that had hidden itself beneath a table on the landing. Still another rabbit was coming up the stairs, and almost upset the White-Haired Woman as it darted beneath her skirts.

"Mercy!" she exclaimed, spinning abruptly, so that the candle flickered and almost went out. "Get him, Susanna!"

"Who? Where?" Susanna demanded, looking over her shoulder from where she crouched on the floor. The rabbit bounded up the stairs, and one escaped from beneath Susanna's arm and followed. They brushed by Daisy's feet.

Susanna spied Daisy then, standing and watching from the stone steps.

"Good even, little bundle of twigs," Susanna said, and Daisy wondered if that was to be her new name. "What think you of our new bunnies?"

Two more came up the staircase beneath Susanna and the White-Haired Woman, surveyed the scene with interest, and leapt off in opposite directions, rounded haunches bouncing.

A brown rabbit went down the stairs; a spotted one came up. Then a big white one, then another brown.

"What am I to do?" cried the White-Haired Woman. "Do you suppose that they're everywhere?"

"I see no reason to doubt it," Susanna agreed, and then she sat abruptly down on her backside, looking from her grandmother to Daisy to the leaping rabbits that seemed to be multiplying before their eyes. She tipped her dark head back and burst into peal after peal of noisy laughter.

"Mercy, Susanna," the White-Haired Woman pleaded.

Susanna's happy laughter sounded like music to Daisy, and silently, she began to laugh too. She made no sound, but the laughter shook her, it tightened her eyes, and almost hurt her mouth.

From somewhere down the dark stairs, an angry bellow sounded.

"Grandmother! Susanna! What in the hell is this?"

Susanna kept laughing.

"Oh, heavens," the White-Haired Woman said, "here comes Julian."

And Daisy noted the Dark Man's name. Julian. She thought it sounded like a nice name. The Mean People in the village were stupid to speak so fearfully of the Dark Man, she thought. She liked his house. She liked his horse. She liked the White-Haired Woman and beautiful Susanna. And now, it seemed, there were as many hares as one could imagine, and she liked them as well.

Daisy hoped they might let her keep one for a pet.

Chapter Nine

Ivy was floating in and out of sleep. Sometimes she dreamed; sometimes she thought she was dreaming, and then she'd open her eyes to find that Julian was real, curved around her body, the soft hair of his chest pressed against her back, his long, hard legs against her own. Her head was cradled comfortably on one of his strong arms, and his other arm was wrapped tightly over her shoulder, his hand cupping her breast. His breath was warm against the top of her head.

Blissful, half asleep, she sighed and drifted off into her dreams again. Faintly, she heard his answering sigh and felt his lips nuzzle into the top of her head.

Who would ever have thought that sleep could feel so heavenly?

When she first heard the voices and laughter, she thought it was part of her dream, and snuggled more closely to Julian. But then she heard it again—Lady Margaret's voice, and Susanna's laughter, and the faint sound of footsteps.

She felt Julian waking. He stretched and pulled her closer.

Far away in the castle, Susanna's laugh sounded, over and over again, like chimes. Something tipped over in the hall behind the closed door and crashed to the floor.

Julian tensed, and the hand that was moving over her breast lay still.

"What the hell," Julian muttered, and sat up.

Ivy opened her heavy eyes and looked up at him, his dark profile outlined by the faint glow of the fire.

From far off came the sound of running feet, and a feminine voice raised in dismayed tones.

Julian leapt from the bed, fumbling for his clothes.

"There's something amiss here," he said quickly, tossing her chemise to her. "Dress quickly."

Ivy sat up, reaching for the tangled white garment. "What's wrong?" she asked, pulling it over her head. It was cold from being on the floor.

"I haven't the least notion, but there's a damned lot of business going on out there for this hour."

He fastened his breeches as he spoke, shaking

178

his hair from his eyes. "And I was enjoying my sleep."

"I was too." Ivy climbed from the bed, shivering as her feet touched the cold floor.

Julian touched a candle to the fire and looked back at her. "Come, Ivy. I know not what's happening, but I intend to find out."

Half dazed, she padded on bare feet across the floor and followed him out into the cold, dark corridor, shivering in the thin shift.

Now Doll's raised voice could be heard joining Lady Margaret's and Susanna's somewhere in the castle.

"What in the hell?" Julian repeated, and Ivy hurried after him.

Something large and furry touched her foot. An involuntary shriek rose from her throat, and she jumped back.

Julian whirled around abruptly, long hair flying over his bare shoulders.

"God's teeth," he said. "Where did that come from?"

Ivy's heart hammered against her ribs. Unable to answer, she followed Julian's astounded gaze down the corridor.

A large white rabbit was scampering away over the stone floor. At the end of the hall it stopped and looked back at them. After a moment, it was joined by a smaller, spotted rabbit. They sniffed with vague interest at each other and parted ways, bouncing off into the darkness.

Ivy gave a startled laugh of relief. "Where did they come from?"

Julian looked after the departing rabbits, his dark brows drawn together. "I don't know," he said finally, "but I've a notion we'll soon find out."

He stood for a second longer, staring after them, and Ivy noticed again how like a pirate he looked, bare-chested with his hair falling in waves and tangles down his back, his long, full breeches hanging low on his slim hips.

He turned to go, and at that moment another rabbit—brown, this time—came hopping toward them. It gave them a bright-eyed glance and sped past.

"Shit!" Julian exclaimed, and the profanity sounded so modern that Ivy was unable to restrain another burst of laughter.

Julian started striding forward, and Ivy hurried after him, trying to catch up. He stopped short as he passed beneath the stone arch that led to the great hall.

"Holy hell!" he thundered, standing absolutely still, his candle upraised.

Ivy hurried to his side and froze.

Rabbits had laid siege to Wythecombe Keep.

They were all over the great hall, an army of rabbits leaping and hopping beneath the great vaulted ceilings.

In the light of the fire and the torches that burned on the walls, she saw a host of rabbits, a midnight party of rabbits, a convention of rabbits.

Black and white, light brown and gray, spotted and striped, with bright eyes and soft tails; they were everywhere. They were hopping in and out of the entranceways, they were climbing on the benches, they were sitting in front of the fire. Some were heading up the staircase, some coming down, some were on their way to the kitchen, some on their way back.

"What the hell," Julian whispered, and if Ivy hadn't been so shocked, the expression of disbelief on Julian's face would have reduced her to hysterical laughter.

"Where are they coming from?" Ivy asked, incredulous.

Julian stared at her as if he had quite forgotten her presence. Just as he was about to answer, a cold wind gusted through the room, stirring his hair and the thin linen of Ivy's chemise.

They both turned and saw the huge double doors leading to the courtyard standing wide open to the black night.

More rabbits were coming in, like furry guests arriving at a ball.

A muscle twitched in Julian's jaw and off he went, taking long strides toward the open door, rabbits leaping away from his feet.

Ivy hurried behind him.

The rabbits were hopping up the stone steps, and in the darkness beyond, Ivy could see more coming.

Julian stood, shaking his head slowly, his mouth open with shock.

A very large gray rabbit stopped abruptly before him, looking up at him with what looked like indignation, as if demanding that he move aside.

Julian looked at the rabbit.

The rabbit looked at Julian.

"Begging your pardon," Julian said with elaborate courtesy, "but we've quite enough, thank you," and slammed the doors with a loud crash.

From somewhere up the circular staircase, Susanna's laughter sounded.

Julian turned slowly, staring across the kingdom of rabbits that had invaded the great hall. His gaze traveled to the staircase, following the laughter.

"What in the hell!" he exploded again, and Ivy had to hurry to keep up with him as he crossed the hall, parting rabbits like Moses parted the seas.

When they reached the top of the staircase, they found Lady Margaret and Susanna.

The good lady of the castle stood, her white hair hanging down her back, her face flushed, holding three rabbits to her chest.

Susanna sat on the stone floor, a large brown rabbit under one arm, its furry tail pointing at them, its feet kicking furiously. Susanna was undone with laughter.

Tears rolled down her rosy face, she shook helplessly, she gasped for breath. The rabbit beneath her arm wriggled free, which made her laugh harder, and she reached for another, with no success.

On the stone step next to her sat a child, a little girl of five or six with bright golden hair, dressed in a voluminous nightshift. In her arms she held a large brown-and-white rabbit, which seemed quite content to be there.

". . . if not a sack," Lady Margaret was saying, "or we could send Doll to the village for a fishing net. Oh, stop that silliness, Susanna, and do help. I think we should close all the doors, and string nets across the halls, and empty one room at a time. Or mayhap—"

"Mayhap," Julian interrupted, "you might explain this."

Susanna's laughter died. Lady Margaret stared aghast at her grandson.

"Oh," Susanna said. "Good evening, Ivy. Good evening, Julian."

Julian looked around as if Susanna might be speaking to someone else.

"Good evening, Julian? Good evening, Julian? Do my ears quite deceive me? 'Good evening, Julian' is not my reckoning of a good explanation."

Next to Susanna, the silent child on the stair regarded Ivy with large, solemn eyes.

"Mercy on us," said Lady Margaret, and if she hadn't been holding the rabbits, her hands might have made the fluttering gesture she so often used. "I'm afraid there really isn't an explanation at all, Julian. They just . . . came, you see."

"No, I really don't see."

"One woke me," Susanna said swiftly, "jumping over my bed. And then there was another, and another. And then more. And here they are."

"We're trying to catch them," Lady Margaret added helpfully.

"Of course, how silly of me," Julian exclaimed. "That explains all, doesn't it? They just came, and you're trying to catch them. Of course, it doesn't sound easy, seeing as we have only two hands each, but what ho! Not to worry. I shall leave you to your rabbit hunt, and take myself back to bed. No great matter."

Lady Margaret let her breath out and beamed. "How very sensible of you, Julian. Good night."

"Good night be damned," Julian roared. "What in the hell is this? By God, I'm waiting for an explanation! I go to sleep, perfectly happy, and wake up to find myself besieged by rabbits! What mischief is this?"

His sister and grandmother exchanged guilty looks.

"Julian," Susanna said softly, "I think you're frightening our little orphan. Pray, don't shout."

Ivy looked at the little girl on the step, who was shivering, clutching her rabbit, and staring at Julian with huge eyes.

"And don't distract me," Julian said, but his voice was softer. "I'm still waiting for an answer."

"Witchcraft," said a voice, and Ivy jumped, whirling to look behind her.

It was only Doll, her light brown curls in tumbled disarray, her plump face set in unhappy lines. Her dress was wrinkled, as if she had been sleeping in it, and she carried two large, roughly woven sacks, one of which she offered to Susanna.

"It must be witchcraft," Doll went on, "for there's no other cause for this. And everyone does know, the Devil appears in the form of a hare, when he comes."

"Doll," said Julian, in a very tired voice, "if you can find him in all these, I shall personally put him into a pot and serve him up, and we shall rid the world of eternal evil, and have a fine supper as well. Until then, kindly close your stupid mouth."

Doll gave him a huffy look, seized a startled rabbit by its hind leg, and stuffed him into the sack.

"Here, Doll, and thanks," Lady Margaret said, and deposited her trio of rabbits into the sack.

"Get down to the hall, Doll," Julian said abruptly, "and fill your sack there."

"But I'm tired," Doll complained. "I was in my bed, all peaceful like, and—" She broke off abruptly at the sight of Julian's face, and hastened down the stairs.

Julian waited until she was out of earshot. "You did this, did you not?"

His voice was low and cool. Ivy stared at Lady

185

Margaret, whose wrinkled face was blushing furiously.

"Oh, Julian . . ."

"Don't fence words with me. Did you do this?"

"Ivy," Susanna said suddenly, "will you take our little bundle of twigs here back to her room? She looks chilled, and I'm afraid she'll take ill. She's in the room next to Grandmother's chambers."

Julian looked behind him, and his face held no welcome when he saw Ivy standing there. Obviously he had forgotten about her.

"Go on, Ivy," he said.

Ivy hesitated only a moment, and then went and put her hand out to the little girl, who sat perfectly still, clutching the brown-and-white rabbit.

"Oh, she can't manage the stairs by herself," Susanna said. "You'll have to carry her to the top."

Ivy bent and scooped the little girl into her arms. Despite her length, the child weighed little more than a cat. Her oversize nightgown dangled below her thin feet.

"Okay," Ivy said, "see you in the morning."

She was halfway up the stairs when she heard Susanna saying, "Okay? What was she saying? Was she spelling something? What is ok, Julian? Do you know what ok means?"

Their voices faded as Ivy reached the top stair, holding the child who was holding the rabbit.

"Come along," Ivy said. "Do you know the

186

way?" She set the little girl down carefully, feeling her unsteady balance.

The little girl didn't answer, but began down the long hall with a slow, awkward gait.

Ivy watched her, following slowly. Mute, Julian had said. The villagers who had hanged her mother had told him that the child was an idiot.

Ivy didn't buy it.

There was a look of keen intelligence in the tired little face, and she seemed to understand what those around her said. Ivy watched the slow, laborious walk, and recognition dawned.

The little girl had cerebral palsy. She wasn't an idiot. She simply had little control of her muscles.

There had been a young man in Ivy's art history class who had the disease, though his limp had not been as pronounced as this little girl's. Aside from an occasional stutter, he had been no different from the other students. Certainly more intelligent than many.

Ivy looked down at the child, wondering what her life had been like, condemned as an idiot, a spawn of the devil, not as good or as worthy of love as the other children.

The child stopped before a partially open door.

"You see," Ivy said aloud, her voice soft in the corridor, "you found your room as easily as I could have. There's not a thing in the world wrong with you. You're as bright as anyone in that damned village, and probably brighter than most. Come on, little one. I'll help you into bed."

She lifted the little girl into the huge bed. The child stared at her with sky-colored eyes, watchful and uncertain.

"My name is Ivy. Ivy, like the plant. Julian brought me here on his horse, just like you." She turned to stir up the fire as she spoke. "So we have a lot in common, don't we? I don't know anyone here, and neither do you. We're both all alone and, as the saying goes, dependent on the kindness of strangers." She looked back at the child, and the large rabbit in her arms, both of them watching her with expressionless faces. "Do you want the bunny to stay with you? I'm sure that won't be a problem. They won't miss him, I imagine. Would you like me to light a candle for you? I hate to be in strange places in the dark, don't you?"

A flicker in the blue eyes.

Ivy waited.

And then, almost imperceptibly, a nod.

Ivy smiled. "All right, we'll light a candle." She took a fresh one from the mantel, lit it at the fire, and placed it back in its holder. "Would you like me to stay while you fall asleep?"

After a minute, the golden-haired child gave a short, awkward nod, and what might have been the beginning of a smile, or not.

Ivy found a chair with a broken arm, upholstered in greenish gold brocade, and dragged it across the room. "There. Maybe tomorrow we could go for a walk or something."

The child's eyes were tightly closed, too tightly for genuine sleep.

Maybe she wants some peace, Ivy thought. She's probably tired and confused.

After a while, the little girl's hands relaxed on the rabbit, and her face fell into the tranquil grace of sleep. To Ivy's amusement, the brown-and-white bunny slept too, nose twitching.

Funny how much better it made her feel to find someone more lost and confused than herself. She wondered how strange everything appeared to this child, who had never been out of her own village in her life.

She wondered how the rabbits had come to be there, and why Julian was holding his grandmother responsible.

She wondered if Julian intended for her to come back to his room.

She sat for a long time in the chair beside the huge bed, her feet propped on the gold coverlet, wishing that she was back in Julian's bed, with his strong body curled protectively around hers.

It was dawn before she made her way back to her own room. Except for an occasional rabbit, the cold halls of the castle were empty.

Julian had forgotten about her. She tried not to think of it, tried not to let it rankle her.

Don't let it bother you, Ivy. It obviously didn't mean much to him, so don't let it mean anything to you, she told herself sternly.

It didn't help. Sleeping in Julian's arms, with his lips pressing occasional kisses against the

189

crown of her head, she had felt cherished, safe, and . . . loved.

Wandering through the empty castle, shivering in the cold, she was miserable. She'd never felt as if she truly fit in, not anywhere. And this was worse.

The sooner she found that damned book and got out of here, the better off she'd be.

She only hoped she could get out with her heart in one piece.

By noon the next day, the village was buzzing with gossip like a hive of bees. True, the gifts of rabbits sent down from the castle were welcome—it was a nice change from the steady diet of fish. But where had they come from?

"A late New Year's gift," Lady Susanna said over and over again, as she stopped at every cottage, every shop, knocking at every door with sacks of squirming rabbits.

It wasn't natural, they said to each other. The fishermen's wives said it to each other, and to the baker's wife, and the baker's wife said it to the innkeeper, and the innkeeper said it to the brewer.

All those rabbits, and fat and healthy ones too, in the middle of winter.

And the way the young lady had laughed, the mischief in her dark eyes! You could tell that something was afoot, and that something smelled of witches.

The baker's wife was afraid to eat the rabbits,

and set hers free. Everyone knew that the devil often appeared in the form of a rabbit, and she was taking no chances.

Doll's sister Agnes, who was married to the butcher, welcomed the rabbits, for it was fresh meat, after all, and she set to work cleaning and skinning, but she also enjoyed her gossip. Didn't her sister work up there, with the whole strange lot of them? Agnes, her apron and arms splattered with blood, repeated gossip to everyone that came to the shop that day. Oh, yes, there were strange goings on up at the keep. That old woman, and Susanna, who was too pretty for it to be natural. And that new one—they might call her a cousin, but that was a lie; Doll had said so. And that red hair! Why, everyone knew what red hair meant.

And Julian—he was a bad one, make no mistake. It fair gave you the shivers just to look at him!

And so it went, from cottage to cottage. Old stories were repeated and new ones examined, and everyone agreed that there was something very strange about Wythecombe Keep, and perhaps something should be done about it.

Chapter Ten

Ivy had the freedom of the castle at last, and was enjoying it.

Left to herself, apparently forgotten by Julian, Margaret, and Susanna, she set off to explore her new home.

She wandered up stone staircases worn smooth by generations of Ramsden footsteps, and down again, into the kitchen where a fireplace big enough for an entire cow blazed. The cook looked at her with suspicion, and Ivy retreated.

She found her way to the minstrel's galley and looked down at the great hall. She could picture it as it must have once been, filled with banners and lords and ladies, alight with torches and with the medieval sounds of flutes and drums filling the air.

She made her way outside and through the silent courtyard, dodging raindrops, and found the buildings of the outer ward, which had once housed soldiers and servants by the score. They were empty now, stone walls cold and wet, cobwebs stirring in the cold wind that blew up from the sea.

She found her way up to the watchtowers and battlements and leaned on the ancient stone, staring across the fields and trees down to the sea. It would be beautiful, she thought, in the summertime.

Even in its lonely, haunted disrepair, Wythecombe Keep was the most beautiful place she had ever seen. She wondered how long it would stand—if she were to go back to the twentieth century and fly over to England and drive down the coast, what would she find?

An empty shell, perhaps, crumbling walls with wild grasses growing where rooms had once been. Maybe a carefully restored and preserved home, open to the public on weekends. Who could tell? The thought made her feel strangely melancholy.

She left the wind and cold of the battlements and walked back down the ancient steps, out into the courtyard, and to the chapel.

It was empty, as she'd expected. Her footsteps echoed under the vaulted ceilings. High under the stone arches were the spaces where windows had once been, but they were empty now. Gray sky showed through the arched openings of stone, and the wind whistled through. In one of them, a few jagged edges of colored glass still framed the sky.

The floor was littered with broken glass and charred wood. It looked as if there'd been a fire.

She bent down and picked up a piece of stained glass, and saw a woman's hand and arm in a blue robe, holding a rose, meticulously fashioned and still beautiful.

She blew off the cold soot that covered it and held it up to the light.

"Are you admiring Cromwell's work?"

Ivy jumped and turned quickly.

Julian stood in the open doorway watching her, his tall figure dark against the rainy day behind him.

His voice sounded cool and indifferent. There was no sign that he remembered kissing her, running his warm hands over her body and through her hair, making love to her, and holding her against his heart while they slept.

She might as well have been a stranger to him.

"Are you admiring Cromwell's work?" Julian repeated, and Ivy realized he was talking about the ruined chapel.

All this damage must be recent, then. Ivy stared again at the broken windows, the empty alcoves in the walls, the piles of burned rubble.

"Cromwell's troops did this?"

Julian nodded and walked over to her, looking at the ruined chapel as if seeing it for the first

194

time. "Aye, they did. In the name of God. What think you of their work?"

Ivy stared at the piece of window in her hand, still beautiful and bright. "It's a desecration."

"That it is," Julian agreed. He put his hand out, and Ivy put the glass into it. He was wearing the same leather gloves that he'd worn the first day Ivy had seen him.

"This window," he said quietly, "was there, above the altar. My grandfather commissioned it as a wedding gift to my grandmother."

Ivy was silent, watching him. If she were a painter, she would paint him as he stood now— standing in the middle of the ruined chapel, dark eyes and dark hair, and his cape hanging over his broad shoulders, his boots covered with raindrops, looking like a sorrowing prince, holding in his hand a fragment of broken glass like a piece of his own life. He stared at the glass with eyes as clouded and sorrowful as the raining sky. After a moment, he tossed the glass to the floor.

"And I could do nothing to stop it. I wanted to fight, I wanted to kill them. Wythecombe was one of the last besieged castles to fall. And in the end, I had to let it. I hid like a rat in a hole while my lady grandmother opened the gates to the Roundhead bastards."

They stood silently, Julian with a gloved finger over his mouth, his face tense and bitter.

"What else could you have done?" Ivy asked.

"Nothing. We were defeated before we started. And running out of food, and outnumbered. If they'd found me, I'd have been arrested and probably executed. I could hardly do that to Grandmother or Susanna. They searched for me for three long days."

Ivy imagined the castle overrun with soldiers, Lady Margaret and Susanna being interrogated. "Where did you hide, Julian?"

He gave her a suspicious look and then shrugged. "I suppose it does no harm to show you. Look."

Ivy followed him across the rubble-strewn floors as he went to the back of the little chapel, behind the altar.

He pressed his gloved hands into one of the empty alcoves in the wall, and to her surprise the heavy wall shifted slightly.

"Here, Ivy, help me push."

She did, the hard stone cold and damp under her fingers, and a portion of the wall slowly moved back, revealing a small room no bigger than a closet.

"A priest's hole," Julian informed her. "From the days of King Henry. We country folk were more reluctant to give up our priests than the city folk were, I think."

Ivy stepped into the room and looked around. Cobwebs and dust, nothing else.

"Were you frightened?" she asked, imagining Julian lying here, listening as the chapel was ransacked.

"No, I was furious. In a killing rage. It took every ounce of my will not to come out and start bashing their brains out."

"And get killed for your efforts," she added. "That would have helped."

Julian laughed a little, and Ivy cheered at the sound.

"You sound like Grandmam," he commented. "God help me."

"It's true. And at least you have your home, and the three of you are still together. That's a lot more than some people have."

"Come out, Ivy, and let me close this place. I despise the memory of it."

Ivy stepped out of the cold little room and helped Julian push the section of wall. It moved slowly, reluctantly, with a scraping noise, and then the doorway was gone. There was nothing but orderly rows of stone.

"Amazing," Ivy said softly.

Julian didn't appear to be enormously impressed. "Come out of here," he said. "This place is oppressive."

Ivy followed him to the door of the chapel. Outside, the rain was falling onto the dark flagstones of the courtyard with a monotonous patter.

"What were you doing in there, by the way?" he asked.

"Just looking. Learning my way around."

"Looking for what, I wonder?" His voice was soft, and immediately an image came to Ivy's mind. The book, *her* book. Where had he hidden it?

"Ivy?"

She looked up, feeling her face glow with a guilty flush. "They have the sight," Doll had said. "They know what you be thinking, like."

Julian was watching her, an inscrutable expression on his sharp features.

"I should like you tonight," he said simply, "after I return from Astley's."

Ivy recoiled from him as if he had slapped her. His words were brutal. There was no affection, no tenderness. Her face burned hot, despite the raindrops that trickled over her, and her throat swelled—with anger or sorrow, she wasn't sure.

And he simply stood there, one dark brow raised, waiting for her response.

"You needn't look so surprised. We had a bargain, if I recall correctly."

"A bargain," Ivy repeated. The words were as bitter as an aspirin stuck in the back of her throat. "How charming, Julian. I'm simply swept off my feet."

"Is that what you expected? To be wooed and charmed? Come, Ivy. You bargained your body and agreed to the terms. And liked it well enough, methinks."

Ivy's stomach twisted with shame. It was true. What had gotten into her? She had clung to him, melted against him, welcomed him into her body. She had touched his hair, his chest, his hips, as tenderly as if she had loved him, with absolutely no hesitation.

A bargain.

She turned her head away, unable to speak, and watched the rain hitting the paved courtyard, turning into little rivers between the stones.

"What, you didn't enjoy it?" he asked. He sounded as if it were a supreme joke.

Ivy whirled to face him, glaring at his beautiful face, wanting to slap the dimples in the corners of his smile.

"No. No, I didn't, Julian Ramsden." *Yes. Oh, yes, I did. I never thought I could feel like that, and damn you for doing it.*

"I thought so," he said, as if he had heard her thoughts. "Well, I'm off to play suitor to Felicity. That should keep old Astley happy for a while, until I can wend my way out of his trap. Perhaps you can help Grandmam with the child until I return. It sounds more useful than poking about in dark corners."

Ivy gave him a final, resentful stare and turned back to the keep, lifting her heavy skirts out of the puddles.

"Ivy?"

"What?" The word was sharp and bitter.

He smiled like a cat and held his arms out. "Do you not think that a proper mistress should offer a kiss good-bye?"

"You crap-head, Julian."

He laughed at that, as if her anger were another joke. "You think not? Well, offered or not, I shall take one."

Ivy stood, stiff and angry, as he wrapped his

arms around her, pulling her into the depths of his cape. He turned her face up with a gloved hand, and her head began to swim.

The spicy smell of his doublet, and the heat of his body in the warm cape, and the rich smell of his leather glove. His mouth was warm against hers.

Her resistance faded into the heat of his mouth; she felt her body growing supple and warm in the circle of his arm. His long hair fell against her cheek like silk.

Damn you, Julian Ramsden. I hate you, I hate you . . . but, oh, you make me feel good.

She opened her mouth beneath his, and his tongue sent hot thrills rushing through her. His kisses were languid and sweet, and then he touched his lips to her closed eyelids, as tenderly as if he truly cared for her.

"That's more like it," he said cheerfully, and the warm arm left her shoulders.

He grinned at her like a clever gambler who had just won a bet. "Oh, Ivy—I've sought a woman like you for some time."

She stood in the cold rain, and the words of the spell echoed in her mind—*I have sought thee over time and land. . . .*

"Keep thee well." He turned on his heel and made his way toward the stables, his jaunty stride completely at odds with Ivy's still, shocked posture.

She stood watching him until he rounded the corner, shivering in the rain, her hair growing wet and limp around her face, her mouth feeling full and hot from his kiss.

She was still standing there when he rode out, and he tossed her a brilliant smile as he clattered past and raised his hand. "Till tonight," he called, and rode through the gates of Wythecombe Keep.

She was driving him mad.

What was she thinking, standing there in the rain, watching him with those huge, dark eyes? Beautiful eyes, like the eyes of a doe, brown and soft, with a strange kind of sorrow in them.

The image stayed with him as he rode down the twisting road toward the sea—Ivy standing in the door of the old chapel, her hair streaming like wet ribbons over her pale shoulders, raindrops glistening on the pale curve of her breasts above the deep neckline of her gown. Her hands, small and pale, holding her skirts out of the rain.

Where in the hell had she come from?

He found himself obsessed by thoughts of her. When he was with her, sitting by the fire and talking, the rest of the world ceased to exist. When he was away from her, his thoughts were always turning back to her. What was she doing, where was she walking, who was she talking to?

He imagined her back at the castle, sitting with his grandmother and Susanna. They would be sitting in his grandmother's rooms, the fire gleaming off the bright, polished wood and the fiery curls that hung down her slender back, and they would be laughing together and talking about . . . well, whatever the hell women talked about when men were gone.

Funny how easy it was to picture. She seemed to fit in at the castle the same way she fit into his arms, the same way their bodies fit together—with an ease and perfection that was almost uncanny.

If she was a spy, she was a clever one.

If she was a witch, she was powerful.

If she was the lost orphan she claimed to be, he was a lucky man. He would keep her there always, and sit by the fire with her every night, and take her pale satin body beneath his, and sleep with her silken head against his heart.

Until he married Felicity.

As placid and docile as Felicity appeared, she would never tolerate his mistress living under their roof, he knew. Nor could he ask her to. There were limits to even his own bad behavior, and he was pushing those limits already.

His horse gave a heavy sigh, its breath showing steamy in the cold air.

Julian laughed softly at the sound, which echoed his own feelings so perfectly, and patted the animal's sleek neck.

"What, Bacchus? Are you downcast as well?"

The horse shot him a quick, backward glance, as if to say, "stupid human."

"Aye, perhaps I am," Julian admitted. "Caught in Cromwell's trap, caught in Astley's trap, and perchance caught in Ivy's as well. And I can no more see a way out than could a blind man."

One thing he could do, though. He would never let Ivy know how well her charms had worked upon him. It would be stupid to give her that power. And if she was a spy, or a witch—not that he put much belief in that foolishness of Grandmother's—it would be insane to let her know how she tugged at his heart.

He turned his horse up the hillside trail, toward the moors. A long ride would do him good. For a while, he would again feel like Julian Ramsden, Lord Redvers, the careless country earl who alternated his time between the gaiety of London and the wild beauty of the coast, with no greater care than the price of a new stallion, or which play he might take his latest mistress to.

"When I was young," Lady Margaret said, "young women never worried about how to spend their time. They had their lessons, they learned how to run their houses, and they never contradicted their elders. Pass me that skein of blue silk, please, Ivy. Thank you, dear."

Lady Margaret had pulled her chair to the window, where the light was better for her needlework. Ivy sat on the window seat, which was cushioned in a breathtaking brocade of hunter green, worked with a pattern of scrolls and roses in darker greens and golds. If she could have taken the fabric home, it would have been worth a small fortune.

Susanna, in a gray gown brightened by white lace and cherry red ribbon rosettes, was pacing up and down the gallery, her low heels clicking a restless drumbeat over the gleaming wooden floors.

The little golden-haired girl sat by the fire, still wearing Susanna's nightgown, the large brown rabbit hopping around her feet.

Susanna interrupted what must have been her fiftieth trip across the room to pet the rabbit. "I can't help being bored, Grandmam. Oh, I wish I'd never heard of Cromwell or his wretched Roundheads. You should have come here before the siege, Ivy. Everything was so gay then! We had visitors all the time, and in the winter we went to London, and it was all so jolly. And Julian wasn't such a sour thing. Nobody comes to visit now. We're a family in disgrace. Oh, why didn't we go to France, like the rest of the royalists did?"

"And leave Wythecombe Keep?" Lady Margaret asked, looking up from her fabric. "Shame on thee, Susanna. Julian would never have considered it, and neither would I."

"I wouldn't either, if I had a home like this," Ivy put in. "It's so beautiful. You don't know how lucky you are, Susanna."

Susanna smiled up at her. "Do you think so, Ivy? Why, what was your home like?"

"Awful," Ivy replied honestly. "It had to be the tackiest place in the world." She could picture the old trailer park, her mother's trailer of faded blue and dirty white with the broken steps. Beyond the scrubby patches of lawn that decorated the tin homes of Bella Vista, the endless desert rolled on as far as the eye could see, monotonous and dry under hot skies. "And my mother—well she was awful too. I know it sounds horrible, to say such a thing about your own mother, but there's really no other way to describe her. She hated for me to read, and she didn't understand me at all. She thought I should just forget all my 'stuck-up ideas,' and just stay in Reno and—" Ivy stopped abruptly, suddenly aware of where she was. Oh, how stupid! She wasn't supposed to remember anything, she wasn't supposed to have a mother, or know where she had come from.

It had just been so comfortable, sitting with Susanna and Lady Margaret in the beautiful room. Lady Margaret had told them stories about her youth, and about Julian when he was a boy, and they had laughed about Doll and what a terrible servant she was, and Susanna had played her lute for them. It had been a lazy, comfortable afternoon. For a while, Ivy forgot she was a visitor across time, and felt like part of the family.

She sat still with shock, and slowly looked from Margaret to Susanna.

Susanna sat on her heels, holding the little girl's pet rabbit, a thoughtful look on her pretty face.

Lady Margaret pushed her needle carefully in

and out of her blue fabric, a faraway expression on her wrinkled face.

The room was silent except for the crackle of the fire.

For the first time in days, the sun broke out from behind the clouds, shining through the diamond-paned windows and gleaming across the golden wood of the polished floors and on the carved paneling of the walls.

"Welladay!" Lady Margaret exclaimed, as if Ivy had never spoken. "Look at that. Cold or no, the sun is a welcome sight. Just what you needed, Susanna, to lift you out of your melancholy. Why don't you and Ivy go for a ride, get out of the keep for a time? Some clean air ought to lift your spirits."

Outside the window, the mists were lifting off the distant sea, and it sparkled, beckoning them.

"Marry, I shall!" Susanna announced, leaping to her feet. "I'd like to take our little girl too."

Lady Margaret made a face at the bundle of soft blue fabric in her lap. "Not until her gown is done. Mercy on us, Susanna, you can hardly take the child out in a shift!"

Ivy wondered if they hadn't heard her, or if they had and were simply pretending they had not.

"No, I guess I cannot. Ivy, go change into the gold gown and jacket, that should do well enough for a ride. Oh, how good it will be to get out."

"But . . . I can't ride," Ivy protested.

206

"Nonsense," Lady Margaret retorted. "You look as if you could do anything you put your mind to. You may take my Buttercup; she's as gentle a mare as one could hope. Go on, you're too young and pretty to mope about with an old woman. And you must learn to ride, if you plan to stay."

But I don't, Ivy thought, I can't.

"You can do whatever you choose to," Lady Margaret repeated firmly.

Ivy startled, and then realized she was talking about the horse.

"Go on, go get dressed," Susanna urged. "I'll get the horses saddled and meet you in the courtyard. Please, Ivy. It's no good riding alone. And only lack-wits like Felicity Astley can't ride. What on earth will Julian do with a stupid wife who cannot ride?"

That did it. Ivy rose to her feet and started for the door. "Okay, Susanna. I'll see you in the courtyard."

"Good girl," Lady Margaret said. "Stay off the moors, in case the fog comes in, and be back well before dark."

"Why," Susanna asked, laughter in her voice, "are you afraid something exciting might happen to us?"

"When I was young," Lady Margaret began, but the rest was lost to Ivy as she hurried toward her room, anxious to see her new world and what lay beyond the walls of the castle.

Chapter Eleven

Riding was easier than Ivy had imagined. Lady Margaret's mare Buttercup was sweet and calm, just as the old woman had assured her. Susanna's younger, more spirited horse led the way down the twisting road toward the village.

The air was crisp and clean, scented with the nearby ocean. The wind felt cool and clean on Ivy's face, and it was hard not to have fun in Susanna's company.

"We might ride through the village," Susanna announced, "or out to the ruins of the old abbey, if you'd like. Unless you'd rather ride along the shore."

"Oh, the ruins of the old abbey, please," Ivy cried, thinking how romantic and mysterious it sounded. "I think I saw them in the distance the first day Julian found me. Old stone arches, that way from the village?" she asked, pointing.

"Aye, that's it. By our lady, Ivy, I've never seen anyone get so excited about nothing. How dull your life must be. Oh, Ivy, shift your weight toward your bent leg, so you don't slide in the saddle. And try not to bounce."

Ivy obediently shifted her weight, but the not bouncing proved to be difficult. "How can I not bounce if the horse insists on it?"

"Just keep your hind end level. Oh, never mind, just don't fall off. Grandmam would have fits, and Julian would bellow at me if you were hurt."

Would *he* care *that* much? Ivy wondered. She arranged her face in a studiously careless expression, but Susanna was so busy chattering that she need not have bothered.

"Doesn't the sunlight feel wonderful? I am so tired of being stuck in the castle. London is the only place to be in the winter. Don't you think Wythecombe is dreadful dull?"

Ivy laughed at Susanna's now familiar refrain. "No, to be honest, I think it's wonderful. The sea and the cliffs are beautiful. And the way the streams rush down the hillside, and the village looks just like a fairy story. And as for the castle—oh, Susanna, I love it. All that history! Just imagine, living where your ancestors have, for hundreds of years. Think of all the things that have happened within those walls. It's part of you, part of history. And think—it will be there for hundreds of years more, and—"

"You sound just like Julian," Susanna said, making a rueful face. They had reached the base of the hill, and Susanna paused her horse, considering the paths. One fork led down toward the village; the other wound into the forest and disappeared. "Here Ivy, let's go round the village, through the wood. I never heard of anyone getting so excited about a bunch of crumbling old walls. When I get married, if I ever do, I shan't stay. I shall have my husband build me a fine house in the city, and go to dances and plays every night. Though they don't have dances and plays much, I hear, since old Crum took the reins. Oh, how I hate Cromwell!" Susanna tossed her black hair. "Don't you, Ivy?"

"I don't know much about it," Ivy admitted, "but he doesn't seem like a likely candidate for the man of the year award."

Susanna laughed at that, and for a few minutes they rode silently through the wood, their horses puffing great clouds of breath into the cold, sunny air. The road was rutted and muddy, tufts of faded wintry grass growing in it.

"There's the old abbey, up ahead," Susanna announced. "We all used to play here as children. We pretended it was haunted, and quite scared ourselves."

Ivy could well imagine. The trees and ferns of the forest gave way to a grassy clearing, and when they rode up to the ruins, a strange quiet seemed to hang over the air.

Grasses and ferns grew in between the cracked and sunken flagstones of the ancient floor. Only crumbling stone blocks remained where once there had been walls, and stone arches vaulted like the ribs of some long-ago animal, dark and imposing against the bright sky.

For the length of the field, pathways and walls formed endless mazes in the wet grass. Trees grew in what had once been rooms. A tumbled pillar lay across a stone path, tangled vines wrapping around it.

Carefully, Ivy climbed down from the immense height of her horse, clinging unsteadily to the saddle.

She walked amid the silent ruins, touching the crumbled walls, her skirts dragging in wet grass where hundreds of women had once knelt in prayer.

What had their lives been like? she wondered. There was a sadness that seemed to hang in the air, a melancholy. And, oddly enough, there was still a feeling of holiness among the ruins, a feeling that the ravages of time could never dispel. There was a beauty to the fallen arches and ancient walls with the wild green of nature claiming them, an ancient magic that whispered through the treetops.

"You like it," Susanna observed. "I somehow thought you would." She slid down from her saddle with a grace born of years of riding, and walked toward Ivy, her dark skirts dragging

211

through the wet grass. "You are just like Julian sometimes."

"I'm nothing like Julian," Ivy protested. "He's loud and arrogant and foul-tempered. And he struts."

"You can hardly fault him for strutting. He's terribly handsome, is he not? And you have a proud walk, Ivy. As if you were saying, 'Don't come too close, keep away from me! I'm the mysterious Ivy, and my secrets are well locked within me.' Not quite a strut, but like this—" Susanna set her mouth firmly, lifted her chin, and tensed her shoulders.

"I don't," Ivy argued, laughing despite herself. Did she really look so haughty?

"You do, indeed. It's driving Julian mad, I assure you. Do you mean to?"

Ivy looked at Susanna, her long-lashed eyes glowing with suppressed laughter, her face lovely and full of color from the cold ride. There was always a hint of mischief in everything Susanna said, as though she found Ivy and her plight wickedly amusing. Or perhaps she felt that way about everything.

"No, I don't mean to drive Julian mad. I don't mean to make him feel anything."

Susanna shrugged, the shoulders of her wine red cape falling gracefully. "If you say so. Pity. I thought that you might fall in love with him, and stay with us." She reached out a graceful hand and gave Ivy's forearm a quick squeeze. "I shall miss thee dreadfully, Ivy, if you go." She walked away down an ancient flagstone path, her skirts bending the grasses behind her.

Her words were a pleasant surprise. *I shall miss thee dreadfully.* Such a simple, truthful statement. And she would miss Susanna, Ivy realized, her laughter and high spirits, even the sly sparkle in her eyes. So like Julian.

And oh, she would miss Julian.

Would anyone miss her at home, she wondered? How long would it be before her mother noticed she was gone? A long time, probably. She always called her mother at Christmas, out of a sense of duty. When she didn't call this year, would anyone care? Would her mother call her?

Ivy stood in the ruins of the ancient abbey and pictured the telephone ringing in her silent apartment, the rows of tidy clothes hanging in the closet, her empty coffee cup waiting on the wicker table next to a pot of white narcissus.

"Nobody home," her mom would say, hanging up the phone. "High and mighty. Too damned good to call her mom on Christmas." She would probably be holding a cigarette in her teeth as she spoke. Then she would turn on the TV set and forget about it till next Christmas.

"Ivy," called Susanna, startling her, "come make a wish at the maiden's well."

Ivy followed Susanna's voice around a mossy stone wall and found her leaning over an old well, uncovered and obviously unused.

"Do you want to hear the story?" Susanna asked. "It's very sad. It's said that a novice here

213

at the abbey fell in love, and with the lord of Wythecombe Keep, no less. Of course, Satan was somehow involved, tempting the poor girl to break her vows."

"Do you mean these rumors have been around that long?" Ivy asked. "Why, these ruins must be hundreds of years old."

"Oh, seven or eight hundred, I would think. Except for the chapel. That was added later, I think. I'm not sure, you would have to ask Julian. He cares about such things. Do you want to hear the story, or chatter about stupid old things?"

"I love stupid old things, but go on."

"The poor novice couldn't resist the wicked lord, and she became with child by him. Of course he didn't marry her; he married the daughter of the neighboring baron, or some such thing." Susanna gave Ivy a sly look. "Can you imagine how she felt? Perhaps you'll know, when Julian weds Felicity. How would you feel, Ivy, standing there, carrying Julian's child, watching him pledge his life to that silly cow?"

Ivy looked at the younger woman sharply. "Don't be ridiculous, Susanna."

Her word were at odds with the sick feeling that whispered through her, the sudden tightening of her throat.

"So the wicked lord married the silly cow, and on their wedding day, the poor novice drowned herself in this well." Susanna peered into the black emptiness of the well, the sunlight dappling through the trees and making patterns of light and dark on the crown of her head. "Do you think that's why this place feels haunted?"

"Maybe. Or perhaps all ruins feel that way. Is the story true?" Ivy could picture it clearly—the careless lover using the young woman and discarding her, the heartbroken novice with no place to turn.

"Likely. There's a grain of truth in all such stories. And such things must have happened often at convents, don't you think?"

It was easy to believe, in such a setting. The air seemed alive with the past, a strange, ominous silence rising from the decaying walls and fallen pillars, from the broken pathways. Beautiful and haunting under the play of light and darkness, the abbey hid its secrets in the past.

"Come, Ivy," Susanna said softly. "The maiden of the well is said to grant wishes to unmarried women, so think carefully on it. I've already made my wish. What would yours be?"

Caught in the enigmatic spell of the silent ruins, Ivy could believe in wishes. She laid her hands on the mossy edge of the well, looking down into the darkness below.

"That's it," Susanna urged. "Now you close your eyes, and wish."

For a strange, long moment, Ivy felt as if she had been there before, standing with Susanna in the quiet forest, watching the sunlight touch the ancient walls and haunted well and Susanna's shining hair. As if she had seen her own hands touching the edge of the well, the careful embroidery on the soft leather gloves.

She closed her eyes and wished.

For a moment she felt dizzy and lost. And then images began to form in her mind, as sharp and vivid as sudden sunlight breaking through the clouds.

She saw herself sitting with Julian before a sparkling fire, laughing over some private joke. He spoke to her with an easy affection, and his eyes were bright and soft as he reached out to squeeze her shoulder.

She saw herself riding down a rocky beach with him, heard the jingle of the horses, the thump of hooves against the eternal crashing of the waves. Julian was happy, his dark hair streaming down his back as he galloped ahead, his laughter ringing out with an abandon Ivy had never heard from him before.

She imagined herself standing in the ruined chapel of Wythecombe Keep. But it was no longer a ruin; it had been restored to jewellike splendor, and sunlight poured through the stained-glass windows. It landed on the gleaming white altar, and on Julian's face, and made patterns of red and blue on the white hair of a priest that stood before them, holding a bundled infant in his arms. "I christen thee," he was saying, but Ivy was looking at Julian's face, the pride and contentment in his eyes as he took her hand in his.

And all the while, in the background of her

visions, Ivy could hear ancient music rising in a holy, clear cant. It was the sound of the haunted abbey, a hundred women singing a mournful, beautiful song for the spirit of a young woman. The music swayed and rose, reaching up to the blue sky in an ancient, holy melody that made Ivy's heart leap and swell with the beauty of the sound.

And then, like a slow, warm shimmer that covered her from head to toe, Ivy felt peace. It was like a perfect sense of happiness, a glowing comfort and contentment, and she thought, Everything will be all right. No matter what happens, I need have no fear. Everything is going to be all right.

Suddenly she was back in the clearing, standing across the old well from Susanna, and the only sounds were the whispers of the branches moving in the wind, and the distant sound of rushing water, and the far-off cry of a bird.

But everything seemed somehow brighter and more vivid than before—the blue of the sky, the pattern of the branches against it, the way the mottled sunlight sparkled on the wet grass. The air seemed alive with the faint song of the long-ago nuns of the abbey. And across the well, Susanna was watching her with brilliant eyes, her face flushed with happiness.

Ivy stared at her, unable to speak.

"You heard it, didn't you?" Susanna cried out, her voice bright with pleasure. "You heard it, Ivy! The singing, and the magic? Oh, I knew it,

I just knew it! Did you hear, Ivy, did you feel it? Grandmother was right, Ivy, you *are* one of us, you are! Oh, I'm so glad!" And spontaneously, the delighted girl swooped at Ivy and hugged her tightly, her happy laughter ringing out.

Ivy's laugh was shaky and uncertain. As shocked as she was, as dumbfounding as her experience had been, she still felt as if something wonderful had happened. And Susanna hugged her with such sincere affection, she felt as if she had found a dear friend, a sister. She suddenly felt as if she belonged to the family, to Wythecombe Keep and the wild, beautiful land around it.

It was a feeling of homecoming, a feeling of belonging.

"That settles it," Susanna announced, turning back toward the horses. "You must stay. It was a message, Ivy. And glad I am too. I needed some company in that drab old place."

She spoke in such a matter-of-fact tone that Ivy stopped short and then started after her.

"Good Lord, Susanna! What *was* that? Does that always happen at the well? Was it real? Did you hear it too?"

"Oh, calm down. It was just a bit of sight, and no, it doesn't always happen. Don't be absurd, Ivy. If such things happened every day, there'd be a never-ending line of wishers, wouldn't there be? Was it real? Don't trouble me with philosophy, I pray thee, I'm very bad at it. What is real, after all?"

218

"I don't really know anymore," Ivy admitted, her voice unsteady. Susanna was brushing moss from her gloves, apparently vastly unconcerned with Ivy's first psychic experience.

"Mercy, I'm hungry," the girl remarked. "I suppose it will be rabbit again for dinner."

"Susanna!" Ivy cried. "How can you be so calm? Like it was nothing? As if you were serenaded by choirs of dead nuns every day of your life?"

"Pretty, aren't they?" Susanna's smile sparkled at Ivy, and the teasing look was back in her eyes. "Some days they can be dreadfully out of tune. Come along, Ivy. Let's ride back through the village. Perhaps we can stop and get a beef pie from the bakers, and give ourselves a change from rabbit." She stopped by her horses, unlooping the reins from a low branch.

"And Ivy—"

Ivy stopped, caught off-guard by Susanna's sudden, urgent tone.

"Julian must not marry Felicity. Do you hear? If he does, something dreadful will happen. I am sure of it."

Stricken, Ivy stared at Susanna.

The girl looked like a pagan seeress as she stood with the field of ruins behind her, the cool wind tossing her black curls and red cape, her beautiful dark eyes intense and staring into Ivy's.

"Ask Grandmother for help, if you must. But you must stay, Ivy. You must marry Julian." Su-

219

sanna broke the tense moment with a sudden, teasing smile. "Anyhow," she went on in her characteristically flippant way, "it would suit me. I should go mad with Felicity about the house. The silly cow."

Shaken and wondering, Ivy hardly paid attention as she mounted her horse and followed Susanna's lead out of the clearing and back toward the village.

She cast a final look back at the timeworn ruins and wondered what it all meant, and what she was to do next.

Susanna made no more mention of the incident, and indeed, seemed to be the most practical of young women as they rode along, offering Ivy suggestions on how best to handle her horse, and pointing out which riding trails went where, and chattering about the new gowns she hoped to buy, if Julian could afford it, which she doubted. She pointed out the cove where the fishermen wintered their boats, the breweries where the local beer and cider were made, the path down to the shore, where there were caves once—and perhaps still—used by smugglers.

At Susanna's urging they stopped at the inn, where she assured Ivy that the beef and mutton pies were beyond reproach. A boy came running to take their horses, and Ivy followed Susanna into the dark, crowded inn.

The smell of cooking food, stale beer, and unwashed bodies assaulted Ivy's nose.

Susanna stopped too, a look of surprise on her face.

Even Ivy didn't need to be told that something unusual was afoot. The room was crowded with villagers, and the sudden silence that greeted their appearance was strained and unnatural.

The long, dark tables of the inn were filled, and some people stood along the walls. Almost to a person, the people of the village were dressed in somber shades of brown and gray and black, unrelieved except for wide white collars. The uniform of Puritans.

Susanna, in her red cape, looked like an exotic bird hovering near a flock of wrens, and Ivy felt conspicuous in her borrowed gown and jacket of dark gold. The heavy brocade seemed suddenly opulent, and she wished that she had confined her copper curls. The women in the room all had their hair hidden under modest white caps, and their eyes showed unveiled disapproval as they watched Ivy and Susanna.

Nobody greeted them, or offered to serve them.

Finally Susanna broke the grim silence with a light laugh. "Your pardon for interrupting. We've been riding, and stopped to buy some pies on the way home."

Still no one moved.

Ivy touched Susanna's shoulder. "Let's leave," she murmured. There was something about the grim faces that sent chills through her.

221

Susanna turned to her, and her eyes had darkened and narrowed. She looked like Julian, arrogant and fierce. "We shall not," she answered simply. She withdrew her gloves and slapped them against her palm with an impatient rhythm, waiting.

Still no one moved.

"I should like some pies," Susanna demanded, her voice clear and sharp, "and quickly, please. One beef, one mutton, and quickly, thank you."

Over by the kitchen doors, a young maid in a soiled apron began to move, but was stopped short as a portly man clamped a hand on her wrist.

Ivy could see Susanna's ire rising. Her spine stiffened, her eyes seemed to snap and sparkle, the rose flush in her cheeks deepened to a wine color.

"Good Mr. Chester," she began, addressing the portly man in a tone that made the word *good* a mockery, "are you quite out of pies today? Or is there a reason that I should be so ill treated?"

The innkeeper, his face reddening above his white collar, cleared his throat, muttered something unintelligible, and looked away.

But not before Ivy had seen fear in his eyes.

"The pies, please." Susanna sounded as haughty as a princess.

"Susanna, let's go," Ivy whispered.

"Yes, you go," a woman ordered suddenly. She was sitting barely an arm's length from Ivy, a woman with a plump, broad face. It might have been a pleasant face, if not for the malicious expression. "You do that. We don't want your kind in here."

"I am not over concerned with what you want or don't want," Susanna snapped. "I am Susanna Ramsden, and if I care to be here, you are nobody to say yea or nay to me, do you understand?"

"No, that we do not." This speaker was a thin, sallow man of middle age, with a fiery gaze. His sparse hair showed beneath a broad-brimmed hat, and Ivy noticed a clerical collar tight around his thin neck. "Save your pride, young woman. You have no title, according to the law of the Commonwealth. Pride is a sin, Susanna Ramsden, and a deadly one. I advise you to guard your tongue, lest it betray you."

"*Dear* Rev. Lang. Such a surprise, to meet you here. Please, Reverend, can you tell me the meaning of this undeserved rudeness? Or enlighten me as to the purpose of this gathering?"

There was a long, pregnant silence, and then the reverend answered.

"We are discussing the presence of the devil here in Wythecombe. It has come to the attention of the town council and the citizens of this town that a problem exists, and action must be taken."

Susanna stood frozen, and Ivy felt the color draining from her face.

"And this town council," Susanna at last said, her voice cold with anger, "I believe that my brother Julian is a member. Why has he not been invited to join this . . . little assemblage, sir? Is that not his privilege, under English law?"

The reverend gave a very unpleasant smile. "Under English law, young woman, a self-admitted traitor and rebel has no rights. Julian has no place in this council. He is subject to our decisions as much as any man in this village."

"And high time too," someone rejoined from the crowd. "You high and mighty have had your day."

"And your time of reckoning has come," the woman with the plump face cried. "You're no better than anyone else."

A murmur of assent ran through the room, and Ivy felt sick as she listened to the rising tide of words.

". . . lording it over us for hundreds of years—"

". . . and what goes on up there, we all know well—"

"It's the old woman, I've always said."

"And just where did Julian get his dark looks? Not from old Denby, that's for sure."

". . . funny things, Doll says, and we know what that means . . ."

Susanna began to quiver with fury. Her nostrils flared, and she pointed a shaking finger. "I won't have this, do you hear? I will not. How dare you! How dare all of you? Why, you've lived on our land for hundreds of years. We've sustained you through wars and famine. You, Agnes, my grandmother saved your baby girl when you thought she would die—how can you speak against her? And you, Henry Toms! How can you speak against Julian? Didn't he give you almost a hundred head of sheep when yours were taken by disease? How many of you come sick and hungry, to be cured at my grandmother's hands, or fed by Julian's charity?"

Silence greeted this outburst.

"You don't feed us no more," pointed out an old man with a face like a boxer dog.

"Of course we don't, you silly old bugger!" Susanna shrieked, rounding on the lone dissenter. "Old Crum has taken everything from us. We can barely feed ourselves. If it's charity you need, go to Astley, if you think that tightfisted old lump will help you. He has everything that was ours."

"The righteous will flourish, and the wicked be brought low," the gaunt reverend intoned solemnly, and a chorus of satisfied "Amens" answered him.

Susanna, quivering with rage, started to speak again, but Ivy grasped her shoulder with a firm hand, pulling her back.

"Stop it, Susanna, before you make them angry. Let's go and tell Julian of this. He'll know what to do. Please don't take this any further."

Susanna took a deep, quavering breath, and then, to Ivy's relief, nodded.

"Very well," she said, drawing her gloves on.

"I didn't really want any pies, anyhow. Shall we go, Ivy?"

Feeling every eye in the room on her, Ivy led the way stiffly out the door. Susanna banged it closed behind them.

Outside, the sunlight had vanished, hidden behind the dark clouds that rolled in off the salty ocean air.

"Are they mad?" Susanna asked, and Ivy could hear fear beneath the anger in her voice. "Is it true that Julian is no longer a member of the council?"

"I hope not. But Julian would know, I bet. Let's get back to the castle, Susanna. I don't like it here."

They rode back through the silent village, past stone houses and over cobbled streets which had just recently looked so picturesque and charming. Now Ivy shivered in the cold wind, and felt that eyes were watching her from behind every shuttered window.

Chapter Twelve

The sight of Wythecombe Keep sitting sentinel on the craggy cliffs had never been more welcome to Julian, and he spurred his horse to a quick pace, anxious to reach home.

A day with Felicity Astley was more than any man should be asked to tolerate, Julian decided. A lifetime with Felicity was a frightening thought.

Certainly there was nothing that bad about the girl.

Except that she was dull.

When she spoke, which was rarely, she never shared an opinion of her own. She simply parroted the words she had been taught. She said only what one would expect from a God-fearing, obedient young woman. Oh, yes, she was dull.

Of course, Julian reminded himself, there were men who would gladly take a wife whose worst flaw was mildness and obedience. Truth to tell, most men would be pleased. So dullness was Felicity's only flaw, and he should be content.

Except that she was rather stupid.

She had no learning at all, aside from being able to sign her own name, and spelling and figuring enough to keep the household accounts. Her father disapproved of learned women. And Felicity was not clever or rebellious enough to overcome such a lack on her own. Still, he supposed she was a skilled housewife and a competent cook. He should be content.

Except that she was a prude.

She wore her modesty as proudly as a crown, and Julian had met that kind of woman before. He tried to avoid them at all costs. Not that he minded a genuinely modest and honorable woman. What he minded was a woman who considered herself immune to the bestial and sinful pleasures of the flesh, and regarded love as a distasteful duty.

Not a good quality in a wife. Rather a quality that would necessitate a man taking a mistress. A mistress who was bright and good-hearted and passionate. Someone unpredictable and lively.

Like Ivy, Julian thought, as he rode up to the gatehouse. Someone had closed the gates, and

Julian muttered impatiently as he reached out to push them open.

They were firmly locked.

His horse pranced impatiently beneath him.

It was the first time the gates had been barred since the Roundhead siege, and a superstitious shiver slid over his spine. Something was wrong at Wythecombe Keep.

An archway of light appeared across the darkening courtyard, and Lady Margaret called to him as she came hurrying to the gates. She must have been watching for him.

He heard the heavy beam lifting, and the wooden gates creaked as they swung open.

"What trouble, my lady?" he asked, observing her tired eyes, her tense mouth. She looked older than usual, he thought. And worried.

"Julian, thank the stars you've come. There's trouble in the village, and I'm frightened for the girls." Julian slid down from his horse and helped his grandmother close the sturdy oak doors.

"Trouble of what sort? Or need I ask?"

Lady Margaret took his arm and blinked up at him. "Witchcraft, Julian. The villagers were having a meeting today, with the town council present. They are speaking against us."

"Damn. Lock up. Nobody comes or goes until I sort this out. Are Ivy and Susanna safely in?"

"Aye, but frightened, Julian. Not so much Susanna, she's far too angry. But Ivy's frightened. She's more vulnerable to charges than we are,

Julian. What will we do if they come for one of us, Julian?"

"We'll thank God that damned book is out of this castle," Julian answered in sharp tones. "And there is to be no more foolishness of any sort, nor talk of any such thing, until this danger is well past. Are we understood, my lady?"

Lady Margaret looked surprised. "Of course, Julian. You have my word upon it. Except, of course, for—"

"No exceptions. Not for any reason. Your attempts to help usually result in chaos, and we can't risk it. Do I have your word, my lady?"

"Certainly, Julian. Though I must say, how very rude of you to demand it so. Now when I was young, there was none of this witchcraft nonsense."

"Oh, please, Grandmother! Wasn't there some sort of uproar about you and the mayor?"

"If he'd minded his manners," Margaret announced in haughty tones, "he need not have had his mouth stuck shut for all that time. That wasn't my fault."

"I daresay," Julian observed, and followed his grandmother into the castle.

" 'Twas not my fault, Julian." Susanna's chin jutted out at an obstinate angle. "And I hardly argued. I said nothing that would endanger us."

"Your very attitude endangers us," Julian informed his sister. "If any of your governesses had stayed for more than a week, you would have learned that Godly young women do not argue with their elders. Or any man, for that matter. You should have left immediately."

Susanna made a face. "Would you have left, Julian? I seem to recall you risking the wrath of an entire village not so long ago."

"That's another matter entirely. I'm a man."

Susanna was sitting on her unmade bed, surrounded by discarded ribbons and gowns and sheet music. She was tying a rosette of multi-colored ribbons to the end of her lute as he spoke, but her fingers fell still at his last sentence, and she looked up, her eyes narrowing.

"How tiresome, Julian. Grandmother says that being a man does not necessarily make a human being superior. She says the day will come to pass when women are equal to men in all things. In business and government, everything. And Ivy quite agrees with her."

"Does she?" Julian sighed. "Why does that not surprise me? Hundreds of women in the world, and here I sit with the three most incorrigible. Three women in the keep is three too many."

Susanna laughed. "Four. You forget our little orphan."

"But she has the distinct advantage of being mute," Julian observed. "That makes her a good deal more tolerable than you, Susanna."

Susanna picked idly at the strings of her lute. "Perhaps Grandmam can teach me how to turn you into a toad, Julian. I could put you into my pocket and feed you flies when you behave."

Julian reached out and caught his sister's hand. The lute fell silent, the last note quavering.

"Heed, Susanna. 'Tis not a joking matter any longer. What you heard today was true. I have no power with the town council. If they chose to come here and arrest any of you, I could not stop it."

Susanna's dark brows rose. "Nothing, Julian? That cannot be!"

"Oh, I would do everything in my power to stop them. Even if it meant barring the gates and fighting them to a man. But we would lose, Susanna. The town would appeal to the government for assistance, and you can be assured that it would come. Cromwell would love the chance to take Wythecombe again. And this time, I fear, I should receive scant mercy."

Susanna was uncharacteristically solemn.

"So no more trouble of any kind, Susanna. Keep yourself within the gates, and keep a tight rein on your tongue. If you must speak with anyone, act as if . . . as if you were Felicity."

Susanna rolled her eyes elaborately.

"You shall have good opportunity to study her ways. Astley is going to London, and Felicity will be staying with us until his return."

"How dreadful," Susanna remarked with heartfelt conviction.

"Aye, but it might help keep us safe until this tempest passes. The council will hardly want to offend Astley. Even in little country politics, morals are subject to the wealth and power of the man."

Julian rose to his feet. "Have you seen Ivy?"

"Oh, wandering about with your little orphan, somewhere. They were in the kitchen, last I heard."

Julian nodded. "Thank you, Susanna. And remember what I've told you. These are no light matters."

He found Ivy in the great hall, sitting on the floor in front of the fire. She had pen and ink-stand on the floor in front of her, and was leaning on her elbows, carefully writing on a large piece of parchment.

She was wearing a cast-off gown of Susanna's, a dusty gold thing that made her wayward hair look even brighter than usual. The sleeves of her white shift showed from shoulder to elbow, full and gathered in knots of gold thread. In the light from the fire, she seemed to glow gold and white—white skin and golden gown, golden lights in the curls that tumbled over her white sleeves.

Across from her sat the mute child, her hair like yellow silk, freshly washed and wearing a new dress of blue brocade. She looked so unlike the half-wild little creature he had carried home that for a moment Julian didn't recognize her.

"B," Ivy was saying to the child. "B for blue, like your new dress, and blue like the sky. B for bread and butter. And B is for bunny."

The little girl's face creased in a smile, and she looked around. After a moment, she pointed toward a bench along the wall. A large, light brown rabbit sat beneath it, chewing on a wilted bunch of greens.

"There he is," Ivy agreed, a bright smile lighting her face. "Mr. Bunny. B for bunny." She replaced the quill pen in the stand and shifted the paper around to face the child. "There, little one. Show me the B."

The child stared at the paper with a blank face.

"You know," Ivy urged. "You can do it. B has a great round belly."

Very slowly, the little girl reached out an awkward finger. Her face was tight with concentration as she put her finger down on the paper.

"That's it!" Ivy cried, and laughed with pleasure. "There you are! Now you know B. Oh, you'll be reading in no time. What an excellent student you are."

The child laughed silently, her face creased with a smile and her thin shoulders shaking.

"What an excellent teacher," Julian corrected.

Ivy looked up as he approached, her smile fading. "Thank heavens you're back. Have you spoken to Susanna or Lady Margaret?"

"Both, in fact." There was a high-backed chair near the fireplace, and Julian dragged it closer. He glanced at it, frowning.

"I don't recall this chair. Is it new?"

"No, it was a broken one that was up in the

234

minstrel's gallery. And the upholstery was torn, so I fixed it. If you notice, you'll see that it's the same fabric as our little one's gown."

Our little one. Ivy spoke casually, but the words caught Julian off-guard.

Thus she would speak, he thought, if we had a child. What a strange, appealing thought. I would come in and find them like this, learning to read. What an easy thing she makes it seem. There would be no harsh tutors with canes, or sour governesses, for my wife would be more than competent.

He leaned forward and looked at the paper on the floor between them. Ivy had written the letters from A to Z in an odd, angular hand. The writing was large, the letters shaped without flourishes.

"Tomorrow," Ivy announced, "we shall learn C and D. I think we should go slowly, so as not to overwhelm her."

"I'm surprised that she can learn at all," Julian said. "It would appear that they were wrong about her."

He studied the parchment again. Around the letters were tidy little sketches. An apple, an ant. A bird. A brick.

"What is that, on the brick?" he asked.

"It's butter," Ivy replied with a frown. "That's bread, not a brick."

"If you say so. Ivy, I need speak to you. Can you put the child into someone's care and come straight back?"

Ivy stood up and put her hand out to the little girl.

"Of course. We were finished anyway. She gets very tired. Come on, little one, shall we go find Susanna?"

The child gave a hesitant smile and pointed toward the rabbit, who had finished his greens and was hopping around a pillar.

Ivy went and scooped up the rabbit and put it in the child's arms. She kept a firm hand beneath the frail shoulders as she led her from the hall. At the bottom of the steps, she bent and picked the little girl up, resting the weight easily on one hip as she made her way up the stairs.

The gesture was as graceful and comfortable as if she had been carrying children all her life, and Julian found himself watching the sway of her skirts and the gentle glow of her face, thinking what a good mother she would be, and what a refreshing quality that was in a woman. Most women of quality assigned the care of their children to nurses and governesses, disdaining such common work as beneath them.

It struck Julian that it was a most unnatural practice. Why should a woman not care for her own child? If Susanna's governesses and nurses were any example, they seemed to be a troublesome lot, and quite unreliable.

He looked down at the arms of the chair he sat on and took note of the careful mending that Ivy had done. It took him a few minutes to find the place where the arm had been broken and set together again, the thin nails hidden beneath the edge of the blue fabric.

Amazing. Perhaps she was the daughter of a tradesman. He had never seen a woman take up hammer and nails before, and for some reason, the picture delighted him.

What a delightful woman she was. Full of surprises. Life would never be dull with Ivy about: he'd wager his life upon it.

When Ivy came back into the great hall, she found Julian peering beneath the chair she had fixed, his dark hair falling to one side.

"Does it pass approval?"

He looked up, smiling. "How ingenious of you. One would almost think you had been trained to it."

Ivy was unprepared for the sudden loneliness that washed over her. She thought of Winston, peering closely at some Victorian tea table, searching for any sign of modern repair. "Never let your touch show. If you must repair, use original materials. I don't care if you have to pull nails from another piece one at a time."

Winston would not have approved, she was sure, of using seventeenth-century fabric on a fifteenth-century chair.

She missed her work. She missed her store. She missed her shower, and her electricity.

"You look so sorrowful, Ivy. What are you thinking of?"

"Nothing. Chairs, I guess." She shrugged, and

then changed the subject abruptly. "What do you think, Julian, of the meeting at the inn today? Are we in any real danger?"

"Any talk of witchcraft is a danger. Until this matter is settled, neither you, Susanna, nor Grandmother are to go beyond these walls. May I have your word?"

"It's not a problem. I was frightened, Julian. Really frightened. I kept thinking about Daisy's mother, and the other women you told us about. What would have happened, had they decided to arrest us?"

Julian looked into her eyes, his eyes dark and intense, his jaw tight, his normally beautiful mouth in a pinched line.

"You do realize, I hope, that this is a very real possibility?"

Ivy pressed an unsteady hand to her mouth and drew a shaky breath before she could speak.

"Oh, Julian . . . oh, it can't be. . . . "

"It is. These witch-hunts are like a plague, like a fever traveling through England. And not just England, but all of Europe. God knows why. In troubled times, it seems that every man wants someone to point a finger at, as if they need an explanation. It answers so many questions, you see. Such a fine excuse for the blows of life. This is why there is war, this is why my crops failed, this is why disease took my wife. . . . " Julian shook his head slowly. He looked very tired. "And who better to blame it on than Satan himself? Do you see the twisted logic of it?"

"Yes." Ivy did see it, and she didn't like it. Wythecombe was a stage waiting for a frightening scene to be played upon it. There were the villagers, whose livelihood had been endangered by the recent wars. Until then, they had been able to depend on the Ramsdens to get them through the hard times, but that security was gone. Add to that the rumors of witchcraft that hung about the castle like a cloud, and the situation was like a thunderstorm ready to break.

"What should I do, Julian?" She tried to sound calm and competent, but there was a slight quaver in her voice.

"The first thing, of course, is to avoid being taken. I shall go see the council myself on the morrow, and see if I cannot influence them to put a stop to this nonsense. If that fails, we must be ready. The gates to the keep are to remain locked, and none of you are to venture outside for any reason."

Ivy nodded.

"Stay out of sight of the courtyard as well, if you can. If anyone should come, be prepared to go into hiding."

"In the chapel?" Ivy asked, remembering the priest's hole that Julian had showed her.

"Exactly. Stay there until I come for you. If things have gone that far, we will need to leave the country. Most likely head for France. And make sure Doll doesn't know about this. I trust her not a whit."

"You have reason not to. Her name was mentioned at the inn today. She gossips, Julian."

"I expected as much. But what am I to do? I fear at this point letting her go might cause more harm than not." The firelight played across his tense, angular face. "I should have put my foot down long ago. I should have kept a tighter watch on Grandmother and Susanna, instead of allowing their ridiculous fancies—" He broke off quickly and gave Ivy a quick, tense smile.

"Enough of that. Let us be practical, Ivy. Listen well—if you are taken, it will be because a complaint has been lodged against you by someone. This is England, thank God, and such crimes are tried by a lay jury, not by a church inquisitor. Take care in all you say and all you do. Give no offense to anyone. By law, without a confession, someone must witness you commit the crime."

"Then I'm safe," Ivy said with a sigh of relief.

Julian reached out and took her hands between his own. "Don't make that mistake. Never think that. None of us are safe. Anyone might make an accusation or swear to anything. And many innocents who are tried *do* confess, Ivy. Technically, a confession extracted by torture is illegal. But there are many kinds of torture, and victims are not always believed."

Ivy's stomach clutched, and it hurt to breathe. She was frightened, more frightened than she had ever been before. Oh, she cursed the day she had bought that stupid book and read that stupid poem. If only she had never come here, she would be safe at home, fretting about electricity bills and the price of coffee.

Much better than fretting about public execution.

"This can't be happening," she whispered.

"Pray, don't fret," Julian said. "I shall take care of this, however I must."

Ivy's laugh sounded a little strained. "You will, will you? And what makes you so certain that you can? What if they take *you*, Julian?"

"Don't be frightened," he urged. "Trust me, Ivy. If they take you, by God, I shall take that jail down a stone at a time before I let any harm come to you."

He meant it. Ivy stared at him and saw that he spoke the truth. He reached out and touched her face with a tender gesture.

"I give you my promise," he whispered. "I did not find you to lose you so soon. It would be intolerable to me."

He reached out and pulled her to his lap, enfolding her tightly in the circle of his arms.

It was like a miracle, Ivy thought, that such comfort could come from the simple touch of another human being. There was safety there, in Julian's arms. Her fears seemed to melt away as she lay against him, her head on his shoulder, her cheek against the warmth of his neck.

There was nothing in the world but she and Julian, sitting before the warmth of the fire, watching the flames dance and listening to each other's hearts beating. Around them, the stone columns rose up to the dark, shadowed ceilings of the silent room, growing darker by the minute as the night deepened. But Ivy and Julian were content, lost in their own world as they held each other in the half-circle of firelight for what might have been minutes, or hours.

At last Julian spoke. "This morn, before I left, Ivy—I made a demand of you. Do you remember?"

Ivy's cheeks flushed. "Yes," she whispered. Damn him, to remind her of their crude bargain just when she was feeling so peaceful, so contented. She could almost have believed that his feelings for her were genuine.

His hand slid through her hair and stroked the side of her neck. "I would take those words back, Ivy. They were ill thought, and less than what you deserve. I am a little arrogant, I fear, and—"

Ivy couldn't stop her sharp laugh. "Just a little?"

"Hang it, Ivy, don't berate me when I'm trying to be humble. 'Tis no easy matter, I assure you."

"Are you trying to be humble?" she teased, but stopped when she looked up at his face.

She had never seen him look like this, soft-eyed and solemn and tender. His gaze met hers, and they held each other's eyes until she felt lost in the mist-colored gaze.

"Aye, I am. You humble me, Ivy. I would like to ask again, and know your answer. Will you come to my bed and lie with me, Ivy? Once was not enough. It could never be enough with someone like you. I would like you to come to my room and kiss me and let me touch you as I did before. Let me make love to you a hundred ways before the sun rises. Let me hear you cry out with pleasure again. But this time, let it be because you wish it, and not because I have manipulated you. It would make the experience so much sweeter to me."

His voice was low and husky, and his words made Ivy's heart race faster than any kiss ever could.

It was still difficult for her to believe that such a man could want her. He was too handsome, and too dashing, and too . . . too good, she supposed. He was the fairy-tale prince, the hero of the late movie, the kind of dream that enchants you on a hot summer night and makes you wish you would never wake up.

And he wanted her.

Not real, she told herself. For a minute she sat quietly, staring at him. It seemed her heartbeat was very loud in the emptiness of the great hall.

She was caught in a dream. What had the poem said?

You, who are lost . . . in enchanted time.

And here she was.

"Oh, yes, Julian," she whispered. There was no other answer possible.

She stood and offered him her hand. He kissed her palm as he accepted it, looking up at her with eyes that made her shiver with pleasure.

They walked from the room together, hand in hand, silent. Ivy's cheeks were warm despite the cold halls, and her hand trembled in Julian's.

She felt that she was walking into the inevitable, and that there would be no turning back.

Chapter Thirteen

Outside the great gray walls of Wythecombe Keep, a winter storm broke. Rain poured from the sky and bent the barren branches of trees. It filled the already swollen streams and quickened the little waterfalls that fell over the craggy cliffs. It ran over the spires and rooftops of the dark village, and ran in rivers over the cobbled streets. The sea raged and boiled, and the waves pounded against the shore in a hard, fierce rhythm.

Behind the locked gates and doors of the ancient castle, Ivy and Julian never noticed. They were lost together, safe and warm in the world between the drawn curtains of Julian's bed, a place as full of light and heat as a summer day.

Ivy had never really thought of men's bodies

as being beautiful, yet she found Julian beautiful. She couldn't touch him enough. She ran her hands over him with an almost reverent touch, intoxicated by the firm swell of his shoulders, the way the dark hair felt over his chest, and the perfect tightness of his stomach. She rubbed her face over him like a cat, sighing as she inhaled the scent of his body.

She was drugged by the perfection of his body, long and lean and hard, exactly like a man's body should be. Her own body seemed to sparkle and sing where her skin touched his, with a kind of silken electricity that heated her very soul.

In London, Julian's mistresses had always been the popular ideal of feminine beauty— lush, plump creatures whose curves were as accommodating as overstuffed pillows.

But none of them compared to Ivy. She was perfect, pale and fragile beneath his dark hands. Her skin was cool to the eyes, but warm to the touch, like luminous silk, like the pale, radiant heat of sunlight. Despite her slender delicacy, there was a vitality to her body that took his breath away.

He could feel the heat, the fire that flowed through her body. She arched and moved to his every touch, her dark brown eyes glowing darker with passion, and the sight of her slender neck bent back in abandon, weighted by her lush mane of fiery curls, stirred him with a fever he had never felt.

There had never been a sensation as soft as her breasts beneath his cheek, nor had anything ever fired him as the feeling of her breasts swelling and hardening beneath his lips. The taste of her skin was like spring flowers, clean and fresh and uniquely hers.

She never shied or demurred from his caresses, but there was nothing of a wanton or jade about her. Her passion was utterly without artifice, almost blinding in its beauty.

The sighs and soft cries she gave at his touch were as spellbinding as the song of a sorceress, and each sound filled him with a primitive joy.

She burned with an incandescent heat wherever his eyes lit upon her, and any vestige of shyness flowed away at the sight of the pleasure that glowed dark and hot in his gaze.

She had never felt so perfectly female.

He had never felt so powerfully male.

When they finally joined together, it was with a consummate harmony, a perfect balance of strength and softness. Each abandoned all thought of anything but the other, and the entire world consisted of their shared breath, their hungry kisses, the heat that flamed where their bodies connected.

She felt that her body might lift from the bed and fly, if not for the strength of him holding her down, and she welcomed each thrust, every hard stroke that pinned her so blissfully to the earth.

She buried her face into the heat of his neck, and her cries were muffled by the satin of his dark hair, the sound rising sharper and more abandoned, until she finally let loose the unmistakable sound of bliss, of fulfillment and joy.

The sound was like a gift to Julian, a tribute to the beauty of their shared passion. He half lifted her beneath him, driving into her as if he could fuse his body with hers forever. He was lost in her sweet, soft grip, in the satin and heat of her body, and then the dark heat that rushed over him carried him away with a silent roar, carrying all thought and logic away, until there was nothing left but a wave of sightless sensation. It poured over him and ebbed away only slowly, leaving him breathless and shaken.

The only thing that brought him back to earth was Ivy, the feeling of her hair beneath his cheek, the sound of her quavering, shaken breath, the touch of the trembling hand she lifted to his cheek.

"Oh, Julian . . ." Her words were so soft that they were almost a breath, more than a whisper, a soft sound that touched his heart even as her hand touched his cheek.

Slowly, reluctantly, he eased his weight off of her, collapsing into the soft down of the bed. He gazed at her, her skin pale and radiant in the dim light that shone through the bed curtains, and pulled her close to his heart, his unsteady hand moving over her silken back.

"Sweetest Ivy," he murmured. He brushed her hair back from her face, her sweet, flowerlike

248

face, so delicate and luminous. "Are you happy, my love?"

The endearment came from him as naturally as his own breath.

"Happy. Oh, Julian, yes." Her voice was unsteady, husky with the memory of their passion.

"Good. Then I shall make thee happy again, and again." His hand played through her hair, delicate whispers of motion that made her shiver with bliss.

They kissed, a kiss that was languid and satisfied, yet shimmered with promises of more to come.

"Ah, Ivy," he whispered, "how I could love thee . . ."

The gentle words were so sweet that they brought tears to her eyes, and for a moment she lay still as if stunned, then closed her eyes and laid her cheek against his chest.

It was enough, she told herself, just to lie there and feel his heart beneath her cheek, and breathe the scent of his skin. It would be tempting fate to wish for anything more.

But it was impossible not to wish.

The sound of the door opening woke Ivy. Julian was still asleep beside her, she could tell by the sound of his breathing, heavy and slow. He was curled up behind her, his long body wrapped around her smaller one, a heavy arm around her shoulders.

The sound of footsteps sounded in the room;

then there was the faint sound of dishes rattling.

Silently, Ivy opened her heavy eyes. The heavy bed curtains were drawn about the bed, and they were enclosed in their own world of damask. Ivy raised herself slowly on one elbow and looked out through the opening of the curtains.

She saw Doll, and Doll was looking straight at her. Her face was set in a sour look, her full mouth clamped into an ugly line.

Julian made a sound low in his throat, a contented, warm sound.

Doll's freckles suddenly stood out on her face as her complexion paled into an ugly, sallow color.

It was the first time Ivy had ever seen anyone green with envy. She had always thought it was just an expression.

Doll shot Ivy a hard, venomous glare, turned on her heel, and left the room. The door crashed closed behind her.

"What the hell?" Julian's voice was hoarse. He cleared his throat and sat up, leaning on one arm. He shook his tangled hair from his face and glanced down at Ivy. "Oh, good. I thought that might have been you leaving."

He pulled her close into the heat of his body, tugging the blankets up against the cold morning air.

"You look thoroughly disreputable," Ivy told him, trying to sound as if he wasn't the most delightful sight she had ever seen, and failing.

He looked very dark and devilish, naked and

tangled in the linen sheets. His smile was lazy and satisfied, his face darkened by a faint growth of beard. "Do I? You look like an angel. A wicked one."

Ivy laughed, pleased and embarrassed. "An angel can't be wicked, by definition." How easily he complimented her. She wasn't used to it. Nobody had ever said things like Julian did—sweet, he said, and beautiful. He looked at her in the morning and told her she looked like an angel.

She blushed and hung her head, and when she looked up, he was smiling as if that too pleased him.

"A humble angel," he observed. "Who was that leaving?"

"Doll. And she seemed really put out, Julian." Ivy snuggled in tightly to the heat of his body, her face pressed against his neck. "I think she's jealous."

"Was she? Too bad for her. She shall have to come to terms with it."

He didn't sound at all surprised, and Ivy tilted her head back, suspicion dawning.

"Julian—would Doll have any reason to be jealous?" Ivy suddenly found herself thinking of Doll's light brown ringlets, her round hips, the way her breasts billowed up above the tight lacing of her bodice.

Julian laughed, trying to look ashamed and ending up looking mischievous instead.

"Julian!" Ivy raised herself up and stared at him, indignant.

"Oh, sweeting! It was naught. And it happened a long time ago, when I was home from university. It meant nothing."

Ivy could feel her cheeks warming. "Apparently Doll didn't think it was nothing," she muttered.

Julian laughed again and pulled her against his chest, squeezing her until she was breathless. "Pray, don't be sullen. I was very young, and it was just a bit of sport. My mother put a quick halt to it, I assure you."

It was the first time Ivy had heard Julian mention his mother. "What happened to her, Julian? Your mother, I mean. If you don't mind my asking."

"Smallpox," he answered briefly. Ivy couldn't see his face, but she could feel the tension in his arms, and hear the terse tone in his voice. "There was nothing to be done. She thought she was safe from the disease, you see. She'd nursed my father years before, and never taken ill. Some people don't. So when there was an outbreak in the village, she and Grandmother thought nothing of going among those stricken and nursing them. Unfortunately, my mother was wrong. She went very quickly."

They were quiet for a minute, and Ivy shivered, thinking how vulnerable those around her were. Perhaps she was too. Smallpox was nonexistent in her own time. She doubted that anyone even vaccinated against it.

"What a morbid conversation," Julian remarked, the teasing note back in his voice. "From youthful follies to deadly plagues. We should make the most of our time before I leave."

He lifted Ivy's chin and kissed her fully on the mouth.

"Where are you going?" she asked as soon as their lips parted.

His hand ran over her shoulder and cupped her breast. His fingers moved softly around the nipple, causing her to press closer.

"To Astley's," he answered in a distracted tone, obviously more concerned with Ivy's breast than his day's agenda. "I promised to escort Felicity back here, until her father returns from London."

Ivy went still, and her hand flew to Julian's chest, pushing him away. "Felicity's coming here?"

He blew a lock of hair from his eyes and looked down at Ivy. His eyes narrowed.

"Aye, she is. And there's naught either of us can do about it, so don't ruffle your feathers. I'm sure Felicity would not think highly of me lolling in bed with my mistress, so let's make the most of our morning."

The slow warmth that had surrounded Ivy was gone. She felt cold and bitter.

Idiot. You let yourself forget what you are to him. You let yourself feel that you were more than you are—and what you are is a convenient piece.

"Will Felicity be sleeping with you?" She

253

hadn't meant to say it, but the words came out, sharp and unhappy-sounding.

"Good Lord, no. She wouldn't dream of it. She's not that kind of woman, you know. Damn, Ivy, where are you going?"

Ivy was already out of the bed, shivering as she reached for her discarded shift, searching the floor for her gown.

"Up yours, Julian."

He looked genuinely insulted. "God's teeth, Ivy! Be reasonable. You know I'm to marry her, and the accusations being thrown about in the village make it even more necessary. We need Astley's protection right now. I don't like it, love, but there it is. Come back to bed."

"Frankly, Julian, right now I'd rather chew glass."

He was infuriating, lying dark and beautiful against the sheets, looking for all the world as if she were insulting him.

"What a very unhappy sort of mistress you'll make, Ivy, if you get sulky whenever my wife is mentioned," he said, sounding aggrieved. "And I was having such a good morning. Leave off with this silliness and come back to bed."

"The hell I will," Ivy retorted, struggling into her gown. "Get Doll to do it."

"Don't be stupid. If I wanted Doll, I could have her. I want you."

"Well, to quote Mick Jagger, you can't always get what you want." Ivy ignored her stockings

254

and thrust her bare feet into her low-heeled shoes.

"He sounds an unpleasant fellow, whoever he is," Julian observed. "God's nightshirt, Ivy, I didn't think you'd get into such a temper. You knew about Felicity, and you know my position. Why not accept it?"

He was sitting up in bed, the sheets falling around his slender hips, the dark waves of his hair falling onto his bare chest. His sharp face was stunning, even lined with sleep.

I can't accept it. Not when you make me feel the way you do. Not when I'm falling in love with you.

Ivy's throat felt tight, her eyes hot and dry.

"Sweetest Ivy, come back to bed," he repeated, and his voice was low and coaxing. "Come back and let me love thee."

If she hadn't wanted to so much, the gentleness of his voice would never have stung the way it did.

"Leave me alone, Julian," she said, and left the room quickly, before he could see the tears in her eyes.

"Insensitive pig," Ivy muttered. She knew she was talking to herself again, but didn't care. It made her feel a little better. Not a whole lot, but a little.

She was in the northeast corner of the castle, a hallway leading from the main keep to the now deserted wing which had once housed the men at arms.

Despite the heavy gown, the numerous under-skirts, and the tawny, fur-trimmed cape she wore, she was still cold. These unused portions of the castle were little warmer than the outdoors. Even in the living sections, she noticed that others would wear their capes when going from room to room.

"If you think I'll stay here and burn at the stake for you, think again," Ivy informed an imaginary Julian. "Or die of bubonic plague. I'm out of here, just as soon as I lay hands on that damned book."

She pushed open a heavy door of iron and oak with one hand and peered in.

She forgot all about Julian. She forgot about the book.

"Bonanza," she whispered, and exhaled softly.

She lifted her torch higher, and the window-less room was illuminated with the warm glow. It was an antique dealer's dream.

Ivy drew a deep breath at the sight of two chairs, obviously from the early fifteenth century. She stepped forward and brushed away a cobweb. The seats were low and square, the backs very straight and tall, topped with a rail of Gothic tracery.

She ran her hand over the carving, as delicate as lace, and shivered with delight. The chairs seemed to whisper stories of ladies in tall, veiled headdresses, of strolling minstrels with pointed shoes.

The backs of the chairs were carved in linen-fold, graceful lines like draped fabric. The wood seemed to be in good condition under the dirt.

Ivy looked around for something to wipe the cobwebs with, and her gaze fell on a bundle of fabric, discarded by the door.

She nudged it gently with her foot, thinking about spiders. When none appeared, she gingerly turned over a fold with her toe.

It appeared to be some sort of banner. She bent down, trying to discern the colors and patterns in the poor light, but then her eye was caught by a chest a few feet away, and then a tall cupboard with doors bearing heavily carved rosettes.

Ivy was breathless. She took a step toward the chest, changed her mind, and turned toward the cupboard, and then looked back at the Gothic chairs. And there was more in the dark corners of the room: carved coffers piled on dusty chests, piles of mysterious objects shrouded in blankets and cobwebs. They seemed to beckon her from beneath their dust.

"Have you found the bodies of Julian's wives?"

Ivy whirled around, a scream caught in her throat, only to see Susanna peering through the door, her dark eyes dancing. The little girl was with her, her frail hand clasped in Susanna's larger one.

"You scared me half to death, Susanna. Quick, bring your candle in."

Susanna entered the room, holding her skirts up with one hand. She wrinkled her nose at the dust. From the door, the little golden-haired girl watched with an inscrutable expression.

"Look," Ivy said softly. "Just look at all this."

Susanna looked, unimpressed. "What a lot of old rubbish."

"Oh, no. These are beautiful things, Susanna. Look at this banner, will you?" Ivy handed Susanna her torch, and unfolded the heavy square of fabric while the younger woman watched.

"Why, that was our coat of arms," Susanna exclaimed. "It must be a tournament banner, to judge by the size."

Ivy shook her head in wonder. The field was dark green, with a wide stripe of black running diagonally across it. A star of cloth of gold was centered in the stripe, six-pointed with radiant curving arms. In the upper right field was a graceful cross; in the lower left was a fierce-looking white ram, looking over his shoulder.

"The ram for Ramsden, of course," Susanna said. "The bend *sable*, the star *or*, the ram *re-agardant*, looking back, that is. The cross of St. Andrew for some particular reason I can't recall. Likely from the Crusades."

"How marvelous," Ivy said. "How proud it must make you."

"Not really. My good looks make me proud. These dirty old things make me want a bath." Susanna laughed a little and looked around. "Why, what is this, Ivy?" She stepped across the room, blowing the dust from a little chest. "It looks like an old reliquary of some kind." She opened it and peeked in. "Thank the stars. Empty. I was afraid I'd find some shriveled old finger of a saint, or some such horrid thing. Come, Ivy, let's leave this mess and go back to Grandmam's chambers. It's cold here."

But Ivy had picked up a piece of old wool blanket and was rubbing industriously at the carved cupboard. A griffin appeared from beneath the dirt, the winged lion of legend supporting a crescent moon.

"Not on your life, Susanna." Ivy was all business, transported by the sight of the work awaiting her. "Go get something old on, and send Doll for cleaning rags. We'll need light, lots of it. And soapy water, and furniture oil and wax if you have it. Who does the cleaning here?"

"Doll, when she has a mind to." Susanna was watching Ivy with a kind of dread. "What are you about, Ivy?"

"Work," Ivy said with grim pleasure, "and you get to help. Doll as well. And that boy in the stables, whoever he is."

"You sound possessed," Susanna muttered.

"I am," Ivy said, gazing with delight around the cold, dirty room. "And you're my assistant. After all, you were complaining about being bored."

"Aye, and so I was, but not as bored as this."

"Lots of candles," Ivy repeated, "and hurry!"

"Come on, little bundle of twigs," Susanna said to the waiting child. "It seems Julian's not the only tyrant giving orders here now."

Ivy was too enthralled with the pale wood appearing beneath her cloth to care.

"Pear wood," she breathed, happier than if she had discovered solid gold.

Daisy had never seen such a day of activity. Lady Margaret seemed very excited by the things in the dark room, and she and Ivy laughed and looked at things. They tied their hair under caps and put aprons over their fine dresses, so that they looked like the village women, but not mean. They were never mean. Even when they were busy, they would stop to pat her shoulder, or stroke her hair.

"Our little one," Ivy called her, and Lady Margaret called her all sorts of silly things, like sugarplum and rosebud and lambkins. All kind names, all pretty names.

Even when she was ignored, they didn't really ignore her. When they became too busy with their buckets of water and rags and oils, they carried her down to the big chair in the huge hall. Lady Margaret wrapped her in a giant cloak lined with fur, and put Bunny in her arms, and there she sat, warm and contented before the fire, and watched the day unfold with interest.

Things were carried into the hall, one at a time. Ivy, her fire-colored hair sticking to her grimy face, called orders to Susanna and Doll, and the skinny horse-boy from the stables, as they all lugged things down the long staircase, pushing and pulling and making a good deal of noise.

Ivy laughed and exclaimed over everything, and kept saying mysterious things about arabesque scrollwork, and Flemish influence and mending arm sumps and fleur-de-lis. It was a mysterious and foreign language, but it made Ivy very happy.

Lady Margaret shook her head with delight, and cleaned whatever Ivy asked her to. "How clever you are," she said to Ivy, quite often, the same way Ivy said it to Daisy when she had found the B. B for bunny and bread and bird.

"B for banner," Ivy told her, spreading a great square cloth out on the floor, and Daisy looked with interest at the dusty symbols and faded colors. Susanna rubbed the star in the center with a paste of salt, and the cloth of gold shimmered like sunlight when she finished.

Ivy smiled when she saw it, and that made Daisy smile too.

"B for banner," Ivy repeated, and to Susanna she said, "B for beating the dust out of it."

Susanna laughed and said, "B for breaking my back, I say."

Doll, the plump girl with the sour face, complained loudly to anyone who would listen as she carried things and hauled buckets and scrubbed away dirt and cobwebs. "Who's giving orders around here now?" she muttered whenever Ivy set her to a new task. Daisy didn't like the way Doll gave Ivy mean looks when her back was turned.

The horse-boy followed orders without answering, or showing any interest at all, not in the work or the things he carried or the women around him.

They ate bread and cheese in the middle of the day, and Ivy didn't quit working even then. She ate with one hand, and rubbed oil into a tall chair with the other. Her brown eyes shone, her face glowed like the moon, pale and bright.

"What's this?" Susanna asked, digging through the contents of an old chest. Cobwebs hung in her dark hair like a veil of lace. "Some sort of old book, I guess."

Ivy, who had been chatting to Lady Margaret about unknown things like grotesques and finials, fell silent. Her cheeks went pale.

"Let me see it." Her voice was urgent and fast. Daisy wondered why. Was Ivy afraid of books? Surely not, for she had told Daisy that books were wondrous good things, and that someday Daisy might read them.

Ivy fell to her knees next to Susanna, holding out her hands. She let out a breath like wind when Susanna put the books into her hands.

"It's not the one," she whispered, and Daisy could not tell if the words were happy or sad. Both, in a funny way.

Over Ivy's bent head, Daisy saw Susanna and Lady Margaret exchange looks. The looks were full of something Daisy didn't understand.

"Why, it's an old book of hours," Lady Margaret said. "What exquisite needlework. I wonder who did it?"

"Oh, some dead woman, I shouldn't wonder." Susanna leaned back into the open chest and continued her search. "When she was alive, I mean. Look," she cried, lifting a tarnished circlet from the chest and placing it on her hair. "I'm the queen of cobwebs."

Ivy put the book down carefully and went back to her chair polishing. Daisy saw that her eyes were sad, and she didn't smile as often as she had before.

What book was she looking for? Daisy wondered. It must be a special one. Perhaps it was the one she had watched Julian hide the day he brought her here on his horse. It must be a special book—he had wrapped it carefully between wool and oiled leather before hiding it between the stones.

One day, if she could remember how to get back to that place, she would show Ivy where it was. Ivy was so nice that Daisy would like to make her happy. B, Daisy realized with sudden delight. B is for book.

Chapter Fourteen

It would be tricky, Julian knew, to try to placate Felicity during her stay without losing Ivy's affections. Not that he would blame Ivy. He tended to be a somewhat jealous lover himself, and he was asking her to tolerate a lot.

He turned his head and looked back at the Astley coach, swaying and creaking as it traveled the steep road up to Wythecombe.

Felicity was traveling with as much baggage as a queen making her progress across the land. Going to survey her new domain, he thought, not without a certain amount of bitterness.

The ironic thing was, it was not Felicity who coveted the ancient castle—it was her father. There had been a time when Astley had been his father's friend. As young men, they had hunted and hawked together, and traveled as far as London. Had Astley set his sights upon Wythecombe Keep even then?

Julian could imagine it: young George Astley riding and fighting and drinking with his good friend Denby, staying in the once luxurious chambers of the keep. And all the while envy growing in him as he walked through the halls, thinking, "But for an accident of birth, this could have been mine."

And then the troubles started. When Denby had been carried away by the smallpox, Astley had ridden over and offered marriage to Julian's mother, even as she knelt by her husband's coffin. She had been horrified and furious. She had never told Julian what words had been spoken, but Astley had been banished from the house.

And when Astley saw the turning tide of the government, he had firmly allied himself with the rebels. Julian wondered if his zest for the Commonwealth was genuine, or simply a road to his desire for Wythecombe. Judging by his haste to marry his daughter to Julian, it would seem the latter.

He rounded the last bend to Wythecombe Keep. The road was muddy, and his horse's hooves made squelching noises with each step. Torches lit the arched doorway to the gatehouse, flickering in the rain.

Julian rode ahead to unlock the gates, and Ben came running from the stables, ducking his head in a futile attempt to stay dry.

Julian dismounted and tossed him the reins. "Pray call Doll and have her help Mistress Astley. There's much to unload."

The boy ducked his head in an awkward nod, looking without much interest toward the approaching coach.

Julian crossed the courtyard to bar and lock the gates behind the vehicle, taking the torch from the gatehouse as he did so. He looked up at the castle, dark and still like a sleeping giant, remembering the days when the windows would have blazed with light, and the courtyard would have been filled with servants to greet them.

The Astleys' coachman was helping Felicity out when Julian approached, and he hurried to offer her his arm. Her hood fell back as she stepped out and looked up at the sleeping castle.

She obviously didn't share her father's zeal to sit in state at Wythecombe. Her placid face revealed little, but for an instant, distaste flickered in her eyes.

Julian studied the face of his betrothed. She was not unattractive, he supposed. Her skin was clear, her jawline pleasantly rounded, like her nose. It was a decent enough face, but not a face to arouse passion, either like or dislike. What then, did he find so disturbing about her?

Perhaps it was her eyes. They were too light, too round. They were eyes that seemed to see everything, but they had a curiously vacant look, as if consciously concealing her thoughts. She would be a good card player, if her religion permitted her to play cards.

"Welcome to Wythecombe," Julian said abruptly. "I fear it will not be as comfortable as your own home, but we shall endeavor to make your stay a pleasant one."

She nodded. "Thank you," she murmured in her soft voice that revealed nothing.

Julian took her arm and escorted her up the stairs, opening the door wide.

He stopped short, staring. The great hall of the castle keep had come to life as if touched by a fairy wand.

It seemed that every candle and torch that could be found had been brought to the room, and the walls and freshly cleaned floor shimmered with unexpected light.

The eight stone columns that flanked the walls were hung with what looked to be medieval tourney banners of the Ramsden green with bend of black, but each bearing a different insignia to represent a different son of the house, or branch of the family. They seemed to flutter with life as the breeze from the open door touched them.

At the end of the long hall, hanging from the stone balustrade that enclosed the minstrel's gallery, was a large ornamental banner, as brilliant as if it had been made yesterday.

Where had it come from? The central star blazed gold against the black bend, the cross of St. Andrew showed brilliant scarlet, the white

ram *regardant* looked back over his shoulder to
the past.

In the niche beneath the gallery, a trestle table
stood on crossed pedestals. A chipped stone gargoyle sat on the edge of the table, its fearsome
countenance made comical by the large candle
wedged in its arms. The gargoyle's furious expression seemed to express resentment at its
new, lowly task as candleholder.

On the wall behind the table were displayed
two long halberds, crossed over each other.
Where such weapons had appeared from, Julian
couldn't imagine. The engraved blades of the
curved axes were shining; the sharp spikes atop
the poles gleamed.

"What is this?" Julian asked, stepping forward
into the brilliant room.

"What think you, Julian?" Susanna called, appearing from behind a chest covered with a
length of jewel-tone brocade. "Do you feel like a
knight returning from the Crusades?"

She was a sight. She was wearing an old dress
that was too short for her and smeared with
grime, and her face was smudged. Atop her head
was an old horned hennin of the fifteenth century, with decaying wisps of veil hanging from
the upturned crescents.

Julian didn't know what to think. He walked
over to the fireplace, where only this morning
had stood a single chair and a rude stool. The
chair was still there, sitting next to a long, low
chest of pale wood with a back so that it could

serve as a seat. Every inch of the gleaming wood was covered with carvings of griffins and dragons and moons and vines. A few tapestried cushions were tossed upon it, with threads of ruby and sapphire and deep green, like the colors of stained glass.

The colors were repeated on the cushions of the two chairs that flanked the fireplace, square-bottomed, high-backed chairs from the days when the Lancasters had ruled England. They looked as if they belonged there, and the carpet that lay between them was certainly a relic from the Crusades. It was faded and worn, but still beautiful, showing intricate patterns of tulips and lotuses, with golden threads sparkling in the faded wine and sapphire patterns.

A low stool with three legs was covered in a fabric of deep claret that he recognized as one of his grandmother's old capes. The stool was a dark wood, patterned with carved Tudor roses around the seat, and a trim of golden tassels set off the wine fabric and dark wood.

Everywhere he looked, something caught his eye—a refectory table topped with a piece of old tapestry, and a gleaming ivory box, an old Welsh crossbow suspended above a doorway, a gleaming coffer on an old chest.

He turned and saw Felicity still standing in the open doorway, her dark wool cape spotted with raindrops. Her wide, light eyes stared at everything, but told him nothing.

"What is this?" Julian repeated, gesturing to

the antiquated furniture gracing the fireplace.

Susanna took the horned headdress off and shook her dark head. "It's a conversation group," she said grandly, "and a very versatile one at that. All the seats have built-in storage units, you know, which is very practical."

"Is it?" Julian asked, wondering what the hell she was talking about.

"So says Ivy. She should be down in a minute. What a slave driver she is, Julian!"

So Ivy had done this. He stared around the room, overwhelmed by the color and light. It was unlike any room he had seen before, and yet the archaic furniture and medieval hangings seemed to suit Wythecombe better than all the modern comforts ever had. The Venetian mirrors, the graceful armchairs and brocaded hangings that had been here before the siege seemed pallid and small compared to the odd mix of treasures that decorated the room.

"It is ghostly," Felicity said from the doorway. "Perhaps in the future you will purchase more appropriate things, sir." She crossed the room, standing before a long table that sat with perfect symmetry between the two arched doorways on the western side of the hall. She picked up a small box and turned to Julian with a small frown.

"Do you see this, sir?"

Julian crossed the room and took it from her hand. It was dark wood and enamel, with pictures of robed and haloed figures wrought in brilliant reds and blues and yellows. Bits of gold still clung to the carefully carved end pieces, and to the halos and patterned robes of the depicted saints.

"It's an old reliquary," Susanna informed them.

"I know what it is, you goose. Where the hell did it come from?" Julian turned it over in his hands carefully. The artist's mark was almost worn away from the bottom, but he could still read *anno domini 1243* engraved in the deep wood. He savored the piece, its air of mystery. Amazing. It was as old as the room they stood in.

"Sir . . ." Felicity's voice quavered slightly, and Julian looked up to see a flush on her cheeks. She was looking at the box with a horrified expression.

"It is an abomination," she said, her voice low and urgent. "It is idolatrous, an abomination forbidden by the Scriptures. Such things should be destroyed; it is the law."

"It is history."

Julian turned and saw Ivy coming down the stairs, his grandmother following her. Ivy's arms were filled with a shaggy fur that looked like a wolf's pelt; his grandmother was carrying a large picture with a heavy frame.

"It's history," Ivy repeated. She looked as grubby as Susanna, if not worse. Her hair was half up and half down, and filmed with cobwebs. Her gown and apron were stained and spotted,

271

her pale skin swarthy beneath a layer of dust. She crossed the room and took the little reliquary from Julian, positioning it carefully on the table. "It's beautiful," she added. "Have you ever seen anything so delicate and bright? It's a work of art, not a political statement. It would be appalling to even consider harming it."

"It is a religious object," Felicity protested, "a shrine of the Roman church, an abomination!"

"There's a shriveled old finger of a saint in there, Felicity," Susanna said, her eyes dancing with mischief. "Or at least I *think* it's a finger. Do you think we should kiss it and see if a miracle happens? Though if it's not a finger at all, perhaps we should not. For all we know, it might be the—"

"Nonsense," Ivy broke in, half laughing. "Susanna, you're incorrigible. There's nothing in there at all, so enough with the shriveled finger business."

"It is rather horrid," Margaret agreed, "but Susanna cannot leave a joke alone."

Felicity did not appreciate the joke at all. Her lips were compressed in a tight line, and she lowered her lids over her generous eyes. "Please, sir," she said softly. "I beseech you to take this thing from this room."

Julian hesitated. It was a stupid request, yet he wanted Felicity's stay to be a calm one.

"Very well, if it pleases you," he concurred.

"Oh, Julian," Ivy cried, her brown eyes darkening, "what a waste of a beautiful object. And we've worked so hard to find everything and clean it. And see how perfectly it fits on the table, the proportion next to the candlestick? And how it picks up those marvelous jewel colors in the rest of the room?"

Susanna gave Julian a cross look. "Devil take thee, Julian," she said, "now you've ruined Ivy's tablescape, and we shall be rooting through the keep for another day, trying to find something of the correct proportions."

"Tablescape," Julian repeated. "Tablescape. Now there is a fine word, whate'er it may be." He took the offending box and handed it to Ivy, tired of the confrontation. "There, Ivy. Take it, and keep it, if it pleaseth you. Just keep it from Felicity's sight."

"For my own?" she asked softly, and she turned the enameled box around in her hands as if it contained precious gems.

"If you like. Where did you find such a thing, Ivy? Where did you find all of this?" He gestured at the hall, the gleaming coffers and chairs, the pillows and Arab carpet and banners.

"In a storeroom," she answered, her eyes still on the reliquary, "by the northeast tower."

And what were you doing there? Julian wondered, but said nothing.

"What a poor welcome we've made," Lady Margaret exclaimed, coming forward to take Felicity's arm. "All three of us in rags, and covered with dust. But isn't it enchanting? I feel as if we've stepped back in time. Ivy is so very clever. I vow, she can fix anything."

Felicity turned her round, cool eyes on Ivy. For a moment, there was a flush of rose on her pale cheeks, and then it was gone. "Indeed, it would seem that she is a most unusual woman. Or so one hears."

What does one hear, Felicity? Julian looked at her sharply, but her face betrayed nothing.

Ivy, on the other hand, looked decidedly uncomfortable. Her cheeks were stained with red under the dust, and she turned away. "I think we've done enough for today. The glue has to set on that corner block on the Flemish cupboard, and it can't be moved till then."

"Thank the merciful Lord," Susanna put in.

Julian looked again around the great hall, shaking his head. What had been an empty and barren space was suddenly an enchanted room. The faded banners and Gothic chairs, the Crusader's carpet and archaic weapons so carefully displayed touched something in him.

It was a sense of history, the continuity of time. Though shorn of his title and money, Wythecombe still stood, as it had always stood. Every object in the room seemed to shimmer with stories of the past, of wars and monarchies that came and went, touching the lives of those in the castle, and moving on. But Wythecombe would survive long after Cromwell was dead and buried.

"Do you like it, Julian?" Ivy asked softly. Her

brown eyes searched his face; her words were almost hesitant.

"I like it well. It is a marvelous gift, Ivy. I thank thee for it."

The familiar "thee" slipped out without thought. Did Felicity notice? It was impossible to tell. Her face told nothing, but her round, pale eyes moved from Julian to Ivy, and back again.

When she was sure that everyone was asleep, Ivy slipped from her bed, pulling her russet cape over her nightshift, and made her way silently to the northeast wing.

The halls of Wythecombe were eerie in the darkness; her own shadow made her shiver. It followed her like a dark ghost through the halls. The wind sighed through the corridors, carrying the faint scent of the sea.

"Come on, Ivy," she urged herself. "Show some backbone."

The door of the storeroom was still standing wide open, the way she had left it. The remaining contents of the room lay in scattered disarray. She lit two more candles from the one she carried, and began her search.

If Julian had hidden the book here in the castle, this was the best place to look for it. She opened a heavy chest and began lifting out moth-eaten clothing. A worn fur, a Tudor-era doublet. A crucifix, tarnished with age. She would have liked to examine them, but she searched on. She touched a pile of letters, and the paper crumbled beneath her fingers.

She pushed a pile of embroidered linens aside, and sighed. Nothing.

She went to the next chest and opened it. The hinges gave a squeak of protest, and the sound made her jump. She lifted out a faded gown of silk, and then shuddered as her fingers closed on human hair.

She leapt to her feet, a hand pressed to her mouth, muffling her strangled cry. Her heart hammered against her chest, and then she forced herself to look.

"A wig," she whispered, and gave a shaky sigh. "For God's sake, Ivy, get a grip."

It lay next to an Elizabethan ruff, and Ivy knew that wigs had been immensely popular in those days, when everyone had been imitating the red curls of the virgin queen. She went to move the red wig aside, and then stopped suddenly, staring at it.

Tangled in the improbably bright curls was an earring.

Not just any earring. An earring shaped like a Christmas tree bulb, made of bright red plastic.

It seemed like a very long time before she drew her next breath. She simply sat there, staring, unable to move. And then she drew the wig out, and gently untangled the earring from the brilliant red curls. She twisted the bauble at the top to set the battery in motion, and it began blinking, on and off, lighting her hands with an unnatural red glow.

276

Blink. Blink. Blink.

Ivy thought of the woman in the antique store, her lurid red wig, her blinking earrings, offering Ivy the paper-wrapped bundle.

"I have something you might be interested in. It's been in our family for years. . . . "

The secret look in the sparkling dark eyes, the soft wrinkles around the pleasant mouth, the plump, wrinkled fingers . . .

"Margaret," Ivy said aloud. But how could it be? It seemed impossible, but what did that mean anymore? Everything was impossible, and yet here she was in the seventeenth century, holding a blinking, battery-powered earring.

It was undeniable. The woman in Enchanted Time had been Lady Margaret. The evidence was there, as clear and undeniable as the red Christmas tree earring flashing in Ivy's hand like a warning light. It seemed so strange, the battery-powered light here in the past. It looked garish and wrong. Ivy twisted the bulb, and the light died.

She leaned forward and began rooting through the trunk. It was all there—she found the ski jacket Margaret had worn folded inside a farthingale petticoat, the shiny polyester pants hidden inside a linen shift. She took out the canvas tote bag the book had been in and opened it. There was a bus schedule for the Seattle Metro-transit, a wrapper from a McChicken sandwich, and three empty bags from Mrs. Field's Cookies. There was a souvenir ink pen from the Space

Needle. When she tipped it, the little yellow elevator moved up and down.

"I don't believe this," Ivy muttered. She pulled out a ticket stub—Lady Margaret had visited the aquarium—and a tube of lipstick.

At the bottom of the bag, she found what remained of the money she had paid for the book. Eighty-one dollars and 67 cents.

"Ivy?"

She leapt to her feet, and pen, money, wrappers, and lipstick rolled to the floor.

"What in the devil are you doing here?" Julian demanded. He stood in the doorway, frowning. His hair lay in tangles over his shoulders, as if he had just come from bed. His full-sleeved white shirt was wrinkled, as if he'd slept in it.

"Oh, Julian . . ." Ivy swallowed, searching for a lie.

He stepped into the room, lifting his torch higher. The mellow light fell on the opened trunks, the cobwebs and dust. It shone on the stone floor, on the McDonald's wrapper, the souvenir pen, and the money.

Julian's dark brows drew together, and he bent down and picked up the bills, frowning. "What is this?" he whispered, staring. George Washington stared back, placid and collected in his baroque green frame.

Ivy stood silent and frozen as he turned the bill over in his hand. He dropped it and picked up the pen, frowning as the little yellow elevator began its descent down the Space Needle. He stared at it for a long time. Then he looked up at Ivy and held the pen up.

"Welcome to Seattle?" He pronounced it see-tle, to rhyme with beetle.

"Julian," she said, and her voice trembled.

"Wait!" He held a quick hand up. "Wait, wait, wait." He picked up a coin that lay by his foot and inspected it carefully.

"Liberty," he read softly. "In God we trust. Noble sentiment, that." He lifted his head, and his eyes met Ivy's, wary and suspicious. "Nineteen eighty-four." He turned the coin over and ran his thumb over the eagle. "United States of America. Quarter dollar." He squinted closer. "*E pluribus unum.*"

"It means out of many—"

"I know my Latin, damn it." His words were tight and harsh. "My dear Ivy. Creeping Ivy, sneaking Ivy. My poor little lost orphan." He laughed, but it was a mirthless sound. "Is Ivy your true name?"

"Yes." She felt a cold, sinking sensation that started somewhere around her heart and plummeted to her stomach.

"And these are your things?"

"No. No, they aren't, Julian."

Impatience showed on his face, and he tossed his hair back like a stallion's mane. "Pray don't trifle with me anymore. I want the truth, damn it." He was holding the bus schedule. "Good until February, nineteen ninety-five. I guess that gives you enough time to explain. Is this true,

279

Ivy? Have you come to us over years?"

"Yes." It was a relief to say, but frightening too.

"From Seetle?"

"Seattle," she corrected. "It's an Indian word."

"The American colonies?" he asked. He dropped the bus schedule and picked up the tube of lipstick.

"Yes." What was he thinking? What would he do?

"I commend you. You must be a very powerful witch, to transcend oceans and centuries. You would put my grandmother to shame, with her poor little invasions of hares and her tawdry love potions."

"That I wouldn't," Ivy cried. "Think again, bucko. I don't even believe in this. I'm not a witch, I'm a businesswoman. And a good one too. I was minding my own business, living my own life, and here comes your grandmother." She kicked at the canvas tote bag. "That—it belongs to her, and the money, and the bus schedule. I had nothing to do with this, Julian, nothing at all. She came into my store and offered to sell me a book, and I bought it, and read it, and flash bang boom, here I am." She drew a deep, unsteady breath.

Julian stared at her, disbelief on his dark face. "She can't do that. She hasn't the skill or the power."

"She can and she did. Look. She was wearing this wig. That's how I figured out it was her. I didn't know it myself until just five minutes ago."

"It can't be so." Julian stared at Ivy and the red wig she was holding.

"It is. She brought me that book, Julian, the book you took from her the day I came. The one that was on your desk. And I want that damned book, Julian Ramsden. I want to get out of here and go home."

Julian looked stunned. He looked up at Ivy with blank gray eyes, and then back at the bus schedule and the tube of lipstick.

"Almost three hundred and fifty years away," he said, and the words sounded melancholy. "Just think, Ivy. When you were born, I would have been dead for hundreds of years, and my corpse rotted away to dust."

The thought shocked Ivy. It was true, of course. Julian would be dead. She stared at him. He seemed so alive, it was terrible to think of it. She would never hear his husky voice again, or touch his neck and feel the warm pulse play under her hand. He would be gone, as if he never existed.

Nobody could ever take his place—her dark lord, her pirate prince. She would go to parties and meet accountants and engineers and graphic artists—sensitive "nineties men" who cared about recycling and getting in touch with their inner selves and saving the earth. She would be bored to tears, and always, always, she would wonder about Julian.

Tears stung her eyes, and she bent over and

began shoving the fallen objects back into the canvas bag.

"Do you have a husband?"

She shook her head.

"A lover?"

"No."

"Do you live with your family, in Seetle?"

"No, I live alone."

"Marry, then! That takes care of everything," Julian exclaimed, and when Ivy looked up, he was smiling, with a self-satisfied expression.

"What do you mean?" Ivy asked.

"Why, you shall stay here, of course! If you have no family to return to, then there's no point in returning. Grandmother likes you, and Susanna likes you, and I think you're an exemplary mistress. Just think, I shall be the envy of all. To have a mistress who can warm my bed and repair my broken chairs!"

"You've got to be joking." Stunned, Ivy sat back on the dusty floor, her cape crumpling around her.

"I'm not joking at all. After all, only I know where that book is, and I have no intention of telling you. And where can you go? Nowhere, so you must needs stay here."

"Julian! You can't keep me against my will."

"Against your will," he repeated, sounding amused. "Come, Ivy. You adore me."

Ivy was unsure whether she wanted to laugh or slap him. "I do, do I?"

"Of course. Oh, this is marvelous. And what

choice have I? I can hardly spend the rest of my life wondering what happened to you. And if you go back to Seetle—"

"Seattle," Ivy corrected automatically.

"As you will. If you go back, I shall be dead. So you would, in effect, be responsible for killing me." He attempted to look sorrowful, and succeeded only in looking mischievous. "And Susanna as well. And poor Grandmother. How could you sleep at night, with all those deaths on your conscience?"

"Julian, this is serious! I can't stay here."

Julian smiled with delight, looking like a satyr.

"You must. You see Ivy, I have come to the conclusion that I can't abide the thought of life without you. So you see, sweetheart, you're trapped."

Chapter Fifteen

"She's probably asleep," Ivy said as Julian banged his knuckles against the door of Lady Margaret's chambers.

The sound echoed through the dark halls.

"I doubt that. She's probably sitting in bed, casting a spell that will turn Cromwell into a newt, in which event I shall wish her luck." He knocked again.

The door opened immediately, and Lady Margaret peered out at them. She wore her fur-trimmed robe, and her silver hair hung over her shoulder in a tidy braid.

"Why, Julian! And Ivy. What a nice surprise," she said, as if she saw nothing unusual in anyone dropping by in the dead of night.

"Is it?" Julian asked. "Is it such a surprise? I

would have thought that you'd have expected it, with your far-reaching powers and your great knowledge of the future."

Lady Margaret stopped short and looked from her grandson's face to Ivy's, and then her eyes lit on the red wig in Ivy's hand. She blinked rapidly.

"What is the matter with the young, these days?" she asked, speaking so quickly that her words ran together. "Imagine bothering a tired old woman at this hour. I'm far too frail for this kind of nonsense, so go back to bed and let me rest. Good night, Julian."

Julian caught the door as it began to close. "I think not," he said calmly and opened the door, gesturing Ivy into the room.

"Oh, bother." Lady Margaret gave a heavy sigh.

She had obviously been awake. The fire in her hearth burned brightly, and several candles glowed around the room, lighting it with a golden warmth.

The nameless little orphan girl was there, sitting in Lady Margaret's favorite chair, bundled in a soft blanket. Her drowsy eyes lit up at the sight of Ivy and Julian, and she gave a timid smile.

"What are you doing awake?" Ivy asked, smiling back.

"Bad dreams, I think," Lady Margaret answered. "I brought her in here, and I've been telling her stories of what a bad little boy Julian was. I never could keep him out of mischief."

"It must run in the family," Ivy observed.

Lady Margaret lifted the little golden-haired girl onto her lap, smiling as if she hadn't heard Ivy. "How nice it is," she said, "to have a little one to hold again. I'm looking forward to holding your children, Julian."

"Are you quite sure you already haven't? Given your ability to move about in the future?" Julian's voice was pleasant enough, but he sat in a wooden chair, a heavy dark piece carved with Tudor roses, and leaned back with the air of one who means business.

Lady Margaret suddenly looked very old and sad. She shut her eyes, and her eyelids looked as fragile as paper. She leaned back in her chair, stroking the golden hair of the child she held. "I see that you intend to have your answers, Julian."

"I'd like some answers too," Ivy said. "This concerns me as well."

"Sit down then, and I shall do my best. It's all a little odd."

"Oh, just a little," Ivy agreed, settling herself on the floor by Lady Margaret's feet.

"Here is where it begins," the lady said. " 'Twas in fifteen-ninety, I think, or was it eighty-nine?"

"And does it matter?" Julian asked.

"You are a cross creature, Julian. Pray be quiet." The good lady shifted and settled the child more comfortably on her lap. "Now, where was I? Oh, yes. I was a young thing, and very

286

pretty. My uncle had found me a position at court, and I was a lady-in-waiting to Queen Elizabeth."

Ivy was thrilled. "Were you really? Tell me about it! What was she like? Who else did you know?"

"Another time," Julian ordered.

"Tomorrow," Lady Margaret promised Ivy. "But that it where your story begins, Ivy. You see, there was a masked ball for the queen's birthday, and we ladies were performing. I was playing the part of Pure Love, and was assaulted by various unseemly characters like Greed, and Lust, and Envy, and Doubt, all played by young men of the court." The old woman smiled. "I was all in white and silver, with pearls in my hair. Of course, Pure Love conquered all, as is the theme of these masques, and the evils all disappeared in a cloud of smoke, and were transformed into Faith and Trust and Honor. And that's when I met my Thomas. Young Thomas Ramsden, the Earl of Redvers. We unmasked at the end of the dance, I looked into his eyes, and I was in love."

Ivy could picture it all. She saw young Margaret, wearing a ruff of pearl-trimmed lace that framed her glowing face like a halo, and the distinguished young man, breathtaken by her youthful beauty. She imagined the room full of courtiers, brilliant in satins and jewels, and Elizabeth I presiding over it all like an approving goddess.

"Which one of the virtues did Thomas play?" Ivy asked, charmed.

Margaret a startled little laugh. "Not a one, I'm afraid. Dear, no. He looked just like Julian, all dark and dangerous. He played Lust, in deep red satin and rubies, and a mask of flames. He was beautifully wicked, and I fell in love on the spot. Can you imagine?"

"Easily," Ivy answered, smiling quickly at Julian. Beautifully wicked. The words could describe Julian's appearance just as easily.

"How very touching," Julian said, but couldn't resist smiling back. "And how does this affect Ivy, or me?"

Margaret sniffed. "It doesn't exactly. But it was the best place to begin. Will you give me leave to finish?"

Julian leaned back in his chair. "Go on."

"We were married within a month. Too soon, everyone cried, but we paid no heed. It is like that, when you meet the right one. There is no doubt. There is the feeling that nobody else would ever compare." Margaret sighed, her eyes far away and soft. "The queen was very angry. We neglected to ask for permission, you see, and both our families were Catholic. The alliance displeased her—it was much safer to marry either of us to a Protestant, to ensure our loyalties. And so we were sent from court.

"Not that I cared, mind you. I'd have followed Thomas to hell in my petticoat, if he had asked me. And when we rode over the hill, and I saw

288

Wythecombe Keep, standing over the valley like a watchful lion, I cared even less. It was summer, and the sea and sky were blue, and the forests green and full of birds, and the pretty village in the valley . . ."

Ivy remembered her first glimpse of Wythecombe. She had felt the same, even in the dead of winter. It was the most beautiful place on earth.

Margaret stared into the fire for a few moments, her plump, wrinkled fingers stroking the cheek of the child in her arms. "I felt as if I had come home at last," she said finally. "And when we rode through the gates, Lady Juliana, Thomas's mother, was waiting. She had known, somehow, she said, though we had sent no word. She welcomed me like a daughter. And for my wedding present, she gave me the book."

"I would rather she'd have given you a set of silver plates, or an emerald necklace," Julian commented.

"Bless thee, Julian, I'm sure. But she didn't. Juliana was very . . . powerful, and very efficient. She had little need of the book, truth to tell. She had the gift of second sight, more than I can describe. She was very dark, and very beautiful, even as she grew older. If she hadn't been so kind, she would have been frightening. I was never very good at spells," Margaret added, with a rueful look. "Something always seems to go wrong. Rather like my cooking. I always seem to put salt in the pudding, and sugar the beef."

Ivy watched the firelight reflecting on the gleaming gold wood of the floor and waited for Margaret to continue.

"We were very happy, Thomas and I. So happy that sometimes it almost frightened me. It felt as though we were tempting fate, as they say.

"When Denby was born, we were delighted. It was an easy birth, and he was healthy. We thought more would come, but none ever did. All the prayers and hopes, all of Juliana's herbs could not change it. 'Never care,' Thomas told me, 'He's a son worth twenty others.' Thomas had a gift, you know, for always saying the right thing. A very charming habit." She paused and shook her head. "And that night," she said simply, "he died."

Ivy felt Margaret's grief as keenly as if it were her own. "No! How did he?"

Margaret's eyes were dark and misted. "God knows. He'd had a chill, just a little cold. Not even anything to care about. He'd gone hunting that day, as he often did. That's how small a thing it was, that wretched sniffle. He went to bed early, saying he was tired. By the time I joined him, he was burning with fever. By morning," she finished simply, "he was dead."

A log crackled in the fire, and Ivy leaned forward to brush a spark back onto the hearth. Julian shifted in his chair and crossed his ankles.

"Even after all these years, it still hurts to think of," Margaret said. "People say that time heals pain, but that isn't true, you know. The

290

pains get farther and farther apart, but when they come, they still hurt just as keenly. I hurt so badly, I thought I might die of the pain. There were days when prayed I would. But of course, I didn't. One never dies, when one wishes to most. And time went on, as it does. Juliana died, and Denby married Judith, and Julian and Susanna were born. Then Denby died, and Judith, and here I was, still at Wythecombe, listening to the wind and the sea, watching the sun come up every morning, and the seasons changing.

"Then one day, when I was going through some of Judith's old things, I found the book. I had given it to her when she came to the house, and quite forgotten about it. Judith was much better at that sort of thing than I."

"Trust Mother," Julian said. "Go on, Grandmam."

"Are you listening too?" Lady Margaret suddenly asked the child on her lap, who smiled a silent, sleepy smile. "And well you may. God knows you won't repeat anything."

The little girl looked at Margaret with clear blue eyes and reached up to pat her face.

"Bless your little heart," Margaret murmured. "Where was I? Oh, yes. Julian was away in London, sowing his oats and growing his hair and whatever young men on their own do—don't tell me, Julian, I'm sure I'm best off not to know. And Susanna was a little dear, but just a child, and here I was, all alone at Wythecombe. I admit, I was feeling very sorry for myself, and oh, how I missed Thomas. It began to haunt me. I thought about him constantly, and how different things would have been had he lived. So I started casting little spells, just to amuse myself. I became rather good at it. Not *too* many things went wrong."

Julian snorted.

"I really am sorry about the time you turned green for a week, dear. That wasn't the object at all."

"I should hope not."

Lady Margaret smiled at Ivy. "I did feel badly, I swear it. But to tell my story, I was reading the book, and I found a charm, or a poem. It was so sad, but so sweet. It might have been written for Thomas and me. I remember I missed him so badly that day."

"I have sought thee over time and land," Ivy said softly, remembering the poem.

"That's the one," Margaret agreed. "I wish I could remember it all, but my wits are not what they once were. There was something about "the other half of my soul, whose body gives heat to the winter, whose breath cools summer's fire . . ." Her voice trailed off.

"Lost, somewhere in enchanted time," Ivy finished.

"I had no idea what it would do," Margaret told them. "I simply read it, and was thinking of Thomas, and then everything went golden and bright, as if the very air was gilded, and things began to quiver, and there I was."

"Where?" Julian demanded.

"Why, London, of all places. But not London as we know it now. The world had changed. And there I was, standing on a street corner, holding the book, and wearing a little gray suit with the smartest little hat. There was a war going on, and several buildings had been bombed, and I was quite confused. The music, the noise, the newsstands and department stores . . . the automobiles! Oh, Julian, the automobiles!"

"What, I pray thee—"

"Later, Julian," Ivy interrupted. She leaned forward and touched Lady Margaret's hand. "What then?"

"I saw him," Margaret said, and tears stood in her eyes. "I saw my Thomas. He was young, in a soldier's uniform, and his hair was shorn off in the most unattractive way. But he was still beautiful, and I knew him at once. He was standing across the street, and having a cigarette with another Yank."

"He was doing what with a what?" Julian asked, but Ivy shushed him.

"I tried to call to him, but he didn't hear, and I tried to cross the street, but those automobiles . . ." A tear rolled down Margaret's cheek, and she wiped it away quickly. "And then these noises started, the most dreadful wail you can imagine, and everyone started running and shouting about bombers and Nazis. Someone dragged me down some stairs to a cellar, until the attack was over. And when I came out, he was gone."

Tears stood in Ivy's eyes, and Julian was silent.

"Ah, just to see him!" cried Margaret, her mouth twisted as if she were in pain. "So many times I thought, if only I could see him again, or touch him once more, or smell his hair. And there he was, and then there he was not. I searched for him all that night, through those terrible black streets, and then gave up. I read the spell again, and came home to Wythecombe. To have come so close, and then to lose him . . . it was almost as if he died twice. It was so painful that I waited two years before I tried again."

"And did it work?" Julian asked.

"Almost the same way. Of course, the second time I was in New York, which was very confusing. But exciting. What do you think of pizza, Ivy?" Lady Margaret asked suddenly. She seemed to be recovering from her sad story, and her eyes shone with enthusiasm.

"I like it," Ivy answered. "Did you see Thomas there?"

"Yes, I did. I was on a tour bus, and couldn't get off, and I saw him getting into a cab on Fifth Avenue, somewhere in the upper seventies. He was older, this time, but I knew him as if I had just seen him that morning. His hair was gray, and longer. It was autumn, and he was wearing a greatcoat that flapped in the breeze like a cape. I cried all the way through Central Park."

"You'll have to translate this for me later," Julian said, "for I confess I'm quite lost. And then what, Gram? Did you come home again?"

"Well, not quite. I booked a room at the Plaza and played tourist for a day or two. Then I came home."

"Extraordinary," Julian said. "And nobody noticed you had been gone?"

"No, indeed. It was as if time had stopped. And then you came home from London, and the troubles started, and what with all the fuss about the war, I quite forgot about it. And then I tried for the third time." Lady Margaret smiled. "And I ended up in Seattle. I stopped to admire all the Christmas lights in the shops, and the trees, and I was looking at a shop window all full of marvelous things, and what do you suppose the sign above the door said?"

"Enchanted Time," Ivy replied promptly.

"Indeed it did. Exactly like the poem. "Ah," I said to myself. "my Thomas will be in there." But he wasn't. There was just this little red-haired woman, sitting at her desk."

"Ivy," Julian guessed.

"It was. And when I looked at her, I had the most extraordinary feeling. I felt somehow that if I gave her the book, she would lead me to Thomas. But it didn't work that way, did it? I went to sleep in my hotel that night, intending to go back the next day and speak to her, but when I awoke, I was back here at Wythecombe, and the book was sitting on the table next to my bed. I might have doubted the whole thing had happened, but for this." Lady Margaret reached for a thin gold chain that hung around her neck, and tugged it loose from her gown.

Ivy's keys were suspended on the end of the chain. They were all there, the key to the store, to the safe, the key to her apartment and to her mailbox.

"They were in the book," Margaret said.

Ivy remembered reading the spell, and the keys falling from her hand onto the open page.

"And then Julian brought you here, and I said to myself, 'something is afoot, here,' and I've been waiting to discover exactly what. By the end of the first day, it became obvious to me that you should fall in love, and I decided to help it out a bit."

"You did, did you?" Julian cocked a dark brow at his grandmother. "And how did you do that, I pray thee?"

"Aphrodisiacs," she admitted, "in spiced wine. I should have known better. I really didn't think you'd force the poor girl, Julian."

"I did nothing of the sort," Julian argued.

"You threatened to turn me out," Ivy reminded him.

Julian scowled.

"How very unchivalrous of you, Julian," his grandmother said. "I certainly hoped that I had taught you better manners than that."

"Don't lecture me, you meddling old woman. You drag a beautiful young woman into my home, and wave her under my nose, and feed me love potions, and then expect me to behave like a proper young boy? Spare me."

Ivy blushed. Beautiful. How easily he said it.

"Perhaps that wasn't very nice," Margaret admitted, "but just see how splendidly it has all worked out. Ivy adores you, 'tis plain to see, and you care for her, and she fits in so well here. I suggest that you marry her quickly, and you give me back my book so that I can find Thomas, and we may all get on with our lives."

"You're quite forgetting a few things," Julian said. He leaned forward and brushed his dark hair from his eyes. "First, if I don't marry Felicity, I shall be dispatched to Ireland, and you taken under Cromwell's protection. I doubt very much that either of us would fare well. I should likely meet with an unfortunate accident during the campaign, and you would likely be hanged for a witch before a fortnight passed. And what would become of Ivy?"

He reached out and ran a hand over her hair, a tender gesture that caused Ivy's heart to flutter. "No, I can't marry Ivy. My plan is much better. I marry Felicity, and Ivy stays as my mistress."

"That's not very romantic," Margaret said.

"But very practical."

"It sucks," Ivy said, her cheeks hot. "Forget it, Julian. If you think I'm going to hang around and watch you marry that ignorant cow, and see you on the sly, think again. The very idea's repugnant." She shivered at the thought of him

297

taking Felicity into his bed, making love to her. And she would have to wait, knowing he'd been with his wife. Second best. Never belonging. Always on the outside of things. Not good enough.

"Damn, you're difficult," Julian said, and Ivy wanted to slap his arrogant, handsome face. "Why not be content? 'Tis better than nothing."

"No, it's not. It's worse than nothing. It's degrading. I say you go get that damned book, and let me go home. Then you can marry Felicity, and I can forget I ever met you."

"Can you, Ivy?" Julian's voice was soft, and he reached out and laid a tender hand on her cheek. "Can you just forget? I must confess, I'm a little hurt. I had hoped that you had come to care for me."

Oh, I do. So much more than I ever should. Forget? No, I'll think of you every day for the rest of my life.

She turned her head away, staring at the polished floor, watching the reflection of the flames on the golden wood.

"You can't blame her, Julian," Margaret pointed out. "It's a lot to ask from a woman in love. I would rather have died than share Thomas with another."

"There isn't a choice," Julian said. "And if she loves me—"

"I never said I did!" Ivy cried.

"—she would rather stay with me, under any conditions," Julian finished, as if Ivy hadn't spoken.

"Not those conditions," Ivy argued. "It's intolerable. Just get the book, Julian, and we can end this before I get hurt."

Julian sat silently for a moment, and Ivy studied his face, as if committing it to memory—his high, proud brow, his sharp nose with the slight bend in the middle, the way his dark brows slanted over his clear, gray eyes.

"No," he said simply.

"No? What do you mean, no?"

"I mean, no, I will not give you the book. Not now, not ever. Intolerable, you say? I tell you what I find intolerable. The idea of being married to Felicity for the rest of my life is intolerable. The idea of being sent on that Godless Irish campaign and waging war against starving innocents is intolerable. The idea of giving that book back to Grandmam so that she can create chaos in our lives is intolerable. But most of all, Ivy, the idea of losing you, when I just have found you—that is intolerable. That I cannot stomach. I have lost enough in my life. I will not lose any more."

Not a word of love. Just, "I will not lose any more."

"You can force me to stay," Ivy retorted, her cheeks hot, "but that's wrong, Julian. I'm not a possession. If you force me, I'll be miserable."

"I think not," he replied with a quick, bright smile. "I seem to please you well enough, at certain times."

"How very indelicate of you, Julian," Lady

Margaret said. "The least you could do is give me my book back. I shall be quite unhappy without it."

"You shall be quite harmless without it. And I'll remind you that there are witch-hunters about. Things are dangerous. One can only imagine what would happen if you were to go about waving your arms and saying 'eenie-beeble' over everything. No, it's simply too dangerous. Ivy stays, the book is forgotten, and that's an end to it. Learn to live with it."

The two women stared at him, Ivy with outrage and Margaret looking offended.

"And now," Julian finished, standing and stretching, "I'm for bed. Ivy, you're welcome to join me."

"Go to hell," Ivy said, quietly.

He appeared more amused than anything else. "Hell is a subjective thing, I think," he said. "Good evening, Ivy, Grandmam. And you too, little one," he said to the tired child in Margaret's arms.

Furious, Ivy stared after him as he left the room, closing the door softly behind him.

"Oh, my," Margaret said softly. "This is a bit of trouble, isn't it?"

"I'll say. He can't mean it, Margaret! He simply can't! How can he be so arrogant? Don't I have any choice in this?"

Margaret's dark eyes were soft and sorrowful. "Are you really so unhappy here, Ivy?"

Ivy put her head into her hands and thought

about it. "No," she admitted. "No, not really. It's beautiful and exciting. And I do care about you and Susanna, very much. I'd miss you awfully, if I were to leave."

"And Julian?" the old woman urged. "Would you miss Julian?"

"For the rest of my life. But it doesn't matter, Margaret. He doesn't love me. I'm an amusement to him, nothing more. And it's become a win-lose issue. You heard him."

"Yes, but it doesn't mean I believe him. What if you had the choice, Ivy? Would you stay, or leave?"

"I don't have the choice!"

"But what if, Ivy? If things were different? What if Julian was not to marry Felicity, and he was to offer you marriage? Then would you stay?"

"I don't know." Ivy sighed. She was tired, her head was whirling from all that had happened. Too much to think about. "I don't think I could really love a man that treated me like a possession. I'm from a different world, Margaret, and I'm used to making up my own mind and choosing my own path. I'm too old to be told, 'Do this, and that's it.' I can't live like that. And anyway, Julian will marry Felicity. He's made that clear."

"If I had my book," Margaret said, "I might be able to alter things. But then, if I had my book, you'd find it and leave. What a muddle!"

"I want that book," Ivy said. "I want to leave while my heart's intact."

"To be honest," Margaret said, "it's already a little late for that, isn't it? It's like that, when you meet the one you love." She sighed and looked at the silent child in her arms. "Time for bed, little sweet. I think you've heard enough for one night. And morning comes early. Tell our Ivy good night."

The little girl smiled at Ivy, her clear blue eyes blinking.

"What are you thinking?" Ivy asked, reaching up to touch the corn-silk hair, the soft cheek. "Those eyes seem to say so much."

Daisy smiled again, looking at Ivy. Ivy was so nice, and patient. And she liked the games with the pictures and letters. A for ant, and apple. B for bread and butter and book. Ivy wanted the book. So did Lady Margaret. But if Ivy had the book, she might go away.

And Julian did not want her to have it. Daisy liked Julian. She wondered why all the people in the village had been so afraid of him. She wondered if he was her father. Old Ethyl had said that once. "Your father be the Dark Man. That's why you're all wrong. One day he'll come and take you away."

That would be nice, Daisy thought, leaning against Margaret's soft, sweet-smelling shoulder. Julian was nice. He patted her head and smiled when he saw her. If Julian were her father, she would be more like the other children.

Maybe they would live in a nice cottage, with flowers. Julian would be her father, and Ivy

302

would be her mother, and they would learn to read together.

No, Daisy decided, she must never tell Ivy where Julian had hidden the book. That would ruin everything.

She didn't open her eyes when Ivy kissed her forehead and left the room. For a long time, she just lay in Lady Margaret's soft, warm arms, listening to her breathe.

At last, the good woman spoke.

"Something," she said, "must be done about this, and if Julian will not give me my book, I must muddle ahead without it as best I can."

Chapter Sixteen

Ivy bent over the rough paper, trying not to spatter the ink, and drew a careful dog. It had a body like a pig, with rectangular legs, and an improbable, undoglike smile, but once the ears and tail were in place, it resembled, more or less, a dog.

"D is for dog." She wrote the word beneath. "D-O-G, dog. You see?" She offered the paper to the thin child, who regarded it with her wide, clear eyes.

Susanna, sitting on some cushions, tossed a log into the cavernous fireplace of the great hall, looked over at Ivy and the child, and laughed. "It looks a sight better than your duck," she observed.

The little girl, sitting on the Persian carpet

next to Ivy, ducked her head and laughed silently.

"You're a lot of help, Susanna. Here, precious, spell dog." Ivy offered the child a large piece of paper, covered with the letters of the alphabet.

Her face tight with concentration, the child extended her tiny finger, and slowly, with great effort, touched the letters D-O-P.

"Good," Ivy cried. "Almost. That's a P, and it looks like a G, almost, but not quite. Try again."

She watched the child happily as she looked at the paper. The blue shadows beneath her eyes were growing fainter with each day, the frail cheekbones filling out. Her eyes were getting livelier, and she seemed to be responding to those around her more readily. As Ivy watched, a proud smile shone on the little face, and Ivy looked down to see her finger on the letter G.

"Bravo! Now you know duck, and door, and dog. How clever you are! I had a much harder time learning to read. Now, what other D words can we think of?"

Susanna looked up from her needlework. "Dull?" she suggested, with an impatient look at her tangled thread.

Ivy laughed and began drawing a flower. "Here we are. Daisy. I like flowers, don't you? This is a daisy. D is for daisy."

The little girl suddenly went still. Her face was perfectly blank, and her hands lay lifeless on her lap. She simply sat, staring at the paper.

Confused, Ivy looked at the paper. It seemed

simple enough. Certainly it was easier to identify than the pig-bodied dog.

"It's a daisy," she repeated.

The child moved then. She shook her head, blinking rapidly, and her hands twitched, rose and fell back into her lap. She shook her head so quickly that her golden braid swung from side to side.

Susanna tossed her needlepoint aside and peered at the paper. "So it is," she admitted, "and quite a nice daisy, given Ivy's skill as an artist."

The child's mouth worked, and for a moment, Ivy had the feeling that she might speak.

"It's simple," she repeated gently, "D for daisy."

The little girl's mouth tightened with frustration. She pointed her finger and pushed it down onto the drawing of the daisy, shaking her head. The ink smeared a little.

"It's not a daisy?" Ivy asked, wondering what was wrong.

The child exhaled and ducked her head in agreement, but still appeared frustrated.

"I should understand better if she had said it wasn't a dog," Susanna remarked. "It's a very nice daisy, considering."

"What's wrong?" Ivy looked from the paper to the child. Perhaps she was going too fast.

The little girl, breathing quickly, brought her hands to her chest and pointed.

"Are *you* a daisy?" Susanna asked, with a merry little laugh.

The little girl stopped short, and then her mouth stretched into a wide, happy smile. Silent laughter shook her, and she began to nod.

"You're a—" Ivy broke off, recognition dawning. "A daisy? Is that your name? Daisy?"

The child's eyes shone, and she almost shook with happiness. Yes, she nodded, and the firelight shone on her smooth golden hair.

"What a turn!" Susanna cried. "I believe you've done it, Ivy! It must be."

"Daisy," Ivy said softly, and the child turned her large blue eyes to Ivy, nodding so vigorously that her entire body rocked with the motion. Her cheeks were pink with happiness; her eyes shone.

Susanna clapped and began to laugh with delight. "Well done, Ivy! Our poppet has a name."

"Just think," Ivy said, gathering the child into her arms and holding her tightly, "how it must feel, Susanna, not to have a name! Oh, this is wonderful!"

Daisy apparently thought so too. She leaned closely into Ivy's arms, still shaking with laughter, and Ivy, thrilled with her discovery, laughed out loud, and then began to sing, "Daisy, Daisy, give me an answer, do. I'm half crazy, all for the love of you. . . . "

That made Susanna laugh harder, and Daisy rocked with delight, and Ivy dissolved into happy giggles.

"It must be a fine joke," Julian said, appearing

from the doorway to the north wing, where his rooms were. "What is here, ladies?"

"Oh, Julian," Ivy cried, forgetting that she was angry at him, "what do you think? Her name is Daisy! We were learning D, and I drew a daisy, and she kept shaking her head and pointing to herself. And we figured it out. Her name is Daisy."

Julian crossed the room and looked at the papers that lay on the carpet and smiled. "Daisy, indeed. Who'd have guessed? That's a fine name. You even look like a daisy, now that your petals are clean."

He touched the child's golden hair with a gentle hand, and she beamed at him. "Good work, Ivy. You're a fine teacher. Your children will be lucky ones."

Ivy warmed to his praise and buried her face on the top of Daisy's golden head, holding her close.

"Now we have a pretty posy," Julian said, "Daisy and Ivy together."

"Why, how poetic you are, Julian," Susanna remarked, "and what a fine mood you're in. Who'd have thought. You don't seem nearly as much of an ogre as you usually do."

"Beautiful women have that effect on me," Julian answered, "or mayhap it's seeing this old hall looking so bright. Just think, Ivy, if you had not come, how dreary our lives would be. I would never have ridden off that day and found our Daisy, and the hall would be dark and empty, and Susanna would be doing nothing but complaining of boredom from dawn till dusk."

"And Julian would be sulking about from morning till night," Susanna retorted, "dreaming of the day when Cromwell is toppled from his stolen throne."

"Ten years of watching Julian sulk," Ivy commented, "now that sounds fun, doesn't it?"

Julian fell silent and Ivy looked up to see his eyes upon her, bright with interest. "Ten years?" he repeated softly.

"About that," Ivy agreed. "I'm pretty certain. I think the Stuarts are restored in sixteen sixty."

"Are you sure?" Julian asked.

Ivy thought long and hard. "Yes. It's an easy date to remember."

"Praise God," Julian whispered, "Only seven more years to go."

"What is this?" Susanna demanded, her eyes dancing with interest. "In addition to being the tutor and carpenter, has Ivy become the local soothsayer?"

Julian began to laugh, and Ivy thought how handsome he was. His smile transformed his fierce good looks, and the glow in his eyes warmed her like a summer day. She found herself wondering what it might be like to stay. She could take care of Daisy, and teach her to read, and maybe have children of her own. Julian's children. The thought filled her with a longing that she didn't expect.

Blushing, she looked up at him, and his face

was warm and approving. It was impossible not to feel an answering warmth, not to smile back.

As she did, the light abruptly died in his eyes, and she followed his gaze to the staircase.

Felicity stood there, her face a pale mask. Her gown was deep brown, her wide collar unadorned by lace or embroidery.

"I give you good morning," Felicity said, and Ivy couldn't help but feel that she didn't mean it.

"Good morning," Julian replied, giving a stiff bow.

"I see that you still have the child here," Felicity observed, her pale eyes focusing on Daisy, still in Ivy's arms. "I am surprised, sir."

"Her name is Daisy," Ivy said softly. She didn't like the way Felicity looked at Daisy. What would happen to the little girl if Julian and Felicity were to marry? She tightened her arms around the thin child.

"Isn't it marvelous?" Susanna asked. "We didn't have the least idea, and then Ivy was teaching her to read, and it came to light."

Felicity's eyes moved from Daisy to Ivy, then back again. "But why?" she asked at last. "Why teach such a creature to read? Surely she cannot learn."

The creature. Ivy looked down and saw that Daisy's face had gone perfectly blank. It was as if she had ceased to be aware of anyone in the room.

Felicity crossed the room and took the high-backed chair with the Gothic scrollwork across the top. She held a length of linen in her hands, and a needle. She threaded her needle almost without looking and began to sew, careful, perfect stitches.

"You are taking an exceeding amount of time," she observed, "in teaching the child. But to what end? It is unlikely that she can learn."

"She *is* learning," Ivy argued. "She's learning quickly."

Felicity's face remained tranquil. "But why? If you wish to teach her, why not teach her something useful? She might be able to work in the kitchens, given time."

"She's not strong enough," Ivy pointed out. "She's not suited to physical labor. And since she can't speak, she should be able to write, so that she can communicate."

"She has no need to speak," Felicity replied with irritating calm. "God has made her thus. And of what use will book learning ever be to such as she? Or any woman, for that matter?"

No wonder it's going to take women almost 300 more years to get the vote, Ivy thought. She moved Daisy from her lap and began gathering up the scattered papers from the floor.

"Perhaps," Julian suggested diplomatically, "an educated woman might prove useful to her husband."

"And then she would be able to read Scriptures," Susanna added, sounding very pious, which was at odds with the sparkle in her eye.

"A woman has no need," Felicity said. "She

311

should let her husband or father read them, and instruct her in God's word as he sees fit."

"What if her father or husband is a horse's ass?" Ivy asked, blowing a fallen curl from her eyes.

Felicity missed a stitch, then picked it up immediately. "She is still subservient to his will," she answered.

"Do you hear that, Ivy?" Julian asked, his eyes dancing. "Women are supposed to be subservient to the will of man in all things. 'Tis the natural order of life."

Ivy tucked her papers under her arm and helped little Daisy rise to her feet. "How fortunate for you, Julian, that your intended wife feels the same. You should get along well over the coming years."

She left the room with Daisy, anxious to be away.

"What a very odd young woman," she heard Felicity say. "Does she mean to stay long, sir?"

"Not if she can help it," Ivy muttered. Patiently, she helped Daisy up the stairs, and she went in search of Lady Margaret, who might be able to provide some ideas of where Julian would have hidden the book.

A week into Felicity's visit, Ivy was ready to quit. She had searched the castle thoroughly, from watchtower to dungeon, and every room between. There were rabbits living in the old falcons' mews, and spiders almost everywhere else.

There were cobwebs, and dusty boards, and once, to her delight, she turned up an old dagger with a carved handle in the shape of a ram's head. She cleaned and polished it, revealing emerald eyes, and presented it to Julian, who was delighted with it.

Lady Margaret watched her progress with anxiety, Susanna with interest, and Julian with a kind of amused indifference.

"I'm beginning to think it's not even in the castle," Ivy whispered to Lady Margaret over dinner one night.

"Mercy upon us, you could be right," the old woman whispered back. "But then we are lost."

That was true, since they were all forbidden to leave the castle.

Ivy tried to avoid Felicity. She disliked Felicity's placid, broad face. She felt it was a mask, covering the young woman's true feelings. But every now and then, the mask would slip, and then Ivy could see the blatant dislike and suspicion in the large, cold eyes.

And Julian—she kept as far from Julian as she could. It was hard to do. Ivy took more pleasure out of looking at Julian than she would ever have imagined possible.

At any time of day or night, she could shut her eyes and picture him clearly—the way his brows slanted, thick and dark, the slight tilt to his eyes, which made him look either very dangerous or very lazy, depending on his mood.

She loved the way he walked, his long-legged,

313

arrogant stride, as if he were always on his way to find a good argument, or coming back from one, triumphant. She loved the way his hair curled in wide waves, and hung long and loose between his wide shoulder blades. She even liked the way he ate, often disdaining his fork and jabbing at things with his dagger. When he spoke during meals, he would sometimes poke at the air with his dagger, when making a particular point.

At night, Ivy would fall asleep listening to the wind crying in the corridors, and dream of the nights she had spent in Julian's arms. Sometimes the memory was so painfully sweet that she would climb out of bed, intending to go to him. But she wouldn't; she would not become any more infatuated with him than she already was.

He sat with Felicity at the morning meal, talked with her in the afternoon when she sat before the fire with her never-ending needlework, and took the chair at her side each night at dinner. Soon, Ivy realized, that chair would be Felicity's, and the castle would be Felicity's, and Julian would be Felicity's.

Why, then, would he not give her the book and let her go?

Though Ivy did not suspect it, Julian was equally miserable. The days dragged by, one after the other. Spring would never come, he felt. Lady Winter had spread her dark cape over the country, suffocating them all with the smell of rain and fog, shutting out the sky.

His grandmother had not seemed well lately. She wore a distracted, unhappy face. She seemed to be growing smaller, and when he touched her, her shoulders seemed frail.

Susanna's mood had changed from argumentative to hostile. It was she who had been charged with keeping Felicity content when he was otherwise occupied, and her patience was wearing thin. He tried to cheer her up, reminding her that when he and Felicity married, she would have a large marriage portion. Then they could begin the pleasant business of finding Susanna a handsome young husband.

To his surprise, Susanna waved him away, looking more like a tired old woman than a 17-year-old girl. "Don't speak of marriage to me, Julian," she said, "for now I see what it is. Like you, I shall never marry for love. I shall simply prostitute myself for financial and political convenience, and die without knowing what it is to be loved."

Shocked by the bitterness in her young voice, Julian tried to make light of it. "Why, Susanna! You're passing young to be so bitter. Take heart—I shall buy you a husband you can love. We shall take care that he is young and handsome, and you shall leave Wythecombe with fifty new gowns and bully him into the grave, if you choose."

Susanna didn't smile. She leaned back in the

window seat, her lute still and silent across her lap, and stared out the window at the endless gray rain falling from the gray sky into the gray courtyard.

Julian noticed that she was pale, and it alarmed him. Perhaps the constant confinement was giving her this melancholy listlessness.

"I promise thee, Susanna," he said softly, "I shall not marry you to anyone who displeases you."

The dark rose flared in her cheeks, but she rounded on him with anger in her eyes. "Devil take thee, Julian!" she swore. "What have you to say about it? Think you that you will be out from Astley's thumb, once you've bedded his daughter? Or out from Cromwell's? I shall marry where it pleases them, and I am sure that will *not* please me."

She leapt to her feet, dark curls bouncing, her fingers clenched tight around the slender neck of her lute. "I shall tell you what *would* make me happy, Julian. Give me that damned book, and *I* shall go to the nineteen hundreds."

"Good Lord preserve us," Julian cried out, throwing his hands up with a despairing gesture. "Not you as well, Susanna! I shall be damned—"

"You're damned already, thank you, having to marry that tedious cow. I hope she quotes Scripture at you until your ears fall off. If you gave me that book, I would read that spell and heigh-ho, I'd be gone. Then *I* would be in the new world, and *I* would go to university, and *I* would drink margaritas and ride on jet skis and eat pizza and drive a Harley! Yes, I would, Julian, so don't look at me as if I couldn't—"

"It's not that I think you couldn't, it's that I'm not clear exactly what it is you're threatening me with. You're speaking a foreign language, Susanna."

Susanna glowered at him. "I don't like you, Julian. I liked you well before the siege, and I liked you more after Ivy came. But now you're toadying to that cow—"

"You go too far, Susanna," he interrupted.

"Don't shout at me! It doesn't frighten me a bit!"

"Has Ivy been filling your head with this nonsense of hurleys and jetskis?" he demanded. "I won't have it."

Susanna hesitated, then shrugged. "Don't tell me, tell Ivy. She's in Grandmam's apothecary, if she'll speak to you, which I doubt."

Julian glowered at Susanna, turned on his heel, and left the room.

Susanna stood there a minute, and then smiled with delight. "Grandmam is right," she said to the silent room. "Men are easy to maneuver, if you just take good aim at the right spots."

Ivy had never been in Lady Margaret's apothecary before. It looked to her like a witch's cavern. The room was behind the kitchens, in the oldest part of the keep. It had been built flush against the cliff wall, which still showed its craggy, dark surface along the back of the room.

Along the beams of the ceiling, dried herbs and flowers hung, lending a spicy, exotic scent to the cool air. Someone had added a fireplace, providing the only light in the windowless space, and the flames reflected off of shelves full of corked jars and bottles.

Some of the jars had quite innocent and friendly labels: "rose and lavender water," "distilled lilac," and "rosemary rinse," and others bore more mysterious words, like "false unicorn's horn," "nightshade," and "sticklewort."

"No eye of newt or toe of frog?" Ivy asked. "Or is it toe of dog?"

Lady Margaret, who had asked Ivy to meet her there, laughed. "What a disgusting idea. No, nothing more sinister than a broken astrolabe, I'm afraid." She was standing above a steaming wooden tub that reached to her knees, and as Ivy watched, she uncorked a bottle, sniffed at it, and dumped the contents in. "Have you any knowledge of astrology, dear?"

"None," Ivy admitted.

"What a shame." Lady Margaret replaced the cork, wiped her hands on her apron, and beamed. "There, Ivy," she said, indicating the steaming tub. "What do you think?"

Ivy peered suspiciously at the steaming contents. "What is it?"

Lady Margaret pursed her mouth. "A bath, of course! You were saying last night how much you missed your tub, so I thought I'd surprise you."

Ivy laughed, a little embarrassed. "That's it? I half expected serpents to be swimming in there."

Lady Margaret straightened the lace cap that covered her white hair and took off her apron. "Now that would hardly make a pleasant bath for you, would it? Where do you get such notions?"

"Oh, I don't know. Maybe being transported hundreds of years away from home scrambled my brains a little."

"That might be it," the old woman said thoughtfully. "But not to worry. There's nothing in there but a little musk and jasmine."

Ivy inhaled appreciatively. "Wonderful."

"Thank you, dear. Shall I help you with your laces, or can you manage?"

"I can manage, thanks." Ivy dipped a hand into the warm water.

"There's soap in the white crock, here, and chamomile rinse for your hair in the jar next to it. I shall leave you to your bath, then."

Ivy had already kicked off her low-heeled slippers and was unrolling her stockings. "It's just a bath, right? If I get in and say, 'Calgon, take me away,' I won't go anywhere, will I?"

"Where do you get such notions?" Lady Margaret repeated, shaking her head.

"Stranger things have happened," Ivy reminded her.

"But certainly not in a bathtub," the good lady

said and departed, closing the heavy door behind her.

Ivy gave a final inspection of the steaming water, deemed it safe, and began to strip, dropping her deep green gown in a heap on the floor, petticoats following, and lowered herself into the fragrant water.

She gave a heartfelt sigh as the steaming water surrounded her. What bliss. She had been washing each day from the basin in her room, but still never felt clean. Once, she had asked Doll how she might go about bathing, and the maid's reaction had been so horrified that she dropped the subject immediately.

"An honest woman needs two baths in her life," was Doll's opinion. "One when she's wed, and one when she's dead. You don't look either, to my eyes."

Ivy dismissed Doll's folk wisdom, and gave herself up to the pleasure of her bath. True, she couldn't stretch her legs out in the round tub, but it was a bath nonetheless, and she was enjoying it with all her heart.

The soap in the white crock was soft and fragrant, and she scooped it out and rubbed it on her pale skin, dipped her head in the steaming water, and rubbed more into her scalp. She ducked her head under, holding her nose, and shook her head from side to side until her hair felt rinsed.

When she emerged from the fragrant water,

Julian was sitting on the tall stool next to the fire, watching with interest.

Ivy sank down farther, her cheeks blazing. "What are you doing, Julian?"

He raised his brows, and his dimples showed in a quick smile. "I came to speak to you."

"Well, speak to me later. I'm taking a bath."

"Obviously. Is there a reason?" He leaned his back against the hearth, tipping the stool on two legs, and making himself comfortable.

"A reason? Because I like to be clean. At home I bathe every day. In private," Ivy added, with a pointed look at the door.

Julian ignored her. "Every day? How odd. What is the purpose of that?"

"Get near enough to Felicity and you wouldn't need to ask," Ivy replied, sounding more catty than she intended to. "The woman smells like an onion."

Julian laughed aloud and smoothed his hair back from his forehead. "What a spiteful thing to say. I've smelled worse, you know."

"That's nothing to brag about. Now will you leave me in peace?"

"I will not. This is the most delightful sight I've seen in some time, and I consider it my great fortune to intrude upon you."

"Who told you I was here?" Ivy asked, suspicious. Lady Margaret was constantly extolling Julian's virtues to her, and she wouldn't put it past the old woman to have arranged this.

"Susanna did. That's why I came looking for

321

you. I want to ask you not to fill her head with nonsense about the twentieth century. She has all kinds of odd ideas about going there, and I want it stopped."

"Send me away, then. Give me that book, and send me home, and you won't have to worry. You can live happily ever after with your onion-scented bride, and I can get on with my life."

"That I won't," Julian retorted. "And do quit making references to Felicity's odor. It's not that bad."

"Not if you like onions," Ivy said. "And you don't smell so hot yourself. You smell like a horse."

Julian raised a disbelieving brow. "Indeed, do I? I didn't notice my skin offending you the last time I took you to my bed. You seemed quite pleased with me. Or do you always cry for more when your dainty senses are affronted?"

Ivy's face grew hot, and she tried to sink a little deeper into the tub, her arms crossed tightly across her breasts. "That wasn't my fault," she said. "You heard your grandmother. She gave us aphrodisiacs. If she hadn't, I'm sure I wouldn't have been the least bit interested."

Julian's smile showed, brilliant and devilish. "Oh, Ivy! What a liar you are."

He stood up, stretching his long legs, and started for the door.

Ivy's relief turned to alarm as he reached over, picked up a heavy piece of wood, and dropped it into the iron brackets that made the bolts.

"Julian! What do you think you're doing?"

He turned and gave her a broad smile that tilted his lazy eyes even more.

"Two things, sweetheart. First, I shall join you in that tub and take that bath you tell me I need so badly. And while I'm there, I shall prove to you that, Grandmam's silly potions aside, you desire me as much as I do you."

"Don't be an ass, Julian," Ivy said sharply, but Julian appeared not to hear her at all, and began unfastening the silver buttons of his doublet.

Chapter Seventeen

"Damn it, Julian, you're not funny," Ivy said, watching as he tugged the sleeves of his doublet, and tossed it carelessly to the floor.

"I should hope not," he agreed, stripping off his full white shirt and bending to take off his boots. "If you started laughing at me now, I should be quite insulted."

"Do I sound like I'm laughing?" Ivy demanded, looking around for something to throw.

"No, you sound utterly terrified," Julian said with infuriating good humor, loosening his breeches, "as if there were some sort of monstrous dragon threatening you, and . . . why, bless my soul," he said as his breeches hit the floor, "there it is."

Ivy turned her head, torn between the desire

to laugh and the urge to kill him. "You ass," she said, well aware that the heat in her face was not altogether due to either embarrassment or anger. She kept her head turned as she heard him approaching her tub, focusing on the herbs that hung from the ceiling.

"Move your legs," Julian said, as cheerfully and casually as if they bathed together every day. "Either move them back, or if you wish to be more accommodating—"

"I don't want to be anything of the sort!" Ivy assured him. "That's it, Julian. If you're getting in, I'm getting out." She leaned over the edge of the tub, reaching for the length of linen toweling that lay there, and trying to present Julian with a view of nothing more than her back at the same time.

Julian was having none of it. As she rose up, he sat down, seizing her waist at the same time. He gave a shout of triumph that sounded more appropriate to a battlefield than a bathtub, and they both went down with a tremendous splash, Ivy still clutching the towel.

Ivy shook the water from her face, sputtering and twisting against his strong arms, and more water cascaded over the top of the tub and ran over the dark stones of the floor.

Julian was laughing, and Ivy's struggles seemed only to make him laugh more.

"Julian! Be quiet! What if someone should hear you?" The warm water wasn't helping; she slipped against his body as if covered in oil. The

feeling of his chest against her back wasn't helping either, or the solid, warm grip of his arms
around her waist, or the way he was pulling her
tightly against his thighs.

"Why, if someone should come, I'd simply call
for help."

Ivy looked over her shoulder through a curtain of wet hair. Julian was too handsome for
his own good, naked with shining droplets of
water trickling over his broad shoulders, and his
eyes sparkling.

"You'd call for help?" she repeated, perplexed.

"Like this," he said, and raised his voice till she
was sure it could be heard in the village. "Help,
someone! For the sake of mercy, break down the
door! She lured me in here, and tried to drown
me, and now she won't let me out! Please, for
the love of God—"

Ivy twisted around, clapping a wet hand over
his mouth. "Julian!"

He wriggled his dark brows at her, pleased
with himself, and placed a hot, slow kiss on the
palm that lay against his mouth.

Ivy pulled her hand away quickly, revealing
his wicked grin.

"That's what I'd do," he said. "But first, I would
do this"—and he bent toward her, taking her
mouth beneath his own. His beautiful mouth
was warm and slow against hers; his tongue
flickered against hers with a delicious, melting
heat.

Ivy was drawn to him like a flower to sunlight,

reaching up without will, her face following the warmth, as if the very essence of her being was created to answer him.

They kissed for a long time, finally silent except for the crackling of the fire and the gentle lapping of the water that slid between their bodies, caressing and touching them like warm, liquid silk.

"Damn," he whispered when their lips finally parted, "I've wanted to do that for days."

He pulled her head to his shoulder, and held her tightly against him, caressing her neck.

Ivy wondered how it was that the minute he held her, her worries seemed to float away like leaves on a rushing stream. As long as she was in his arms, the rest of the world ceased to matter. Such security, such comfort from a touch. If she could stay here forever, held in the circle of his arms, with his hand moving in her hair, she would.

Only Julian, she knew, could ever make her feel like this. Her head fit perfectly into the curve of his neck, his chest and lean torso curved exactly to fit her spine, his long legs accommodated her smaller ones like a missing piece of a puzzle sliding perfectly into place.

He reached down and took her hand in his, gently, turning it over and examining first her palm, and then her fingers, one at a time, as if the sight were something new, something he had never seen before.

"How well your hand looks in mine," he said

quietly, as if it were a small miracle.

Ivy felt too full to speak. It was simply her own hand, but somehow, held in his, it became a thing of beauty.

Was that love? To be transformed by another's touch, by his words? To suddenly be aware of a million things she had never noticed before? What a marvel it was, just to listen to the sound of his breath, and what beauty his voice had.

Everything was different when Julian held her. The water that surrounded them, and the golden reflection of the fire shimmering across its surface. The dark, shadowy corners of the room seemed soft and comforting; the glow of the fire was like rich gold against the darkness.

And Julian—he was beautiful, too beautiful for words. She reached up and outlined his face with her finger, as if drawing its lines into her heart. The crooked nose, the angular cheekbones, the high, broad brow, the almost too perfect mouth.

He watched her silently, his eyes soft and dark, and though he said nothing, his eyes seemed full of promises that made her heart swell with a wordless joy.

They kissed again, moving toward each other at the same time, a rich, lingering kiss that left Ivy feeling as if wine ran through her veins.

She shifted and lay half against him, her breasts aching and pressing against his chest, the water warm and limpid between the two of them. He kissed her forehead, and her cheekbones, and her eyelids. "You have dove's eyes," he whispered to her.

She tilted her throat back, and he kissed it, his hands moving over her arms and to her breasts. The bathwater trickled from his hands and dripped over her pale skin like sparkling tears.

Beneath the warm water, she could feel him grow hard against the curve of her hip, and she pressed against him with a sigh. Her hands ran over his body, leaving glistening water wherever they touched, until both of them shimmered in the warm firelight.

The water overflowed and ran to the floor as they moved, but neither of them noticed. They were too fascinated by the discovery of each other's bodies, learning, as if for the first time, how a hot breath felt against a throat, the way a hand curved around a thigh, or the way their lips fit together.

Julian lifted handfuls of water to her neck and watched it flow over her shoulders and trickle down the hollow of her spine, and then traced the warm path with his mouth.

He kissed her shoulders, and her breasts, and her stomach, until she was shaken and dizzy. His hands, wet and warm, slid over her body, touching her everywhere.

Occasionally he whispered words to her, telling her that she was beautiful, that she was perfect, but even if he had remained silent, the adoration in his eyes would have been praise enough to intoxicate her.

Her body moved wherever his hands led, swaying in answer to his touch. She only demurred once, when he lifted her hips through the limpid water and parted her pale thighs so that she lay exposed to his gaze, but he tightened his grip, and with his other hand he brushed the curtain of hair back from her blushing face.

She met his eyes, trembling with emotion and desire.

"Don't," he murmured. "Sweet Ivy, hide nothing from me. It would be a crime to hide such a sweet sight from my eyes. That is a garden I would gladly wander through, with your leave, and leave no blossom or bud untouched. Grant me that, I pray thee."

Her breath quavered as his fingers traveled over her, warm and wet and gentle, caressing and stroking until the melting heat chased all thought from her mind.

He pulled her over him when she began to utter soft cries, wordless, gentle sounds of need that ended in a low, long utterance of delight as he drove into her, filling her with the heat and strength of his own need.

He held her hips tightly against him, moving until she was mindless with the joy of it, with the untamed, perfect sensation. It started like a fire at the very core of her being, flaming through her veins and shaking her body over and over.

She opened her eyes when she heard him answer with a low, fierce sound, and their gazes locked as he gave a final, powerful thrust into her body, his head falling back in ecstasy.

Shaking, he pulled her against his chest, and she rested her head there, stunned, listening to his heart beating, fast and hard, and then gradually slowing.

They lay there, silent and still in the fragrant water, and she thought that the sound of his heart beating was the sweetest sound she had ever heard, until he spoke.

"How I love thee," he said softly.

Her breath shook as she exhaled, and a warm tear trickled from her eye, flowing down her already wet face and onto his wet chest.

"If I had my book," Margaret exclaimed for what seemed to Susanna the hundredth time, "then we could get things done. I'm sure that there would be some way to send Felicity packing. I don't trust that girl."

"You haven't your book," Susanna said, impatiently, "and if you did, what would it help? I thought the only spells in there were spells for good. Is there a *good* way to be rid of someone?"

Margaret frowned at her needlepoint. "Move that candle closer to me, sweet. Thank you. A good way to be rid of someone. Let me think. Well, there must be. If I had my book . . ."

Susanna rolled her eyes and looked at little Daisy, who was sitting on the floor by the fire, playing with her rabbit.

"Perhaps," she suggested, "you should quit

worrying about Felicity, and find a way to get Julian to tell you where he's hidden the book."

"Hopeless," Margaret proclaimed. "He's too afraid Ivy will leave him."

Susanna settled cross-legged on the floor, the skirts of her plum-colored gown spread around her, and took up her lute. Idly, she plucked at the strings.

Daisy watched, fascinated, her blue eyes wide.

"Grandmam," Susanna exclaimed suddenly, "I think I have it."

"Have what, dear?" Margaret asked, blinking.

Susanna's dark eyes sparkled, and her cheeks flushed with a rosy glow. "Do you remember when I was little, and your ruby necklace went astray?"

"Went astray, indeed. A necklace is not a runaway horse, dear. It was stolen." Margaret gave an indignant sniff.

"Very well, so it was. But you said that charm, remember? The one that makes anyone keeping a guilty secret confess it?"

Margaret's eyes rolled. "For all the good it did me. That dreadful little maid confessed her crime to the groom, and they went off together and set up housekeeping in London. And 'twas my necklace she used for her dowry."

Susanna waved an impatient hand. "Well, that part was bungled a bit. But if you were to try the same charm on Julian . . ."

Lady Margaret's face lit up, and she clasped

her hands together. "I see! And then we keep him in our company—"

"Who else could he confess to?" Susanna finished, triumphant. "Do you think you can remember the spell, Grandmam?"

Lady Margaret bristled. "Of course I can! I know I'm getting on in years, but my head is as clear as it ever was."

If Susanna had any doubts, she decided to keep them to herself.

"Almond custard," Margaret said.

"I beg your pardon."

"The powders that loosen the tongue can be hidden in almond custard, and that's Julian's favorite."

"Is it?" Susanna asked. "Are you quite sure?"

"Perhaps it was Denby's. No, it's Julian's, I am sure of it. Run and tell Edith to make almond custards, dear, and we shall have the truth after our sweet tonight."

Lady Margaret stood, shaking out her skirts, and Susanna raced from the room, her dark curls bouncing over her shoulders.

"Now," Lady Margaret said to Daisy, "what were the words, exactly? A guilty secret, in thy heart . . . shall press upon thee like a weight. . . . To ease the weight, they lips shall part . . . to speak the truth shall be thy fate." She smiled with delight at Daisy, who smiled back. "There, I knew I could remember. Oh, this promises to be a fine night! Julian will have no choice but to speak."

Amy Elizabeth Saunders

Daisy buried her face in her rabbit's soft fur, which made him squirm. She hoped that the spell would make only Julian speak the truth. It would be a bad thing if she were to speak. She remembered clearly how displeased her mother had been at the sound of her voice. It was too bad, too, because Daisy liked custard very much.

Ivy stood in her room, trying to comb her damp curls into some kind of order. Over her shoulder, Julian watched from the bed, his reflection faded in the mottled glass of the mirror.

"Put those blue ribbons in your hair," he ordered. "I like it that way, all wound round like a crown."

Automatically, Ivy reached for the ribbons, then stopped. "No, I think I'll just wear it tied back." She tried not to laugh at his affronted expression.

"I like the blue ribbons," he repeated, reaching for the enameled box on her bedside table and turning it idly in his hands. He looked inside, found it empty, and replaced it, picking up a sheaf of papers and looking through them. "More reading lessons for Daisy?"

"Yes, she's doing very well. She wrote her name, and mine, and she's drawing the sweetest pictures." Ivy began braiding her hair. "She's a very bright little girl."

"She has an excellent tutor." He picked up a rumpled chemise from the bed and held it up, smiling as though imagining Ivy inside of it.

334

Ivy tied the end of her braid, smiling back. "I'm ready. Shall we go down?"

He leaned up on one elbow, shaking his hair back from his face, frowning. "You forgot your blue ribbons."

"I did not," Ivy said, fixing a lace cuff. "I deliberately ignored you."

"Did you? Whatever for?"

"Because," Ivy said, taking her rumpled chemise from his hands and tossing it to the floor, "you have a terrible habit of giving orders. 'Put in the blue ribbons,' you say, instead of asking. That may be completely acceptable to a seventeenth-century woman, Julian, but I'm a twentieth-century woman. If you're going to force me to stay here against my will, we'd better establish that right away."

"Damn," he said, "how unpleasant for me."

"Too bad."

"Do you intend to argue with everything I tell you to do?" he asked, sitting up on the bed.

"If I must, to make my point."

"Damn," he repeated, aggrieved. "I thought that you loved me."

"I do," Ivy answered softly, "but one has nothing to do with the other. You know the old saying, 'If you love something, set it free. . . .' "

"I've never heard that old saying, and I think it's particularly stupid."

"Well, maybe it's not that old. The rest of it goes, 'if it doesn't come back, it was never really yours to begin with.' The point is, I would like the choice."

Julian thought about that for a while. "So what you're saying is that if I provided you with the means to leave . . . the book, in this case . . . you might choose to stay, or not? And if you chose to leave, it would mean that you did not love me?"

Ivy hesitated. "Or it might mean that I love you, but can't live under the conditions you propose. At any rate, we'll never know if you don't give me the book."

"Good," Julian said. "I have no intention of letting you go. I've laughed more today than I have in a year or longer. It did me good, and I have no desire to stop. Now let's forget this ridiculous conversation and go down to dinner."

"I have no intention of forgetting about it," Ivy retorted. "Julian, if you honestly care about me, let me have the dignity of making my own decision. You, of all people, must know what it feels like to be manipulated into a position where you have no choice."

Julian stopped, and his face became very still and solemn. He stood by the door, his face half-turned in dusky shadow. Again, Ivy thought how he looked like a painting by Rembrandt, dark and thoughtful, his long fingers resting on the latch.

Ivy waited, holding her breath.

"I'm sorry," he said finally, and left the room.

Ivy stood, staring after him. For a moment,

she had thought that he might offer her the book, and a choice. But what if he had? And if Felicity wasn't a factor, would she choose to stay?

She gazed around her room, at the battered stool, the enameled box with the pictures of the saints on it—all the dearer because Julian had given it to her. She looked out her diamond-paned windows, over the dark courtyard toward the sea. She loved Wythecombe, and Margaret, and Daisy, and Susanna.

And especially Julian. But was she certain enough to sacrifice the life she had built for herself, to stay in this unpredictable, dangerous place?

"I love thee," he had said. But did he really mean it? Were those three simple words worth risking her life for?

Ivy pressed her hands to her temples. "Dear Abby," she said aloud, "I have a real doozy of a problem. I think I'm in love with a three-hundred-and-fifty-year-old man, and he wants me to relocate to the past, even though he's going to marry someone else. Also, he's unemployed. The food here is terrible, his grandmother is a real witch, and the villagers are getting ready to storm the castle, but he says he loves me. What should I do? Sincerely, Wondering at Wythecombe."

From the minute Ivy sat down to dinner, she felt as if something was afoot. Margaret seemed distracted and absentminded, but her dark eyes sparkled with interest as she looked from Ivy to Julian.

Susanna was gayer than she had been in days. She laughed and chattered throughout the meal, teasing Julian about everything from his nose to his worn-out boots, and occasionally darting sly looks at Ivy.

Felicity sat and ate silently, her pale eyes watching everything, gowned in a sage green dress with more lace than Ivy had ever seen her wear before.

Was she trying to please Julian, Ivy wondered? Did she suspect? Ivy tried to behave casually, but she was acutely aware of Julian at every moment. Each time she caught his eye, the memories of their afternoon together flooded through her mind. She would look away, and then worry that she would be noticed looking away.

Doll served the fish and soup with her usual air of sullen ill-grace, and Ivy thought she felt Doll's disapproval, strong and silent, each time the buxom girl set a dish down near her.

Only Julian seemed perfectly at ease. He ate heartily, and laughed at Susanna, and made polite conversation with Felicity, and told Doll to compliment the cook on the sturgeon.

Margaret, at the end of the meal, complimented Julian on his good mood. "It's a delight to see you so happy again," she said, handing Doll her empty plate. "And look, Julian, here's something to please you even more. Almond custard, your favorite."

Julian looked down at the steaming dish Doll set before him. "My favorite? Thank you, but no. I'm not fond of custard, really. Eggy things don't sit well with me."

Lady Margaret's face fell in dismay as Julian handed the dish back to Doll.

"Mine looks wonderful," Ivy said, taking up her heavy spoon.

"I'm sure it is excellent," Felicity said politely, accepting Julian's rejected bowl from Doll.

"But . . . but . . . it was meant for you," Margaret said helplessly, and her hands fluttered. "I ordered it for you, Julian."

"Now it must needs be Felicity's favorite," Susanna said, leaning forward on her elbows. She tilted her dark head, her eyes shining. "For she has the specially large custard that was to be Julian's."

"It's your favorite," Lady Margaret repeated, her wrinkled lids batting, her soft mouth tight.

"What a tempest over a custard," Julian said. "Bring me one, Doll, if it means so much."

Lady Margaret didn't appear soothed. Her own custard sat untouched, while her hands fussed with her falling collar, patting at the lace.

Susanna laughed as she stirred at her own dish, Ivy ate the sweet, almond-flavored pudding with pleasure, and Julian poked at his. Felicity ate silently and methodically, as she always did.

"There," Julian said. "I thank you, Grandmam, it's very good."

Margaret waved a hand at him, as if to say it didn't matter. "Thank you, Julian, but I'm quite beyond caring," she said, her voice tired.

"Oh, do be quiet, you babbling old woman," Felicity said suddenly.

Ivy dropped her spoon and looked up abruptly, wondering if her ears had deceived her.

Julian stared at the pale girl, his mouth open.

Susanna choked into her napkin.

"I must confess," Felicity went on, dipping her spoon into her dish, "it's surprising I have not gone mad in the past fortnight. I have never met anyone given to such needless chatter. If you put as much energy toward your household, it would be a good deal more comfortable here."

"Oh," was Margaret's answer. Her voice sounded very thin.

"Felicity," Julian asked softly, "are you ill?"

Felicity took another bite of custard and swallowed. Her pale eyes met his directly, and she actually pointed at him with her spoon.

"Ill? Am I ill? Nay, that I am not. Though I do feel the need to say, sometimes I feel quite ill, being trapped here. Father would never have made me come, you know, except that he says I must watch you."

"Does he?" Julian asked, his eyes glittering. "And why is that, pray tell?"

"Why, you think you are so vastly superior in

intelligence, Julian, I am quite surprised that you are not telling me," Felicity said. "He and Lord Cromwell know full well that you are not as poor as you pretend to be, and that you are somehow giving what little you have to the rebels. You think that I am so stupid, it should be no great trick for me to discover you, and then Father shall have you neatly under his thumb, which is just where you Ramsdens belong."

Susanna gave a shriek of laughter behind her hands, Ivy stared openmouthed at the usually silent Felicity, and Margaret's eyes were round and shocked.

"Oh, Julian! Tell me you're not involved with anything like that. It's so dangerous."

"Good," Felicity said, "perchance he will be caught and hanged for a traitor. I should like to hang him myself, the demonic lecher. Do you have the slightest notion," she went on, eating her custard as though everything was perfectly normal, "the slightest idea how he infuriates me? He sits with me and makes conversation that I'm sure he thinks is charming, and all the while he's staring at that little"—her spoon jabbed in Ivy's direction—"that little carrot-headed Jezebel. That merry-legs, that lightskirt."

The table was utterly silent, and Felicity continued eating, apparently unconcerned.

"Have some more custard, Felicity," Susanna said, twirling a dark curl around one finger.

"I rather think she's had enough," Margaret said mildly.

Julian leaned back in his chair, his glittering eyes darting from his grandmother to his sister, and then to the fateful custard. "By law," he said, "I am entitled to beat you."

"I should sincerely hope you would not, Julian," his grandmother replied indignantly, lifting her white head.

"No, indeed not, but sometimes the idea is very tempting."

"It would be good for Susanna," said the new, forthright Felicity. "That little vixen needs to be taught her place. She bedevils me from morning till night with her sly ways. When I am mistress of Wythecombe Keep, things will be very different."

Julian fixed his eyes on the young woman, his face expressionless. "Really, Felicity? And how is that?"

"*I* shall be in charge," Felicity replied, treating Julian to a fierce glower. "Not my father, not you, not your doddering old fool of a grandmother or your cackling little sister. *I* shall decide what is to be done, and what is not. Nobody shall command my fate anymore. 'Supervise the cook, Felicity, talk to the laundresses, Felicity, polish the plates, Felicity, marry young Ramsden, Felicity.' I shall be done with all that. And if you give me trouble, I shall have you clapped into jail. So there."

" 'Who can find a virtuous woman?' " quoted Susanna. " 'For her price is far above rubies.' "

"Be quiet, you little witch," Felicity said. "The

342

words of the Good Book are an abomination upon your mouth. And I have seen and heard enough to be rid of you, so mind your step. Give me your custard, please, Julian, if you do not intend to eat it. I vow, I have never enjoyed a custard so much. Is it not simply marvelous?"

"I'm not sure marvelous is the word," Julian said. He looked stunned, but handed Felicity his dish.

"I would not ask, but the food here is so meager that I am always hungry. That will change, of course, when this is my castle. That will be the first thing to change. No, the second. The first thing to do is to get rid of your mistress merry-legs, there, with her big brown eyes."

"Up yours, Felicity," Ivy said, joining in the spirit of things.

Julian looked with alarm at Ivy's half-eaten dessert.

"Not to worry, Julian," Margaret assured him. "Ivy's response was entirely natural."

"If ill thought," Julian said.

"And that idiot child," Felicity went on, ignoring them all. "She goes too. I will not have her under my roof. She and the whore go. And I mean to have my way, Julian Ramsden."

" 'Whoso findeth a wife findeth a good thing,' " Susanna recited. "Felicity taught me that, Julian."

"This isn't funny, Susanna." Julian looked at Felicity as she ate. "Tell me, Felicity, is there anything else you haven't told me? Any other plans afoot that concern Wythecombe?"

"Your stupid maid is a spy, and fueling the villagers with a lot of nonsense about witchcraft. And aside from that, only that my father is waiting in London with the lord protector, and as soon as I can find the details of your meetings with the rebels, I shall send word. Then the marriage can proceed."

"How utterly delightful," Susanna said, giggling.

"Congratulations, Julian," Ivy said. "She's a charming girl. I'm sure you'll be very happy."

Julian rested his elbows on the table, dropping his forehead into his hands.

"Do you have a headache, dear?" Lady Margaret asked.

"Do you need to ask?"

"I am very tired," Felicity said, "and anxious to be away from you. It is amazing to me that I like not one of you, and would rather be alone in my room. How tiresome it will be to have to share a room with you, Julian, not to mention a bed. I'm not looking forward to that at all."

The young woman sat, looking at Julian as calmly as if she had been discussing the weather. "Well?"

"What do you expect me to say, Felicity?" Julian asked, throwing his hands up.

"I don't expect you to say anything, nor do I care overmuch what you do say. I'm waiting for you to pull my chair out."

"Of course, how stupid of me." Julian stood

and pulled back Felicity's chair.

She stood and smoothed her green skirts. "I wore this gown," she said, "to show everyone how much prettier I am than that redheaded witch. Do you like it, Julian?"

"It's very charming," Julian said, still staring at Felicity as if he had never seen her before.

"Thank you. How rude of you not to mention it before.

I bid you all good even."

Julian stood still as Felicity swept from the room, his hand still frozen on the back of her chair.

"What a good idea," Margaret said in a bright, false voice. "I think I should retire as well. Good night, Julian."

"Sit down, damn it," Julian said. "You and I, my lady, need to speak." He looked across the table at Susanna, who had collapsed with her head on the table, shaking with silent laughter, and at Ivy, who stared back at him with wide, shocked eyes.

"In truth, we should all speak. What happens next will concern all of us. We must needs lay our plans, I think. Will Felicity remember this tomorrow, Grandmother?"

"I think so," Margaret admitted. "But I'm not sure, Julian. Things have a way of getting out of hand, you know."

"Do they?" Julian asked, his voice heavy with irony, "How so, pray?"

"Now don't get vile, Julian . . ."

"Julian," Ivy said urgently, "is it true, what she said? Are you secretly meeting with royalists and financing them?"

"I am," he admitted.

"Oh, Julian, how very dangerous!" Lady Margaret exclaimed. "You promised me you would not!"

"And what of your promise to me?" he returned. "I suppose that I should thank you for it, now that Felicity has shown her hand. But first, let us make plans. If Felicity sends word to her father that they are undone, they may decide to take action quickly. We may," he added, looking sadly around the room, "have to flee Wythecombe."

Chapter Eighteen

Ivy stood on the front battlements of Wythecombe, her gloved hands resting on the ancient
stone. The wind was blowing up from the sea,
cold and sharp. It had scattered the fog that
clung around the rooftops and spires of the village, and was tossing the clouds from the winter
sky, pushing them inland. There would be no
rain today.

The cold wind stung her cheeks, despite the voluminous hood of her cape. It caught her skirts,
and they snapped and fluttered like banners. But
the winter sunlight felt good, and the sea air was
delightful to breathe. She wondered what it
would be like in the summer, with the ocean clear
and sparkling, and the grass green on the hillside,
and the barren trees lush with leaves.

She might never see it. Julian had said that they might have to flee to France, waiting with the other exiled royalists, until the Commonwealth fell.

"There you are," Julian called, and Ivy turned to see him coming toward her, looking like a swashbuckler from an old movie as he strode past the battlements, hair and cape tossing in the wind.

"You look like Errol Flynn," she greeted him.

"Should I be jealous?" he asked, drawing her into his arms and holding her tightly.

She breathed in the scent of him, his doublet of faded black, and the scent of his leather gloves, and the scent that was simply Julian.

They stood that way for a while, looking out to sea and enjoying the warmth of each other. Ivy wondered what it would be like to live here in a time of prosperity, to be Julian's wife. She would sleep next to him every night, and on summer evenings they would stand like this and look out to sea while they listened to the sounds of their children playing in the courtyard, or on the grassy field beneath the stone walls.

She closed her eyes, leaning close to him, and for a moment it seemed that it was so, that she could smell the scent of grass and wildflowers in the summer sun, and hear the soft laughter of children. They could go riding along the rocky coast, or to the ruins of the abbey. It would be green and sunny there, with ancient roses growing wild and climbing over the fallen walls.

If only there had been no Cromwell, no Astley, no Felicity . . .

"Felicity is gone," Julian said, as if he had heard her thoughts.

"What do you mean, gone?" Ivy asked, her eyes flying open. Her daydream was gone, it was cold winter again. Only Julian was still real, solid and strong and warm.

"I mean that she is gone," Julian said. "Where to, I have no idea. She has gone, and left a letter, very poorly written and badly spelled, though she makes her point."

"Which is?" Ivy asked, not sure whether she should be glad or worried.

Julian laughed, but there was an edge to it. "Good tidings, or bad, depending on the angle you look at it from. This is the bad. She writes that she was bewitched, that we are all sorcerers and necromancers of the most evil sort. Doll, you see, told Felicity that Grandmother was in the kitchen, stirring something into that accursed custard and saying a spell, with young Daisy at her side. Beyond Felicity's testimony, she now has a witness. That is all one needs, under law, to bring charges of witchcraft."

"Will she, do you think?" Ivy asked, her hands tightening on Julian's shoulder.

"She may. She will either attempt to reach her father in London, or stay near and present her case to the court. Probably she will seek her father's advice."

"After last night, I'm not sure," Ivy said. "I get

the impression that Felicity is a lot more inde-
pendent than we've given her credit for."

"God knows. And Doll has gone with her,
which makes me suspect she'll testify. If that is
the case, we'll find out soon enough."

"And then?" Ivy asked, trying not to think
about witch trials. Women were hanged, and
burned.

"We simply keep the gates locked, and if they
attempt to make an arrest, we escape."

"Escape to where?"

"That remains to be seen. Out of England, that
is certain. But cheer yourself," Julian said, giving her a squeeze. "There is still the good news."

"I can't imagine what," Ivy said. The idea of
leaving England was terrifying. As unpredictable and dangerous as life at Wythecombe might
be, it had begun to feel like home.

"Felicity writes me this. She will not marry me
under any circumstances, not even if she is
beaten or imprisoned. On one hand, it puts me
in a bad situation. Astley is sure to be furious.
On the other hand, we shall likely have to flee
anyway, so there is no great loss."

"Only Wythecombe," Ivy said softly. She
looked up at the great stone towers, dark and
powerful against the blue sky, watching over the
endless sea.

"Only Wythecombe." Julian's voice was low
and sad, and he pulled Ivy closer, resting his
chin on the top of her head. "Why, Ivy," he exclaimed suddenly, "what a long face. Sometimes

I think that you love this old heap of stones as much as I do."

"I do love it," Ivy said. "I think it's the most beautiful place in the world. It makes me sick to think of losing it, and having it fall to ruin."

Julian kissed the top of her head. "I doubt that. Wythecombe is built of stouter stuff than that. And, if you're correct, we have only ten years until the monarchy is restored. If I live ten more years, which I intend to, I have no doubt that all my holdings will be restored. I shall probably get a nice new title as well."

"Ten years is a long time."

"Come, think of it as an adventure," Julian urged. "True, living abroad as an impoverished exile is not what I'd planned, but we shall have to make the best of it. And think, Ivy: you could return to England as a countess, at least. Would that please you?"

Ivy's heart stood still for a long moment. She wondered if she had misunderstood.

"What do you mean, Julian?"

"What do you think I mean? We shall be married, of course, as soon as we can. If I must risk all, then I intend to please myself in the bargain. I considered sending you safely off home to Seetle—"

"Seattle," Ivy said, without thinking.

"You'd be safe there, no risk of arrest, no crossing channels in leaking boats, no noble but miserable poverty. But then I decided that I would be quite lonely, and that the best thing

351

for all concerned was for you to marry me."

"Did you think of consulting me?" Ivy asked. "Did you, Julian? Or did you just decide this, and now I'm being informed? You're asking me to give up everything, everything I've worked my whole life to build. It frightens me, Julian."

"I thought about it. I spoke to Grandmother. Aye, we live in a dangerous world, but so do you, Ivy. Grandmother has told me of the times you live in. There are guns, and robbers, and there are still diseases. You could be hit by a car, or an airplane could fall on your head, or you could step in a mine field—"

"Oh, Julian! A mine field? They just don't lay them around anywhere!"

"Don't be contentious; you know what I mean. The world is dangerous. It always has been, and always will be. There are always risks."

"But," Ivy answered, "I would like to be the one to decide what risks I'm going to take. I feel like I'm just standing still, and things are happening, and I have no control over my own life anymore."

"Do you know," Julian said, lifting her chin with a gentle hand, "I had imagined this very differently. I thought that you would be quite happy, and fall into my arms. Somehow I seem to have bungled things. Let me try this again."

He cleared his throat and shook his hair back from his face.

"You set such a damned high value on the matter of choice," he said. "It is really an awkward thing, when you think about it. Life is so much easier when women simply defer to men."

"Easier for men," Ivy agreed, wondering if he was joking or not. He might be. His eyes sparkled with mischief; a hint of a dimple showed at the corner of his mouth.

"I have been laying plans all night," he said. "My first plan was simply to tell you what to do, and have you do it. That would be the easiest. My second plan, which is not as effective, involves risk. Also, it involves humbling myself, which I don't care for."

Ivy tried not to smile. "It's not something I think you'd be good at, Julian."

"You leave me no choice, you difficult creature. But since you insist, let's have done with it." He reached into his doublet and brought out a piece of paper, folded and sealed with wax.

"Here. This is my gift to you, Ivy, and evidence of the trust I place in you."

Ivy took the paper in her hand and looked at it.

"I know that I am asking much, and I know full well the comforts and safety I am asking you to sacrifice. True, I say I love you, and I do. I would not ask you to share my fate if I did not." He drew a deep breath and covered her hand with his own.

"On that paper, Ivy, is written the location where I have hidden that damnable book. It is your escape, if you will, should you decide not to cast your fortune with mine. I ask, though, that you not share this information with anyone else. My grandmother's writing is in that book. It would mean her death, if she were to be found with it. If you use it, take it with you."

Ivy stared at the piece of paper. There it was. She had the means to leave, to go home. It was that simple.

"But consider," Julian said softly, "I pray you, consider that I love you. And you have said that you love me as well. I would not care to live my life as my grandmother has, always aching for a love that will never return. Always, I would be wondering where you were, and what I might have done differently. It is a pain that I would not like to live with."

Ivy felt tears sting at her eyes. "Do you mean that, Julian?"

"With all my heart. There would not be a day of my life that I would not think of you, and long for you. I had hoped that you would feel the same."

Ivy stood, still and silent, watching the streaks of white clouds blowing off the sea. From high up here on the battlements, it was like looking off the edge of the world.

Julian reached out and closed her hand over the paper tightly.

"I know I'm asking much," he said. "You need not answer right away."

They stood there, hands clasped, listening to the wind and the sea, until they heard Susanna's voice below in the courtyard.

She was laughing, leading Julian's horse. Daisy sat astride it, clutching the saddle with both hands. She was laughing her silent laugh, and sitting proud and tall in the saddle.

"Good God," Julian said, "I hope Susanna had the sense to tie her in."

He leaned over the battlements. "What horse thieves are these?" he called, and Daisy's face creased with smiles as she looked up at him.

"Damn, she looks proud of herself," Julian remarked, smiling at Ivy. "It is good to see, isn't it?"

Ivy laid her hand on his arm. "You're a good man, Julian," she said softly. "And thank you for that. You never had to take Daisy in, or care for her, but you do. For that matter, you could have turned me out, but you didn't."

"I could never have turned you out," he admitted. "I'm kicking myself right now for giving you that damnable paper."

Ivy hesitated for a moment. She looked at Julian, at the way the wind tossed his dark hair around his face, and the way his gray eyes seemed to take their color from the very stones of the castle.

"Thank you for it, though," she said. "Thank you for letting me choose, and for letting it be my decision."

"I'm damned sorry I did," he said, his voice studiously light, "because I think I know what your answer is to be."

"That," Ivy answered, "is part of your problem,

Julian. You simply think that you know everything."

She looked down at the paper, heavy and cream-colored, already creased from being held so tightly.

For a moment, she imagined tearing it into a million pieces, tossing them into the air, and watching as they fluttered away on the breeze.

She couldn't.

"I don't know what to do," she admitted. "So many times, Julian, I thought that if I had the means, I'd go without another thought. And now that I can, I'm not sure I want to."

Julian said nothing for a while. "Are you sure," he asked at last, "that there is nobody else?"

"Not a soul, Julian. I really don't even have close friends. Well, Winston, I guess. I'd miss him."

"And who is Winston?"

"For heaven's sake, Julian. He runs the gallery across the street, and he must be about Margaret's age. He's just a friend. But it's more than that, Julian. It would mean giving up everything I've worked for, all my dreams. Home might not be exciting, Julian, but it's safe. I know what to expect."

"I did not take thee for a coward, Ivy," he commented. "Is your love such a pale thing that you would sacrifice it so easily?"

"It's not easy," Ivy argued. "If it were easy, my decision would have been made. You don't understand, Julian. I've never fit in, not really, not

356

anywhere. And I worked hard to make a place for myself in the world. It's all I have. If I stayed here, what then? I belong less in this world than I do in my own."

"What utter drivel," Julian remarked. "You belong at Wythecombe. I am sure of it. Grandmother thinks so, and Susanna as well, and so do I. Do you know, Ivy, how many times I might have been married by now, if not for Wythecombe? But I will not leave the place, and no woman wants to give up her fashionable city life, or the petty intrigues and politics of court life. But you, I thought you were different. I see the way you look at the old place, as decrepit as it is. The same way you look at the sea, and the countryside. You see the beauty of it, the enchantment of it. I thought that you felt the same way I did."

"It's the most beautiful place in the world," Ivy admitted.

"And you belong here," Julian insisted. "With me. I am certain of it. I will not lie to you, Ivy. These are bad times. If we have to leave for the continent, I cannot answer for our safety. The idea of crossing the channel with three women and an ill child in a leaky little boat . . . well, it's risky, at best. And when this is over, God only knows what we will have to return to. We will all be risking our lives."

Ivy stared out at the sea, trying to imagine floating away into the winter winds, out into the unknown.

Julian's hands caressed her shoulders. "I know. I'm asking you to gamble your very life in the hopes that fortune will turn. Don't give me your answer yet. Don't decide until the time we leave. Till then, let us be happy together. And when the time comes, you will either cast your lot with me, or say farewell."

He held Ivy tightly against him, and they stood together for a long time, looking out to sea, and wondering what the future would hold.

"I am too old for this," Margaret said. "I never thought to leave Wythecombe."

She stood in the dining room, watching as Ivy and Susanna took down the tapestry of the hunting party and laid it flat on the floor. Margaret did look old, Ivy realized. Ever since Julian had told them that they must be ready to go, a melancholy seemed to have settled over her. Her eyes misted over as she watched them work, packing and storing whatever could not be carried with them.

"We shall be back," Susanna assured her. "It isn't forever."

"I feel as if it is," Margaret answered softly. "Each time something is packed, I think, 'this is the last time I shall see this.' Ten years is nothing to a young woman. It flies by, and you are still young. But at my age, I may not have ten years. I know you hate me to say it, but it is true. I should be greeting my great-grandchildren and sitting by my fire."

"You will," Ivy said. "You have to believe it, Margaret. We don't have a choice."

"No, we don't. Forgive me an old woman's melancholy. 'Tis a mood, I'm sure, nothing more." She sat down, easing her back into a chair, and watched as Ivy and Susanna began rolling the great tapestry. Another piece of her life to be bundled up and hidden away.

"As to the great-grandchildren," Susanna added, "I'm sure they will not be long in coming. We shall leave that to Ivy and Julian, and I'm sure that there will be obnoxious little Ramsdens running about the place in no time."

Ivy blushed, and Margaret laughed a little.

Good, Ivy thought. She was worried about Margaret. Travel, Ivy knew, would be both uncomfortable and dangerous, and she wondered if Margaret was strong enough to tolerate the trip across the channel.

She and Susanna rolled the tapestry into a long bundle and tied it with strips of canvas.

"Into the priest's hole," Ivy announced.

"Is there still room?" Julian asked, coming into the room. He went immediately to Ivy, squeezing her shoulders in a quick hug and kissing her full on the mouth.

"There they go again," Susanna said, rolling her eyes. "Have you no shame, Julian?"

"None at all," he admitted cheerfully.

"The young these days," Margaret said, but she smiled as she spoke.

"I've come to take your slave driver away," Julian said. "That should make you happy, Susanna."

"Away to where?" Ivy asked, wiping her dusty hands on her gown. "There's so much to do, Julian. . . ."

"It can wait. We need to speak, and alone, thank you. Leave off with this work and come along."

"Please," Ivy reminded him.

"Damn, you're difficult. Please, then."

Ivy smiled, satisfied. She followed Julian from the room and out into the great hall.

As soon as they were alone, he took her into his arms and kissed her again, with a hard, fierce urgency.

Ivy gave herself up to it, loving the way his body felt against hers, the way he touched her hair, the way his mouth fit over hers.

"You make me dizzy," she said, when their lips parted.

"Good. It's my intention to make you dizzy. Eventually you will lose all your good sense and allow me to make your decisions for you." He kissed her neck as he spoke, and his breath was hot against her throat.

"What an insidious plot," Ivy murmured. "Is that why you dragged me out here?"

"No, but it's a damned fine idea. Shall we go back to bed?"

Ivy laughed. "Again?"

She had given up her own room, and now slept in Julian's, in the great carved, curtained bed with the ram's heads carved into the spiraling posts. Each night, he drew the dark blue bed curtains, and she lost all thought of the world beyond.

The winter breezes stirred the curtains from without, but inside they were warm, heated by their desire. They made love over and over again, and slept in each other's arms, and woke up to make love again. Sometimes they stayed up until the small hours of the morning, just talking. Julian told Ivy about growing up at Wythecombe, of how he had dreamed of being a great soldier, and organized the village children into troops, and how they built camps on the wooded hillside, and ran screaming across the battlements. He told her of going to London as a young man, and his friend Christopher, and their escapades in the alehouses and gambling dens.

Ivy told him of the twentieth century, about bank machines and airplanes and electricity. She told him about growing up in Nevada, and moving to Seattle.

By silent, mutual agreement, they spoke of nothing unpleasant, of the impending escape or Margaret's unhappiness. For a few days, Ivy allowed herself to pretend that they were safe in their little world, and that it would always be like this. She never touched the folded paper Julian had given her. It sat unopened in the enameled box he had given her.

"I have bad news," Julian said.

Alarmed, Ivy stared up at him.

"Pray, don't fret. It is this. I must go to London and leave you here for a few days."

"Why?" Ivy clung to his shoulders. The dream world they had been living in faded.

"Money. There is no way around it. If we are to live as refugees, we must have funds. My friend Christopher is in London, and I must ask him to advance me money. I would rather not go—it's dangerous, and I don't know what damage Felicity may have caused. But I won't tarry. I shall ride quickly and come straight back, and we will take our leave on that night. Until then, stay here. Leave the gates barred, and admit nobody."

Ivy nodded.

"Make sure that anything of value is hidden, and that everyone is ready to leave." He hesitated, and then took her chin with a gentle touch, tipping her face back. His eyes were solemn, the color of the winter sea.

"I have a gift for you," he said. He took from his pocket a bracelet, a wide copper cuff.

Ivy took it, turning it in her hands. It was old, older than anything she had ever held. The gleaming surface was covered with elaborate, runic markings, Celtic swirls and knots. It was probably pre-Christian.

"Here," Julian said, and slipped it over her wrist. "It suits you. The same color as your hair, almost."

"Where did it come from?" Ivy turned her

wrist, which looked very small beneath the wide cuff, admiring the mysterious-looking designs.

"Nobody knows," Julian said. "There are two of them, actually. Identical. One is for Susanna, the other for you. My mother wore one, I remember, and Grandmother did as well. If you look in the painting in the dining hall, you can see that Susanna of Denbeigh is wearing them. They just show beneath the edges of her sleeves."

Ivy traced the design with her finger. The copper felt warm and almost magical.

"I can't take this, Julian. It belongs to your family."

"You ridiculous thing, you are part of my family," he said softly, and his hand covered Ivy's. "I told you you belonged here, and I mean it. This is simply a token. Even if you leave, Ivy, keep this with you, to always remind you of us, and Wythecombe. The time is almost here when you must give me your answer. I know that I may lose you, but for some reason, I think I could bear it a little more easily if you were to take part of us with you. If you wear this, I would feel bound to you across time. Even if I never see you again in this life."

Ivy stared at the bracelet. She imagined going home, back to the ritual of her former life. She would get up each morning, and shower, and dress in her tasteful wools and cashmeres, and go to work each day. She would go to parties and out to lunch and to auctions and estate sales, and every day, look at the gleaming copper on her wrist, and think of Julian.

Tears stung her eyes.

"I have a present for you too, Julian," she said.

"Have you? Is it a new pen?" Julian had appropriated Margaret's souvenir ink pen and run it dry within a week.

"No, better than that. Come on."

Ivy led the way from the great hall to Julian's bedchamber. He followed silently and watched as she crossed the room and opened the enameled box with the pictures of the saints.

Inside lay the fateful paper, the wax seal still unbroken.

Ivy held it for a minute and then, without pausing, turned to the fireplace and threw it in.

The edges turned black, curled up, and flamed. The wax seal sputtered and melted, and then the paper burst into flame.

Ivy looked at Julian, his face reflecting the golden light of the burning letter. He seemed shocked.

"There," she said. "I don't want the damned book. I don't want the spell, I don't want to leave. Where you go, I go. Forever, if you like."

He stared at her, and then a brilliant smile broke across his face, lighting his eyes with a soft glow. He held open his arms. "Come here," he demanded.

Ivy went, not bothering to tell him that he was

giving orders again. There would be years to break him of the habit.

"I love thee," he murmured against her hair.

The letter in the fire turned to ash as they kissed, but neither of them noticed as the heat of their desire flickered and flamed.

Ivy felt a freedom, a liberation from the uncertainty that had eaten at her for days. She had cast her lot with Julian's, and from this moment on, her fate would be intertwined with his, like the Celtic knots on the copper bracelet.

Chapter Ninteen

"I am depending on you," Julian said, "to keep Susanna and Grandmother safe. Whatever happens, none of you are to leave. Bar the gates behind me, and don't open them until I return."

The sky above them was just beginning to lighten to a heavy gray. The sound of the sea seemed closer than usual in the silence of the early morning. The fog was thick, covering the walls and stones of the courtyard with a sheen of wetness. The tops of the towers disappeared into the thick clouds.

It looked like a ghost castle, silent and deserted, and Ivy shivered, clinging to Julian's shoulders. "I wish you weren't going," she said, "or that I was going with you."

"It will only be for a few days," he said, holding

her close. "You'll be safe here."

Ivy closed her eyes, pressing her cheek against the soft, worn velvet of his doublet, savoring the sound of his heartbeat, the scent of his skin, the feeling of his hands in her hair. Safe. This was where she felt safe, locked in his arms.

Beside them, Bacchus stamped his hooves on the ground and nickered, impatient to begin the journey after his days of confinement.

Julian kissed her, slowly and tenderly.

"If I don't leave now, I shall have to take you back to bed," he murmured.

Ivy attempted a brave smile, but it felt shaky. "What a terrible threat."

"Frightened, are you? Just wait till I return."

They walked together toward the gatehouse, and Julian lifted the great oak beam that barred the gates. "Can you manage to get it back on by yourself?" he asked, lifting it aside.

Ivy nodded. "I'm stronger than I look."

He swung the gates open and stood for a minute, looking out into the fog.

"Nobody is to enter or leave," he said for the hundredth time.

"I wish you didn't have to go," she said for the thousandth.

They stood silently, hands clasped, unwilling to say good-bye.

"I love thee," Julian said abruptly, his hand tightening over hers.

"I love you," she echoed, and it seemed after that there was nothing more to say.

He turned and climbed onto his horse. "God keep thee, Ivy."

She stood in the open gates and watched as he rode away into the sea-scented fog. Even after he disappeared into the mist, she stood there, listening to the sound of Bacchus's hooves striking the dirt road, until that sound, too, was swallowed by the fog.

She pushed the ancient wooden doors closed and struggled with the beam as she barred them. It was heavier than it looked, but she managed to drop it into its iron brackets, where it fell with a hollow thud.

The sound was as heavy as her heart, and her shoulders drooped as she turned back to the sleeping castle.

"Hard work," Ivy told Susanna, "is the best cure for boredom."

Susanna made a disagreeable face. "Trust you," she said. "But I would rather sit by the fire and play my lute."

The great hall was almost empty. Banners and tapestries, cushions and carpets had all been bundled off and carried to the priest's hole in the chapel. The hall was as empty as it had been the day Ivy arrived.

"What do you suppose France is like?" Susanna asked, brightening at the idea. "I hear that it is warm there."

"I've never been," Ivy admitted. Only Susanna seemed to be looking forward to their exile. She thought of it as a great adventure, and chattered about it incessantly.

Everything was ready, waiting for Julian's return. The priest's hole was almost crammed full of the few treasures Wythecombe still owned, and the rooms were cold and empty. Only Margaret's rooms were still comfortable, and it was there that Daisy, Susanna, and Ivy spent most of their time. It was easier, Ivy pointed out, to keep only one fire burning, and so it was there that they took their meals. At night Susanna and Ivy and Daisy bedded down on the floor there.

The truth was, Ivy couldn't bear to sleep alone in Julian's bed. The sheets and pillows smelled of his skin, and the room seemed empty without him. His boots and breeches and shirts lay around where he had thrown them, as if he had just walked out the door.

Ivy thought that she might feel better if she cleaned up, and tidily arranged his clothes in the cupboard. It made her feel worse, as if he had left forever. Feeling a little silly, she threw them back around the room.

After the first night alone in the bed, she announced that they should all sleep in the same room, to conserve firewood.

Their clothes were bundled and packed into small chests and bags, the rooms were emptied and cleared of any valuables, and all that remained to do was wait for Julian.

Margaret had found an old cape that she had once worn, and was remaking it for Daisy, lining the hood with soft fur, and taking neat, patient stitches in the rose-colored wool. She sighed as she worked, and her eyes were sorrowful.

She was working on it today, when Ivy and Susanna went to find her. Daisy sat at her feet, playing with her rabbit, who sniffed with interest when they came into the room.

"A miracle has happened," Susanna announced, going to kiss her grandmother's cheek.

Margaret looked up, hope springing into her eyes. "Is Julian back?"

"No, a greater miracle than that. Ivy has run out of work for me to do. I thought the day would never come."

"I might think of something else, if you push it," Ivy said, settling herself onto the floor.

"And to think I've always longed for a sister," Susanna remarked. "Now that I have one, I should like to send her back." She smiled as she spoke, and her gray eyes, so like Julian's, sparkled at Ivy.

A sister. The words surprised Ivy, and warmed her. She was part of a family. If only Julian would come back, she would be perfectly happy.

"It can't be much longer," she said aloud.

"No, it shouldn't be," Susanna agreed, following Ivy's train of thought with ease. "Then you can calm down and quit your slave driving."

To Ivy's shock, Margaret suddenly dropped her fabric onto the floor and covered her face with her hands.

"I cannot bear it," she said, and her voice quavered.

"What?" Susanna cried, sitting up straight, her eyes wide with alarm. "Are you ill?"

Margaret took a deep breath and shook her head. "No," she whispered. "I . . . I don't want to say it."

"What's wrong?" Ivy asked, reaching out to take Margaret's hand.

Margaret looked from Ivy to Susanna, and tears shone in her dark eyes. "It's a feeling," she answered at last. "I have tried to ignore it, but it will not leave me. I'm certain I shall never see Julian again."

A chill raced down Ivy's spine, and a sickening feeling clutched at her heart. "You're wrong," she said automatically. "You must be."

Margaret shook her head, despair in her eyes. "No," she said. "No, I'm not. I am sure of it. I will never see France, and I will never see my great-grandchildren, and I will never see Julian again."

"Don't say such things," Susanna cried. "Don't! You are wrong, you must be. Julian will be home, and everything will be fine."

Daisy sat silent on the floor, her wide blue eyes looking at the old woman.

Margaret managed a shaky smile. "Shame on me," she said, "for giving in to an old woman's fancies. I'm frightening my little sweetheart, for no good reason."

"You're frightening me as well," Ivy said,

squeezing Margaret's hand anxiously.

"Oh, my dear, I am so sorry. Forgive me, please." Margaret dabbed at her eyes. "I am just tired, I think, and worried. It is so hard, seeing the place empty, feeling as if my life has been hidden away, and wondering what will come next. I'm an old woman, I fear, and not as able to deal with change as the young."

She picked up the fallen fabric at her feet, but didn't take the needle into her fingers.

Susanna and Ivy exchanged worried looks.

"Like as not," Susanna said hastily, "it is our incessant company that's got the better of your nerves. I do chatter, and Ivy has been pacing the room for six days now. Why don't you rest, and Ivy and I shall take Daisy out for some fresh air."

"Has it stopped raining?" Margaret asked, with a worried look at Daisy.

"If we waited for it to stop raining," Susanna observed, "we should none of us ever leave the keep. Marry, Grandmam, a little rain won't hurt us. And I think you need the quiet. We shall saddle up Buttercup, and let Daisy ride her round the courtyard."

Daisy smiled at that. Next to reading and drawing, she liked riding better than anything in the world.

"Will you be all right?" Ivy asked, still frightened.

Margaret waved her hand with a dismissive gesture. "Aye, of course. I pray thee, Ivy, don't worry."

But Ivy was worried, and as she and Susanna led Daisy from the room, she said a quick, fervent prayer that Julian would come that day.

"What a horsewoman you are, Daisy," Susanna declared. "I vow, you are a better rider than Ivy."

That made Daisy laugh. She knew that it could not be true, that she could do something as well as Ivy. Ivy was too clever. Ivy could read, and fix broken things, and sing songs, and draw funny pictures. But Susanna and Ivy praised everything that Daisy did.

Yesterday, for example, she had tried to draw, like Ivy did. She had made a castle, which she meant to look like Wythecombe. It did not, really. The lines were wrong, and the pen splattered ink in dark blobs. And she had drawn herself, and Ivy and Julian and Susanna and Margaret, looking out the windows, smiling. She had tried to draw the village below, and the place of fallen walls, and a horse. None of it looked right, to her eyes.

But Ivy had exclaimed over it, and Margaret had propped it up on a table, saying that she wanted to look at it every day.

Margaret knew what each drawing was. That was the wondrous thing about Lady Margaret. Sometimes she seemed to know things without being told. "Look," she told Susanna, when she showed her the picture, "Here we are, and there is the village, and there is the old abbey. What a keen eye our Daisy has."

Riding the horse around the courtyard, with Ivy and Susanna praising her, Daisy began to wonder if her mother had been wrong, if all the Mean People in the village had been wrong.

She was not bad. She was not stupid. She was clever; she was learning to read. She had a keen eye. She had a rabbit, and a beautiful blue dress with lace like spider's webs, only better. She was going to have a hooded cape, like the one Ivy wore, only rose-colored, instead of autumn-colored. Every single day, Ivy braided her hair, and tied ribbons in it, and told her how pretty she was.

These things could not happen to someone who was bad, Daisy reasoned.

Sometimes, lying in her soft bed, with her warm blankets and her bunny next to her, she thought of the village. Sometimes she dreamed that she went back there, riding Julian's big black horse, and wearing her fine blue dress. In her dreams, she could speak, and she would taunt the other children, as they had once taunted her. They would look with wonder at her horse, and the lace on her dress, and they were sorry.

Sometimes, the dreams were bad. The gray-haired man who took her mother would be there, and he would chase Daisy, and in her dreams her horse could not run fast or far enough to evade him. She would think she had lost him, but then there he was again.

When she woke up from dreams like that, she would cry. Even though she cried without sound, Lady Margaret always seemed to know that she was awake, and would come to her, stroking her hair and holding her until the fear went away.

Daisy tried not to think about those dreams, or the village. She was safe here, with the great wooden gates closed, and Ivy and Susanna leading her around and around on the gentle horse.

"Shall we stop?" Ivy asked. "Daisy's looking tired."

"Aye, we should," Susanna said, looking up at Daisy. "Her balance falters after a while."

Daisy would have liked to have kept going, but she sat quietly while they untied the sash from her waist and helped her down.

Susanna led the mare back toward the stable, and Ivy took Daisy's hand and led her back toward the keep.

"What a fine rider you are," she said. "One day we'll ride through the forests and down on the beach. Won't that be exciting?"

Daisy smiled.

"One day," Ivy went on, "we'll have enough money to buy you your own pony. You'll feel safer on that, I think. And then—" She broke off suddenly, turning back to the gates.

"Do you hear that?" she asked. Daisy liked that, the way that Ivy asked her questions, as if she expected her to answer.

Daisy listened. Someone was coming up the

road to the castle. It was a way off, but she could hear the faint sound of horses.

"Julian," Ivy whispered, and her face was rosy, and her brown eyes glowed. "It must be. Let's look."

"Where are you going?" Susanna called, returning from the stables.

"Someone's coming up the road. It must be Julian." Ivy's hand was tight on Daisy's, her voice bright with excitement.

"Is it?" Susanna asked, frowning. "That was passing quick. I didn't expect him back for three more days, at least."

Ivy was going toward the watchtower quickly, so quickly that Daisy stumbled.

"Shame on me," Ivy said, and scooped Daisy into her arms. "Hey, are you getting heavy," she added.

"Aye, she is," Susanna agreed. " 'Tis a wonder what food will do."

They climbed the stairs of the dark gatehouse, their voices hollow and echoing in the emptiness. Daisy wished Ivy would not squeeze her so tightly.

"There," Ivy said when they reached the top stair, setting her down quickly and leaning out the narrow window.

Daisy had a keen eye. She knew the moment Ivy looked out that it was not Julian coming home to them. Ivy's shoulders grew stiff, and the happy laughter stopped immediately.

"Who is it?" Susanna asked.

The horses hooves were coming closer. It was not one horse, Daisy could tell. There were four, or maybe more.

Susanna crowded next to Ivy, looking out the narrow window, draping a hand on Ivy's shoulder.

Daisy shivered. It was dark in the tower, and cold. She didn't like the smell. There was no glass over these windows to block the wind out.

"Who are they?" Ivy asked.

Daisy sidled in between them, and Ivy's hand rested on the top of her hair, but it was an absent touch.

"I don't know," Susanna said, frowning.

Daisy looked up at them, anxious and worried, but neither woman looked at her.

"What if something's happened to Julian?" Ivy's voice shook.

"I would have known," Susanna said, speaking quickly. "I would have known."

Daisy was frightened. She tugged at Ivy's dark green sleeve.

"Do you want to see?" Ivy asked, but the smile she gave was not a real smile. She picked Daisy up and let her look out the window.

Daisy could count them then, the men coming up the hill, crossing the field that led to the castle. One, two, three, four, five, six, seven. Seven men, seven horses. They wore clothes of dark gray and black and brown, like the colors of winter.

"That's the mayor in front," Susanna exclaimed suddenly, "riding the chestnut with the white blaze. Who is that with him?"

Daisy looked, and knew. She knew his black hat with the high crown, knew the gray hair. If he came closer, she would see his cold eyes and sharp chin.

She closed her eyes, and wished, wished with all her might, but when she opened her eyes, he was still there, bringing the bad men. Here, to her castle.

"Run away," she wanted to say, but her throat hurt. It felt like a rock was there, or a fist, growing and tightening. The floor dropped away, and came back, and her heart pounded like the coming hooves.

"What can they want?" Ivy asked, and her arm was tight around Daisy's shoulder.

"Whatever it is, they cannot have it," Susanna said, sounding more cross than frightened. "They can turn around and go home. Julian said not to open the gates, and so we shall not."

It was like a bad dream, one that Daisy couldn't stop. They had found her, even though she was far away over the moors and down the sea and over the tumbling brooks. They had found her, and they would take sweet Ivy and Susanna and Margaret, and they would make them dead, and Julian would not come in time to help them.

Daisy closed her eyes so tightly that it hurt. The fear in her grew and grew, like something alive, like an animal clawing and fighting to get out. It pushed and fought, shoving her stomach into her heart, and tight against her throat, until she thought it might tear her in two.

"What can they want?" she heard Ivy say, from very far away, and Daisy saw the rope around her mother's neck, rough and dark against the pretty hair, she heard the solid thump of wood, the air whistling past, and the snap of the slender neck.

The thing in Daisy's throat came out with a raw, horrible explosion. It was words.

"Nooou!" she screamed, twisting away and pulling at Ivy and Susanna. "No! No! No!"

"God have mercy," Susanna cried, and Ivy was saying her name, "Daisy, Daisy," over and over again. They were holding her, rocking her, and talking back and forth over her head in high, frightened voices. Daisy was blind with fear, or tears. The bad man was coming, like he came in her dreams, and there was nothing she could do.

"Bad," Daisy sobbed, "Oh, bad, bad." And there was nothing to do but hide her face against Ivy's soft, fire-colored curls and cry.

Gradually, their voices started to make sense. They told her not to be afraid, that they would not let anyone hurt her, that everything was going to be all right.

Daisy clutched at Ivy, shaking, wishing that the sounds of the horses would go away.

"Stand firm," Susanna said, "and don't let them frighten you." Her words were brave, but there was no laughter in her pretty voice.

"Who are they?" Ivy asked. "What will they do, Susanna?"

"Why, we shall soon find out," Susanna said, tossing her dark curls. "As to who they are, they are accursed monsters, the lot of them. And that one in front, with the Puritan's garb? Look well at him, Ivy, for that, I'd swear, is the most evil man in all England. Unless I'm dead wrong, that is Josiah Feake, witch-hunter general."

And Daisy gave a long, pained shudder as she heard the name of the man who had killed her mother. She clung tightly to Ivy's skirts. She would not let Ivy go.

"Don't be afraid," Ivy said, but Daisy was horribly afraid. She buried her face in Ivy's waist, hiding beneath the autumn-colored cloak as she listened to the horses come to the gate.

Ivy held the frightened child tight, and she and Susanna exchanged silent glances. Susanna's eyes were unreadable, like smooth gray silk.

"She spoke," Ivy said. "She spoke, Susanna."

Susanna gave a quick, humorless smile. "Aye, she did. But I would rather she'd have said, 'Look, the tinkers are coming' Or the brewer, or anybody."

"What do we do?" Ivy asked, keeping her voice low. She could hear the low voices of the men beneath them, and was grateful for the stout gates, the thick oak beam that stood between them.

"Since we can't pour boiling oil on their

heads," Susanna said, "we shall have to brazen it out. Take heart, Ivy."

Ivy jumped at the sound of them banging on the gate, the solid, hard sound of the iron ring striking the wood.

"Margaret Ramsden," called a voice. "Margaret Ramsden, open the gates."

Ivy could feel Daisy's heart racing. Despite her own fear, she gave the child a reassuring squeeze. Julian, she thought, oh, Julian, come home.

"Margaret Ramsden," shouted the voice again, "we demand that you open the gates."

Susanna tossed her dark curls and drew a deep breath. "Here we go," she whispered to Ivy. The girl lifted her chin and leaned out the narrow window of the gatehouse tower.

"What rudeness is this?" she demanded.

Ivy marveled at her clear, strong voice. Only her fingers, clenched into pale fists on the stone sill, betrayed her fear.

"Susanna Ramsden, open the gates."

Ivy moved to a narrow slit in the wall, once used by archers. Daisy clung to her, impeding her progress.

Peering out, she could see the assembled men. She thought she recognized two or three from the day she and Susanna had stopped at the inn. But the one that commanded her attention was the man on a sturdy gray-and-white-spotted horse. He was dressed in black from hat to boots, except for a solid white collar and neck-cloth.

His face was gaunt, framed by coarse, close-cropped gray hair. It was a face of sharp, unforgiving angles, with deep lines by his tight mouth. He was pale, a colorless man. Only his eyes had life. They were burning, hard eyes. The eyes of a fanatic.

"I simply cannot open the gates," Susanna informed them. "My brother has expressly forbidden it, and being an obedient girl, I will not defy him."

The man on the chestnut mare, a stout, sturdy man in brown, frowned at her. "Do not fence words with us, Susanna Ramsden. Your brother has no say in this. We have a warrant, as set forth by the laws of England. Open the gates."

"Nonsense," Susanna retorted. "Come, my lord mayor, there are no criminals within these walls."

"There are two!" the mayor called back, and Ivy could see the agitated flush that stole over his solid face. "We have taken depositions, we have witnesses. By law, you must admit us."

"I can't," Susanna repeated. "Julian has forbidden it."

"No man is above the laws of the country." It was the man in black who spoke. He had a voice like thunder, strong and hard. "Obey God, and honor the king, sayeth the Good Book. Would you defy the words of your Lord, woman?"

"The king is dead," Susanna snapped. "And

my brother has authority over me. I will not defy him."

"Susanna Ramsden, do you dare to defy the law of the Commonwealth of England?"

Susanna hesitated, and Ivy could tell that she was treading dangerous ground.

"How do I know you really have a warrant?" she demanded.

The mayor held up a paper.

"I can't read it from here," Susanna exclaimed. "Marry, that could say anything, or nothing at all. It could be a penny ballad sheet, for all I know. Now pray thee, go home, and do not tempt me to defy my brother in his absence."

The gaunt man in black turned to his companions. "Do you hear," he asked, "how she defies you, and attempts to turn your heads with her pretty voice? 'The lips of a strange woman drop as an honeycomb, and her mouth is smoother than oil: but her end is as bitter as wormwood, and as sharp as a two-edged sword. Her feet go down to death, her steps take hold on hell.' So she says the word of God; do not let yourselves be deceived."

"Mercy," said Susanna. " 'Tis a harsh condemnation, sir."

"We have a warrant," the mayor cried out. "A warrant for the arrest of Margaret Ramsden, and the child Daisy, born of the condemned witch Bess of Westford. Open the gates, Susanna Ramsden, and deliver them to us, and you will not be harmed."

383

"And if I do not?" Susanna asked.

Ivy thought she might be sick. She thought of gentle Margaret, sitting unaware in her cozy rooms, sewing Daisy's warm new cape. And Daisy—surely they could not arrest a child of that age!

"They cannot," she whispered to Susanna. "Susanna, they can't arrest a child."

Susanna leaned back from the window. "Tell that to old Mother Demdike, of Pendle," she murmured. "For as well as taking the old woman, they took her grandchildren. Allison, Janet, and James. The oldest one was ten, I believe. All hanged."

"Listen to me, Susanna Ramsden," called the gaunt man with the fiery eyes. "I am Josiah Feake, witch-hunter general, and I have much knowledge of these matters. If, indeed, these women are innocent, you have nothing to fear. They are entitled to a trial by jury. God will not let innocents perish unjustly. His hand will stay the jury."

Susanna's cheeks flushed brilliant red, and her tilted eyes darkened. " 'Tis not God I fear, but you, Josiah Feake, and those who listen to your evil prattle. Hear me well. I shall not open the gates to you, not today or ever. Get yourself away from this place, and keep away."

"Is that your final word?" called the mayor.

"It is." Susanna's mouth was set in a tight line.

The men turned away and conferred. Ivy held Daisy tightly, rocking her stiff, trembling body back and forth. And then she saw one of the men lifting a small keg from his horse and carrying it to the gates.

"Damn," Susanna whispered. "Oh, no. Oh, Ivy."

"What is it?" Ivy asked, her voice shaking. "Susanna, what is it?"

"It is gunpowder," the girl replied, and her voice was grim. "They will blast those gates off their hinges, Ivy, and we are damned."

Chapter Twenty

Susanna and Ivy stood, staring at each other for what seemed an eternity. Daisy, clinging to Ivy's skirts, shook violently.

"Hide her!" Susanna cried, "Hide her, quickly. I'll get Grandmother. Don't come out until Julian or I get you."

Ivy didn't need to be told twice. She scooped Daisy up in her arms and raced down the spiral staircase. Her skirts tangled around her knees, and she pulled them up as best she could. Daisy's arms were tight around her shoulders, and her feet banged against Ivy's legs as they ran.

"Hurry," Susanna urged.

Ivy's throat was too tight to answer. She raced across the slick stones of the courtyard, hardly aware of the heavy child in her arms, seeing only the chapel door.

As she pushed open the heavy door, she saw Susanna, dark curls and red gown flying behind her as she rushed to the doors of the keep, moving so quickly that she looked like a red bird.

"Hurry, Susanna," Ivy whispered, and the thought of Lady Margaret being taken brought tears of panic to her eyes.

She pushed the door closed behind her and raced across the silent chapel, stumbling over charred timbers, broken glass cracking beneath her feet. Daisy's face was buried in her neck; the child's breath was shallow and quick.

"It's all right," Ivy whispered, even though it was not.

She reached the alcove in the wall and tried to set Daisy down, but the little arms were firm around her neck, clenched with surprising strength.

"Just for a minute, sweetheart," Ivy begged, trying to pry open the tight fingers. "Please . . ."

She glanced at the chapel door, praying for Margaret to come through. "Hurry," she repeated, not sure whether she was speaking to Susanna, or Margaret, or herself.

She pried Daisy's finger's apart, and the child slid to the floor, her arms wrapping around Ivy's waist.

Ivy pushed at the alcove that released the door, and pushed again.

"Oh, please!" she cried, and her voice echoed

weirdly in the silent chapel. "Please!"

There was a slight give, and then the wall moved. The sound of the stone scraping was loud, so loud that Ivy thought it might be heard outside the gates.

"Come on, Daisy," she said. "In we go." It was unnecessary; Daisy was firmly attached to Ivy's waist, and obviously had no intention of letting go.

The little room was almost filled to the ceiling with the precious tapestries and silver, tables and cupboards Ivy and Susanna had hidden there. Ivy seized the dark green tournament banner and threw it to the floor. It would be better than sitting on bare stone.

She hesitated, unwilling to close the wall until Margaret was there with them, safe behind the thick walls. Her face was wet, and she realized that she was crying.

"Oh, Margaret," she whispered, "hurry."

She kept her eyes fastened on the chapel door, but it didn't move. Her heart was beating in a furious rhythm against her ribs. Too late, too late, it seemed to say.

An explosion sounded out in the courtyard; she heard the sound of splintered boards falling against stone. The impact could be felt through the stone floor of the chapel. A triumphant shout went up.

Ivy's hands covered her mouth; her face tightened.

Too late.

She pushed the wall of the priest's hole closed. Each breath she took was an effort; her throat felt as if she were being strangled. Daisy was like a lead weight, fastened to her waist.

The last crack of daylight glimmered, and disappeared.

Shaking, she slid down the wall, gathering Daisy tightly to her heart. Her tears were falling onto the silken hair.

"Julian will come," she whispered to Daisy. "Everything will be all right."

She prayed she was right.

She gathered her cloak tightly around the trembling child in her lap, grateful for its thick fabric, and leaned against the cold stone of the wall.

The darkness was oppressive, solid, unrelenting black, without a shadow. She closed her eyes against it, grateful for Daisy's company. It gave her something to think about, aside from the cold and darkness.

She was afraid to think what might be happening outside the solid walls of the chapel. Would Susanna be arrested, or only Margaret?

She wondered how long they would be here, trapped without food, or water, or light. How long would it be before Julian came?

"I didn't expect him back for three more days at least," Susanna had said when they first heard the sounds of the approaching horses.

Three days. What would have happened by the time Julian returned? Ivy wiped the tears

from her face with a cold hand and tried to remember everything Julian had told her about
witch trials.

*In Essex County alone, thirty women hanged
and burned this year. In all of England, twice that.
In Scotland, they say, a full hundred a year. In
Germany, too many to count—and there are no
laws against torture there.*

Ivy shuddered.

Don't think about it, she ordered herself.
Think of practical things. How long can we go
without food? Would it be possible to sneak out
and find some? Perhaps, if it was in the darkest
part of the night. But how will I know when
night falls?

She stroked Daisy's hair and felt the cold tears
on the little face.

"Don't worry, Daisy. Susanna will come, or
Julian. Everything's going to be all right."

Her whisper sounded eerie in the darkness,
like the lie it was. What if nobody came?

For a long time, she was afraid to move, afraid
to make a sound that might betray them. Her
breathing seemed loud and harsh in the dead
silence, and only Daisy's quicker, soft breaths
could be heard in their shared prison.

She had no idea how much time was passing.
After a while, she felt Daisy's breath rising and
falling in the easy, rhythmic pattern of sleep.
Her left leg was stiff, prickling pins and needles,
and she shifted the child's weight.

Time passed slowly in the dark. She wished

that she could sleep, but she knew it was impossible. She counted sheep, she counted backward from a thousand, she made lists in her head. Anything, just to shut out the frightening reality.

She prayed that Julian would come.

She dozed, she woke. She dreamed, strange, disjointed dreams of Margaret and Julian and Susanna. She would wake and not be sure that she was awake. Only Daisy was real, solid and warm against her. Her backache was real, and the cold air, growing colder all the time. Did that mean that it was night?

She lay down on the floor and gathered Daisy tightly against her body, covering them both with her cape, drawing it over their heads. The air was warmer that way.

She was thirsty, and she needed to use the privy. Daisy was awake. Her tiny, cold hands touched Ivy's face, seeking reassurance.

"Everything will be all right," Ivy said, over and over again. She tried to remember stories, and told them to Daisy. Goldilocks, and Cinderella, and Little Red Riding Hood. When she told about Red Riding Hood's grandmother, Daisy cried, and Ivy knew she was thinking of Margaret.

After a while, Daisy slept again. Ivy lay silent, listening, listening for anything, until she thought that the silence might drive her insane.

When at last she heard a sound, she thought she might be imagining it.

She listened again.

Was it a faint scraping? The sound of a footstep? A voice?

She prayed, prayed that it would be Susanna or Julian.

The wall scraped and began to move.

Terror engulfed her. She lay still and flat, pushing herself into the floor as if she could become part of it. Her eyes were tightly closed, like a child—*if I can't see you, you can't see me.* The smell of fear—she had heard the expression, but never known what it meant. But there it was. Her fear was so great that it had become a separate presence, and she could smell it, sharp and ugly.

The wall moved, and the scraping of stone was as loud as thunder.

"Ivy?"

She tried to speak, but the relief was so great that she couldn't. She began to shake.

"Ivy? Are you there?"

Susanna. Ivy tried to speak again, and couldn't. She made an effort. "Here," she managed, trying to sit up.

"Praise God."

It must be night. Ivy could see no light, though she knew the door was open. She thought she could see the faintest shadow of movement, and then the door closed.

"Where are you, Ivy?"

"Here, on the floor."

"I didn't dare to bring a lit candle. I thought

they might be watching. They think that you and Daisy are with Julian."

Susanna stumbled over Ivy's feet.

"Here we are," she said, and there was the heavy sound of something hitting the floor. Ivy could tell that Susanna was sitting down.

"What has happened?"

"Just a minute, let me light this, and I'll tell you."

Ivy sat silently, watching as sparks flickered into the darkness. One of them caught something at eye level, and then she could see Susanna, breathing into a tinderbox, igniting the fluff into a minute flame.

"There," the girl breathed, with obvious relief, and lit a candle from the tinder.

Ivy blessed that light, that pale, golden flame that brought relief to her dark world. Susanna's hands seemed beautiful, touching the dark candlestick, setting it carefully on the floor, closing the little pewter tinderbox with a loud click.

Daisy sat up, her blue eyes wide, her rosebud of a mouth half open.

"Here," Susanna said, and reached for a bucket she had brought. "Bread and cheese." She drew out a bottle of wine and pulled the cork. "It was the best I could find in the dark."

Ivy took it in a shaking hand and tore the bread in half, giving part to Daisy.

Susanna sat silently, watching them. Her face was pale in the candlelight; her beautiful eyes

Amy Elizabeth Saunders

had dark circles beneath them. She had been crying.

"Use the bucket," she said after a minute, "if you need to. I know it's disgusting, but I didn't think to bring a piss-pot."

Ivy was beyond caring what was disgusting. "Thank you," she said, around a mouthful of bread. The cheese was sharp, pale, and crumbling.

Susanna had brought candles and clothes. An ivory comb and ribbons.

"I've probably forgotten something," she said fretfully, "but I'm not thinking clearly."

"I'm grateful," Ivy said. "Tell me, what has happened?"

Tears welled in Susanna's dark eyes, and she put a fist to her mouth for a moment before she spoke. "Oh, Ivy," she said, and seemed unable to go on.

Ivy waited.

Susanna cleared her throat and shook her head. "Pardon. It is so awful...." She drew a deep breath and reached for Ivy's hand. Ivy gave her a reassuring squeeze. Their identical copper bracelets gleamed, shining in the golden light.

Susanna looked at her lap and spoke quickly, as if the words hurt her.

"I was not fast enough. They blew the gates clean off, and they met us as we were coming down the stairs. I tried to fight them, but there were so many. And Grandmam said no. She said for me to stop, that she had nothing to hide, and

394

would gladly go, and that God would prove her innocence." Susanna wiped a tear from the corner of her eye.

"They bound her hands, Ivy, and made her walk. They would not even let me saddle Buttercup for her. Oh, she looked so small!" Susanna choked, and drew her hand away from Ivy's, dashing tears from her eyes. "She is so old. Cannot they see how old she is?"

Ivy felt tears slipping over her own face.

"They were ready, Ivy. They held the trial in the church, the better to fit in all the crowds. Trial! That is what they call it, but it was a sham. It was like a bear-baiting, Ivy! They all sat there, and catcalled, and taunted her. You could not hear her answers, Ivy."

Ivy was cold with dread. She gathered Daisy next to her, pressing the little golden head to her breast, and covering the tiny ears, as if she could shield her from Susanna's words.

"And the witnesses! The things they said. They have seen her flying on a broomstick, on an oat straw! One man said that she had led him to the stable, and slipped a harness around his neck, and turned him into a horse!"

"A horse?" Ivy echoed, incredulous.

"Aye, and when he woke up"—Susanna paused and gave a bitter laugh, a laugh that edged on hysteria—"when he woke up, he had horseshoes nailed to his feet! Then he took off his boots and showed the jury his foul feet. There was something on one, it might have been a scar, or not. But they listened, Ivy, *they listened.* And," she added softly, "they believed."

"Susanna!" Ivy was sickened. "They couldn't!"

"Oh, and the questions they asked—did she know the Devil, had he given her a secret name? Did she sign her name in his book? How often has she sacrificed children? What is the name of her familiar? How many times a month is she visited by demons? Has she had carnal union with the devil? Has she borne him any children?"

Susanna dropped her head to her hands and cried.

Ivy cried too, silently, trying not to frighten Daisy.

Susanna lifted the edge of her skirt and wiped her eyes. "The most damning piece of evidence, if you can swallow this, was a pair of torn breeches."

"Torn breeches?" Ivy asked.

"Oh, yes. It seems that while Grandmother was flying about on her broom, she picked up a farmer from his bed and flew him three times around the church. On the final time, she dropped him, and if his breeches had not caught on the steeple, he'd have fallen to his death! The breeches were brought forth, and handed round the jury."

"But that's ludicrous!" Ivy cried out.

"Not according to Josiah Feake. It is proof." Susanna's mouth twisted into a line of ugly grief and rage. "Proof, Ivy."

396

"It's proof that some horse's ass tore his pants," Ivy snapped.

"It was proof enough for the jury," Susanna said, and she laid her face in her hands.

Ivy's heart stopped and twisted. She wanted to ask, and did not want to know.

Susanna lifted her face, and it was white with rage. "They found her guilty, Ivy! Guilty! She is locked in the jail, and they will hang her tomorrow morning. And Josiah Feake, damn his bastard soul to hell, will be paid seventy shillings!'

Susanna's sobs tore through Ivy's heart.

"Seventy shillings," the girl cried, "for my grandmam's life!"

Ivy's heart ached, and then broke. Blind with grief, she reached out for Susanna and drew the shaking girl into her arms.

They rocked together, crying like two lost children, and Daisy watched with silent misery.

After a while, Susanna's sobs ceased, and she sat, silent and grim, staring at the floor.

"There must be something we can do," Ivy said.

Susanna lifted her hands and let them fall.

If only Julian were here, Ivy thought for the millionth time.

"We could dynamite the jail!" Ivy cried, grasping at straws. "Get guns and kill the jailers! Drug them, perhaps! Susanna, can we drug them?"

"They emptied the apothecary," Susanna whispered. "Evidence, you know."

"Oh, if only she could work a charm," Ivy said.

"Is there any way she could just . . . disappear?"

"There is only one spell powerful enough for that," Susanna said softly. "And it is in the book, Ivy. Wherever that may be."

Ivy thought of the paper Julian had given her that told the location of the book, and wanted to cry.

She had consigned that paper to the fire, and in doing so, sealed Margaret's fate.

"Oh, if only I had it," she cried. "If only we had the book, and some way to get it to her."

"But only Julian knows," Susanna said. "And where Julian is, only God knows."

"We cannot give up," Ivy said. "He could return at any moment, Susanna. He may get here in time."

"Or not!" Susanna cried. "Oh, Ivy! I *would* sell my soul to the devil, if only for that book! I would, I swear it." She raked her dark curls from her forehead with a gesture so like Julian's that Ivy almost cried.

Oh, Julian, where are you?

"The book," Ivy whispered. "The way out is in the book, Susanna. She could go, and find her Thomas, and be safe. Think, Susanna, where could Julian have hidden that book?"

Susanna shook her head wildly. Her eyes glittered, and Ivy could see that she was too upset to be of much help.

Daisy tugged at Ivy's sleeve, and Ivy looked down.

The child's eyes were bright, despite the red

around them. Her mouth worked, and she made a soft sound.

"What's the matter, sweetie? Are you hungry?"

She shook her head, and then again, the soft sound. A *puh, puh, puh* noise, like soft, repeating breaths.

"She's trying to say something," Susanna said, her voice very soft.

Daisy's face tightened, and her eyes screwed tight. She tilted her head back, and then it burst from her throat.

"Book," she cried. The word was unsteady and hoarse, but it was there. "B-buh-book!"

Ivy and Susanna stared at each other, and Ivy could feel the same wild hope in her eyes that she could see so plainly in Susanna's.

Daisy stumbled to her feet, and her tiny fists began to beat on the stone wall.

"Book," she cried. "Book!"

"It can't be. . . . " Susanna whispered.

"Daisy," Ivy cried, whirling the child about by her shoulders, "do you know where the book is? Lady Margaret's book? The one Julian hid?"

Relief showed on the frail little face, and she began to nod, *yes, yes, yes.*

"Can it be?" Ivy asked.

"It is!" Susanna cried. "It must be!"

She dropped to her knees and held Daisy tightly. "Do you understand, truly, Daisy? Can you take us there?"

Daisy began to nod.

"Say it, Daisy," Ivy urged. "Say it."

"Mmmm, yes. Yes, yes." The hoarse, flat voice was the most beautiful thing Ivy had ever heard.

"Dare we believe her?" Ivy asked, trembling.

"Dare we not?" Susanna demanded. She pushed on the wall, and it opened, revealing the dark chapel. Moonlight streamed in through an empty window, sparkling on the broken glass.

The little girl stepped out, and the moonlight touched her golden head. She turned and put out her hand to Ivy.

"Book," Daisy said.

Chapter Twenty-one

They followed the little girl across the wet, moonlit courtyard and through the open doors into the great hall.

"Can it be," Susanna whispered, "that it was here all the time?"

Ivy thought of the days she had spent searching for the book. It seemed impossible, but the idea that Daisy was wrong was too terrible to contemplate.

Faith, she told herself. Have faith.

Susanna stopped and took one of the spiked halberds from the wall, where Ivy had hung them above the refectory table. She poked the air with it, and Ivy thought that she looked like some ancient Celtic spirit as she wielded the long weapon, with her pale face and unbound hair. The moonlight shone dimly on the ax blade.

"If anyone tries to stop us," Susanna said, "I shall run him through."

Ivy had no doubt that she meant what she said.

Daisy stopped at the bottom of the dark staircase and looked back at them.

"Come on," Ivy said, and together they followed the child as she made her way up into the darkness, with her slow, awkward walk.

The halls of Wythecombe had never seemed so dark, so haunted. The ever-present wind made a soft sound, like a sigh, as it moved through the night.

Daisy moved in the shadows with a slow but certain step, looking like a fairy child. Only her silvery hair guided them.

They followed her to Lady Margaret's chambers, and Ivy's heart ached as they entered the silent rooms. A few coals still burned faintly in the fireplace. Daisy's new cloak lay in a heap on the floor in front of Margaret's empty chair, the silver needle shining in the darkness.

"She must be wrong," Susanna whispered. "It cannot be here, Ivy. We would have found it."

"The book, Daisy. Where is the book?" Ivy didn't want to believe Susanna's words, but she feared that it was true. If the book was in this room, one of them would have known.

Daisy nodded, and went to the table that stood by Margaret's chair. She stopped and pointed at the floor, a frown creasing her face.

Ivy looked and saw a plate of water, and another of wilted greens.

"We'll find Bunny later. The book, Daisy."

"Bunny is in prison, too," Susanna said, a slight note of hysteria in her voice. "They say he is a familiar."

Daisy lifted a heavy sheet of paper from the table and brought it back to them.

Ivy knelt by the fireplace, frowning. It was the drawing that Daisy had made, and Lady Margaret had beamed over and displayed so proudly. The crooked castle on the hill, with five smiling, bubble-round faces in the window. The square clusters of cottages that were the village, with spirals of smoke issuing from the chimneys.

Past the crooked village, a collection of trees and blocks, with an impossibly large horse standing among them.

Ivy stared, looking for a clue, and finding none.

Daisy's tiny finger touched the paper, pointing at the horse.

"Horse," she said, in her rough little voice.

Frustrated, Ivy nodded. "Yes, there's a horse, Daisy." Did it mean something?

Daisy pushed at the paper with her trembling finger.

"Book," she said, her voice rising slightly, "horse."

"The book is with the horse?" Ivy asked. Stay

calm, she told herself. Don't push too hard.

Daisy nodded, then shook her head. Her little face was pinched with frustration.

Susanna was leaning over Ivy's shoulder, so close that her breath stirred Ivy's hair.

Tears gathered in Daisy's eyes, and she stared at them both with mute frustration. Her shaking finger never left the paper.

"The abbey," Susanna whispered.

Ivy's heart stopped and began to race again.

"The ruined abbey," Susanna repeated, her voice rising. "It must be!"

Ivy stared at the childlike drawing, the giant horse on its toothpick legs, standing amid a chaos of squares, rectangles, and trees. She lifted her eyes to Daisy's face.

The child was smiling, despite the tears in her eyes.

"Is that it, Daisy? The ruined abbey? The place in the woods, with the fallen walls?"

Daisy nodded, her smile stretching across her face.

But how could it be so? Ivy wondered. Daisy had not left Wythecombe since the day Julian had brought her here on his horse. But she must have seen the abbey, to have drawn it into the picture."

"Is it true, Daisy? Is the book at the abbey? Did someone take you there?"

Daisy nodded, and then she spoke again.

"Oh, Julian!" she exclaimed, in a tone so like Lady Margaret's that Ivy and Susanna stared at each other, and then, despite the horror of the day, they laughed.

"Oh, Julian, indeed!" Susanna cried. "Thank God for you, Daisy, you jewel."

"Thank God," Ivy echoed, and drew the child tightly into her arms.

"Make haste," Susanna said. " 'Tis late, and we must somehow get the book to Grandmam before dawn. You carry Daisy down, and I'll saddle Buttercup and Guinevere. It will be rough going in the dark, but we'll make better time than walking."

"But once we find the book," Ivy said, "how will we get it to Margaret?"

"We'll sort that out on the way," Susanna replied. "First things first. Let's to the stables, and quickly."

"Horse," Daisy agreed happily, because Daisy loved nothing more than she loved being on horseback, moving quickly and proudly over the ground.

If the abbey had seemed haunted by day, it was doubly so at night. The moon cast a faint glow through the thick trees, turning shadows into ghosts, branches into arms, and the fallen walls into a spectral fortress.

A faint fog crept over the ground, like pools of ghostly water. It swirled around the horses' hooves, and around the hem of Ivy's gown as she slid to the ground. Her heart pounded with a strange excitement.

They would not fail. She couldn't consider the possibility. Faith, she repeated to herself, like a magical incantation. Faith.

She looked at Daisy and Susanna and smiled. What a strange trio they would seem, if anyone were to look.

Little, frail Daisy, with her hair shining silver in the moonlight, like a fairy child with her enigmatic smile, and Susanna, standing above her, her cape hanging over her shoulders, her midnight hair streaming wildly down her back, carrying the medieval pole-ax over her shoulder, like some kind of warrior goddess.

"You look a little ghostly yourself," Susanna said, as if Ivy had spoken aloud.

It didn't surprise Ivy a bit. Nothing was beyond possibility anymore. The line between the real world and the magic beyond was no longer clear; it was blurred and misty, like the ground beneath the silken fog.

Lost, somewhere in enchanted time.

Daisy was looking around, her pale brows drawn together. She began to walk, slowly, gazing around her.

Then she stopped and pointed. "Book," she whispered.

She was pointing at the ancient well.

Of course, Ivy thought.

"If Julian threw that book down the well," Susanna said, "I shall run him through without regret."

"He couldn't have," Ivy replied. "Have faith."

She took Daisy's cool hand, and they walked together toward the well. Somewhere in the forest an owl hooted, and Ivy jumped.

Daisy stood for what seemed a very long time, staring at the moss-covered stones. And then she bent down and ran her tiny fingers between the crevices. "Book," she said. "Book."

Immediately, Ivy and Susanna were beside her. They dug their fingers into the cold, damp cracks between the ancient stones, scraping away moss and dirt, trying every rock.

A stone moved under Ivy's hand.

"Oh, please," she cried out. "Please!"

The stone came loose and fell out, striking her bent knee. She scarcely noticed. There was a dark space behind it. The next stone followed with almost no resistance, and she felt rough fabric beneath her cold fingers.

She fell back onto her heels in the wet grass and pulled the bundle out. The rough fabric unrolled, and then a length of soft, oiled leather, and the book fell onto her lap.

She clutched it like a child to her heart, running her fingers over the smooth leather of the covers, smelling the musty odor of the pages within. It was cold and damp, but there it was. Her book. Margaret's book, and hopefully, Margaret's salvation.

A wind whispered through the trees, like a sigh of relief.

"The lady of the well must have been guarding

it," Susanna observed, and her voice was only half teasing.

"Remind me to send her a thank-you note," Ivy replied, holding the precious book to her heart.

They stood and started back, Daisy on one side of Ivy, clutching her free hand, Susanna walking on the other, her slender arm around Ivy's shoulder.

"Are you afraid, Ivy?" Susanna asked softly. "Can you manage the rest? I would go myself, but they know me too well. If I were seen in the village, they would surely raise an alarm. Our only chance is that you will not be recognized."

Afraid? Ivy considered. Her heart raced in a strange, rapid beat, and the blood in her veins seemed to sing with a strange electricity. She should be afraid, but she was not. She was filled with a sense of purpose, and inevitable duty.

"Afraid? No. But I think I know how a soldier must feel right before he rides into battle. It doesn't matter, Susanna, whether I'm afraid or not. It's too late in the game."

They stood by the horses, and Susanna reached for Guinevere's reins, untying them from a branch.

"Remember all I've told thee. The jail—"

"On the village square, across from the church and two doors from the inn," Ivy repeated. "Leave the horse tied at the end of the high street and go quietly, on foot. Leave the moment the book is in Margaret's hands, and ride straight up the hill to Wythecombe. Go straight to the priest's hole, and there we wait for Julian."

Susanna smiled a tense smile. "And pray," she added, climbing to her horse.

Ivy kissed Daisy's soft, cool cheeks and held her close. "You're a good girl, Daisy. The best in the world. You hold tight to Susanna, and I'll be back soon. Then we can all wait for Julian."

Daisy clung to her for a moment and then nodded, wiping a tear from her eye.

"I'll be there soon," Ivy repeated.

She helped Daisy put her foot in the stirrup, and helped Susanna lift her. The child settled comfortably in front of Susanna, who still held the old halberd in one hand, its engraved blade gleaming in the soft light.

The horse shifted impatiently.

"Godspeed, my sister," Susanna said softly.

Ivy repeated the ancient wish. "Godspeed, Susanna."

Ivy climbed onto Buttercup and took the reins into her hands, the book held fast under her arm.

Without another word, Susanna deftly turned the horse and rode away through the fallen walls and mist. Ivy sat still, watching until she disappeared into the foggy forest, and the sound of the jingling harness and soft hoofbeats were swallowed by the darkness.

"Okay, Buttercup," Ivy said, "it's you and me, girl."

The old mare twitched her ears and quivered.

Ivy looked around, wondering if she would ever see the ruined abbey again. It was still holy and beautiful in the night—the fallen columns, the crumbling, vine-covered walls and flagstone paths, the empty arches that stood in black silhouette against the night sky.

The clouds around the moon shifted and moved, a silver circle of light illuminating their billowing valleys.

Ivy squared her shoulders and started forward. She paused by the ancient well, remembering the day she had stood there with Susanna in the brilliant winter sunlight, listening to the story of the long-ago maiden who had so loved the lord of Wythecombe that she could not live without him.

She remembered Susanna, her dark eyes laughing and full of mischief, her hair gleaming in the dappled sunlight.

Come, Ivy. The maiden of the well is said to grant wishes to unmarried women, so think carefully on it. What would your wish be?

Tonight Susanna would not have had to ask twice. Ivy bowed her head and whispered aloud.

"Let me be strong. Let me get to Lady Margaret in time and save her from Josiah Feake. Let Daisy and Susanna get safely home." Ivy drew a deep, quavering breath.

"And please, let Julian come home to me. I want to hold him again, and marry him, and bear his children. I want to stay by his side until the end of my days, and see our grandchildren

410

playing in the great hall."

Ivy waited, but there was no sign. Only the gentle moonlight, and the fog, and the dark road that led to the village.

The ruins lay silent; the ancient well kept its secrets.

"Damn," Ivy whispered, dashing an unexpected tear from her eye. "The first time in weeks that I actually *want* something weird to happen, and nothing."

She turned her horse toward the village and started toward the dark road.

Julian, come home.

"Knock it off, Ivy," she said to herself, and the sound of her own voice strengthened her. "This is no time to get all mystical and stupid. You have work to do, and you'd better do it well. Get tough, girl."

The book under her arm was solid and real, Buttercup's back solid and warm beneath her.

"You flake," she told herself, "whining to mythical nuns."

Buttercup stopped abruptly and laid her ears back. She tossed her mane and whinnied, shying and turning in a half circle.

"Whoa! Hold on there, girl. I'm not—"

The words died in Ivy's mouth, and her heart stopped.

The novice was standing by the well, a young woman in shimmering white. She seemed to have been made from the fog at her feet, from the white veil that covered her head to the long

411

sleeves that fell over her graceful hands.

She was looking right at Ivy, a tranquil, peaceful expression on her beautiful face.

Slowly, the ghost of the young woman held out a hand with a shimmering, balletic motion.

And though she was silent, Ivy could hear the beautiful, ancient words of Ruth:

Intreat me not to leave thee, or to return from following after thee: for whither thou goest, I will go; and where thou lodgest, I will lodge: thy people shall be my people, and thy God my God: Where thou diest, will I die, and there will I be buried: the Lord do so to me, and more also, if ought but death part thee and me.

The pale hand lifted like a blessing, and shimmered, and was gone.

Ivy sat staring at the silent ruins, the lonely well, her hand shaking on the reins.

As if by instinct, Buttercup turned and started forward at a quick, even clip, carrying Ivy toward Lady Margaret.

Ivy.

In the rude inn, Julian woke with a start.

He sat upright in bed, his hand automatically reaching for his waist, where the money for the journey was sewn securely into the lining of his doublet.

What had woken him? His dagger lay next to

him, the precious relic of Ramsden history that Ivy had unearthed in her explorations of the castle.

He took it in his hand, looking into the corners of the dark room for any sign of whatever had jarred him from his sleep.

He saw nothing, and the door was still bolted.

For a moment he sat listening. Somewhere in the far distance, a dog barked and then was silent.

He climbed from the narrow bed—he had paid extra for clean sheets, which annoyed him—and went to the shuttered windows and opened them.

He saw only the dark innyard and the long, low stables beyond. A motley-looking hound slept by the wall. It looked up at him as he stood in the open window, and cocked its head, trying to decide whether or not he was worth barking at.

Apparently not. It lifted a hind leg, scratched halfheartedly at a flea, yawned, and went back to sleep.

Beyond the stables, the rolling, grassy hills were shadowy under the moonlight.

"What the hell," Julian muttered, and turned back to his bed. He had ridden hard; he needed his sleep. Tomorrow he would be back at Wythecombe.

Ivy.

The name seemed to pierce his mind, and he

sat upright on the bed, looking around the room again.

Nothing was amiss. Likely he had been dreaming. He lay down, trying to arrange the lumpy mattress into some kind of order. He punched his pillow a few times and stretched out, closing his heavy eyes.

Ivy.

"God's nightgown!" He sat up for the third time, glowering at nothing. The name was so clear, so vivid in his mind that it might have been spoken aloud.

The room was empty, just another room at another inn. His bucket boots and haversack lay by the bed where he had left them.

"I'm going to sleep now, thank you very much," he said aloud to the voice in his head.

He lay back, pulled the blanket up to his shoulders, and closed his eyes. After a moment, he opened them again, peering from side to side.

Iv—

"God bless us!" he exclaimed with great disgust, throwing the blanket off and sitting up. "As if I hadn't had grief enough. All I wanted was one damned meal, and a good night's sleep! But, no. That's just asking too damned much."

Bleary-eyed, he shoved his feet into the soft leather of his boots, muttering about damned second sight, blasted inner voices, incessant premonitions of danger that wouldn't let a man take a decent night's sleep, and—

He stopped in the middle of his grumblings.

414

The skin prickled on his arms, and the hair on the back of his head tingled.

And again, the sense of premonition. There was danger, and whatever danger it was, it was close to Ivy.

"Damn!" He threw on his cape without hesitation, thrust his dagger through his belt, swore again as he jabbed himself in a most unheroic fashion, and reached for his bundle.

Waking easily had never been one of Julian's qualities.

Within minutes he had roused the landlord from his bed, settled his account, saddled Bacchus, and was riding across the moors, his heart pounding in time with the relentless beat of the horse's hooves on the rough turf.

Above him, the moon was bright in a halo of clouds, lighting the endless grassy hills that lay between him and Wythecombe.

Chapter Twenty-two

The village was silent, the good townspeople asleep behind their locked doors and shuttered windows. Ivy was grateful for the fog as she moved down the narrow street. It hid her, a protective blanket that covered the village from the moonlight.

"Across from the church, two doors from the inn," Ivy whispered.

A dog barked, and Ivy froze, pressing herself against a damp stone wall. A voice yelled, the dog whined, and then all was quiet.

Ivy released her breath, pulled her hood farther over her face, and started forward. Her skirts were damp and heavy, the thin leather of her shoes clammy. She passed the churchyard, where the fog softened the old headstones. It was eerie, a scene from a Vincent Price movie.

"No ghosts," she muttered. "My quota is one per night, thanks. I'm not in the mood."

If there were any dissenters among the inhabitants of the churchyard, they wisely kept their spectral silence.

There was the inn, a candle glowing in the window to welcome travelers. Upstairs, one room glowed with light, and Ivy knew as surely as if she could see inside that Josiah Feake was in there. She could imagine him sitting at a table making neat entries in his book. *One witch, Margaret Ramsden, seventy shilling fee.*

"Two down from the inn," Ivy repeated. She looked around, saw that she was alone on the empty street, and raced across. She had barely reached the corner of the inn when the door flew open, letting a stream of light into the foggy street.

Ivy pressed herself flat against the wall, clutching the book to her chest.

Two men walked by in thick boots and dark jackets. They were so close that she could smell the smoke that clung to their clothes, and the smell of ale from their breath. Their voices were slightly thickened from drink.

". . . wouldn't confess to nowt," one was saying. "But where there be one, there be more."

"It's the young one, certain enough," agreed his companion. "They'll get the old girl to confess by morning, I imagine. Than that high and mighty Susanna Ramsden will see what's what."

"Shame. She's pretty enough, in't she? I'd like to be there when Mr. Feake strips her down to search for witch's marks!"

Ivy's rage boiled at the sound of their laughter. The hypocrites! They would too, if they could. They would hunt Susanna down in the name of God, and watch her naked and abused with their lustful eyes. Then they would watch her die, and piously tell each other that they had rid themselves of an evil presence and could sleep well that night.

And Josiah Feake would drop another seventy shillings into his retirement fund.

Anger overcame Ivy's fear. "Not while there's breath in my body," she whispered.

As soon as the footsteps were gone, she raced around the back of the inn and moved north. The sound of the sea was louder here in the village than it was up at the castle, and she was glad. The sound of the wind and hiss of the waves would muffle her footsteps.

Past one stone building, then the second. A faint light glowed behind the barred window. Ivy closed her eyes and prayed for courage. The book was warm within her cloak.

She crept up to the window and peered within.

The stone room was no bigger than a closet, and what little light there was came from behind the door, which had an iron grate set into it. It fell in faint stripes over the straw-covered floor.

418

The air was rank with the smell of old vomit and urine.

And there was Margaret. She sat on the floor, huddled against a wall, her eyes closed. Her deep blue gown was smeared with filth, the heavy collar of falling lace torn, and stained with what might be blood. Her white hair was un-bound and tangled across her shoulders.

She lay so still, so silent, that for one horrible moment Ivy thought that she was dead, that she had somehow cheated the hangman.

"Oh, Margaret," she whispered, sorrow twist-ing in her heart.

Margaret's eyes flew open. Slowly she turned her head. Her eyes were watery and bruised-looking, but when she saw Ivy at the barred win-dow she smiled, and her eyes began to sparkle.

Slowly she rose to her feet and made her way to the window. She reached out a shaking hand, and Ivy took it into her own. Margaret's skin was like ice.

Ivy tried to speak, but her throat seemed to swell, and she felt tears gathering in her eyes.

"Sshhh." Margaret patted her hand. "There, Ivy. Don't fret for me. Are you all well? Susanna, and Daisy?"

"Yes," Ivy choked.

"Stay in the priest's hole," Margaret said, her whisper so quiet that Ivy could barely hear it. "They mean to take Susanna in the morning. And they will take you as well, if they find you. Josiah Feake will not want to leave town with only one witch fee. It is not, as you would say, cost effective."

"He won't take us," Ivy said. "He won't. Nor you either, Margaret."

Margaret gave a little fluttering wave of her hand. "Oh, Ivy. 'Tis too late for that, I fear. I have only a few hours. The sky is already turning toward morning. But don't cry, darling. True, I hadn't expected death, but it will put me so much closer to my Thomas. I'm not afraid, dear. Truly I'm not."

"Margaret, listen!" Ivy glanced over her shoulder. "Go to Thomas!" She lifted the book from beneath her cloak and shoved it through the bars.

Margaret stared, stunned. Her hands shook as she took the book, and then she closed her eyes, and an expression of joy and relief flooded her lined face.

"Praise God," she whispered. "He delivereth me from mine enemies . . . that rise up against me: thou hast delivered me from the violent man. Therefore I will give thanks unto thee, O Lord, among the heathen, and sing praises unto thy name." She opened her eyes, and they sparkled with tears of joy. "Do you know that, my dear? 'Tis from the eighteenth psalm, I believe. Or maybe the seventeenth. No, the eighteenth, I think. I can't be sure. My memory, you know . . ."

"Margaret!" Ivy looked over her shoulder. "Hurry! What if someone comes?"

"Oh. Well, that would be dreadful, wouldn't it?"

Ivy almost laughed. "Yes, I think so."

She stood pressed tightly against the wall, shivering, while Margaret began leafing through the book.

"Hmmm. I never could get this one to work. And here's that impossible recipe against gout. Useless. Difficult and useless. Where is it?"

"Farther back, I think," Ivy whispered.

"Ah, here we are. Do you really think I shall find my Thomas this time?"

"Yes, I do. You must believe it, Margaret. You simply have to. And if you end up in Seattle again . . ."

Margaret looked up with interest.

"Do you still have my keys?"

Margaret drew the chain from around her neck, and the keys jingled.

"Okay. There's the key to the store, and this is for the safe. There's money there. And this is for my apartment. My bank card's in the top dresser drawer—"

"How exciting," Margaret said. "I wanted to try one. Card in, money out. It's so simple!"

"Well, too simple, unfortunately. But there's enough in there, for a while. The code is six-three-four-seven. I have trouble remembering numbers myself, so if it's easier to remember, it spells a little word. M-E-G-S, Megs . . ."

Ivy stopped abruptly, and their eyes met.

"That should be easy to remember," Margaret

said, her eyes dancing. "Meg was what Thomas called me. So the bank card was Ivy's, but now 'tis Meg's."

Ivy shook her head. "That's weird, Margaret. That's really, really weird."

"Nothing surprises me anymore," the old woman said. "Now, be good to Julian, and give him my love. And Susanna as well, and don't let her get too saucy. And Daisy—be sure and rub her legs every night; it seems to help. And—"

"Here, who are you talking to?"

Ivy dropped to the ground as Margaret whirled around.

"Why, I'm talking to myself," she informed her jailer in pert tones. "We old women do that, you know."

Ivy began crawling away. There was a barrel next to the wall. Silently, she hid next to it and curled up as tightly as she could.

"You do, do you? We'll see about that."

Ivy heard the door of the cell creak as it opened, and after a minute, a beam of light showed on the ground near her. It seemed a long time until the voice spoke again.

"Nobody out there, or if there was, they're gone." Another pause. "Hey, what do you have there?"

Ivy buried her face in her hands. *No, not the book.*

"Why," Margaret replied, "are you mad? This is the book that Josiah Feake gave me. It is full of prayers and sermons, and he bade me study it, that I might find salvation before morning."

Good, Margaret.

"I don't remember that." The jailer sounded suspicious.

"Well, my good man, you're not as young as you might be. Perhaps your hearing is going."

"I don't know. I'd better get Mr. Feake."

A beat passed.

"Do so," Margaret replied coolly.

Ivy waited until the door closed and then rushed to the window. "Now, Margaret! Before he's back!"

Margaret nodded and opened the book. "Here it is. Pray, Ivy, give my love to the children—"

"I will, Margaret, but please . . ."

Margaret lifted her white head and smiled at Ivy; gentle tears shone in her eyes. "I bid thee farewell, Ivy. I have come to love thee well. If not for you, I would not have lived through this."

"I love you too, Margaret," Ivy whispered. "I hope that you find Thomas."

"Why, I'm sure I shall. And one more thing, please—"

"Anything," Ivy promised.

"Make Julian cut his hair. I know 'tis fashion, but I cannot bear it hanging down like a spaniel's ears. The young these days . . ."

"Margaret!"

Margaret cleared her throat and softly whispered, "I pray I find thee, Thomas." And then she began reading:

"I have sought thee over time and land,
And found naught but more seeking.
I have sought thee through dawn and dusk.
I have sworn that I would seek no more."

Margaret's skin began to glow with a pale, pearllike incandescence. She glanced up at Ivy and smiled quickly.

"Good-bye, Margaret," Ivy whispered.

"But my sorrow is undimmed.
Most certain is my heart
That I long for more than longing's sake.
And so I call thee."

Ivy heard footsteps approaching along the street. "Hurry," she whispered.

". . . I said, I know I didn't see any book." The jailer's voice.

"The work of the devil. I will have this evil thing, this book of shadows." The voice of Josiah Feake, deep and angry.

The stinking jail cell was alight with a radiant gold shimmer. The straw on the floor began to quiver and move, as if touched by a magical wind. Ivy stepped back from the window, away from the iron bars that vibrated beneath her cold fingers.

"I speak to the other half of my soul," Margaret read, her voice gaining strength.

The door of the jail banged, and Ivy could see both men through the bars on Margaret's door. The jailer was fumbling for the key.

"Whose body grants heat to my winter
Whose breath cools summer's fire—"

The door of the cell swung open. The jailer stood rooted to the spot, staring at the radiant, smiling woman, the shimmering light, the bits of golden straw that danced in a whirlwind around her.

"Emissary of Satan!" shouted Josiah Feake. "Oh, foul sorceress. Unhand the book, written in the blood of your victims!"

Margaret simply stood, smiling, her white hair falling around her, and continued.

"You, who are lost
Somewhere between dawn and dusk—"

Josiah Feake, his gaunt face purple with rage, lunged forward and grabbed the book, trying to tug it from Margaret's hands. But somehow, through some power, the frail hands held fast.

"In enchanted time."

Ivy took another step back as the walls began to shake, as the straw rose and fell in a shimmering cloud. Sparkling light began to rise and fall, a shower of Fourth of July brilliance, surrounding the smiling woman and the enraged man whose words became a mindless bellow.

There was a blinding flash, and the last thing Ivy saw was the smile Margaret sent her, and a delighted, mischievous wink.

The cell was dark and silent. Margaret was gone. . . .

And so was Josiah Feake.

Ivy stared in wonder.

The jailer was on his hands and knees by the door, whimpering, his head buried in his hands.

Everything else was silent, except for the distant hiss and slap of the waves.

After a moment, Ivy turned and sped down the dark street, where Buttercup was tethered and waiting. Panting, she climbed onto the mare's sturdy back and raced toward Wythecombe Keep.

The sun was beginning to break as she rode through the splintered wood of the gates. She paused to dry Buttercup and tie her in the stables, making sure that she had oats in her trough. To her relief, Susanna's Guinevere was there, chewing contentedly.

Dazed and exhausted, she wandered through the kitchen, stopping to take some dried fruit and sausages and cheese, and made her way through the empty hall, out into the courtyard, and into the chapel.

She stumbled over the debris on the floor as she made her way through the chill room. It took her two tries to open the secret chamber.

Susanna was sitting against the wall, and a candle burned beside her. Daisy was solidly asleep, her head in Susanna's lap.

Trembling with exhaustion, Ivy closed the entry and slid down the wall, closing her eyes with relief.

"Ivy? Did she manage?" Susanna's voice trembled.

"Yes. She got away."

"Praise God," Susanna whispered. "Ivy—do you think she shall find Thomas? Truly?"

"Susanna, let me tell you something." Ivy opened her eyes and smiled at the dark-haired girl. "The last normal day of my life was December twenty-third, nineteen ninety-four. Then I came here. And since I've been here, I've learned one thing. Anything is possible, Susanna. The only thing that isn't possible is what hasn't happened yet."

Susanna smiled and kicked at Ivy's foot. "Philosopher," she mocked. Then she smiled again. "I am glad to see thee, Ivy."

"And you too," Ivy replied. It wasn't so terrible hiding in the priest's hole with Susanna there. And they had food and light. And soon Julian would come, Ivy was certain.

"I hope that bastard Josiah Feake doesn't stay long," Susanna said.

Ivy began to giggle. Perhaps she was tired, but it struck her as terribly funny. She tried to imagine Josiah Feake in his Puritan's garb, dropping into the middle of a busy New York street, or maybe an Eskimo village. Perhaps he would wander into the debutante party of a southern belle, or stumble into the gunfight at the OK Corral.

"Ivy! What is it?"

"Josiah Feake is gone," Ivy informed her. "Lost. History. Somewhere in enchanted time."

Susanna stared with wide eyes, and then, for the first time since the witch-hunt had begun, her merry laugh rang out, filling the tiny room like silver bells.

Chapter Twenty-three

It was sunset when Julian caught his first scent of the sea, the scent that told him he was home. He breathed it in fully, drinking it as a parched man drinks water.

He stayed away from the main roads, traveling the treacherous trails that wound down the craggy cliffs, out of sight of the village. For all he knew, Cromwell might have issued warrants for his arrest, and he intended to take no chances until he and his family were safely on their way to Calais.

He looked fondly at each wooded trail, each rushing stream that he had played in as a child, ridden by as a young man. He would come back. He would come back with Ivy and their children, God willing. And they would prosper, as the Ramsdens always had.

He rode through the ruins of the ancient abbey, spurring Bacchus to move a little faster, now that they were home.

Then it caught his eye. The rocks were gone from the side of the maiden's well.

"Damn." He rode closer and stared in disbelief.

The missing stones lay on the ground, along with the canvas and leather he had wrapped the book in.

The book itself was nowhere to be seen.

"Oh, Ivy," he said softly.

Would she be there when he rode to Wythecombe Keep? Or would she be gone, vanished into the mists of time? What had happened here while he was gone?

His face settled into grim lines. He turned his horse to the trail leading to Wythecombe and broke into a gallop. Whatever had happened here, it boded ill for him, he could feel it.

When he rode to the castle gates and saw the splintered wood, the bent hinges hanging askew, his heart sank. Dreading what he would find, he rode forward, and when he saw the doors to the great hall hanging open to the wind, he swore, a long and terrible string of oaths.

He left Bacchus standing in the courtyard and walked into the hall.

It was empty, a hollow shell. Not a sound reached his ears, no voice raised in greeting. The wind whistled through the stone columns, and a few dust motes shone in the light of the setting sun.

"Susanna! Ivy! Grandmother!"

He raced up the stairs, going from empty room to empty room. He went back down again, and to the kitchens. There had not been a fire there for some time. The ashes in the hearth were cold. A piece of moldy bread lay on the table, looking like a mouse had been at it.

He opened the door to Margaret's apothecary, and when he saw the shelves torn down, the bottles and jars and bags gone, he knew what had happened. The witch-hunts had reached Wythecombe.

The damning book, gone from its hiding place. The empty castle. The rumors that had reached him, that the witch-hunter was in the west country.

"I cannot bear it," he said simply, and his voice sounded lost in the empty castle.

He walked back out to the great hall, and then into the courtyard.

Bacchus looked at him reproachfully, wondering why he had not been fed or watered.

"Piss off," Julian said, not bothering to care that he was swearing at a horse, and a horse that had just carried him a great distance, at that.

He stood in the courtyard, smelling the sea wind that rushed over the battlements and through the open gate, watching the hazy golds and reds of the sunset over the sea.

He did not want to check the priest's hole. He could not bear it if it were empty.

He knew he had to. "Get it over with," he told himself.

He went quickly, broken glass and wood crunching beneath his boots. He did not allow himself time to pray, or time to hope, before he pushed open the hidden door.

"Do you know how to knock?" Susanna greeted him, frowning over a hand of cards.

His relief was so great that for a moment he couldn't move. There they sat, Ivy and Susanna and little Daisy, safe and whole.

Ivy looked at him with a radiant, beautiful smile. She stood up, the cards in her hand scattering across the floor.

And then she was in his arms, her beautiful hair soft under his cheek, her slender arms wrapped around his neck. Their bodies seemed to melt together; their lips met, parted, and met again.

"I love thee," he whispered.

"Oh, how I've missed you," she whispered back. Her hand moved across his face like silk; her brown eyes shone with tears.

"Thank you, Julian," Susanna said from her seat on the floor. "I'm glad to see you too."

Julian, holding Ivy tight, smiled over her head at his sister. "Wait your turn, monkey. We'll have—"

He stopped, and fear seized him.

432

"Where is Grandmother?"

"Safe," Ivy assured him.

"Gone," Susanna informed him. "Off to find her true love, Julian. It was that or hang, so don't get angry. And she's likely having more fun than I am. This is so boring Julian, being trapped here."

"Susanna," Ivy cried, "I would think you'd had enough excitement to last you a lifetime!"

"What has happened here while I was gone?" Julian demanded. "Tell me everything, at once."

"Please," Ivy corrected, smiling at him.

"Sorry," he answered automatically. "*Please* tell me everything that's happened here. At once."

"Oh, Julian!" exclaimed little Daisy, sounding exactly like Lady Margaret.

Ivy and Susanna laughed at his shock.

"What has happened here?" Ivy repeated. "A lot. Close the door and sit down and I'll tell you everything."

He held her in his arms as she told the story of the witch-hunter, and how Daisy had led them to the book, and of Lady Margaret's rescue. As she spoke, he sat silently, occasionally touching her copper curls, her pale hands, her soft face.

" 'Twas dangerous, what you did," he told them when Ivy finished. "I can see that I must never leave you alone again."

"As if I'd let you, Julian Ramsden!" Ivy exclaimed. "No, you're in for it now. 'Whither thou

433

goest,' as they say. No, you'd better not leave me again. I'm stuck here forever, so if you change your mind, I'm in serious trouble."

"Change my mind? I promise, Ivy, I shall not change my mind. The next few years may be unsettling, and I have little to offer you except my heart, and that I give you fully. But this I promise—one day, we shall return to Wythecombe and never leave. I want to grow old with you here; and when that bastard Cromwell is dead and turned to dust, our children and grandchildren will still be here, prosperous and happy within these walls. They will play in the forests and ride on the beach, and I'll tell them the story of how I found their grandmother lying on the sand, like a gift from the sea."

"One of the famous witches of Wythecombe Keep," Susanna observed, rolling her eyes. "That is what they shall say."

"I don't care what anyone says," Ivy told Julian, pressing her face against his neck. She touched her lips to the warm pulse that beat there. "My place in the world is next to you, and that's all I want."

"Then I am perfectly happy," Julian said. "Bless Grandmother and her stupid book, wherever they may be."

Winston Arthur left his gallery at exactly 10:30, carrying a carefully wrapped painting beneath his arm. He had paid far too much for it, he knew, but that was one of the drawbacks of this business.

Every now and then, just when he thought he'd become immune to it, a piece went by that seized him, that caught his fancy for no good reason.

Like Ivy and her book of spells, he thought.

He waited at the edge of the sidewalk as a bus rumbled by, and made his way across Jackson Street. The traffic had melted the snow off of the city streets, but it still frosted the dark branches of the trees and the cornices of the old brick buildings.

Bad weather and holidays did nothing to slow down the pace of city life. Lawyers hurried to their offices, artists to their rented lofts, waiters and vagrants to their various restaurants and street corners.

Winston liked that about the city. There was always something happening.

This morning, for example.

He paused for a moment, his attention diverted by the sight of a police car and an ambulance parked in front of the coffeehouse on the corner.

A police officer and the ambulance driver were trying to subdue a tattered man who had climbed onto a planter box of greenery and was refusing to come down.

"You can step on down," an officer was saying, "or we can take you down, but you're coming down, fella."

435

The vagrant seemed to have other ideas. "I am sent by order of the lord protector," he shouted to the amused crowd, "to weed the evil out of your midst. Lay hands on me at your peril, demon! I am the witch-hunter general."

"You are, huh? Well, we all have a job to do, and my job is getting you down from there." The policeman turned to the ambulance driver. "Live wire, this one."

The vagrant was very excited. His gaunt face was flushed red. "See you not the dragons on your streets?"

"Yeah, we do, fella, but we had to haul St. George in last week. Come on, time to get down."

"I am the witch-hunter general!" the vagrant screamed as the policeman took his arms and hauled him toward the ambulance. "I am the witch-hunter general!"

"Well, we'll just take you up to Harborview, and you can hunt all you want."

Winston shook his head as they hauled the deranged man toward the ambulance.

"I have orders from the Crown," the vagrant screamed as the doors of the van swung closed.

The ambulance driver and police officer exchanged cynical chuckles and shook hands. "Takes all kinds," the police officer observed. "Last week I arrested Catherine the Great up on Fifth Avenue. Did you know she was a six-foot-tall man with a beard?"

Winston laughed as he turned toward Ivy's shop, anxious to show her his latest acquisition. The sleigh bells jangled as he opened the door. He sniffed the air appreciatively, the mingled smells of cinnamon and furniture polish and evergreen.

Ivy was someplace in the back room, he guessed. He could hear the teacups ringing together.

"Wait till you see this," he called to her, laying the painting carefully on the pseudo-Gothic horror that Ivy called her desk. He pulled his camel-hair greatcoat off and tossed it to a waiting chair as he unwrapped the painting. "I went to New York to purchase an entire lot, and came back with one painting. What possessed me I shall never know."

He leaned back, shaking his head with mingled disbelief and pride at his purchase. It was not large, as far as seventeenth-century works went, but it was perfect.

It was an English painting, but with the soft lines and delicate tints and shadows more common to the Dutch. A traditional family scene, but painted with a unique liveliness.

They sat in a wooded hilltop of summer greens and golds, and through the trees, one could see the brilliant blue ocean, and on the hill beyond, a magnificent castle, ancient and mysterious.

The gentleman in the painting was a handsome devil, tall and dark, with a mischievous

437

gleam in his eye. His hair hung long over the shoulders of his blue-black satin doublet, and the lace of his falling collar and cuffs was rich and thick, exquisitely painted. Like many fashionable men of the Stuart court, he wore a gold ring through his ear, but instead of a foppish air, it made this man look barbaric and dangerous, despite his fine clothes.

His wife leaned at his side, looking up at him with an adoring expression. It was she who had first caught Winston's eye when he had seen the painting—probably because of her amazing resemblance to Ivy.

Her eyes were dark in her pale, delicate face; her hair was caught on her head in a knot, with ringlets of coppery gold flowing over her pale shoulders. Her gown was of brilliant satin, the color of the sky, and it seemed to catch the light. The low bodice was trimmed with a band of gold brocade and white lace, and the same fabric showed between the split skirt of her overgown. Iridescent pearls hung in magnificent strands from her slender throat, and decorated the lace at her wide, ruffled sleeves. Every bit a lady of fashion, except for the odd, wide cuff of copper at her wrist. It seemed an odd choice for a formal portrait.

The children around them were attired with equal elegance—two tall boys, dark and mischievous-looking, despite their Restoration finery, the lace collars and satin doublets. And four girls, two dark, one copper-haired, their full gowns perfect replicas of their mother's, in various shades of rose and yellow and lavender. The youngest girl looked to be about two, her dark curls peeping from beneath a white lace cap, framing her plump, rosy face.

The oldest girl was a mystery to Winston. She had neither her father's dark coloring nor her mother's ruddy ringlets. Her hair was smooth and straight, as golden as corn silk. She sat on the grass, her beautiful skirts of rose satin around her, and in her arms she held a large gray rabbit, instead of the typical parrot or monkey that the aristocracy usually chose for a portrait.

They looked a healthy, noisy brood. There was a quality of merriment about the painting, as if the sitters had just shared a good joke and were about to share another. The gentleman, in particular, seemed to be looking out of the picture and straight into the eyes of the viewer, as if he expected that, whatever his private jest was, the viewer should get it.

On the back of the heavy frame, the dealer's tag read: *Lord Redvers and his family, about 1670, artist unknown.*

"Ivy! Come and see this, will you? And one teaspoon of sugar in that tea, please."

He held his hand out for his cup, listening to her step behind him, but still transfixed by the painting. Why had it stirred him so? Looking at the happy, healthy family from long ago, he had been seized by a sudden remorse about his bachelor state. Very unlike him.

"Do you see the resemblance?" he asked, turning.

It wasn't Ivy.

Who was this woman standing in Ivy's store, holding out his tea to him as though she had a right to?

She was about his own age, small and curved, with a sweet, round face and sparkling eyes, dark brown and knowing. Her white hair was gathered into an elegant knot at the back of her head; she wore a simple dress of deep blue wool.

For a moment she simply stared at him. And then she did the most extraordinary thing. She reached out a small, plump hand and touched his face.

"Excuse me," Winston said. He would have said more, but he was suddenly struck by the feeling that he knew her. Yes, that was it. He simply *knew* her, as well as he knew himself. She liked fires in the evening while she read the paper, and port after dinner, and collected needlepoint pillows. Her favorite things were the color blue, lilacs, and (for some reason that evaded him completely) old Western movies. And he *knew*, even as he accepted his cup, that she had forgotten the sugar.

It was uncanny; it was ridiculous. Was he losing his mind?

She was watching him with tears in her dark

eyes. "I shall likely say this wrong," she said, "but here it goes."

She cleared her throat and recited softly:

"If ever I forget thee,
what would I be then?
A barren sea,
A starless sky
A nightingale turned to wren.
If ever I forget thee,
The sun need never rise.
The only dawn
for which I long
Is breaking in thine eyes."

For a long time they stood in silence, the gray-haired man in his tweed jacket, and the small, dark-eyed woman with her plump hand upon his cheek.

He started to speak and then stopped. He shook his head as if to clear it, started to speak again, and looked around as if he had lost something.

"What is it?" she asked, her voice hesitant.

"I'm not sure. For a moment I felt as if I'd quite lost something."

She stood, waiting, trying not to let the teacup tremble in her hand.

"Ah, there we are. Tea." He took the cup and sipped. "Damn, Meg. You've quite forgotten the sugar."

She let her breath out and closed her eyes

against the sudden sting of happy tears. "Have I?" she asked with a soft, light laugh.

"Don't you always?"

"I suppose I do."

"You haven't said what you think of the painting," he reminded her. "Where shall we hang it?"

She smiled at the painted family, and it seemed to Winston that she was sharing their long-ago joke.

"It's beautiful," she told him. "Put it somewhere where I can see it every day."

He put a hand on her shoulder and patted it. "Why? So that you don't forget that we have it?"

"Come!" she chided him. "My memory isn't that bad. If something's important, I remember it well enough."

"Is the sugar in my tea important?"

"No," she admitted, taking the cup, "but you are."

"Good. Take care not to forget."

She laughed as she made her way through the antique shop. "Silly man. The heart never forgets."

AMY ELIZABETH SAUNDERS

Passionate, Sensual Historical Romance By The Bestselling Author Of *Forever*.

Sweet Summer Storm. Rude, snobbish, and affected, Christianna St. Sebastien is everything Gareth Larkin despises, but she's the most breathtaking creature he's ever beheld. Determined to steal the beautiful aristocrat's heart, Gareth sets out to teach her that the length of a man's title and the size of his fortune are not necessarily his most important assets.

_3650-9 $4.99 US/$5.99 CAN

Wild Summer Rose. Torn from her carefree rustic life to become a proper city lady, Victoria Larkin bristles at the hypocrisy of the arrogant French aristocrat who wants to seduce her. But Phillipe St. Sebastien is determined to have her at any cost—even the loss of his beloved ancestral home. And as the flames of revolution threaten their very lives, Victoria and Phillipe find strength in the healing power of love.

_51902-X $4.99 US/$5.99 CAN

Dorchester Publishing Co., Inc.
65 Commerce Road
Stamford, CT 06902

Please add $1.75 for shipping and handling for the first book and $.50 for each book thereafter. NY, NYC, PA and CT residents, please add appropriate sales tax. No cash, stamps, or C.O.D.s. All orders shipped within 6 weeks via postal service book rate. Canadian orders require $2.00 extra postage and must be paid in U.S. dollars through a U.S. banking facility.

Name_____

Address_____

City _____ State_____ Zip_____

I have enclosed $_____in payment for the checked book(s).
Payment <u>must</u> accompany all orders.□ Please send a free catalog.

Timeswept passion...timeless love.

Forever by Amy Elizabeth Saunders. Laurel Behrman is used to putting up with daily hard knocks. But her accidental death is too much, especially when her bumbling guardian angels send her back to Earth—two hundred years before she was born. Trapped in the body of a Colonial woman, Laurel arrives just in time to save a drowning American patriot with the kiss of life—and to rouse a passion she thought long dead.
_51936-4 $4.99 US/$5.99 CAN

Interlude in Time by Rita Clay Estrada. When Parris Harrison goes for a swim in the wild and turbulent surf off Cape May, she washes ashore in the arms of the most gorgeous hunk she has ever seen. But Thomas Elder is not only devastatingly sexy, he is also certifiably insane—dressed in outlandish clothes straight out of a ganster movie, he insists the date is 1929! Horrified to discover that Thomas is absolutely correct, Parris sets about surviving in a dangerous era—and creating her own intimate interlude in time.
_51940-2 $4.99 US/$5.99 CAN

Dorchester Publishing Co., Inc.
65 Commerce Road
Stamford, CT 06902

Please add $1.75 for shipping and handling for the first book and $.50 for each book thereafter. NY, NYC, PA and CT residents, please add appropriate sales tax. No cash, stamps, or C.O.D.s. All orders shipped within 6 weeks via postal service book rate. Canadian orders require $2.00 extra postage and must be paid in U.S. dollars through a U.S. banking facility.

Name _____
Address _____
City _____ State _____ Zip _____
I have enclosed $_____ in payment for the checked book(s).
Payment <u>must</u> accompany all orders.☐ Please send a free catalog.

An Angel's Touch

*Where angels go,
love is sure to follow.*

Time Heals by Susan Collier. Tired of her nagging relatives, Maeve Fredrickson asks for the impossible: to be a thousand miles and a hundred years away from them. Then a heavenly being grants her wish, and she awakens in frontier Montana. Saved from the wilderness by a handsome widower, Maeve loses her heart to her rescuer—and her temper over the antics of his three less-than-angelic children. As her angel prods her to fight for Seth, Maeve can only pray for the strength to claim a love made in paradise.

_52030-3 $4.99 US/$5.99 CAN

Longer Than Forever by Bronwyn Wolfe. Patrick is in trouble, alone in turn-of-the-century Chicago, and unjustly jailed with little hope for survival. Then the honey-haired beauty comes to him, as if she has heard his prayers. Lauren has all but given up on finding true love when she feels the green-eyed stranger's call—summoning her across boundaries of time and space to join him in a struggle against all odds; uniting them in a love that will last longer than forever.

_52042-7 $5.99 US/$7.99 CAN

Dorchester Publishing Co., Inc.
65 Commerce Road
Stamford, CT 06902

Please add $1.75 for shipping and handling for the first book and $.50 for each book thereafter. NY, NYC, PA and CT residents, please add appropriate sales tax. No cash, stamps, or C.O.D.s. All orders shipped within 6 weeks via postal service book rate. Canadian orders require $2.00 extra postage and must be paid in U.S. dollars through a U.S. banking facility.

Name_____
Address_____
City _____ State_____Zip_____
I have enclosed $_____in payment for the checked book(s).
Payment <u>must</u> accompany all orders.☐ Please send a free catalog.

THERE NEVER WAS A TIME

GAIL LINK

"Gail Link was born to write romance!"
—Jayne Ann Krentz

Sitting alone in her Vermont farmhouse, Rebecca Gallagher Fraser hears a ghostly voice whisper to her. But not until she stumbles across a distant ancestor's diary do the spirit's words hold any meaning for her.

Drawn by inexplicable forces, Rebecca journeys to the once resplendent Southern plantation where her forebear loved and lost a Union soldier. And there, on a jasmine-scented New Orleans night, she discovers that passion unfulfilled in one lifetime can defy fate and logic and be reborn so much sweeter in another.

_52025-7 $4.99 US/$5.99 CAN

PREFERRED CUSTOMERS!

*Leisure Books and Love Spell
proudly present
a brand-new catalogue and a
TOLL-FREE NUMBER*

*STARTING JUNE 1, 1995
CALL 1-800-481-9191
between 2:00 and 10:00 p.m.
(Eastern Time)
Monday Through Friday*

*GET A FREE CATALOGUE
AND ORDER BOOKS USING
VISA AND MASTERCARD*

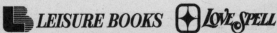

LEISURE BOOKS · LOVE SPELL